Praise for *Our Only Shield*

"Michael Goodspeed is an excellent storyteller. In *Our Only Shield*, his protagonist Rory Ferrall continues to joust with his nation's enemies, this time in Nazi-occupied Holland at the start of the Second World War. His writing embodies excellent character development. He superbly situates his story within an accurate historical context. Reader beware: prepare to be not only highly entertained, but also educated."

DAVID BASHOW, Editor, *Canadian Military Journal*

"As a Dutch-born Canadian whose family experienced the German occupation, I could not put down this powerhouse book by Michael Goodspeed. I felt right in the action beside the characters. A wonderful read."

PETER STOFFER, Member of Parliament for Sackville–Eastern Shore, Nova Scotia

Praise for Michael J. Goodspeed's
Three to a Loaf: A Novel of the Great War

"A compelling account that is fiction in name only. Goodspeed's research and personal military experience make this fast-paced story powerful and authentic, as real for World War I as *The Red Badge of Courage* was for the American Civil War."

MAJOR-GENERAL (RET.) LEWIS W. MACKENZIE

"An exciting Great War story of soldiering and spying. Goodspeed's book is almost unique for being well-written and accurate militarily…"

PROF. J.L. GRANATSTEIN, author of *Canada's Army: Waging War and Keeping the Peace*

"A great read ... didn't put it down until 1 a.m. ... a full-bodied, compelling espionage thriller. Goodspeed has captured the horror of life in the mud and blood-filled trenches of World War I as only an experienced soldier with a great eye can. On top of that, he's got down pat the cultural differences in the manners, mindsets and methods of the Britons and Germans among whom his Canadian hero finds himself."

JOE SCHLESINGER, award-winning CBC journalist and foreign correspondent

"Michael Goodspeed's debut novel that's set in the First World War will appeal to fans of both historical fiction and the espionage genre."

PAUL BACHMEIRER, *National Post Book Reviews,* July 19, 2008

OUR ONLY SHIELD

A NOVEL OF THE SECOND WORLD WAR

Michael J. Goodspeed

Blue Butterfly Books
THINK FREE, BE FREE

Blue Butterfly Book Publishing Inc.
2583 Lakeshore Boulevard West, Toronto, Ontario, Canada M8V 1G3
Tel 416-255-3930   Fax 416-252-8291   www.bluebutterflybooks.ca

Complete ordering information for Blue Butterfly titles can be found at:
www. bluebutterflybooks.ca

First edition, soft cover, 2010

LIBRARY AND ARCHIVES CANADA CATALOGUING IN PUBLICATION

Goodspeed, Michael J. (Michael James), 1951–
    Our only shield : a novel of the Second World War / Michael J. Goodspeed.

ISBN 978-1-926577-05-0

    1. World War, 1939–1945—Fiction. I. Title.

PS8613.O646O87 2010   C813'.6   C2010-904445-2

Design and typesetting by Gary Long / Fox Meadow Creations
Text set in Monotype Bulmer
Cover photo © Bigstock Photo / Erik de Graaf
Title page photo © Bigstock Photo / Denise Ellison
Printed in Canada by Transcontinental-Métrolitho
Text paper contains 100 per cent post-consumer recycled fibre

Mixed Sources
Product group from well-managed
forests, controlled sources and
recycled wood or fiber
www.fsc.org Cert no. SW-COC-000952
© 1996 Forest Stewardship Council
FSC

Blue Butterfly Books thanks book buyers for their support in the marketplace.

To Simon, Samantha, Andrew, and Pamela:
four people whose enthusiasm and daring
have always been an inspiration

1

Pemmican Lake, Manitoba, October 1939

THE FAIRCHILD FLOATPLANE skipped and bounced twice as it touched down on the northern lake. The engine roar intensified as the plane slowed, and the cloud of mist thrown up around the exposed cylinder heads bloomed into a circular rainbow. To Chief Superintendent Rory Ferrall, sitting in the passenger seat, the instant rainbow looked as if some clever engineer had designed the aircraft to have its own good-luck charm with each landing. With his one good eye, he stared out at the shoreline of granite, jack pine, and birch, wondering if he would ever be lucky enough to see these north woods again. He shifted restlessly in his seat after the long flight. His life had changed dramatically in the last few days. Just a week ago he had been in charge of the Royal Canadian Mounted Police in northern Manitoba. Now he was flying out to say his farewells before being posted overseas. This was his last stop on that parting journey.

Exactly a week ago he had received a brief and cryptic telegram from Ottawa advising him politely that "if he should choose to volunteer," the RCMP would second him to the War Office in London for "unspecified duties." Rory had a good idea what those duties would entail. He spoke fluent German and had served on clandestine operations within Germany during the Great War. With another war now declared, some desperate soul in an office had dug up his file and they wanted him back.

As the Fairchild neared the dock, a small crowd of handsome, cheering, copper-faced Indian children ran down the hill. In the isolated northern Manitoba village of Pemmican Lake, the unannounced arrival of a floatplane was still such an infrequent occurrence that it created a stir in the community. The children waved and shouted greetings in Woodland Cree; and while the happy mob applauded their village's latest arrival, a small boy in a red-chequered flannel shirt triumphantly seized the mooring line.

Rory smiled at the children's enthusiasm. There was something infectious about the way kids up here laughed and roared when a plane came in. There was a sense of genuine zest in their hilarity, and he loved it. But these days, laughter was something he had to work at. Ever since his wife had died four months ago, he found some days a struggle. On the good days, he thought he was getting over his loss. He had told himself that he was a fatalist, that he understood that life was inherently unfair. That kind of thinking got him through the Great War, and he supposed it helped make him a reasonably efficient policeman; but on the dark days, it wasn't enough. He looked from the children on the dock down to the aircraft's floor. He still wasn't certain how he got himself through those dark times.

As boisterous as this meeting with the native children was, it also left him with an uncomfortable twinge. The kids out there were like all the children who remained back in these isolated settlements: happy and energetic. The others, the majority of Indian children, those who had been sent to the residential schools, seemed perpetually dejected and tired, like transplanted flowers wilting in a neglected garden. Rory wrestled with the handle on the plane's door. It seemed that all the new ideas after the Great War had proven to be catastrophic failures. Communism and fascism were the two colossal disasters. But even up here in the North, the great social engineering project to integrate native children wasn't working the way it had been planned. He couldn't put a finger on it. How else would you run schools for a population so sparsely distributed across tens of thousands of square miles of bush? Maybe it was the schools them-selves, or maybe the way they ran the system. He wasn't close enough to the project to know, but it was a problem begging for a solution. What was strikingly obvious to him was that the kids in this remote village were happy.

Happiness is a strange thing. Rory had always believed you had to cultivate it yourself. He had come back from the war highly deco-rated, but missing an eye and three fingers on his left hand—and with more ugly memories than he cared to think about. Happily, life had gotten steadily better for him. He joined the Mounted Police, and years later married a wonderful Chinese woman from a small prairie town; and despite the protestations of his father at both of his choices, Rory had found married life and his career in the police force deeply satisfying. It was true, there was something about police work. If you weren't careful, it had the potential to turn some of the most optimistic men into cynics. Maybe that was true for other pro-fessions as well, but as he had seen some wonderful men become embittered, long ago he had deliberately set out to counter that.

By the time Rory's duffel bag was unloaded, the boy in the red-chequered flannel shirt had established for everyone within earshot that he was to be the one carrying it to the Mountie's cabin. As the procession got under way, Sergeant John McWilliams and a heavy, grey-bearded black Labrador jogged down the rock-strewn path from the village. Although McWilliams was several years younger than Rory, an extra twenty pounds, thinning hair, and a bushy grey moustache made him look much older. Unlike his commanding officer, McWilliams was dressed in a mixture of Royal Canadian Mounted Police uniform and Indian clothing. He wore a Mountie's peaked forage cap, a buckskin jacket, regulation yellow-striped trou-sers, and moccasins; and as usual he was smiling broadly.

"Got your radio message last night, sir. Didn't expect you to come up for another month. Everything okay?"

"Everything's fine, John. It's a routine visit. I've brought some books and newspapers, and I've got some spices, books, and maga-zines for Angela as well." Rory looked around him, drinking in the scenery with obvious satisfaction. "I'm posted out of the division and they let me do one last set of rounds before I head off. The new divisional commander hasn't been designated yet. Thought I'd come up and see you folks. I'm going to miss this part of the world."

"Where are you going, sir? I was sure you'd be with us for at least a couple more years. It's only been nine months. Is there some kind of problem?"

"No, no problems. It sounds like I'm going to England—some-thing to do with the war. They've let me do one last circuit. I get to tidy up some loose ends, and then I go to Ottawa and then off to Lon-don. I suppose I'll find out what's in store for me later, but from what I can make out, they're being tight-lipped about what's going on."

Surrounded by a cluster of happy chattering children, the two men walked up the path from the dock. The birch trees were still a dying yellow and most of the scrub bushes had already lost their leaves, exposing a floor of pale green lichen-covered granite. There was more than a touch of autumn in the air, and it struck Rory that up here only the maples resisted this turn of the seasons with one last defiant but futile crimson flourish before winter's iron frost.

At the cabin, McWilliams's wife, Angela, a sturdy, black-haired woman with a ready smile, was tying a braid in her three-year-old daughter's hair. Angela stood up and gave a mock curtsey, and then, instantly turning serious, hugged Rory. "Rory, I was so sorry to hear about Ruth. It was all so sudden."

"Thanks, Angela. Yeah, it was sudden. One week she felt ill and complained of stomach aches, and five weeks later she was gone. To be honest, I still haven't gotten used to the idea of her being dead." For a few seconds nobody spoke. It was a tacit moment of remem-brance and commiseration. Rory shrugged. He felt choked, and despite these two being among his closest friends, he didn't want to lose control, not now. He took a deep breath. "Life has to go on, I guess. So tell me, how have you two been since I was up here in the spring? You both look great."

Angela spoke. "We're fine. We still love it, just like you did when you were up here with us. That seems like a long time ago now. I suppose some day John and I will have to go back down south, but until then, we're happy here."

Anxious to change the subject from married life, Angela gave a small shrug. "Just now, except for the three of us and the village grandmas, we're the only adults within a hundred miles of here. Everyone else has gone downriver for the autumn goose hunt. They'll be back in a week or so."

Later, followed by two shy, giggling girls and a puffing Labrador, Rory and John McWilliams strolled through the village. They were in no hurry and stopped to chat with the elderly women who sat in front of their cabins expecting to see their visitor. Although Rory could only remember a few words of the language, he was gratified to see how fluent his old friend had become in Cree and how he was genuinely accepted by the native elders. That wasn't always the case with some of the officers up here.

When they returned, Angela had a simple supper laid out in their cabin's front room. They talked cheerfully for an hour, then Angela excused herself to put their daughter to bed. She followed not long after.

Rory was pleased that the conversation meandered throughout the evening. In truth, there wasn't a lot of police work to discuss up here. The Mounted Police functioned more as a steadying influence than as enforcers of the law in these truly isolated communities, a practical link to the more intensely settled world rather than the long arm of the outside world's law. As it was, Rory probably didn't have to come here. He could have said his official farewells by letter, but Angela and John McWilliams were special friends; and there was something in the North that exerted an irresistible pull on him. No matter what the time of year, he loved the rock, the lakes, and the woods. But it wasn't just the outdoors. For those with the Northland in their soul, there was a perceptible sense of freedom and simplicity up here. On the Canadian Shield, life was lived to the unhurried rhythm of the seasons rather than the ticking of a clock and the shuffling of paper.

Late in the evening as the two men sat outside around a stone fire pit watching the flames, Rory grew serious. They had exhausted their small talk. For those who had spent many years living amongst the Indian communities, they understood that a trusting silence was a kind of conversation in itself. "Have you heard anything about Tommy Many Dreams?" Rory asked. "I guess I haven't seen him for over a year now."

McWilliams stirred the coals with a stick. "He's gone downriver with his daughter and her husband and his grandchildren. He lives with them in the Eagle Lake band now. I think he's doing quite well. Someone was telling me about him a month or so ago. His limp hasn't gotten any worse, and he has no trouble keeping up with the others." He winced at the heat from the fire. "You know, you Great War veterans keep pretty close tabs on one another. I suppose that's only fair. Come to think of it, one of the last things Tommy said to me was that I had to say hello to you for him when I saw you next."

They stared into the fire for a long time. John asked, "Why are you going back, Rory? I can't imagine you don't have a say in this. You've already done your share. Anybody who knows you, knows you've done your bit."

Rory didn't answer right away. He poked the fire with a stick, squinting as a draught of wind blew flame toward them. "I suppose I could have said no. In fact, even though I'd prefer to stay here, I think I could have done some useful work if I went to Ottawa at the end of this posting in Manitoba. But this war just isn't the same as the last one. We can't lose it. I've no doubt: the Nazis are completely different from the Kaiser."

He stopped and gazed at the fire as if trying to read a pattern in the coals. "If we lose this war, it really will be the end of our civilization as we know it. That's not me repeating propaganda. I believe it. Not only do I believe it, it scares the hell out of me. So, I think I have to go where I'm needed. Besides," he said with a wry smile, "unlike you, I don't have a family to raise. I can afford to be altruistic."

The log Rory had been poking suddenly collapsed in a crash of sparks and crackling. "The fire's dying and I suppose it's time to go to bed; my plane'll be back first thing tomorrow."

Rory was up long before the others. He made himself a mug of tea and went outside. The wind was rising and low clouds were driving in from the north. He put his mug on a rock, stretched his arms above his head, and twisted to the left and to the right, slowly stretching the muscles in his back as he looked out over the lake. He was surprised that the socket of his right eye felt so good. Normally, the lingering effects of a short night's sleep and the smoke from last evening's fire would have left his eye feeling irritated. His glass eye and the missing fingers on his left hand had been a constant reminder that he was a survivor of the cauldron that was the Western Front. Now, with the passage of time, his disfigurement served more as a reminder to be grateful for each day instead of a stimulus for the intermittent anger he had endured for so many years after the war.

Far off, out in the middle of the lake, whitecaps were forming. Rory walked down to the community's small dock, made from rough planks and a log-and-rock crib. The wind was cold. As the sky in the east brightened and the waves lapped along the shoreline, he watched a large flock of geese rise and circle and then shake into their V formation before flying low out from the reeds at the end of the bay. There must have been a hundred of them. They were honking and calling out to each other as they winged their way southward. Staying far out from the settlement, they passed the cabins at the lake's narrows—well beyond shotgun range. They were smart birds, no doubt about it. And their calls, whatever it was they said to each other, made for a lonely song. Nothing epitomized the sound of the north woods in autumn like the distant call of Canada geese on the wing. At the same time, Rory thought, they were an odd sort of bird. They lived in flocks, but it wasn't unusual for several to join another flock if they couldn't keep up, or if in their perpetual honking at one another they had some kind of falling out. In flight, they regularly rotated their leaders throughout their journey of thousands of miles in their aerodynamically efficient wedge. And unlike most birds, the big grey, brown, and tan geese mated for life. If one mate was killed on the migration, the other stayed in the vicinity until the days grew so short and the wind so cold that it absolutely had to go. Up here amongst these lakes, Rory had often seen grief-stricken Canada geese lingering around for weeks after their mates had been killed. The survivor would be there, out on the water or strutting up and down a rocky headland, day after day, alone, and always out of shooting distance; and then one day it would be gone. Rory didn't need the food and had stopped hunting geese a long time ago.

Above the wind and the cries of the geese, Rory thought he could hear the faint drone of a floatplane. It was time to get his things and say his goodbyes.

2

"Reinhold, hurry up or you'll be late. Everyone has to be seated at least forty-five minutes before the Führer arrives and we can't leave the taxi waiting."

Reinhold Neumann smiled. Maida, always such a worrying little hen. Hadn't he managed to become Austria's youngest Major in the Schutzpolizei? Now he was well on his way to becoming the youngest Oberstleutnant in Greater Germany's newly integrated Geheime Staatspolizei—more fearsomely known by their acronym, the Gestapo. Not to worry, he'd get them to the investiture on time. That wasn't anything to fret about. His rise in the Reich's police ranks wasn't going to be slowed down by something as stupid as being late for the most important ceremony in the history of the Austrian police. Neumann thought that Maida, as pretty as she was, should stick to her three primary worries: their boy, Klaus; their baby daughter, Monika; and of course, anything to do with fashion.

Neumann adjusted the swastika on his pocket and smoothed his grey tunic in the mirror. He looked good: wavy, thick brown hair, a healthy complexion, and an aggressively downturned mouth. At twenty-six years old, he was eagle-eyed, fit, and ruthlessly efficient looking. He turned his head to catch the light. Not bad. Today he conveyed the precise sense of authority and vigour that such an occasion demanded.

In the last three years his situation had improved more than he could have imagined. Who would have thought? But then, his career path hadn't happened by accident. He had made the right moves. Marrying Maida, the daughter of one of Vienna's deputy chiefs of police, had given him legitimacy and status in some people's eyes. He was well aware that a poor boy from a small walk-up flat on the seventh floor of a tenement in Vienna's Simmering District would ordinarily have taken decades, and a lot of good luck, to attain that kind of social position. He never let on to anyone that Maida's family didn't like him; and although he never told Maida, the sense of hauteur her family exuded when he was around left him resentful and angry.

A year after marrying Maida, he'd boosted his career once again by joining the Austrian National Socialist Party, even though at the time it wasn't something most people would have described as a clever move likely to result in promotion. Most of Maida's family were quite cool with him after he became a National Socialist; and while he didn't know it then, there were a few senior officers who tried to have him and his fellow Nazis run out of the police force. Happily, those days—and those officers—were long gone. Three years ago he had been a struggling police cadet walking a beat in a Viennese slum. His good judgment was paying off faster than he could have imagined. In 1936 he'd joined the party, a frustrated young man looking for a means of venting both his energy and his anger at the world. It had been the right thing to do. He'd shown courage and insight. He certainly had a knack for predicting how things would work out, and he knew it.

Neumann had always been inspired by the Nazi talk of a "Greater Germany." For him, it was inevitable; anyone could see that. If you believed in the survival of the fittest and the strengthening of species, then it was quite obvious that the German race, led by the Nazi Party, was destined to dominate inferior races. Sure, the party had more than its share of windbags, and it carried a certain amount of dead weight; but Neumann was certain that would change in a few years.

In a curious way, Reinhold Neumann had always felt at home in the party. It gave him a sense of solidarity and purpose; more than that, there was something about the concept of national destiny and racial hierarchy that appealed to him in a strange way. He thought it was the same sense of direction some people found in their faith, although even as far back as his first year in secondary school he had regarded the religiously devout as psychological weaklings. Religion was for those who needed something external to prop them up. National Socialism was for those unafraid to take responsibility for the future into their own hands. But there was more to it than that. The party, under the Führer's leadership, brought a sense of order; it stood for things you could understand and see. The party knew what had to be done. In a few years it had returned Germany and the German people to a position of strength and respect. It had united Germany and Austria, and was in the process of bringing back all German peoples into a single and mightier Greater Germany. Who could argue with that?

In forging a new national consciousness, the party had unequivocally identified the nation's enemies, the people who sucked the life blood out of the nation: Jews, communists, homosexuals, gypsies, capitalists, and farther down the scale, weak-kneed church leaders, the pseudo-intellectuals, and the liberal artists. It was a good, comprehensive list; it explained what was wrong with society and it provided an indication as to where action was required to fix things.

Now, this afternoon, he was off to attend Austrian Chancellor Seys Inquart's reception for the Führer. Only a very few other police officers, and no others of his rank, had been accorded that honour; but then, none of the others had been in the party as long as he had.

Downstairs, Maida cast an appraising eye over him and coquettishly brushed imaginary fluff from his lapels. She reached up on tiptoes and kissed him ever so lightly on the nose so as not to brush off her lipstick. "Do you really think when you're promoted to Oberstleutnant that we'll be posted to Berlin, Reinhold? I'd love to spend a few years there."

"There's a good chance of it. We'll find out soon, so keep your ears open at the reception and do your best to flatter Scheidler. He's close

to Himmler and he's the one deciding which Austrians to send on
the new Reich Senior Security Officer's Course. That's the route to
promotion, especially now that war has been declared."

* * *

AMSTERDAM WAS BASKING in the midst of a glorious late autumn
warm spell, and to Annika Hammerstein it seemed that all the city's
young men and women were out this evening. Throngs of them in
shirtsleeves and pretty summer frocks ambled aimlessly along the
pathway beside the Prinsengracht Canal. She gave up trying to ride
her bicycle, and in an aggressive stop-and-go manner pushed it
determinedly through the crowds.

It was already a quarter to the hour. She had to be home by eight
to take her husband, Saul, to a surprise birthday gathering at his sister's. Tonight she was flustered. She was running behind schedule;
twice she had almost had her violin case knocked from her bicycle's
basket. Annika's string quartet had been late in starting practice and
they were late ending. They could have used more rehearsal time.
It bothered her that the quartet's interpretation of Allessandrini's
"Eighth Sonata" was nowhere near ready for their recital in two days
time at the Institute.

But, as she told herself so frequently when she felt frustrated, she
was a practical woman. She could cope with whatever hardships and
anxieties life had in store for her. At thirty-four, she had weathered
more than her share of misery and sorrow. When she became gloomy
or impatient, she reminded herself that she had lived through hardships that were much more difficult. In her teens, she had been the
sole support for her mother through a long fatal illness. And after
her mother's death, she had, entirely with her own resources, gone
on to finish her degree with first-class honours in modern languages
and music.

Now, she was a lecturer and research assistant in the Music Conservatory at the University of Amsterdam.

Annika was a thoughtful woman, and grateful for having been

born and raised in a level-headed, comfortable, and safe country like the Netherlands. The rest of the world looked like it was once again in the process of disintegration, but thankfully this tiny oasis of neutrality and common sense would once more keep itself isolated from whatever calamities the rest of humanity was foolishly preparing for itself.

She wheeled her bicycle around a handsome blond couple in their early twenties. Both of them had their heads thrown back, laughing together at some private absurdity. In a way, she envied them. Not that she wasn't happy with Saul, but this couple so obviously had their whole future before them. They would probably spend the rest of their lives enjoying this comfortable, civilized lifestyle and raise a family together. It seemed that Saul and she would never have a child now. For the last year this had been a source of wrenching unhappiness; sometimes, even the sight of happy couples without children brought this deep-rooted anguish to the surface.

It all seemed so unfair. She and Saul had overcome so much together. Theirs was a mixed marriage: she was a Christian, he was a Jew. Relatives on both sides had been aghast when they announced their intention to wed. For Annika, it was less of a problem than it had been for Saul. Annika was an only child and both her parents were dead, so she had fewer upset relations to deal with. There was of course her cousin Margrethe in The Hague, who had written her a long, scolding, arrogant letter, but she had ignored both the letter and Margrethe. Things were different for Saul. The Hammersteins were a large and close family. Many of them were not happy that Saul had flouted their traditions and their wishes, and married a gentile. Still, Saul and Annika had their own circle of friends, and tonight a number of Saul's younger relatives as well as their mutual friends had quietly chosen to ignore their elders' concerns. Even so, for two otherwise gregarious people, it meant now that their lives were effectively restricted to a smaller circle of close relatives and friends than would otherwise have been the case.

Although Holland was, by European standards, a very tolerant country, it wasn't the same as being an accepting country. Not a day went by without both Annika and Saul being made in some small and painful way aware of that unpleasant fact.

Annika became more aggressive pushing her bike forward through the crowds. No point in wallowing in self-pity. What else was life if it wasn't a series of obstacles to overcome? She felt a surge of energy. She wasn't going to be late for something as simple as a birthday party.

3

London, 9 December 1939

"GENTLEMEN, THANK YOU for coming here today. I know that some of you have journeyed very long distances and that you have been given precious little explanation as to what is expected of you."

Geoffrey Harris, a moustached and anxiously precise man dressed in the red collar tabs and khaki uniform of a British colonel, looked at the solemn faces staring back at him from around the government-issue oak table. The room was overheated and stifling. London's late afternoon sunlight shone tenuously through dusty windows. Harris was doing his best to inject a sense of gravity into his briefing. His audience was a group of seven sceptical-looking middle-aged men dressed in conservative wool suits. The colonel was younger than most of the men before him, and he was conscious that the differences in their ages could stimulate resentment.

"I'd like to be able to tell you with some certainty how the war is likely to turn out, but, I'm afraid, any of your guesses are likely to be as good as those from the experts here in the War Office." Harris had a deep, crisp voice with a penetrating timbre that could have brought him success as an actor. Today, however, he was speaking softly, almost inaudibly. It could be intensely irritating to those he was speaking to, but it was a ploy he used frequently to command attention.

"I'm afraid the problem we will soon be forced to come to grips with is that we shall have to prepare contingencies to deal with what happens when the war gets going in earnest. I think we're in a period that we could safely call a phoney war. It's true that we're at war, but everyone is staying politely entrenched behind their lines and nobody is getting hurt. That situation isn't going to last long."

Harris turned away from his audience and looked out the window into London's hazy, refracted sunshine. He put his hands in his trouser pockets and jingled loose change, waiting a second for effect. "There's a small group here in London, soldiers and politicians, who believe that when things get nasty, as they inevitably will, we may well be pushed right out of Europe. That's certainly our worst-case scenario, and it's the one we have to plan for." He exhaled loudly and wheeled about.

"Frankly, I also think being pushed off the continent is the most likely possibility. Jerry has an army that is much better trained than ours. He has the initiative, and he has been earnestly equipping, preparing, planning, and exercising for exactly this scenario for the past ten years. For some of you here, what I'm saying will come as no surprise whatsoever. That's one of the reasons, amongst others, that we have asked you to join us."

Four of the civilians sat forward in their chairs. Although most of them had considered the probability of abject defeat at the hands of the Germans, this was the first time they had heard it expressed officially. No one had been forthright in speaking about the possibility of looming catastrophe on the continent. This kind of talk wasn't heard in the House of Commons, in the newspapers, or even in the pubs. The atmosphere in the room changed noticeably from scepticism to rapt attention. None of them spoke.

Harris nodded almost imperceptibly and then went on. "If that happens, the army we so hurriedly sent off to France on the outbreak of war might well be lost entirely. We've never had that happen to us before. But even if we lose that army, it won't be the end." He looked around the room determinedly. "I need not remind any of you that whatever is said here stays here. All of us are bound by the Official Secrets Act." He paused again.

"We have failed to keep Germany in check diplomatically, and our military response has been sluggish, defensive, and ineffective. To make things worse, Prime Minister Chamberlain has effectively refused to consider military catastrophe as a possibility. Many of us at the War Office think he is still hoping that there can be some kind of negotiated settlement, and the war can be ended without too much bloodshed. I'm afraid it's the curse of being perpetually optimistic." He paused again for effect.

"Unsubstantiated faith in the future is a wonderful trait in school teachers, but it's a disastrous one in wartime prime ministers. There are many of us who believe that when they are ready, the Germans will go on the offensive. And, as more than a few of us in the army and elsewhere believe, we are now almost preordained to suffer a serious calamity. From that heretical perspective, which is both our worst-case and most likely scenario, no matter whether we sue for peace or not, sooner or later, we'll find ourselves fighting for our lives again. Like many of you, I know the Germans and Corporal Hitler far too well, and neither Hitler nor the Germans intend to let us off easily. They'll be at our throats again whether we sign a peace treaty or not."

There was an uneasy silence and more shifting of hard wooden chairs around the table.

"First off, neither I nor the people I work with have any intention of acting overtly or covertly to influence Britain's political outcomes over the foreseeable future. I hope to put your mind at rest on that account. We understand that we are here to protect democracy, not overthrow it or supplant it. However, we do have to be prepared to react to the worst possible scenario, and our worst possible scenario is a decisive German victory on the continent. And that, for reasons of wishful political thinking, is currently viewed as an heretical and unthinkable possibility."

Harris quickly scanned the room, looking each man at the table in the eye. "I hope, gentlemen, that you will agree with me that it's our job to think through the current difficulties as we see them, and then quietly and unobtrusively insert a degree of common sense into the political process. And if we can't do that—and I might add, we have been entirely unsuccessful in doing that over the last five years—then we have to be ready with an alternative plan when all the unworkable alternatives have come crashing down on us." Harris's speech slowed and he began to sound somewhat uncomfortable. "Secondly, although I'm in uniform, I'm not addressing you as soldiers. I see you gentlemen as the first of a new style of fighter. If you agree to fight with us, you will be the first of a new kind of shadow army. It will be the beginning of a civilian resistance unlike anything the world has seen before."

He paused again and stared out the window.

"So what exactly are you coming to here, colonel?" The impatient question came from Rory Ferrall, the Canadian with the eye patch and missing fingers. He looked irritable, and to reinforce his point, he looked at his watch. Two other men at the table muttered agreement.

Harris fixed the Canadian with a penetrating stare. "Yes, well, that's precisely where we are going, Chief Superintendent Ferrall. If we're driven off the continent, we fully intend to go back some day. With, of course, the help of the Dominions: nations like yours, Australia, South Africa, New Zealand, and, of course, Empire troops—and I don't know how, but with any luck, we have to get the Americans onto our side as well. But I fear that's a long way down the road. Who knows? This could take decades. I personally agree with Churchill's private assessment of the Nazis: they're a scourge and it may take the world's free nations generations to defeat them. So let me come to the point. If that's the case, we have to start preparing now for a war that could last decades. If we get run off the continent, we intend to set up a network of behind-the-lines saboteurs: men and women who will wage guerrilla war, assassinate key leaders, harass the enemy, and provide us with accurate intelligence from which to base future operations."

A ruddy-cheeked gentleman with a Scottish accent steepled his hands and spoke before Harris could continue. "So, colonel, I just want to be clear. Have you brought us here to organize some kind of resistance for you? A resistance for which there isn't a legitimate or a politically sanctioned need; or are we somehow to be involved in exerting this political influence you speak of?"

"I don't want you to do anything just yet," Harris said. "What I am asking of you is to start thinking about what we might do when we lose on the continent. Please bear with me. Each one of you has been brought here after a very careful selection and vetting process. Two of you had direct experience in the last war in military intelligence operations in Germany. Three of you have been selected for your demonstrated organizational skills, and two for your knowledge of the German security services. All of you have been carefully vetted for your common sense, trust, and loyalty. Despite such qualifications, we haven't been authorized any money, people, or equipment to prepare for this kind of eventuality. Given what I've just said, that's not surprising. But that should not stop us from thinking about how we shall proceed, if and when we find ourselves with our backs to the wall."

Harris clasped his hands behind his back. "So, yes, I'm not asking anything of you just now, except for you to think about how we are going to do this. I'd like you to stay right where you are. Remain in your jobs until such time as we need you. And we will be contacting you, trust me, on that score. But for some of you, we need your help to convince a number of those in key decision-making positions that we should be planning actively for the desperate situation we're going to find ourselves in. And, yes, for all of you, I'm seeking your support in creating a resistance to a possible Nazi occupation of Europe."

* * *

"Reinhold, you must admit that the Führer is even more impressive in person than he is on the radio or when you see him on the movie reels," said Oberst Scheidler, sipping enthusiastically at his glass of sekt. Oberst Scheidler, of the Schutzpolizei, was one of Vienna's three deputy police chiefs and an influential man who was clearly going to continue to rise in both the Nazi Party and the Reich's police ranks. "I had the impression tonight that we were witnessing history being made: the Führer giving a speech that was being broadcast to all Germans, describing for us his vision of the future. Mark my words, this is a man who holds destiny in his hands."

Major der Schutzpolizei Reinhold Neumann nodded and smiled, but unlike Scheidler and the other senior officers at Vienna's Imperial Hotel, Reinhold Neumann hadn't been impressed by the Führer and his speech. And for that matter, he wasn't much impressed by his police Oberst either. He had always thought of Scheidler as being somewhat stupid. And worse, Scheidler was often naively obsequious around his superiors. Neumann was well aware that Scheidler wouldn't have made it to the rank of Oberst if he wasn't a Nazi. But since the Anschluss—the union of Austria and Germany—his rise had been meteoric. Aside from his demonstrated skill in flattering the right people, Scheidler was an unremarkable policeman, an indifferent plodder who barely got the job done; there was no real spark that distinguished him from other senior officers. But Scheidler had one talent, and that was an unerring ability to get close to and stay close to the right superior. So, even though Scheidler might be a plodder, Reinhold Neumann was shrewd enough to appreciate that Scheidler's single strength was the one he needed to exploit and cultivate in himself if he were to rise.

"I think you're right, Herr Oberst," Neumann said, smiling.

In truth, Neumann thought the Führer was much more impressive on the radio than in person, although he certainly wasn't going to admit it here. Scheidler would never understand. The Führer was wooden, his entire performance predictable. Neumann had heard it all before: the themes of sacrifice and hardship and the inevitable furious crescendo aimed at Germany's enemies. It wasn't that Neumann disagreed with what Hitler said; he was impatient with the Führer's theatrics and wanted to see the Third Reich's expansion sooner rather than later.

Neumann was wise enough to keep those thoughts to himself, and smiled self-deprecatingly. He said to Scheidler, "Oh, there's no question that the Führer understands where he's taking us, Herr Oberst. I'm just delighted that I'm alive now to serve him." He rocked back on his heels and looked down at his wine glass as if he was unsure of himself. "I'm glad to be a part of the Reich, even if it's just in a small way."

"Your part may not be quite as small as you think, Reinhold. You and I were amongst the first police officers to join the party. This story, as we heard tonight, has a long way to go yet. And you know, being in the police is going to be a much better spot for a man with your talents. Once the fighting ends, the best place to be in the Third Reich will be in the SS—especially in the SS's police and security services—not the army. The army is good, but it's not the future for the Reich. This is where we think men like you, men with talent and ambition, will advance the interests of the police and the SS. The SS is the future of the Thousand Year Reich, and you are lucky and smart enough to be one of its early members. That will be something to tell your grandchildren."

Neumann shrugged and smiled self-deprecatingly again. Out of the corner of his eye he could see Maida absorbed in some tedious conversation with Scheidler's shy, fat, garishly dressed wife. "Herr Oberst, for me, joining the party seemed like the right thing to do at the time. It was obvious where the country needed to be taken. And lots of good men have joined since."

Scheidler beamed. It was what he wanted to hear. Like Neumann, he'd joined the party when influential officers frowned upon it. Not that his superiors disagreed with what the party stood for; but in the early days, Austria's Nazis were regarded as a déclassé bunch, scruffy and dangerous—the kind of people who routinely ended up in Vienna's jails on a Saturday night. That image had changed now and Reinhold Neumann was proud of his new status.

"Look around you tonight, Reinhold," said Scheidler. "This is a splendid example of how well the party has fared here in Vienna, but there aren't many police uniforms here. Yours, mine, and handful of others. And that's the very point: you joined at the outset and you stayed on even after the party was outlawed. That showed insight and allegiance." Scheidler looked around the room and lowered his voice. "And tonight, I think I can tell you that we are both going to Berlin very shortly."

Neumann nodded and fixed the older policeman with his most captivated stare.

"Yes," said Scheidler, "Himmler himself has directed that we are to send our most promising officers to Berlin. I received the order this afternoon. There is to be a course to standardize our procedures and to develop methods to make certain that when our enemies are defeated, we have the processes in place to ensure that our new territories are properly governed and are no security risk to the German state."

Neumann didn't have to pretend that he was pleased with the news. He smiled broadly. "I'm truly honoured by this, Herr Oberst. As I said earlier, I feel we're at a crossroads of history, and it's my good fortune and privilege to play a part in it."

"Oh, we shall both be playing a part in the historic days ahead of us, and very soon. Mark my words, Reinhold." Scheidler gestured towards his medals, nearly spilling his wine in the process. He leaned forward, until he was almost in Neumann's face. "Your generation is much luckier than mine. We endured the Great War, only to be betrayed by Jews, socialists, and the rich; but you and your generation will enjoy our final triumph. The Third Reich is going to be something we can all dedicate ourselves to building. Before long, the war is going to heat up again. Believe me, when we are ready, we will be on the move, and we will crush the British and French and take our rightful place in Europe. This time things will be very different."

Neumann was listening intently and waved away a waiter with canapés. Scheidler's voice grew low and he leaned forward even closer. "We will also get ourselves 'Lebensraum' in the east. We will have land to expand and grow Germany in that direction. It's our destiny. It's not just talk, Neumann. Trust me. I heard this from Himmler himself at our briefing this afternoon. This is not just wishful thinking. The next year will be the most momentous period in all of European history. We are going to smash the German people's traditional enemies and carve out for ourselves and future generations the Greater German Empire. Our destiny has been sleeping since Charlemagne, but not for long now. What this means for people like you and me is the opportunity to distinguish ourselves in the service of the Reich."

Despite his previous scepticism, Neumann felt a frisson of pride and enthusiasm. The disdain he felt earlier was rapidly disappearing. He had undergone this transformation in the past. It happened so frequently now that Neumann didn't even notice it. He had often been ambivalent about the party, but his ambition was kindled by the prospect of opportunity, and this created an uncritical kind of enthusiasm. The rapid change from cynic to disciple was no longer quite so remarkable. Reinhold Neumann had come such a long way from a Viennese slum, and now his talents were clearly being recognized for what they were. It was hard not to feel exultant.

* * *

ANNIKA'S SURPRISE PARTY for Saul was a tremendous success. Everyone she'd invited had come, and they were joined by people she had never seen before. It didn't matter. They were all friends of friends. Saul's sister's house was crowded with dozens of their colleagues and associates. The air was blue with cigarette smoke, and two dozen people were talking at the top of their lungs. A gramophone trumpeting out a scratchy swing-band tune was losing hopelessly against the chattering of so many boisterous conversations.

Annika sidled up to Saul, who was talking animatedly in German with a small circle of guests. In another part of the room she could hear a conversation in French. In the background someone else was speaking English. One of the things Annika loved about the Netherlands was the nation's fluency in so many languages. It was a skill that made them unique in Europe. It also helped keep the country prosperous, as it gave them a great trading advantage over all their

largely unilingual neighbours. Both she and Saul, like all their educated friends, spoke Dutch and German, and could get by in either
English or French. She slid her arm around his waist.

"Annika," Saul said enthusiastically, "I want you to meet Pauli
Herschel." He introduced her to a tall man with a fair complexion,
horn-rimmed glasses, and thinning brown hair. "Pauli has just come
from Germany. I was explaining to him that next semester he could
probably get a spot teaching a tutorial in the law school. I'm sure he
could eventually get a job here at the university."

Annika nodded vigorously. "Yes, of course. I don't know what
positions are open, but I hear that you have excellent qualifications.
Where exactly did you come from in Germany?"

"We lived in Stuttgart, but we managed to get out three months ago
via Switzerland. We're lucky to be here in the Netherlands. Things
were getting unbearable at home. I got my immediate family out. I
used to have a small office specializing in business law, but I haven't
been allowed to practise law for several years now. It's hard to believe
what it was like living in that environment."

"Will you be able to sell your house and have the money forwarded
here?" someone from the circle of guests asked.

Pauli laughed bitterly. "No, not at all. We were lucky to get out
with the clothes on our backs. Jews must have travel permits and special exit visas to get out of Germany. We had a phoney set of papers
made up for us, identifying us as non-Jews, but I won't tell you how
we got them. Others are still using the system. But no, there's no possibility of getting money from your bank account or from any kind
of sale. Still, I think we were lucky. We had to leave home separately,
without luggage, and we met at the train station. My wife took my
daughters and I took my son. We travelled separately; travelling as a
family would have been too suspicious."

"What would have happened if you were caught?" Saul asked.

"Jews who break the law are sent to a special prison camp at
Oranienburg. I've heard conditions are pretty grim there, but nobody really knows, as everything we've heard about it is some kind of
rumour. As far as I can see, the Nazi plan is to isolate the Jews from

the population and strip them of their possessions and their liveli-hood. We've heard rumours about the possibility of mass deporta-tions, but they're only rumours. We've been progressively restricted in our contacts with German society, yet we can't legally emigrate. I don't understand it."

"We've been reading about this in the papers for several years now," said a fair-haired woman with a bright red headscarf wrapped around a tight perm. "I believe you, Pauli, but I lived in Germany ten years ago. Things were tense, but I know the Germans: they are fun-damentally decent people. I know them. I have friends in Germany. They are not so unlike us; this is just so hard to understand."

"Hard to understand, like a nightmare is hard to understand," Pauli said. "In the last three months, I'd have to say that most people I've met don't want to believe it. It's too inconvenient. If they believed it, what would they do? It's only been a year since Kristallnacht—the Night of Broken Glass. Jews right across Germany and Austria were driven from their homes, vandalized, robbed, and beaten while the police watched or helped. The rest of the world seems to have conveniently forgotten already. In Switzerland, we were treated with suspicion. We were almost sent back as vagrants. We were lucky; we went to a Swiss synagogue and were forwarded along a chain that led here; but even here, in the Netherlands, we aren't guaranteed of find-ing a home. Yes, this is hard to imagine."

The woman with the headscarf was not going to be put off. "I have a difficult time with all of this. I know the Nazis are criminal louts, but this is the culture that gave us Wagner, Goethe, Bach, the printing press. Germans are practically related to us Dutch. The Nazis are a stopgap, something to protect the Germans from com-munist anarchy."

"They won't last forever," someone else chimed in. "Besides, the Germans were treated abominably after the war. The Treaty of Ver-sailles was a travesty and they suffered so much. Hitler at least has led them out of all that. I'm sure the German people will sooner or later put a stop to all the rest of this. People all over the world just want to live in peace. We all know that."

Pauli said nothing. He looked disbelieving and jaded.

Members of the circle swirled their drinks pensively or fumbled about busily lighting cigarettes or searching for lost items in handbags. Saul was the first to speak. "Well, Pauli, you're here now, and you're right, I don't know what we can do, but we're grateful that you are here tonight and that your family's safe." The others burst into smiles, relieved at not having to find a solution to the problems of Germany.

4

London, 6 January 1940

RORY LOOKED AT HIS WATCH as he waited on the sidewalk for Ewen
Crossley, his immediate superior and an old friend from the Great
War. It was not at all like Crossley to be late; the man was normally
a stickler for timings. Rory shoved his hands into his coat pockets
and shrugged, loosening his neck muscles. A minute later when his
friend arrived, Rory was surprised to see that he had brought with
him another man.

Crossley beamed. "Very sorry. I'm running late, Rory. Shall we
walk?" Crossley swept the three of them along and set off at a brisk
pace. His smile disappeared and he looked around furtively. "Let's
talk a little ways on, shall we?"

It was early morning, still cold and damp, with wispy remnants
of the night's smog lingering in the alleys. The closeness of the city
unnaturally amplified the sounds of their footsteps. Despite the
recent imposition of petrol rationing, London's air was no more
breathable than it had been before the war. Rory thought that wartime London's streets had a severe feel about them, as if the entire
metropolis was consciously readying itself for the coming struggle.
Depressingly, it seemed almost everyone in London was once again
wearing some kind of uniform. It wasn't at all the same city Rory

had known even five years ago. When he was last here, the city had the jostling self-assurance of one of the world's great capitals. Now, like a failing invalid determined to beat a mortal illness, London had become grim and resolute.

Ewen Crossley seemed mildly apprehensive this morning. Rory's old friend had at last been given a title in his new organization. His papers had come through. He was no longer officially a member of the Secret Intelligence Service working under cover of the Foreign Office. His new designation was the deputy director of operations in the Ministry of Economic Warfare. Crossley walked slowly beside Rory.

Beside shared military service, the two men had much in common. Both bore scars from their time in the trenches: Rory's less obvious glass eye, and Crossley's jagged scar, which ran from his left cheek to his ear. Rory was pleased to see that over the years the contour from Crossley's wound had faded from a disfiguring angry red slash to a more subtle white line. Despite the scar, Crossley's face was open and perpetually cheerful. His obvious good nature overshadowed the scar's testimony to his violent past.

From appearances alone, the two friends might have been from different generations. Rory, wearing a stylish black fedora, strode forward with his hands thrust deep in his trench coat pockets. Crossley was bare-headed. His hair was still a thick disordered thatch but had uniformly turned grey—quite a difference from the shock of red curls on the man Rory had known two decades before. The other man was much stouter. He also wore a fedora, as well as a heavy wool coat and thick, round, tortoise-shell glasses. He said nothing and stared straight ahead as the other two talked.

Crossley swivelled about, looking up and down the street. Satisfied that there was no one within earshot, he slowed his pace and said, "Rory, I want you to meet Harold Thornton. Like me, Harold's come over to join us from MI6. He's part of the recruiting team, and I thought if we had our meeting while we walked to Aston House, we'd save time and get a lungful of fresh air while we're at it."

Rory and Thornton shook hands hastily. Rory nodded impassively and grinned as if at a private joke. He'd been expecting some kind of interview but was surprised at the matter-of-fact way his new employers had chosen to spring it. "Fresh air here in London? You're kidding me, Ewen. Northern Manitoba, now, there's fresh air."

Crossley put his head back slightly and gave a good-natured obligatory laugh to the light-hearted but not very funny observation. "I suppose you're right. Rory, now that we have some time, maybe you can give us an indication of what you've been up to for the last twenty-odd years."

"Okay. Can I assume then that your interview's officially begun?"

"You can't have been a policeman all these years and still think I really wanted to go for a stroll to chat about old times, can you?" said Ewen, smiling. "I'll be honest, Rory, I have to make a report to Harris. He needs to confirm what kind of work he can task you with. All the others are getting the same routine—only, with your background, we have much higher expectations."

Crossley and Rory had known each other on and off since the Great War. Back then, Ewen Crossley had been in charge of training Rory for a clandestine mission in Imperial Germany. Their contacts had been infrequent in the intervening years; in fact, apart from Christmas cards, they had only met twice on business, but there was still a strong bond of trust between them.

"I haven't seen you, Ewen, for what, five years now? But you know, even back then, in one way or another, we hoped the Nazis would somehow just disappear. We were all wishful thinkers. Somehow we hoped that the German people would simply overthrow them. I guess the signs were there to read if we'd cared to. Doesn't seem like five years though, does it?" He paused and they walked in silence for a short distance.

"There's no point in playing games," Crossley said. "So, Rory, for Harold's sake, let's start where we left off at the end of the war. You left England in 1919, and now, twenty years later, you're here. What happened in the meantime?"

"Okay. I'll give you a brief outline and if you have any questions, just ask." Rory looked upwards and vigorously rubbed his chin as if he were about to make some kind of a decision. Instead, he said nothing for a few moments. "When I demobilized, I went back to Montreal. I suppose the biggest surprise to everybody was that I didn't join my father's firm. He was disappointed; still is. The last I talked to him, he still wanted me to quit the RCMP, go back, and help run the business for him. He's getting on, and things are picking up for him now that there's another war on. He runs several small- to mid-sized textile and manufacturing companies that have been quite successful. But it's never had any interest for me."

Rory paused, as if he didn't really believe what he had just said. "So, to make a long story short, in 1919 I ran into a friend of a friend and I ended up in the Royal Canadian Mounted Police. They even let me in missing an eye and two fingers on my left hand. They made a number of exceptions for otherwise fit veterans in those days. I've been in the RCMP for nineteen years and served mostly in Western Canada. Spent a lot of time in the North and in isolated locations. I liked it. I liked the people. It was useful and challenging work."

"I envy you," Crossley said. "You sound like you've had a more interesting time of it than I have. Tell me more about your police work."

"I've been reasonably successful as a police officer. Of course, I started as a constable, and that raised a few eyebrows. Some of the people I knew thought I was taking a step down from being a major, but I never looked at it that way. I've always figured that if you're going to learn a new line of work, you learn it from the ground up. Besides, I was young and I had no other choice, and my fellow constables were top-quality people. Since then I've had a variety of very good jobs. Worked with some wonderful people in and out of uniform. Put some not so wonderful people away where they belong. I never specialized in anything. I preferred it that way. I've been a general investigative officer, initially running a beat in northern Manitoba; later on, I had several commands in rural and isolated areas, and in small cities, mostly in the Prairies and the North. I'll probably not make the highest ranks. I don't have the right instincts, and to tell the truth, I'm just not that interested in doing some of the administrative jobs that will get me there, although the war probably rescued me from a posting to Ottawa. Who knows? I might have liked that." He shrugged. "I'm happy where I am, or where I was a month ago, anyway."

Crossley smiled briefly. "I can see you being a police officer."

"Yes, well, I've preferred to work in the field. It gives me a sense of accomplishment. How am I doing so far, Harold? Is this the kind of thing you were expecting to hear?"

"Pretty much. You know I'm going to have to ask you later to commit a brief summary of this to paper." Harold had a wonderfully crisp, theatrical voice and a Liverpool accent that he made no attempt to conceal. "I'm sorry, but they also have psychologists vetting our new officers now. This is one of these new wartime efficiencies. I had to go through the same silliness when they brought me over from MI6. This interview is the first step in screening and everybody gets it."

Crossley nodded. "Rory, tell us about your family life."

"I don't have one now, apart from my elderly parents. My dad is working himself into the ground and my mother does volunteer work in Montreal. I was married for nine years. We didn't have any children. My wife died a few months ago."

"I'm sorry to hear that," Thornton said. "Of course, I knew it. I am sorry just the same. I read it in your file. How are you getting on?"

"I'm all right. It was so fast but it was still a terrible thing watching her go the way she did. I miss her tremendously. But I suppose you need to know if I'm sufficiently recovered from my grief to be of any value in operations. I think so. In fact, I think doing something will focus my mind more than it has for a while. I'm physically fit and emotionally sound. Going through the normal grieving period, I guess. Not really out of it yet."

"Are you angry at all?" asked Harris.

"Not now. I was, but I'm pretty much over that. There was a time when I thought, 'Why her, why us?' But I suppose that I've come to accept it. It seems there's a randomness attached to suffering and death. I don't understand it. I never have." He shrugged. "I don't pretend to."

"How do you feel about the war?"

"When I was last over here, when I returned to Germany five years ago and had a good look at the Nazis, I thought it was inevitable. I had no doubt that we were headed for another major war, and felt we should have fought sooner rather than wait and fight it on Hitler's terms. We didn't have the moral courage to do it then. Now, God knows where this one will end. So far, it sounds as if we're likely to lose—at least, we'll probably lose Europe initially. Generally, I agree with what Harris has to say. I think he's painting the worst case, but I agree, it's also the most probable case."

"Do you think we should make some kind of accommodation with the Nazis? A lot of people are suggesting that. Some say that's what Prime Minister Chamberlain is secretly holding out for. They say war has become too dangerous. We've too much to lose, that sort of thing. What are your thoughts on that?"

"Absolutely not. You can't come to terms with someone who has already made up his mind that he's going to destroy you and knows he has the power to do it. I know a lot of people here feel that somehow we can avoid a fight. The Nazis are as much a scourge as the Mongols were. They have to be stopped. Unfortunately, those who don't see it that way are mostly wishful thinkers, and refuse to believe the truth because it means something horribly unpleasant becomes a certainty. There are a few others opposed to the war, but they're a minority we'll have to deal with. A few days after we declared war, we locked up the mayor of Montreal as a fascist sympathizer. Lots of people are howling over that; but if we're going to win against these people, we have to do it with all our efforts focused."

Crossley nodded knowingly while Thornton made a face that could have indicated perplexity or lack of interest.

Rory went on. "I really am in favour of free speech, but this is a war for survival. The time for debating has long passed. We should have acted against Hitler a long time ago. Intellectually and morally, I've no problem with fighting if you have a just cause. I don't want to fight, but I believe that now we have absolutely no choice. The issues have probably never been so black and white."

Thornton interrupted. "Ewen tells me you served in a clandestine role in Germany in the last one. You're part German. How has that affected you?"

"I don't think my clandestine work or having a German parent made much difference to me. I was more affected by my time in the trenches. That was a nightmare, but those of us who survived got through it."

Rory stopped walking and looked around him. They were across the street from a bus stop and a small crowd had gathered, patiently queued up on the sidewalk. "I've often thought about the killing and the deaths of good men. It haunts you. I don't think I'm different than thousands of others. I was lucky. I guess I always have been. I often wonder why I survived and others didn't; but in the end, I survived and I was fortunate enough to get on with my life. Now, it looks like we're going to do it all again. I don't want to do it, but when it's over, we have to get it right this time. The thing that angers me is that we should never have fought the Great War."

Thornton and Crossley exchanged worried looks.

Rory shrugged his shoulders. "Sacrilege, right? I know what you're thinking, but in hindsight we were all so foolish. The Germans, the French, the Russians, us: nobody understood what was coming. What were the great ideals we were fighting for? The Germans weren't so different than we were in 1914. Yes, they violated Belgium's neutrality to get at France; but they were forced to fight a two-front war. We probably would have done the same if we were buying time to prevent a Russian army from occupying our capital."

Thornton and Crossley glanced at each other again.

"So, we all made a mess of that one. We made a mess of the peace treaty, and as a result we now have two of the most malicious and murderous ideologies in history to contend with: one in Russia and one in Germany. Unfortunately, we can't do anything about the Russians for the time being, but they're going to be another mortal threat to us."

Rory stopped and looked hard, challengingly, at the two men beside him. Crossley nodded as if in reluctant agreement, but Thornton said nothing. He forced a cough, covered his mouth, and broke eye contact.

"As you both know," Rory went on determinedly, "five years ago, I spent three months on an assignment for your previous employer. I came to London and then went on to Germany to find out information for the War Office. Like so many others, I reported at the time that Hitler and the Nazis were a deadly menace. Nobody in power listened to me or to the scores of others who returned with exactly the same report. I went back to Canada and continued to work in the RCMP. I was promoted to chief superintendent and given command of D Division in Manitoba. The rest you know... What else can I tell you?"

The two Englishmen looked at each other knowingly. "Rory," said Thornton, "we aren't fighting the Russians. Why are you so concerned about them?"

"The war's expanding. Russia just occupied half of Poland. We entered the war because Germany invaded Poland. Do you think for a moment that with Russia and Germany staring at each other across an imaginary frontier in Poland, things will remain settled on that front? Hitler hasn't moved against France yet. Ask yourselves, why hasn't he done that? The second most hateful thing to the Nazis after the Jews is Communism. Nazism and Communism are mortal threats to each other. Sooner or later Germany and Russia are going to be at war with one another. I'd take Harris's theory a step further. Hitler is probably biding his time, deciding whether he's going to attack us in the west first or go after Stalin in the east."

Both Crossley and Thornton looked annoyed and uncomfortable.

"Have either of you read Hitler's book?" Rory asked. "It's all in there."

The other men looked sheepish. Thornton spoke. "We don't read German. I know about it from what I've read in the papers. They say it's not worth reading."

"It's not great literature, but it is Mr. Hitler's philosophy spelled out for you. At the risk of being patronizing, I think you should read it. If our enemy has provided us with a complete overview of his philosophy and a summary of his plans, we should at least take the trouble of reading and studying what he has to say. We're in the business of estimating what our enemy intends to do and defining our options. Several years ago, every politician, army officer, newspaper editor, and intelligence officer should have read Hitler's book very closely. How foolish can we be? You can't even buy a paperback translation of it anywhere; not in Britain, not in Canada, not in America. In some ways, we don't deserve to win. Instead of making a tough decision, we've chosen to believe what we want to believe: that maybe things will somehow work out all right. We're going to pay a heavy price for that kind of thinking."

The three of them walked on in silence for a few moments. "Forgive me for getting on my soapbox," Rory said. "You wanted to know what I think and why I came over. First off, Hitler wants to build a greater Germany, which we've already let him do. The next thing he wants is Lebensraum in the east and he wants to create a new German Empire. He wants to dominate Europe and unite all the Germanic peoples in a Third Reich. People like Mr. Chamberlain and France's Daladier have already given him the first of these. We went to war because of the second, but he's not finished. He'll want more than half of Poland, and he'll go after the third objective soon enough. That's why I figure we have this period of phoney war. He hasn't decided what he's going to do yet: finish off his plans for Lebensraum or conquer his Third Reich."

Rory pulled his coat collar up higher around his neck. "I'm sure that Stalin hasn't overlooked that, and we can bet that the Soviet intelligence services have read and translated a copy of Hitler's book. As for your earlier question about coming to some kind of accommodation with the Nazis, if you think you can be safe living with a violently lunatic Nazi Empire that's armed to the teeth and eventually extends from Moscow to the English Channel, then by all means let's cut a deal with Hitler."

"Very interesting," said Thornton. "You know, Rory, you do have allies outside, people like Harris and ourselves. There are people around here who think like you do about the Nazis. More people are coming around to your line of thinking every day—people like Winston Churchill. He's been a voice in the wilderness for ten years; it's just that Churchill's not running things. What do you think's going to happen next?"

"Harris has it right. We have no choice. We dig in here in England and get ready for a long war."

* * *

"Gentlemen, the Reich's enemies are larger and physically stronger than our German army, but we are in many ways much better prepared to destroy them. So please, let us make no mistake about it: we will destroy them."

The man droning on at the podium was Karl Dortinger, one of the National Socialist Party's founding members. But as far as Reinhold Neumann was concerned, Dortinger's lecture didn't have the ring of destiny nor what the papers described as the new Nazi speaking style. Instead, the lecture sounded more like a country parson's sermon. Nonetheless, it was still a break from the seemingly endless stream of bureaucratic directives read out by senior police officers here at the new SS Police Academy's Führerschule.

Neumann looked about him. Most of his fellow students were men just like him. They were police volunteers recently inducted into the Schutzstaffel, more popularly known as the SS, the Nazi Party's most privileged security organization. All the others were intently focused on the elderly party functionary. Neumann and his colleagues sat in the comfortable lecture hall on the third floor of Berlin's Natural History Museum. The museum's auditorium was now temporarily being used as the Third Reich's recently created Security and Police Services Staff College. Natural history, they were told, would now have to wait for the ultimate triumph of National Socialism.

Karl Dortinger, a noncommissioned officer in the German army in the Great War, had been an early convert to the Nazi cause. Over the last three days, Neumann had become used to this sort of ideological intermission sandwiched between more practical lectures. It was the second time they had been exposed to Dortinger's droning tirade.

The lecture hall was filled to capacity with a hundred middle-ranking police officers from across Germany and Austria. Behind Dortinger was a very large map of Europe, flanked by two swastika flags. Neumann couldn't help but notice that every time Dortinger looked up from his notes, the stage lights reflected back from his round steel-frame glasses, making him look like one of those hapless characters in an American cartoon. He tried to suppress a laugh.

The good-natured Bavarian officer sitting next to him turned and grinned. "You find this clown as hopelessly boring as I do? That's reassuring. Look around. Everyone's pretending to be enthralled by this bullshit."

Neumann immediately became mildly alarmed and whispered, "What? Herr Dortinger has interesting views on the destiny of the German people. I only hope we have time to hear him expound on them. I think the last time he spoke it was much too short."

The officer beside him let out a long exasperated breath. "Absolutely. How could I forget?"

Neumann responded in a scolding tone, "Of course, he's made some excellent points, especially about the nature of the threat posed by Germany's traditional enemies." He glanced around, but no one was paying any attention to this exchange. "No, Herr Dortinger is very good indeed. The future of the German people is not something to be taken lightly."

At the podium, Dortinger continued. "Germany is now united in its efforts to realize the vast potential of this country. You have seen how in just a few short years National Socialism has brought the Aryan nation to life. Germany has pulled itself up from its near moribund state of unemployment, debt, and dishonour. We have united the Austrians and Sudetan Germans, and we have rescued our Prussian brothers, who were confined by the treachery and fraud of the Versailles Treaty and locked into an artificial Polish state. Can you imagine Germans having to live under the domination of Slavs!"

Reinhold Neumann looked about him. The faces of his fellow students were expressionless.

"Now," said Dortinger, "our Führer, Adolph Hitler, has shown us that it is our destiny to take on the role that history has always demanded the Aryan peoples should rightfully assume. Our armies are ready, and in the last two years we have developed a doctrine for the occupation of hostile countries. We shall implement that doctrine in the neighbouring territories that will make up the new frontiers of the Third Reich. The army will conquer and the police and security forces will subdue and organize our new territories. You gentlemen will play an important role in that respect."

The officer beside him shifted uncomfortably in his seat and looked over at Neumann. Dortinger went on. "So, in addition, don't forget the part that you, the leaders of our police forces, will play in helping us solve the Jewish question. I can tell you that many solutions have been bantered about. I have heard that the Führer himself believes that all of Europe's Jews should be deported. And I have it on good authority that Madagascar is one of the places they are considering deporting them to, although I have also heard that they may simply be removed to Russia when the time is right. For me, I say, let them colonize Siberia. Slavs and Jews deserve each other. They have polluted Europe and sapped Germany's vitality for far too long. I could tell you stories about the Jews and the Communists."

As Dortinger wound up his speech, fantasizing about ridding Europe of its undesirables and describing how Jews, capitalists, and Communists had desecrated Greater Germany, Neumann began to drift off into his own reverie. He kept his eyes fastened on the bespectacled old crank at the front of the room and wondered where all this was taking him. If, as they were telling him, the Reich expanded within the next two years, he would certainly have more opportunity than he could ever have dreamt was possible when he was a simple Anwärter der Schutzpolizei rounding up drunks on Vienna's street corners. Now, the next step was to get himself onto the staff of the newly created Department D—the New Territories Police Agency. So far, things hadn't gone badly. In the last three years, he had done incredibly well for himself. By being on this course, he was halfway to realizing his ambitions.

As for Dortinger, the old fool had some value. He was describing the official blueprint for career success in the Reich's new police forces: crush the Fatherland's enemies and transform the occupied territories into docile and productive colonies. These were achievable tasks, ones that he could see himself playing a useful part in. Neumann had already made up his mind, and going back to regular police work in one of the German-speaking cities was no longer an option. That would only be a ticket to a plodding, conventional career. Six weeks ago, who could have imagined him being here?

Things were quite different now. If he played his cards right, in a couple of years he might find himself head of a major department for all of the Third Reich, or better still, sent back to Vienna as a deputy chief of police. Wouldn't that make Maida's family cringe! She had no idea he felt so strongly about her family; but he'd often daydreamed about it. They had a thousand ways of putting him in his place. Neumann hated his overbearing in-laws and just thinking of the possibility of having one of his smug brothers-in-law arrested made him smile. A few hours of stiff interrogation by some thug of an underling would hurt no one. Then, of course, he would step in and release the brother back to Maida's family with the wretched man telling them how grateful he was for Neumann's intercession. The way things were turning out now, that kind of fantasy might just come true someday.

"But this is where you gentlemen come in." Dortinger was finally summing up. He had walked away from the protection of his podium and changed his tone of voice. The old goat always seemed to cheer up at the end of a lecture. Maybe he was happy it was over. Neumann glanced at the lecture schedule in his notebook and mentally rolled his eyes. Over the next two days they had another two hours of this insufferable man on the timetable. There was a price for everything.

In the hallway on their break, amongst a milling, stretching, and chattering crowd of police officers, Neumann lit a cigarette. It would be a mistake, he thought, to look too bored by any of this. The Bavarian beside him had made a stupid mistake. In the worst case, simple boredom could be interpreted as disloyalty. One thing could lead to another, and disloyalty in the SS had only one punishment. At best, the other students would ostracize the Bavarian for being a know-it-all. There was a danger in that too, thought Neumann. Being isolated from one's peers in this line of work could lead to problems down the road. He shook his head. In all other respects the Bavarian seemed intelligent. It never ceased to amaze him how naïve some men could be.

Neumann drew in a lungful of smoke and exhaled noisily. For some reason he felt jumpy. He'd been feeling that way a lot lately and it was hard to put his finger on why that should be. He knew he should just focus on what he was doing now, get his mind firmly settled on doing well on this course.

He flicked the ash from his cigarette. Perhaps he was putting too much pressure on himself, worrying about getting promoted. That was certainly part of it, but there was also the matter of Maida. She was really at the back of his mind. Maida had been out of sorts lately: distant and frequently surly, and she wouldn't say why. It worried him. She was beginning to behave like the rest of her family. She claimed to be happy about being in Berlin, but even before they came here, he had begun to sense a gradual change in her.

Maida used to be a hot-blooded little vixen, but now most of the time she was cold and unresponsive. Some days she was downright sullen. It was a worry. She hadn't made friends with any of the other wives of the officers on the course. He was certain she wasn't having an affair. And then it struck him for the first time. Just possibly Maida had ceased to love him. Maybe whatever flame they had once shared was now gone. That wasn't how things were for him. He had never seriously wanted another woman. He had always been faithful. He couldn't imagine Maida with another man. He had done nothing to her to merit this. He had never been cruel or inattentive. He didn't drink to excess. He was successful in his career. He was a good provider. He was a good father to their children. There had to be another explanation for her behaviour, but for the life of him, he couldn't figure it out.

Down the hall someone was announcing, "Time, gentlemen. Time. Cigarettes and pipes out. Your next lecture begins in two minutes." At least the next hour would be more interesting than the last period of National Socialist hot air. The timetable indicated this one was to be given by an Oberführer Heinrich Müller from the Reich Main Security Office. It was entitled Gleichschaltung "Building the Reich: Night and Fog in the Occupied Territories." Silly sort of name, Neumann thought, but it was probably going to be something useful. Not like this endless crap about the meaning of being Germanic, the greatness of the thousand-year Reich, and the wisdom of the Führer.

As a group of officers stubbed out their cigarettes in the hallway's steel ashtray, Neumann nudged the Bavarian police officer who had sat beside him. "You know, about Dortinger, he's not a good speaker, but he's a man with insight and the ability to see things clearly. We need more leaders in the police with that kind of aptitude. Don't you agree?"

5

RORY FERRALL STARED DOWN listlessly at a scarcely touched pint of bitter and wondered not for the first time why he had been so quick to accept the request to come to Britain. It was a Saturday night, he was a stranger in a strange pub, and he was depressed and angry. Despite strenuous attempts to force himself to look on the bright side of things, it was a struggle believing that he hadn't been duped.

He looked about him. The lights in the Ship and Flag were dingy, the room was draughty, and the beer lukewarm. Groups were seated in the corners talking animatedly. In an hour, he was supposed to go out to dinner at Ewen Crossley's house in Ealing. Until then, he was stuck. Rory didn't know anybody else. He was starved for conversation and needed a change of location, but going to a dinner party wasn't what he wanted to do, not tonight. He always found it much easier to keep to himself when this kind of mood enveloped him. When he thought about it, his feelings were ridiculous. Tonight he was even angry at himself for feeling ungrateful about Ewen's invitation. The Crossleys certainly didn't have to have him, and he was sure that they were holding the party for him.

Rory had been in England for upwards of five months now, and the work he had expected to be assigned had only been hinted at in a few disjointed conferences. Twice, briefing officers implied that the war effort was going to get into high gear any day now and before long he would find himself feverishly engaged in work more suited to his background and talents. It all sounded empty.

He took a deep drink of his beer. He had left a career and a job that he enjoyed only to find he was working by himself in a shabby office analyzing outdated military reports and worthless diplomatic intercepts. The work was boring, probably pointless, and he couldn't discuss it with anybody. How did he let himself get into this situation? He put the beer glass down. One was enough. Drinking to cheer himself up wasn't an option.

Something had to give. He wanted a new job. He had no real desire to go back to war, but he certainly wanted a change from what he was doing. In a way, it was humiliating. He had been happy as a policeman. In Manitoba, he had a position of influence and value; more importantly, he had self-respect. Here, he found himself anonymously dropped into a junior position where he was subordinate in rank to younger men of lesser ability, and there were no tangible results for his efforts. It rankled him.

He toyed with his beer glass and listened to a small but boisterous trio of soldiers in khaki battle dress uniforms in the background. They were young Canadian officers on their first leave, obviously enjoying themselves. Other than troops at training centres, the Canadian Army was the only large armed organization left in Britain, and the newspapers made much of the fact that some of the Empire's finest troops were manning Britain's defences. What the newspapers didn't say was that the Canadian Army in March 1940 was almost completely untrained. It had been hastily recruited and shipped over to England with only the most rudimentary preparation and none of its major equipment. Like almost all the troops left on this island, they weren't ready to fight anybody yet.

Rory looked vacantly at the blackout curtains over the windows. He wasn't in a situation much different than these young men, except that they all seemed to be good friends and they had a sense of purpose, while he was living like some angry urban hermit.

The towns around London were rapidly filling up with troops such as these from the Dominions and the Empire. In the last few months, thousands of similar young men had been arriving across the country, most of them untrained but enthusiastic and willing to risk their lives in the service of a higher cause. In spite of their enthusiasm, so far the war effort looked like a huge bungle.

He knew he should go over and say hello to them, introduce himself as a fellow Canadian, a veteran, someone who was proud that they had volunteered to come here. It was the right thing to do: wander over, engage them in friendly conversation, and have a sociable drink with a few of the boys from back home. They were probably people he would like. Twenty-five years before, he had been in exactly the same situation. But tonight he was feeling tense and irritable. He needed a change.

He pulled on his coat and hat and stepped into the blackout and the icy March drizzle. Few people were on the streets. Those who were out seemed to loom up at him in the dark like something in a haunted house. Perhaps people who had two eyes and proper depth perception didn't experience the blackout that way. Ruth had once told him that he looked like a hawk, because he had a habit of imperceptibly scanning back and forth to get a sense of distance. She'd laughed, but he took it as a compliment.

Rory walked briskly, struggling to put himself in a better frame of mind. A year ago who would have thought he'd be here: single, and doing his bit for the war in a relatively junior position.

He'd never agreed with much of the thinking so prevalent after the Great War. Since then, too many people who should have known better chose to view men as cogs in a machine, with little control over their lives. It was worse in the new violent ideologies in Germany and Russia; fascism and communism stripped men of their free will. In those creeds the destruction of individuality had become a philosophical foundation stone. He pulled his collar higher up around him. As long as he was alive, he couldn't go along with that kind of thinking. It was no accident that both fascism and communism held the view that individuals were impelled by an inevitable mass destiny. History sucked people along like so much debris caught in the undercurrent of a river. It was a kind of fatalism that bred disaster on a colossal scale with massive social turmoil and unending repression and bloodshed.

He pulled his hat lower to keep the wind off his face. Perhaps that kind of tyranny and misery was inevitable for less fortunate nations. Even in stable countries, he had to admit, the range of individual choice for those trapped at the bottom of society's pyramid was pretty much restricted. But there was still choice.

Then again, he might have looked at things differently at the end of the Great War had he been carried off a troopship in a wicker stretcher, missing limbs and permanently shell-shocked. No, he was fortunate. He was lucky enough to have survived and he lived in a decent country. Stable democracies gave people security. Although democracies weren't perfect, they provided a greater range of choices—not an equal range, but certainly at all levels there was less repression and more opportunity. On an intellectual level, he certainly believed in what he was doing; but in his more despondent moments, like this one, he wondered if that lofty thinking was what really lay behind his volunteering to come over here.

Was there something else to it, something that he hadn't admitted or even worked out? Despite people asking him every time he turned around, he'd avoided thinking too deeply about his motivation for coming here. He wasn't certain why. As a police officer, he'd spent much of his professional life examining the motives of others; and here, in his own case, where he had so much to lose and so little to gain, he found himself evading the subject. If Ruth hadn't died, would he have stepped forward so readily? He wasn't certain what her death had to do with volunteering. In his most private moments, he suspected there was a connection with which he hadn't come to grips. Maddeningly, he wasn't certain what it was. It hovered at the edge of his subconscious like an elusive fragment of a dimly remembered dream.

Maybe it was a sense of obligation. Life had been good to him. He'd never wanted for much. Pre-war life in an exclusive Montreal suburb had been a sheltered existence—maids, gardeners, private schools, summers in Germany, travelling back and forth across the Atlantic in first-class berths, spring and autumn weekends at the cottage by Lac Saint-Pierre in the Laurentians. School had never been difficult, and university had come just as easily. And then came his time in the trenches, his wounding, his recruitment in England, and his period as a spy in Germany.

He had come back from the war more disoriented than angry. His father became exasperated and told him he was one of those men who couldn't settle down after the war. But that hadn't been the case. The war had unquestionably been a turning point in his life. God, how could it have been anything else? But he hadn't spent a lot of time drifting afterwards. He tried working for his father for a few weeks. One sunny morning late in May of 1919 he left the business's ledgers and order books and went off impulsively on a canoe trip to northern Quebec.

In the North, he'd met a retired Mountie who ran a fishing lodge. Despite their difference in age, they had a lot in common. The ageing pensioner seemed to understand what he had been through, and the pensioner's descriptions of police work appealed to Rory. It was a thinking man's life, with a healthy balance between activity and deliberation. That was almost two decades ago. It seemed like last week. He smiled. Had he become a cliché? Not likely. He knew his life had hardly been routine and he never regretted his time in the Mounted Police.

He walked quickly for forty minutes, and with the exercise, the rain, and the fresh air, his mood shifted. A few blocks from Charing Cross he called a cab. With the exception of a dull pain in the socket of his missing eye, a pain that he always got in damp weather, by the time he got to the Crossleys' he was feeling more like somebody whose company he might enjoy.

Ewen Crossley met him effusively at the door of their large brick house. "Rory, so good to have you here at last. Sandra and I have been meaning to have you over for so long now, but this damn war, it's always been getting in the way." Crossley laughed good-naturedly.

His wife was attractive, probably at least a decade younger than her husband. Slender, wearing a tight-fitting blue cashmere sweater and a tweed skirt, she had her dark hair pulled back dramatically in a bun. She smoked a cigarette in a long tortoise-shell cigarette holder. Sandra Crossley could have stepped out of a Noël Coward play. Everything about her was a fashionable cliché, but she was genuinely friendly and more than attractive enough to get away with it.

When Rory first saw them together he was surprised that Crossley's wife was so pretty and chic. From outward appearances there was a huge difference between the two. Ewen had matured into a pleasant, unassuming, and nondescript sort of man—the perfect individual for an intelligence officer. He was shrewd and personable, but entirely forgettable, while Sandra wasn't the sort of woman one forgot easily. Despite these differences, Rory knew that they were both astute judges of character. They were a good match. Crossley was a solid type; Rory had known him on and off for twenty-odd years. He was a decent man, likeable with a strong character and a perceptive and alert mind. Rory had met Sandra on at least two other occasions. He enjoyed her company but couldn't say he knew her well. They were one of those couples you instinctively like. They were completely relaxed in one another's presence.

The evening at the Crossleys' turned out to be more enjoyable than Rory expected. Ewen had invited some old friends he had known since his army days, and several other couples who cheerfully presented themselves with vague introductions of "... actually Ewen and I have worked together for years." It was evident that in this line of work it was a forbidden conversational gambit to pry into anyone's background. As for himself, he responded equally as imprecisely, "I'm in police work. I've spent years in northern Canada and I'm just here doing the odd job for the war effort." It was a successful ploy. Nobody asked about his present employment, but he soon had a small circle of jolly looking faces quizzing him about his past exploits, and questioning him at length about his experiences in northern Manitoba.

"Did you ever have to go long distances by dog team?"

"Well, yes. Most of the major outposts are accessible by ski plane in the winter, but to get to the more remote locations we generally took dog teams up the frozen rivers." This response earned him a cheer, an energetic round of "well dones," and a flurry of questions on life in the North. It seemed that few in this small and friendly crowd seemed interested in anything but Rory's life in the depths of winter, and he found himself fending off questions as to how often he had managed with frostbite and did he ever have to arrest mad trappers or whisky runners.

It wasn't until later in the evening that Ewen joined him in one of these animated circles. "You seem to have made a big hit, Rory," he said.

"No, not me. It's a great party, Ewen."

Ewen abruptly changed the subject and turned so his back was to the group, allowing a degree of privacy. He changed his tone. "I know that you've been sidelined since you've been here, and I want you to know that I'm aware that you are seriously underemployed. I'm sorry."

"Fair enough. So what do we do now?"

"Well, I'm afraid there's not a lot that I can do about it just now. You see, Colonel Harris, he's got it into his head that he's saving you for some other project. When the time's right, he's going to pluck you out and give you something dramatically different."

"You could have left me in Canada to do that. How many others in our original group have you kept on ice like this?"

"None. All the others are from this side of the Atlantic. They've gone back to their original jobs. You're the only one that we actually have a line on. The others all still have a degree of independence until we call upon them. Harris thought things would have turned out differently by now, but he's still convinced that the situation is going to go downhill quickly once this phoney war ends. He's very stubborn. Look, Rory, I'm really sorry about this. I've talked to Harris repeatedly. He's a good man, honest as the day's long, but he's not an easy man to deal with. For one thing, he actually thinks you're gainfully employed. He really does. He reads everything you put out and he likes it."

Rory chuckled. "That's not a good sign. We aren't producing anything anybody with an ounce of common sense hasn't figured out already."

"If we push him into a corner, he's as likely to do something he knows you don't want just to prove he's in control. Rory, I shouldn't say it, but he's one of those leaders who doesn't quite know what he wants, but he's damned certain that whatever it is, he's going to control it."

"We've both seen a few of those in our time. Anyway, I appreciate you telling me this."

Ewen gave an understanding smile and turned back into the circle and struck up a conversation with the couple to his left. The moment of conspiracy was over.

6

Berlin, 12 March 1940

HE LET THE PHONE RING JUST ONCE. It was late at night and Major
Wolfgang Erhlichmann of the Oberkommando der Wehrmacht planning staff wanted to go home. He had already drunk so much coffee
that his nerves were on edge and his mouth had that metallic taste.
He'd have difficulty again sleeping. Erhlichmann had been working
for months on "Case Yellow," the plan for the invasion of France
via the Low Countries and across the Maginot Line. He had been
assigned to this one operation for so long now that he could run
through every possible move in his head, like a chess prodigy able to
play several games simultaneously, blindfolded. He rubbed his bald
head and took off his glasses. The voice at the other end of the phone
was clipped and to the point.

Erhlichmann put the telephone down and spoke quietly to Major
Carl Faber across the desk from him. "They want us to brief them
again on the Manstein plan, first thing tomorrow morning. They
want us to emphasize the detail of striking through Holland and Belgium, and only provide a broad brush outline for the breakthrough
into France. Apparently there's some concern with those close to
the Führer as to whether or not we can do it. This time the task has
been given to Colonel Brandt. He's just finished the weekly plan-

ning conference and has to go before the Führer himself at the end of the week. The Führer has announced that he will personally decide which plan we'll use."

Major Faber leaned back and put his jackbooted feet up on the desk. He was a quiet individual, a tall, athletic, and perpetually youthful-looking man with a dry wit. "They can use whatever plan they want. No matter how you look at it, we're going to steamroll through Belgium and the Netherlands." He laughed and gestured with a grease pencil. "We have two perfectly good plans. Tell the Colonel to inform the Führer that they can choose whichever one they want and let us go home to our families. At this point, we all know how the invasion will turn out. I think the Führer's aides are all just a bunch of bureaucrats, playing some kind of political game to see who curries the most favour with him. Whatever plan he chooses, we're going to pulverize the Dutch and the Belgians. The real test is whether or not we can break through the French and then separately defeat the English and French armies. Because in the end, if either the Dutch or the Belgians give us any trouble, we're just going to bomb them into submission. There's nothing terribly sophisticated in the preliminary phase of the operation."

Major Faber began spinning a pencil in the crook of his thumb and forefinger. Abruptly he stopped and looked up with a mischievous smile. "Don't you find all of this kind of boring? I'll tell you what: let's flip things around. Tomorrow, you do the manoeuvre briefing for the Colonel, and I'll brief the logistics plan with all the options spelled out. I can recite your parts with my eyes closed. You describe the actions of the units in contact with the enemy; I'll go through all the supply and transport details. I don't need notes. You're always telling me the fighting bits are the easy part. We've gone over this so many times I could stand in for you without notes. It's simple. I'll review in broad detail all the major supply options, give them an assessment of everything: the overall daily tonnage summaries, rail, motor transport, and forage requirements, fuel, rations, ammunition, casualties, go through the unique railroad coordination measures, road requirements, harbour areas, dumping programs, rear area signals, use of civilian telephone exchanges, water points, airfields and airheads, likely points of resistance in the rear, and rear area security plans."

He looked pleased with himself. "It's easy. See if the old goat would even notice we were briefing each other's parts. We both know the detail well enough to do it."

"Don't be ridiculous," said Erhlichmann. "The Colonel will catch us out. Besides, he's so keyed up now he's going to think we're making fun of him. Even on a good day, the man has no sense of humour."

"Okay, better still, let's do the whole briefing as we always do and then ask him how he thinks we should react in the event of a possible French or British counter-attack north in support of the Dutch. Everybody just presupposes that the French and British will stay put and give us the initiative. He's so wooden, asking him to think on his feet will throw him off his stride for days."

"You're probably right, but he's sly enough to know how to handle that kind of question without having to think it through."

Major Faber crumpled a sheet of paper and threw it across the room into the wastebasket. He had a self-satisfied grin. "I know his answer already." He changed his voice into a high-pitched rasp. "For fear of offending us, neither the French nor the British have even conducted a map exercise of a major offensive movement north into the Low Countries; and neither of them have built in sufficient logistic capacity to conduct large-scale offensive action against us even if they wanted to. They're tied to a rigid linear defence providing a shield right around the French perimeter, while we're thinking in terms of a series of sharp spear thrusts into their soft areas." Dropping back to his normal voice, Faber added, "He'll tell us it's going to be like taking an ice pick to a balloon. And you know what? He'll be right."

* * *

ANNIKA'S IMPATIENCE with Professor Snijders was beginning to show. "There are a lot of things Pauli Herschel could do, perhaps not in our department, but I know he could teach a course in the law department. He's well-qualified."

"Annika, you don't understand," said Dr. Snijders. He leaned back and began removing his glasses so that he could polish them on his tie, a gesture the portly gentleman always used when he wanted to buy time. "It's not that your friend Pauli Herschel isn't qualified, but there have to be circumstances other than the fact he's a refugee from Germany before we go ahead and start urging our colleagues here in the university to hire him. There are procedures we have to observe."

Annika's inability to conceal her displeasure was never a trait that endeared her to her superiors. Today her exasperation showed in every movement. Snijders had known her since he first hired her five years before, and he wasn't going to allow her an opening. "Mr. Herschel isn't the only well-qualified refugee we have, by the way, and you haven't provided me one shred of evidence that his qualifications are as you and he say they are."

Snijders stood up quickly and began arranging papers on his desk. "Annika, I don't doubt that Mr. Herschel is legitimate, but we just can't jump up and hire someone because we think they've had a bad time of it."

"No, of course, you're right. But we aren't talking about a theoretical situation here." Annika's voice became louder. "In the last war, the Netherlands took in over a million Belgian refugees. What's happened to us? We see what's going on next door and we not only turn our heads, but we make pious pronouncements about our self-interest and the need to maintain balance with our relations. We know we have an entire religious group being persecuted in Germany. These people are suffering. We can't become officious when they start arriving as refugees. We should assist those who've shown up on our doorstep in need of help. You believe in that kind of charity don't you, Professor Snijders?" Annika's argument about charity was spoken in a much more conciliatory tone. "Please, please."

Snijders continued to pretend he was busy with his papers. He looked up momentarily and then lowered his eyes, holding up his right hand in a defensive gesture. "Let's not be personal about this, Annika. I have every sympathy for your friends from Germany. We can agree to help them, but we can't go breaking our own rules and putting their interests above the legitimate interests of Dutch citizens. Helping these people doesn't mean we give them preferential treatment. Besides, the government has set up a camp for such people at Westerbork. That's where such people should be held. There's an established procedure in place. The regulations were put in place to keep out communists and dangerous agitators; and I certainly don't disagree with that. Why are you trying to go around the regulations? That kind of attitude's not going to help your career here at the university." Professor Snijders threw the papers he had been shuffling down onto his desk and snatched his reading glasses from his face. "I have a lot to do this morning, so if there is anything else that you want to discuss, do so now."

Annika lowered her voice. "Where else do you suppose we could find some kind of suitable employment for Pauli?"

"I don't know. And your friend won't be the only one. If you make room for him today, there will be twenty more clamouring at us tomorrow. We don't want German refugees in the Netherlands. We can't accommodate them, and to attempt to do so will ruin trade relations with our largest partner as well as strain diplomatic relations between our two countries. In case you haven't noticed, it's not a good idea to antagonize Mr. Hitler. I'm sorry, Annika, but that's how it is."

Outside, in front of the conservatory building, Annika felt stunned. Her cheeks burned as she unlocked her bicycle from the crowded rack. It was as if she had somehow humiliated herself. Now she felt awkward and unsure. This morning when she came here, she thought she would be able to accomplish something positive, that she would make a difference. She didn't expect to be rebuffed here at the university.

Thinking about it, Annika realized how important her life at the university was to her, especially now that things were so different at home. Saul wasn't the same. After the party he had been strangely quiet; and whenever they discussed the Herschels' situation he merely nodded in agreement. She knew him well enough to know that he wasn't being defeatist, but was deep in thought. It still irritated her when Saul went into one of his uncommunicative moods. There had been far too many of those lately.

For a full minute Annika stood in front of the university buildings holding her bicycle, staring expressionlessly at the cobblestones beyond her front tire. Slowly she began to push the bicycle. Her movements were tentative, almost as if she was reluctant to go somewhere. After walking fifty metres, she swung onto the bike and began pedalling steadily.

For twenty minutes she cycled across Amsterdam, through streets lined with trees, arriving finally in front of a large building surrounded by a high brick wall with a crowded bed of red tulips at its base. At the gate, Annika did her best to sound authoritative when she addressed the young, freckled, blond man of about seventeen who manned the entrance. "I've come to see Mr. Van Zuiden. I'm his nephew's wife."

"Do you have an appointment?"

"No. It's very important. I must see Mr. Van Zuiden now."

It was only then that Annika noticed the small brass nameplate discreetly nailed beside the control booth's door: *Samuël Van Zuiden, Diamond Merchant. Appraisals, Cutting and Sales.* The building, with its manicured grounds, was immaculate; there was nothing industrial about it. It could have been a private school or an embassy. The young man looked at Annika suspiciously and indicated that she wait outside on a bench by the wall beneath a large chestnut tree. He picked up the telephone, spoke briefly, then hung up.

"He'll see you now," he told Annika. "He's very busy this morning."

Annika merely nodded her head in a chilly display of thanks and was led inside to a small, tastefully appointed office with a large desk and two leather armchairs. The pale green walls were lined with framed antique technical charts showing various cuts of diamonds.

Samuël Van Zuiden came in a few seconds later. He was in his early sixties, with a grey Van Dyke beard, and dressed in a smartly cut dark suit.

"What can I do for you, Annika? We don't see you or Saul very often. Is something the matter?"

"No, Uncle Samuël. I know the family should get together more often. You're busy so I'll get to the point. Nothing is the matter with Saul or me, and thank you for asking. We have refugees from Germany staying with us, Jewish refugees. They arrived two days ago with nothing but the clothes on their backs. I've been trying unsuccessfully to find them work, something to help get them on their feet. Mr. Herschel is a lawyer. I've tried at the university, but everywhere I go, I don't seem to have any luck. I'm beginning to think nobody cares. They're absolutely destitute and they can stay with us as long as they wish to, but I know they want to be self-supporting. They're proud people, Uncle Samuël."

"And so when you have run out of places to go, you come to me. Does Saul know you are here?"

"No."

"I see." Samuël rubbed his jaw and said apologetically, "Please sit, Annika. You know what I'm thinking?" The two of them sat beside one another in the leather armchairs.

Annika nodded. "I know, we haven't seen much of the family since we got married—"

Samuël interrupted. "It's good of you to show such concern for these people, Annika. I assume you want me to help you in this search of yours?"

Annika said nothing.

"I can tell you that there isn't much that I can do for them here in my business. I have no openings, but I know some others who might be able to employ them temporarily."

"Thank you, Uncle Samuël, this is such a relief."

"Don't thank me." He patted her hand. "These are bad times; we have to do what we can. I wish there were more like you. These people, do they have children?"

"Three—two girls and a boy. All under the age of ten."

"Well, they're all better off here than back in Germany. God knows where that will end. I really do have another appointment to go to just now, but Annika, can I call you in a day or two? I'll find something. It probably won't be much and nothing like a lawyer's job, but leave it with me."

Samuël stood up. As he was showing Annika the door, he turned and touched her elbow. "You know, Annika, we really would like to see you and Saul some time. Families shouldn't feud like this. Can you speak to him about it?"

"That would be nice," she said with a smile. "Why don't you come over some time; in fact, why don't I call you next week and we can arrange for you to meet the Herschels? You know, for the first time in ages I think that things are going to work out."

* * *

Northampton, 9 April 1940

COLONEL GEOFFREY HARRIS was in a three-piece suit and wore the striped tie of the Staffordshire Regiment. He chewed his lower lip as he walked across an enormous oriental carpet in the portrait-lined drawing room of Ramsford House in Northampton. He thrust his hand forward in greeting. "Rory, I'm awfully glad you could make it tonight; things are heating up faster than we predicted." He was breathless. "I don't know if you've heard or not, but the Germans have just attacked Norway late this afternoon. I'm sure you've heard that they invaded Denmark this morning. From what I've heard, the poor old Danes are capitulating, and there's scattered but fierce resistance from the Norwegians. Of course, all this changes things substantially for us."

Rory merely nodded.

"You don't seem surprised by any of this," said Harris with a note of suspicion. "What do you make of the news?"

"I don't think anyone predicted it would happen like you've described. Nobody expected they'd go after Scandinavia first. But there's no question now. Hitler's going to attack France and Britain next. For now, the Russians get a by."

"I think you're right. In fact, no news to you, a lot of the work that your group has been preparing for us seems to support that view. From what we've been able to determine, the Germans haven't moved any divisions, or even so much as a major unit eastward for some time; and they're still quietly moving equipment and supplies by train in and around their western garrisons and airfields."

Harris fished in his jacket pockets for his cigarettes. "As you can see, things are changing and I wanted you to see this house." He was jumping from subject to subject, but despite this, he now seemed less breathless, more in control. "What do you think of the place? So far we've got ourselves two of these stately homes. We plan to use them as training schools. This one's the first. I think you'll find once Jerry comes at us in earnest the government will be more agreeable about giving us the use of these places. They'll make ideal training centres: they're reasonably isolated, lots of bedrooms, a large kitchen, drawing rooms that can be used for lecture rooms, and with their grounds they all have an attached training area. Anyway, come upstairs. Crossley's waiting for us. We have news for you."

This was not the first occasion Rory had seen Harris agitated. He was an odd sort of individual. One day he was distant, icily professional and commanding, and the next he seemed tense and unfocused. Rory suppressed a sudden impulse to tell Harris that he thought he was over his head, that he had been wasting his time for months on end, and that he had almost no confidence in him; but he took a breath and consciously restrained himself. That sort of an outburst would be pointless; it wasn't entirely true; and it would only get him sent back to Canada. He said nothing and followed Harris out of the drawing room. Although he had wondered previously about Harris's suitability for the job, it was the first time his doubts had erupted so spontaneously in anger. As he rationalized things with himself, and just as suddenly brought himself under control, he wasn't at all certain if his anger really was directed at Harris, or was simply a vent for so many months of frustration.

Upstairs, one of the larger bedroom suites had been haphazardly converted into an office. The furniture contrasted abruptly with the floral wallpaper and gilt trim. Lost in the corners of the room were two plain wooden desks. By the windows was a government-issue conference table strewn with manila files. Rounding out the room's improvised military appearance, a large map of Europe was tacked to the wall. Crossley was talking on the telephone. He put it onto its cradle almost as soon as the two men entered the room.

"Hello, Ewen," Harris said. "Before we go down to dinner, I want to run a few things past Rory. Ewen, please flesh out any details that I might miss. Rory, pull up a chair."

Rory looked about warily and sat on a wooden office chair. Every sense told him he was going to be offered a change of employment. Ewen was wearing his professional face: expressionless and reserved. Whatever the reason for the meeting, Rory thought his personal preferences wouldn't trouble Harris. He wondered if Ewen's comment about Harris's need for control had been some kind of a warning. With his languages and Great War experience, he suspected he was about to be asked to go to Germany. France seemed unlikely. But something about Harris's behaviour tonight put him on his guard.

Harris spoke first. For a fraction of a second it appeared as if Ewen raised an eyebrow.

"Rory, let me start from the beginning. We've brought you here because of your clandestine work in Germany, your languages, and because you have such splendid police experience. All of these qualifications make you an ideal candidate for running a large operation in either Germany or France. Unfortunately, no one is going into Germany just now, and we haven't figured out how to fix that."

He raised his hands in a defeated gesture. "Unless we get some kind of spectacular defections, I'm afraid we've missed the boat there. We should have developed that area ten years ago, but back then no one with any influence was thinking in those terms. We had no money and, as you know, we didn't cultivate any sources within the Nazi Party. Incredibly short-sighted of us when you look back on it, but that's where we are. Now, and for the foreseeable future, Germany's a closed shop to us. Their security measures are much too well developed for us to have any reasonable chance of success and any mission there would be a suicidal waste of talent." Uncharacteristically he shrugged.

"France is another matter. However, in France we have a rich supply of usable agents who speak good colloquial French and know the country well. We don't anticipate any problems there. You, on the other hand, have the resourcefulness and the experience that makes you suitable for work anywhere on the continent. We need you for the time being to go somewhere else. So, despite the fact that you don't speak another language—" He stopped and for a moment almost looked embarrassed. "I'll get to the point. We want you to work initially in the Low Countries."

Harris stopped talking and watched Rory closely. Rory exhaled deliberately and imperceptibly, doing his utmost to appear impassive. He didn't respond. There was a moment's uncomfortable silence.

"How do you feel about that?" Harris said.

"I'll withhold comment, for now. I'd like more information."

Crossley jumped in. "Rory, I know this sounds a bit hasty. But we've thought it through, believe me. If the Germans come at us across the Maginot Line and we have a long stretch of stalemated trench warfare like everyone thinks, we'll pull you out and re-employ you. But if they come from the north and violate Dutch and Belgian neutrality, like we think they will, Jerry will get in behind the French and roll up the country fairly quickly. I don't have to tell you that's always been our worst-case scenario."

"You see, Rory," Harris interjected, "there are two things we have to reckon with in the Low Countries. Let me begin with the military situation. We don't think the French army is up to much. They're well equipped, but our private assessment is that they're almost certainly going to buckle." He held up a hand in mock restraint. "No question, they've got lots of good units, excellent equipment, but at the senior levels they're still feuding with one another, and the quality of their army is too uneven. There will be holes in their line. On top of this, civilian morale is extremely low. We fear they don't have the stomach for a serious fight."

As Harris paused for a breath, Ewen Crossley added, "It's even worse than the last time Colonel Harris briefed you on this. The French are going to break, and break early. And the best way for Jerry to make that happen will be with a short, sharp campaign launched from an unexpected direction where they drive deep into the French rear area. If that happens, France will probably buckle and sue for peace in a matter of weeks."

Harris nodded. "Should that occur, again assuming they strike into France from the Low Countries, like we think they will, we'll have a British army stranded in France with Jerry occupying all of northern Europe. We'll need people in the Low Countries. And the way things are going tonight, we're probably going to need them in position very soon."

"All right," Rory said, "so let's assume that things turn out as you suggest and you send me into ... where in the Low Countries? ... Holland? Belgium?"

"Holland," Harris said flatly.

"Okay. What do you expect me to do once I'm in Holland?"

"Nothing's changed there," Harris said. "We want you to build a resistance movement. Get things started. Then we want you to come back and put your experience to use organizing an army of agents that we'll be developing back here."

Harris stopped talking and looked at Rory for a moment. "I do have something else to tell you about going into Holland, Rory. We've had some very bad luck there in the last few months." He paused. Again Rory thought he sounded like he was making some sort of confession.

"You probably aren't aware that we had a serious intelligence setback in Holland in November. It's not common knowledge. We lost two agents. It was a trap and we fell for it hook, line, and sinker. We were in touch with what we thought was a dissident group in the

German army. We were led to believe that certain sections of the German Officer Corps were about to attempt a coup, kill Hitler, and stop the country sliding further into war. In fact, this may explain some of the prime minister's optimism. There have been a number of people who felt that if they pushed the right buttons they could avoid a prolonged war. We were foolish. Well, to make a long story short, two of our agents were lured to the Dutch border town of Venlo. They were captured by Abwehr agents and taken into Germany."

Crossley took up the story. "It gets worse, Rory. We think that, as a result of this, every one of the SIS's intelligence contacts that we've cultivated in Holland has been compromised. We know that following this kidnapping, several of our Dutch contacts were murdered or simply disappeared. We believe Holland is next to be attacked, and we're now in the position where we have no reliable network sources to work with."

"It's not entirely bleak, Rory," said Harris. "Obviously, one of your first tasks will be to establish a network. There are two positive notes in all of this. The first is that you can go in clean. We're confident that Jerry will know nothing about you. Even if the Nazis have an agent working here in London on this, you don't have to worry about that end of things. The second advantage is that our agent who was picked up worked for MI6, not us. That's another reason we think you have excellent prospects for success. So far, our organization, which doesn't even have a name at this stage of things, is effectively limited to the handful of men you have already met and the other men I briefed along with you last autumn. I hope to be getting some more people shortly, but you can be certain that when you go in you won't have been compromised. That's more than SIS can count on these days."

The colonel pursed his lips, put his hands in his trouser pockets and turned away without speaking.

After a moment, still facing away from Rory, Harris continued. "As I said to you several months ago, we expect to be in this business for several years, and frankly, Rory, right now we don't know much about it. I'm the first to admit it privately, we're bloody amateurs. I'm sure it hasn't escaped your notice that we've been making it all up as we go along. The only people who've really been in control of events have been the Germans."

Both Harris and Crossley gave humourless smiles. There was a strained silence. They exchanged awkward looks and Harris turned about and spoke. "I'm sorry we've left you in the dark, really since you arrived here. I didn't expect it to take so long to get to this. And you can imagine, we've had political constraints imposed on us."

The two men looked at Rory for some sort of affirmation. Rory spoke quietly, "Okay, I still want to hear more detail."

"You're right," Harris agreed. "You deserve to know more, but for the time being we can't tell you too much because you'll be going into the field. And, if you're captured, I'm afraid you're going to have to trust us." Harris was choosing his words carefully. "The short answer is that you are about to be working for a special committee reporting directly to the prime minister. For funding and administration, we have, as you already know, created a cover organization in the Ministry of Economic Warfare. This committee and whatever we build from it will remain entirely separate from the War Office and the Secret Intelligence Service. You move over to us this week. No one in the armed services or SIS knows about us. If they did, they'd find a means of snuffing us out."

Rory nodded imperceptibly. "Sounds a bit out of character for Mr. Chamberlain, don't you think? First, you tell me he's dancing on one foot hoping for the German army to stop Hitler, and now he's setting up a new clandestine service designed to subvert and sabotage a Nazi-occupied Europe."

Harris spread his hands. "What can I say? Chamberlain certainly went as far as he could appeasing the Nazis, but I think he sincerely hoped he'd avoid another war. I'm told he's even given an order for the air force not to bomb German munitions factories or harbours. He's an enigma, no doubt about it. On the other hand, he's hedged his bets in a number of areas. He's a more complicated personality than the papers give him credit for. I don't think he'll be prime minister much longer, but this whole resistance movement, believe it or not, is his idea."

"It's not just Chamberlain who's on side, though," Crossley added guardedly. "We have the backing of some influential politicians. A lot of people are pushing for Churchill to take over the reins. And of course Churchill himself has been pushing strenuously in private for something like this for months now. My guess is that our project is only getting oxygen as a means of appeasing Churchill in cabinet, which answers your doubts about Chamberlain's support. That would also explain why not even the secretary of war, Oliver Stanley, is aware of what we'll be doing, but we have been told that he'll be brought in later when the prime minister thinks the time's right. Since the war broke out, we've been nothing more than a tiny planning cell and we've been busy getting the administrative groundwork right. There's been no need for many people to be in on this; and I'm sorry, but that's why you've been kept working on the sidelines. All this is probably going to change now that the Germans have started to move. But for reasons that I'll explain to you, it's viewed as being highly desirable that we remain completely independent from any existing organizations."

Rory made a sceptical face at this. "I can see problems in that."

"We know," Crossley said. "Starting up a separate intelligence and clandestine strike force won't make us any friends. But we have two advantages by being separate. First, as I mentioned before, we don't want to be given away if the Germans succeed in penetrating one of the larger organizations—and we aren't certain yet that they haven't already done that. And secondly, we believe that nothing bold, imaginative, or innovative is going to come out of the stuffy old hierarchies of either the War Office or MI6. We want to build something different, an organization that will exploit the talents and energy of the entire British Empire, and that's not likely to come from the regular army or the peacetime intelligence service."

"The other aspect of this," said Harris, "is that we don't have time to wait around for the other security branches to get their act together.

The incident at Venlo that we just described to you is proof SIS isn't up to the job of fighting the Nazis. We're not going to build another incompetent old boys' club. We need to react quickly and we'll have to expand rapidly; and to do that we need innovative minds. Our next project is to start recruiting an organization to fight the Japanese, and I'm afraid we just can't get anything like the numbers or the kinds of people we'll need in the places where SIS and the smart regiments recruit their officers."

"So, Rory," said Crossley, "we've probably told you more than we should have. We really should get to the point. Are you in?"

Rory rubbed the back of his neck and smiled before answering quietly. "Of course I'm in. I haven't been sitting around here for the last six months for the fun of it. If that's what you wanted to know, my answer is yes, definitely; now, let's go downstairs for dinner."

7

ANNIKA WAS TAKEN ABACK. She stood in the living room of her town house, her right hand unconsciously raised to her mouth. "You mean you're leaving Amsterdam tomorrow? But Pauli, I think I've managed to get you a job through Saul's uncle. You can start a new life here. It'll be wonderful. Your family—they'll be safe and secure and we can help you with the adjustment. This is the Netherlands. It's not like Germany."

Pauli shook his head. "Annika, Germany hasn't been like Germany for ten years now; Europe's turning into a madhouse. You've been very kind, and I'm really grateful for the help you and Saul have provided on no notice when we just turned up on your doorstep, but last night, after we went back to your place, my wife and I decided we're not staying in Europe."

"This will end, Pauli. We need people like you here. Where will you go?"

"You obviously haven't heard the news on the radio. Germany just attacked Denmark and Norway."

Annika said nothing. She crumpled backwards into an armchair, stunned and numb, as if she had been given a strong and unexpected electric shock. It wasn't just the news of disaster from a distant country. She felt personally stung with the sudden understanding that the future would not be what she hoped it would be. The news left her frail and embarrassed. Her mouth went dry. "It can't be true. We could be next. It's unbelievable."

Pauli's voice sounded remote, as if he were speaking from another room. Unaware of Annika's distress, he continued. "I went to Saul's synagogue today. It was just a hunch, but apart from yourselves, the only other man I had any connection with in Amsterdam was a distant cousin on my mother's side. I found someone at the synagogue who knew of him and he gave me his address. My cousin was smart. He left Stuttgart when things really started getting ugly in 1935. I'd almost forgotten about him. He lives here in Amsterdam, but last week he sold his business and he's leaving for South Africa next Thursday. He has connections with a Dutch shipping line. He's offered to arrange our way to Cape Town. We can pay him back when we're on our feet in South Africa. We sail to Lisbon tomorrow on the first leg of the journey. In ten days, we'll be in South Africa."

"Pauli, do you really think the Germans will come here? We haven't done anything to harm them."

"Neither did we. Neither did Norway or Denmark. For that matter, my father was even wounded in the German army in the Great War. We've been living in Germany for hundreds of years. What did any of us do to deserve this?"

"Pauli, I feel like such a fool. I've always believed people were essentially civilized, and that if you treated them decently they'd behave the same way. Even with the Nazis and Hitler, I thought they were just an aberration, something caused by an unjust peace treaty. I thought the invasion of Poland was the worst thing that would happen, and even then I thought that it could be justified in some measure because they intended to absorb the Danzig Germans. But now, Denmark and Norway. What could they have possibly done? What does this mean for us? They really might try to enslave us all. Is this possible?"

Pauli gave her a look of resigned finality. "Oh, it's not only possible, it's happening. Europe's going into a dark age; but my family's not going to be a part of it. We sail at eleven tomorrow."

* * *

Kaldenkirchen, 9 May 1940

IT WAS MUCH TOO WET for the beginning of May. By late afternoon, the rain had picked up in intensity and was drumming on the roof of the 1935 Opel Olympia. The car had been parked for the last three hours in front of a grubby and shuttered electrical repair shop in the German village of Kaldenkirchen near the Dutch border. Major der Schutzpolizei Reinhold Neumann was sprawled in the back seat watching the puddles grow on the far side of the cobblestoned street. It was still much too cold for this time of the year, but that wasn't what was troubling him. Neumann had to remain stuffed into the back seat of this cramped car until they were called forward some- time after first light tomorrow when the invasion of Holland began. It was chilly and damp, and to save fuel they were forbidden to run their engines. To make things worse, he was getting a cold. His throat was sore and his head ached.

Neumann would have gone back to bed if he could have gotten away with it, but by early afternoon the army's Feldgendarmerie had placed all units of the 26th Infantry Division into their pre-invasion Order of March. Patrolling the flanks of the columns were grim- looking helmeted military police with rifles.

Neumann thought the army's nickname for the MPs, "Chain Dogs," was appropriate. Around their necks they wore a distinc- tive brass neck plate. And come to think of it, Neumann had never seen one of these men smile. Not once. They served their purpose, though. They kept curious onlookers away and ensured that no German soldier strayed from his allotted spot in the assembly area. Besides, Neumann knew he couldn't go back to bed anyway; the hotel that he had been billeted in the previous night was now out of bounds. If he was caught there he'd probably be summarily shot for desertion.

Down the street, the enormous smiling figure of his driver, Rottenführer Dieter Schmidt, lumbered towards him. Schmidt was a tall, gangly, fresh-faced Austrian in his late twenties. Before being transferred to the Ordnungspolizei and then into the Schutzpolizei, Schmidt had been the senior member of a two-man detachment in a small Tyrolean village. He was rustic to his roots. He even told Neumann that before he was transferred to the larger police force he did his rounds on a bicycle. When he transferred to the SS, some clown must have acknowledged his supervisory status and made him a non-commissioned officer. Neumann wondered how he was ever posted into his unit as a driver.

Neumann smirked at the thought of this monster of a man struggling up and down hills on a small bicycle, keeping order amongst the cowherds and pig farmers. What were they thinking, posting mild-mannered men like this into the SS? Schmidt was the kind of yokel who gave Austrians a bad name in the new German security apparatus. Neumann regarded him as far too rustic for the kind of hard police work National Socialism demanded—much better to have cold-blooded men from the cities about you rather than farmers' sons who longed for the smell of cow shit and an evening's yodelling.

Schmidt fumbled along cheerfully, juggling a green wine bottle, two loaves of bread, and a large paper bag in his arms. Neumann had let him go forward within the vehicle column to see what kind of luck he might have scrounging food to supplement their army hard rations. He had obviously been successful.

Holding the bag under his chin, Schmidt tugged open the car's back door. Neumann made no effort to help him. The junior policeman was dripping wet but smiling. "Herr Major, some things to make the night pass a little more quickly. I bought them from an old man who lives in that apartment building by the traffic circle." He was excited and obviously pleased with himself. "The signals troop leader a few blocks farther up says he's seen the first motorized infantry battalion leave the assembly area. They passed not twenty minutes ago. It's really going to happen."

"Get in the front and close the door. Of course it's happening; you think we're here for the fun of it?"

Schmidt shrugged, climbed in behind the driver's seat, and gently closed the door.

Neumann shifted in his seat. "Let's see what you managed to find. Did you think to get us glasses?"

Schmidt rummaged in his coat pocket and triumphantly produced two small tumblers. "Yes sir! And some pork pâté!"

Neumann grunted. "Good. Pour me some wine and pass me some of that bread and pâté." Neumann sniffed and made a face. "Schmidt, did anyone ever speak to you about that cologne or aftershave, or whatever it is you're wearing? It's revolting. Don't wear it again. You smell like a Hamburg pimp."

"Yes, Herr Major." Schmidt paused for several seconds. "It was a gift from my wife. But you know, I've never smelled a Hamburg pimp before." Schmidt turned away and sipped his wine and then busied himself breaking the crusty loaf.

Neither man spoke and the implied rebuke hung in the air between them. Neumann could punish Schmidt for that kind of insolence. He didn't have to explain anything to anyone. That's what discipline was. On the other hand, Neumann thought, someone quick witted and resourceful like Schmidt could be useful, especially in Holland. Who knew what waited for them there. It would probably be advantageous to have him onside. It wasn't that long ago he had been walking a patrol beat himself. Still, it burned to be made an ass of by his driver, especially when Schmidt was being gracious and Neumann knew he had behaved like a swine.

For a brief moment Neumann debated with himself whether to say something now or jolly Schmidt along later. He could teach him a lesson by letting him sweat it out for a while, worrying that there would be some kind of reprisal for his impudence; then again, maybe it might be the wiser just to brush it off now.

"Schmidt, I'm going to stretch my legs for a few minutes." Neumann grabbed his hat, opened the door, and stared down the street. "And Schmidt, thanks for the food. How much do I owe you for my share? You know, I have a terrible headache."

Schmidt beamed. "Not to worry at all, sir. Four marks, and we'll say we're even."

Neumann gave him a mirthless smile and stared at him for a second. Schmidt couldn't have paid more than a mark fifty for the lot.

Outside, Neumann stood up and stretched. Nothing had gone right today. He reached back into the car and grabbed his Tyrolean hat, the expensive one with the grouse feathers and boar bristle plume. He liked that hat. It was a hat that made a statement. When dressed in civilian clothes, most Gestapo officers wore a green leather trench coat and a dark, wide-brimmed fedora, pulled down low over their eyes. Neumann thought they were imitating the gangsters in American movies. This hat was clearly Austrian and Neumann privately resented it that so many "German" SS officers half-jokingly ridiculed him for being Austrian. After all, the Führer was an Austrian, and when he was in civilian clothes he frequently wore a Tyrolean hat. Nobody dared make jokes about the Führer's clothing.

Behind Neumann's Opel was a requisitioned Daimler bus filled with uniformed police officers. He gave them only a passing glance. He didn't want to appear too interested in them. Better to exude confidence in front of his men.

Some of the men on the bus tried to read in that fading light, some were sleeping in uncomfortable positions; others smoked and stared vacantly out at the world, thinking their own thoughts. The war pulled them away from their normal jobs, their families, and the routines they had once known. His car and the bus accompanying them made up the first police contingent designated to go into Amsterdam. They were assigned to occupy the police headquarters. In his briefcase, Neumann had a long list of priority tasks they were to accomplish on their first day in the city. They were going to be busy.

By midnight, the rain stopped and the clouds blew away, leaving wisps of vapour trailing across a crescent moon. Neumann had managed to sleep fitfully for a few hours; Schmidt, despite being crammed into the driver's seat, was sleeping like a baby. In one of the trucks farther down the street, there were cigarettes glowing, and Neumann could see the silhouette of troops in helmets with rifles slung. They were talking in low tones. He wondered when they would all be going home. But another problem nagged at Neumann. Tonight he wasn't quite sure where his home was.

Maida had moved back to Vienna. He had got the letter from her the day after he left Berlin. It was the last he had heard from her. It was so matter-of-fact, a heartless, one-page note informing him of her move. There was none of the old chatter about the children. He wondered how Klaus and Monica were doing. They were probably in their pyjamas, fast asleep, still clutching their teddy bears at this time of night.

It was no use asking Maida to wait for him back in Berlin; she wasn't going to stay there. She said in her letter she was going to be staying at her parents' house; she had already asked her mother to put the children's names down for an expensive private school. The implication was clear. She had no intention of following Neumann in his career. Even worse, there was no suggestion that he should come back to Vienna when this was over. He rubbed his hand across his mouth. What the hell was going on with that woman? What could have caused the change in her? This was all so sudden. Did it mean she wanted a divorce? She had no grounds. The party didn't take kindly to that sort of thing. Families in the Third Reich were meant to stay together. It hurt. And on top of it all, it didn't look good. It was humiliating.

The only good news in all this was that Maida's father had been retired prematurely. Maida had offered no explanation. She simply wrote that Daddy was now retired from the police force. That was good news. It meant he would never have to feel beholden to her family for anything again. Not that they had ever done much to help him. It was his participation in party activities that had given him the boost he needed. Besides, the party didn't like these old-guard families anyway. Now, no one could ever say his future achievements were anything but his alone. Still, he had to admit that the tension between him and Maida's family never did anything to help their relationship.

He exhaled deeply. It sounded more like a sigh. Maida had never shown the slightest interest in his family. Not that Neumann was much of a family man in that sense. He hated his father, who he had not seen in six or seven years; and he had never been at any great pains to be close with his mother, or his sister and two brothers. He wasn't sure where his brothers or his sister even lived now. He fumbled for his cigarettes. He should quit these; they made his throat sore. But in a funny sort of way, he'd hoped to have had a better life with Maida and his children than he did growing up. He didn't understand Maida sometimes. There were times when she could be a proper little bitch; then he chided himself. He didn't want to be angry with her. Whatever it was, perhaps it would blow over.

He turned and tried to make himself comfortable. All this would have to wait until the war was over and he could go back home on leave. With any luck, he might get home before the end of the summer. He couldn't do much to fix things from here. But maybe in late August or early September he could convince Maida to join him in Amsterdam if things improved. Who knew?

Shortly after one in the morning the first flight of aircraft roared overhead. Neumann was surprised at how low they were: wave after wave flying low and in formation, all of them making a tremendous din. The noise of their engines reverberated in the box-like street. It was a disturbing and frightening sound, but at the same time it was strangely thrilling. In the dark it was hard to tell what kind of planes they were. They had big engines, that was certain. Neumann thought they might be bombers, but, then again, maybe they were transports carrying paratroops. Whatever kinds of planes were ploughing overhead through the night, Neumann knew that the soldiers in them were soon going to be killing Dutchmen who were probably now sleeping. That didn't bother him. He hoped that if they were bombers, their bombs rained down on Dutch soldiers, inflicting massive casualties. Better to have the Dutch army suffer than our own troops.

The soldiers in the truck forward of him jumped out of the back of their vehicle and began shouting and slapping one another on the back and waving up at the sky. The prospect of the coming violence was invigorating. Neumann smiled at their enthusiasm. Another flight of planes thundered above them, and the windows and shutters in the buildings of the village shook.

As energizing as this moment was, Neumann didn't regret that he had never been a soldier. He didn't care for the possibility of getting killed or wounded in battle; who did? By the same measure, Neumann didn't like the discomfort, or the discipline, and he didn't like living and working at close quarters with so many others. That kind of life had never appealed to him. In fact, when he really thought about it, Neumann didn't like the idea of spending time in groups. He was more of a solitary man. Police basic training was something to be endured, but since then he rarely had to work in a team. It was just as well, too. Neumann didn't want anyone else taking the credit for his work.

Although he certainly never wanted to be a soldier, he revelled in the sense of power that the German army infused in the nation. He was proud of the Third Reich's military. Those planes overhead, these young soldiers in front of him, even those menacing Feldgendarmerie troops made Germany a nation to be feared; and tonight they were going to seize Greater Germany's rightful place in the world. Even Austria—as much as he loved its slower pace and unassuming character, he knew in his heart of hearts that it was stronger and more vigorous now that it had fulfilled its destiny as a part of a greater Germany, and the German army was somehow inseparably bound up in that sense of destiny.

He smiled as the soldiers in front of him whooped and cheered and made obscene jokes about the unsuspecting Dutch. Tonight, even some of the military police who wandered over to the vehicle lines were smiling. No one should ever get in the way of the might of the Third Reich. Tonight he was proud to be a part of that new nation.

8

Northampton, 10 May 1940

STILL SWEATING from his morning exercise, Rory Ferrall walked around the flower beds of Ramsford House. The old estate no longer had its small army of gardeners, maids, and footmen. Everyone under forty had left for military service, and those too old or unfit for the army had been drafted into better-paying jobs in the munitions factories. Rory noticed that the weeds were already winning in their fight against the perennials. He enjoyed it out here in the countryside. He took a deep breath of the cold, damp air. He could smell last night's rain soaking into the moist, rich earth. The months he had spent in London had left him fatigued and unfit, but in these last four weeks he had been exercising intensively every day and there was a huge difference in his energy level.

It was still frustrating. There was no word yet as to when he was to go to the Netherlands. He chafed at being kept perpetually in the dark. The only information he had received was that the plan developed for him had not been approved, as no one wanted to be seen to be undermining the Expeditionary Force's efforts with the French. He would be advised as soon as a decision was made. In the meantime, he should continue to prepare himself.

Rory had driven himself hard this morning. After a good sweat he thought more clearly. He stood back on the lawn, looking over the house and its grounds. Since moving here a month ago, he had spent fifteen hours a day preparing himself for his task in the Netherlands. Still, he wondered how much he had accomplished. He had organized all of his training by himself. Harris's section was still running on vapours; as far as he could tell, the much promised infusion of new staff was a long way from ever happening, and there was no one else in the Ministry of Economic Warfare who knew anything about Holland. There were fewer still who knew anything about clandestine warfare; but there was no point in being pessimistic.

At least now he had a passable cover story. Harris, Crossley, and he had agreed that he would travel in Holland as Martin Becker, a German- and French-speaking Alsatian businessman from Strasbourg. Even though it was deadly serious, it had been fun for the three of them making up Becker's persona. They created Becker together one night over a bottle of brandy in front of the fireplace in the estate's study. Wherever possible, Becker was given a similar background to the one Rory had used as cover in Germany in the Great War. And so it transpired that Becker had been seriously wounded while fighting the French on the Marne. He had served with the 9th Landwehr Division and was invalided home. This meant reluctantly becoming a French citizen after the Versailles Treaty. But Becker was a man with an easygoing disposition; his late wife, who he greatly missed, was half-French.

If questioned, Rory would only admit to speaking German and French. Becker would be travelling in the Low Countries, intending to expand his seed and fertilizer business on behalf of an old but sickly friend back in Strasbourg with whom he had been employed for eleven years. To flesh out his cover, someone in London prepared Becker a dog-eared French passport and a wallet-sized card with a picture of his deceased wife on one side and a memorial prayer printed on the other. He had yellowing discharge papers, a prescription for migraine headache medication from a French doctor in Strasbourg, a library card, and in his briefcase he would carry a series of

letters and files from several Dutch farmers and agricultural distribu-
tors to an address in Strasbourg. Rory had even travelled down to a
wholesale seed distribution firm in Kent, spending two days learning
some of the fundamentals of the seed and fertilizer business.

Now he spent each day reviewing and strengthening his cover
story, doing his physical exercises, practising Morse telegraphy,
shooting at the pistol range, studying Dutch, and reading anything
he could get his hands on that was remotely connected with the
country or the agricultural supply business. His days were full, but it
was exasperating. Nobody in the Ministry of Economic Warfare was
prepared to risk compromising his security, and because the Dutch
were still obsessively neutral and hoped to escape the war, he had
been forbidden to make contact with anyone in the Dutch embassy.
As a result, Rory found himself in the ludicrous position of preparing
to risk his life on a clandestine mission without benefit of actual prior
contact with a Dutchman. He shrugged his shoulders and rolled his
head to stretch his neck muscles. There was no point, he thought, in
getting worked up about it. If you were going to be successful in war,
or anything else, you had to be accommodating about things that
were beyond your control and ruthless in pursuing the things you
could influence.

In one respect, Rory conceded that he was fortunate. In the last
two weeks he had been able to practise his German and French with
four newly arrived trainees. They were mostly expatriate Polish officers, and he knew them by their cover names only. They were an optimistic bunch, anxious to fight the Germans. Amongst this group
were two who could speak fluent German and French. On the other
hand, having the chance to talk to them was not always a great comfort, as Rory found his French and German were rusty and he often
struggled for simple words. It was an asinine way to prepare for a
deadly serious mission. And notwithstanding his attempts to stay
optimistic, whenever he saw Harris, he told him what he thought
about the training regime.

He walked slowly up the stairs leading to the front door. Despite his misgivings about the mission, he liked it here. The great stone house was a magnificent example of Elizabethan construction, and over the centuries the landscaping had been steadily updated by some of the world's finest designers. The house and grounds were a glorious illustration of what could be done when good taste and money converged over several generations. Someone once told him at dinner that the southern wing of the building had been designed by Christopher Wren. The glass in the front door could possibly be three hundred years old.

For the last two weeks Rory had been packed and prepared to leave Ramsford House on short notice. But even these final preparations hadn't been easy, and getting a radio proved to be a serious trial. In the end, he had badgered Ewen Crossley and was given one of the first new, experimental, long-range Morse sets that the section had been allocated. The radio and its specially designed electrical hand crank weighed almost forty pounds and took almost all the space in a large leather suitcase. He only had one other smaller case for his revolver, two hand grenades, his clothes, false papers, false letters, money, and emergency rations. Both pieces of luggage were packed and sitting by his bed.

As he climbed the stairs to his room, one of the clerks from the newly formed administrative section came tearing breathlessly after him. "Mr. Ferrall, sir! There's a call for you downstairs in the orderly room. It's Colonel Harris and he says it's important."

He took the call in one of the converted drawing rooms.

"Ferrall speaking."

"Rory, thank you for taking this call before breakfast. I do hope I haven't disturbed your exercises."

"Not at all, Geoffrey. What's happening?"

"I don't know if it will come as any surprise to you, but the Germans launched their invasion of France and the Low Countries this morning. The news will be on the radio within the hour. The Phoney War's over. I've just finished speaking to my superiors, and I think you have a very good chance of travelling as we've planned. I can't be any more specific as this is a civilian telephone exchange, but can you be ready to leave Ramsford House by noon?"

"I can be ready in five minutes if you like." Rory's heart quickened and he did his best to sound controlled.

"No need of that. Take your time. I'll have a car pick you up at noon."

* * *

IT WAS A BEAUTIFUL DAY, and like so many other shocked residents of Amsterdam, Annika and Saul had been drawn to the city centre in the days after the Dutch government surrendered to the Germans. There was nothing festive or jolly about their desire to come together. It was like a family being close after the sudden and tragic death of a loved one.

It was such a shock. The Netherlands had done nothing to deserve this. It seemed so unreal, a steady stream of uniformly bad news. It was as if they had lived through a nightmare and couldn't wake from it. Even now, it was hard to remember what had happened in the proper sequence. German paratroops had landed on the first day; those were followed up by a ground invasion with tanks and motorized infantry. Pitched battles had been fought for three days, in which the Dutch were steadily hammered by the larger, stronger, and more professional German Army. And finally, on the fourth day, Rotterdam had been pulverized from the air. More than a thousand civilians were dead and tens of thousands of homes destroyed. The Germans threatened to repeat the bombing, and so the Dutch government signed an armistice.

It seemed like it was over before it started. The royal family had fled the country and was headed for Canada. And now there were German troops in Amsterdam in large numbers. There were even rumours of thousands of Dutch prisoners of war already being marched en masse into Germany to work in war factories.

Sitting at a café beside the Emperor's Canal, Annika and Saul spoke in hushed, worried tones. It all seemed so inconceivable. Across from them were Oscar and Nina Van Sittart. Oscar Van Sittart worked with Saul at his law office.

"Saul, I don't think we can stay here. Your German friend Pauli had the right idea. We Jews should just down tools and get the hell out of here."

"You mean just sell everything and leave?"

"No, I mean just leave. Lock the door and get out. Give the key to a gentile friend and get out while the going is good. Maybe they could sell things later."

"Where would you go?" Saul asked despairingly. "They're still fighting in France. Half that country is overrun."

"Make our way to America, Canada, South Africa, Australia, Ireland. Hell, I don't know; anywhere but here. This is no longer just a bad premonition of disaster. This is a disaster."

"What do you think they'll do—uproot us, ship us off to some place like the Polish ghetto? You think we should just give up everything we've worked at for so many years? So we'll be an occupied territory. This isn't the seventh century. The Germans aren't the Mongols. Civilization has progressed, and even the Nazis can't destroy a thousand years of progress. No, we should stay here and resist this on our own terms. The rest of the country will stand by us, and the Germans will eventually come around to the rule of law. It's in their blood. There may be some dark times, but we can see this out. I don't believe in running."

Annika was frustrated. "Saul! You said that to Pauli and he's gone. I agree with Oscar. It's long past time to get out. Yes, we leave everything. We won't starve to death. We start new somewhere else. We won't be the first to do that."

Saul nodded and took a deep breath. "I agree, things are bad, but the Dutch people will stick together. What are the Nazis going to do? Mass executions for disobedience? We still have our courts, our ways, our traditions. They won't break these overnight."

"Don't be a fool, Saul," said Oscar. "What do you think they just did to Rotterdam? They flattened half the city. Thousands dead.

Why? Because the Dutch army showed resistance when their country was invaded. Why can't this happen here? Are we any better than the Russians? Russia has been a bloodbath for twenty years. It's been completely out of control for years. Why can't some people just interpret what they see for what's really going on. This isn't the worst of our troubles—with German troops invading, it's the beginning. What's to stop Hitler now? The British have been driven out of continental Europe. The French army has come apart. Look at Rotterdam. Nobody knows how many are dead. Why do think our army capitulated? Why did the Germans bomb Rotterdam? Now they're bombing Paris. What have any of us done to Germany?"

"Saul," Annika said, her voice rising, "I've never seen you so blind and so obstinate. But let me say something: I don't want to raise children in a country like this. The Netherlands is fine. Raising a Jewish family in the Third Reich is not. I won't do it. Oscar and Nina are going to try and get out of here, make their way to Spain and on from there. I want to go with them."

As Annika spoke, three trucks of motorized German infantry followed by a police sedan drove at an insane speed down the Spiegelstraat. The drivers of all the vehicles in the convoy were leaning on their horns. There was something menacing and inhuman-looking about these soldiers, with their coal-scuttle helmets and their rifles. They were gone in a minute. All conversation stopped, and the waiter cleaning crumbs at the next table stopped and stared. "Where do you suppose they're going? And how many years will we live under an army of occupation? Who would have thought it would ever come to this?" Everyone at the café's tables stared in silence across the canal.

Saul was the first to speak. "It's bad, but we'll survive. We're not quitters. We can talk about this again tonight. I gave my word to Uncle Samuël that I'd go and see him this afternoon. It's not as simple as it sounds. I spoke to him this morning. He's not well. He's been talking to his doctor and they think he's seriously ill. That's why he's anxious to see the family get back together again. He's probably only got a few months left. Until yesterday he hadn't told anyone except his wife. I promised to go and see him this morning. We'll mend fences.

This is no time for us to be running out on him. Annika, why don't you go home with Oscar and Nina? I'll meet you back there in two or three hours. I should go see Uncle Samuël myself. We'll talk later."

***

Amsterdam, 19 May 1940

AS THE BLACK OPEL OLYMPIA squealed on the cobblestones at the corner of Amsterdam's Weesperstraat, Reinhold Neumann struggled to sit upright in the back seat. His driver, Dieter Schmidt, was grinning with his hand firmly on the horn. Driving at high speed in a military convoy through the streets of Amsterdam was the most exciting thing he'd done in days. He shouted over the blare of the car horn, "Sir, who would ever have thought the army would be able to drive their trucks this fast?"

"Keep enough distance between us and them so you can stop if you have to. I don't want to die stuck to the back end of a Wehrmacht lorry."

They were under strict orders not to stop, and it was unlikely that this column had any intention of slowing for anyone. Neumann knew the insane driving was in part melodramatic and they did it for the effect it would have on the local population. Aside from getting to their objective quickly, they wanted to convey the impression of merciless speed and efficiency. Resistance in the face of this display of strength and purpose would be utterly useless. As far as Neumann could see, these tactics were having their intended effect.

This was Neumann's third high-priority objective of the day. His first two had gone smoothly, much more smoothly than he could have guessed two days ago when he was first warned of his secondary occupation tasks. And today, if he was successful, he would almost certainly be in line for another promotion. The Reich was growing at a great rate and it would need more senior police officers. He remembered reading somewhere that success was ambition's strongest stimulant. Today he was feeling stimulated. The ease with which his team had carried out these police raids certainly kindled his daydreams of commendations, promotion, and glory, and he had to struggle to keep his mind on what he was doing now. So far it had been a good day.

Just before dawn, at his first objective, Neumann and his team had arrested the foreign minister. They ringed his house with troops and before anyone knew what was going on, they broke his door down with a sledgehammer. The poor old fool was dragged out of his house in his nightshirt, demanding to know under what grounds he was being arrested. That task went smoothly enough. Nobody in the house expected he would be arrested and the family was clearly terrified. There wasn't so much as a second's resistance.

After a quick breakfast of coffee, black bread, and cheese at the main Amsterdam police headquarters, Neumann's team moved on to the day's second objective, the Dutch Mint. He watched the streets of Amsterdam flash by and the shocked look on people's faces as his column raced through their streets. He smiled at the thought. There was a certain professional satisfaction in knowing how easily the much more sensitive second operation went. That was one that had the potential to go wrong, but his team of police and infantry handled it superbly. Nobody expected them, and once they had clubbed the guards' shift supervisor, clapped handcuffs on him, and thrown him into the back of one of the trucks, the remaining guards turned over all their keys and willingly demonstrated how to synchronize the unlocking procedure so they didn't trip any alarms. He left two sections of infantry to guard the building, and he still had the better part of a company to handle the rest of the day's work.

Things were going so swiftly. At this rate, he'd probably be finished by noon. There were only two more tasks on his assignment sheet. Both of these were in the same area. He had to secure two addresses in the diamond-cutting and trading section of town. When he briefed the infantry and his policemen that Amsterdam's diamond industry was run by Jews, there were loud guffaws and cheers. Personally, he didn't like that sort of display. Not that he particularly liked Jews, but if you are going to be professional in your police work, you shouldn't allow the rank and file to behave like they were drunken louts at a village soccer game. Soldiers, police—it didn't matter—they had to concentrate on what they were doing, and that required discipline and focus.

Whoever had mapped out these police objectives had done his homework well. Someone, well before the war, had exhibited real professionalism in this kind of detailed planning, and now things were going flawlessly. A platoon of infantry had been assigned to each Gestapo squad and so far there had been no resistance. Neumann liked that.

Neumann also liked what he had seen of Holland. It was such a sensible little country. The people were good looking, the towns and cities clean. There was an obvious sense of order and purpose to the place. In its own way, it was as Germanic as Salzburg. The café on the other side of the canal looked like it could have come out of a Viennese postcard: people enjoying the early summer sunshine, drinking coffee, reading newspapers. It was a shame it had come to war between them. But when you thought about it, compared to the Great War, the casualties in this operation had been insignificant. That's how it should have been.

Neumann lit a cigarette and exhaled as they careened around another corner in one of the narrow streets north of the Herengracht Canal. He had to admit that whoever had decided that the Netherlands should be incorporated into the Reich certainly knew what he was doing. Oh, for now, there were sullen and hostile stares from most people on the street, but Neumann was confident that would all change once they got over the initial shock of being invaded. Besides, he had heard there was a group of Dutchmen that had actually been on hand to welcome the German army. The Dutch Nazi Party had urged a sensible armistice and made a small ceremony of welcoming their brothers in arms. That was wise of them. There was no point in taking casualties for what was a foregone conclusion. Their numbers weren't large, but National Socialism had definitely taken root here. It just hadn't had time to blossom yet. There was hope for the Netherlands. With their Aryan blood and their Germanic sense of order, someday they would be a part of the Reich itself, and not just one of the countries in its Empire.

The column came to an abrupt halt. The lead lorry stopped and infantry were fanning out around the block, preventing anyone from entering or leaving the cordoned area. These diamond factories shouldn't take too long to deal with. Just like at the mint, he would arrest the owner, place a guard on the property, and then move off to his final objective for the day.

Neumann got out of his car and flicked his cigarette into the street. He straightened his Tyrolean hat and adjusted his tie in the reflection from the Opel's window. He noted the small bronze sign beside the front gate tactfully advertising *Samuël Van Zuiden, Diamond Merchant. Appraisals, Cutting and Sales*. He glanced at the sheet listing his daily case file. He was at the right place. The only difference between the sign and his file was that the case file noted "Juden" behind the name of the business. Neumann smirked and wondered by how much this place would increase the Reich's coffers.

The infantry platoon leader doubled up to him and saluted smartly. "The cordon is in place, Herr Major."

"Fine. Send in the entry team. I'll be here at the car. Report to me personally when the grounds are secure and we'll do an inspection. Keep a section in reserve in case there are any problems."

Neumann loitered about the car for several minutes, and then as he grew impatient, he walked up and down the cordon. The infantry stood in full fighting order: rifles, helmets, water bottles, leather ammunition pouches, respirators, and polished jackboots. The soldiers were spaced ten metres apart, every other man facing in opposite directions, allowing them to keep watch over the windows and doorways on both sides of the street. None of the soldiers' eyes met Neumann's and nobody spoke. Neumann looked at his watch. The entry team should be out by now. He paced halfway around the block again. Seconds before he was about to go in to see what was taking so long, a procession made up of three soldiers and a civilian in handcuffs came out the front gate.

"The premises are ready for your inspection, Herr Major. We had some problems with Herr Van Zuiden, but I think he understands the situation. Things are in order now."

Samuël Van Zuiden had his head down. A trickle of blood ran from a cut above his left eye and his shirt was torn at the collar.

Neumann jerked his head toward the waiting vehicles. As the soldiers pushed Samuël Van Zuiden toward the truck, a sweating man on a bicycle cycled furiously up to the cordon.

"What's going on here? What do you think you're doing? This is my uncle; he's done nothing wrong." Saul let the bicycle fall to the pavement with a clatter. As he did so, two soldiers stepped forward and one of them pushed the butt end of his rifle into Saul's chest.

"Stop! He's my uncle. He's done nothing wrong. I'll take care of him. Please, release him." Saul took a deep breath and looked around. Recognizing that Neumann was in charge he stepped toward him. "Please, sir, please."

Neumann snapped his fingers. "Take him with the rest of them. I'll do my inspection now. We have another cordon to complete before noon."

9

Annika bit her lip and began to pace the length of Oscar's and Nina's living room. She was exhausted. Saul had been "missing" for three weeks now, although she had few doubts as to where he was. And that knowledge made things worse. Her imagination ran wild. She was unable to see him, communicate with him, or get any information about him. Saul had suddenly become a non-person. Over the last days she had made a dozen inquiries and merely got shrugs and sympathetic looks.

Three weeks ago, when Saul had not returned to their apartment, Annika went searching for him at the Van Zuiden Diamond Factory. There she spoke to the young, blond gate guard. He confirmed what she didn't want to hear. Yes, he had seen both Samuël and Saul being arrested. He shrugged in an idiotic sort of way and looked away. The Germans took them away, that's all he knew.

Annika's voice turned shrill and she shouted, "Where did they take him? Why the hell haven't you phoned anyone?" When the security guard merely shrugged again she became furious. Her face flushed and her hands went clammy. She took a deep breath, struggled back onto her bicycle and, cursing at the idiot guard, began pedalling frantically the two and a half kilometres to the Amsterdam Central Police Station.

At the police station her pulse was racing, but she had recovered her composure. Although the officers on duty treated her respect-fully, something wasn't right. Despite having never met these men before, she had no doubt that the sergeant and the constable at the front desk were behaving in a strange manner.

All the time she was in the building a steady stream of helmeted German soldiers with rifles slung across their backs and clickers on their boots were carrying document boxes through the front door. The police sergeant blinked rapidly, acting as if he couldn't see them. He was polite and sympathetic, but there was no question: he wasn't telling what he knew. He kept his voice unnaturally low and refused to make eye contact. "I really can't say, madam. The Germans have made a number of arrests, but none of us in the Amsterdam police know who they are or what they've been charged with. We aren't allowed to visit them. There are a number of prisoners downstairs."

He shrugged in exactly the same way the gate guard had an hour ago. And it struck her that these men weren't being stupid or uncon-cerned. It was probably a peculiar mix of shame, humiliation, and fear. She was still very angry, and her flash of insight didn't make her feel any better. The Dutch police couldn't or wouldn't tell her anything about Saul or Samuël, and at the same time, they shied away from any other questions. It was as if they knew exactly what was going on but weren't saying anything. The police sergeant found some reason to leave the room and ordered the constable to take the particulars of Annika's query.

The constable had been no better; if anything, he had been even more uncommunicative. The behaviour of both men seemed unnat-urally muted, as if they were in shock or suffering from some griev-ous news themselves. There was nothing reassuring in their manner, and their behaviour only served to increase her anxiety. Finally, the constable told her she couldn't stay there. There was no information on either Saul or Samuël. Once the Dutch police knew something they would be in contact with her. They took her phone number and her address, and without speaking, escorted her through the door.

As Annika stood alone on the concrete steps of the police station, a pair of black German staff cars with swastika pennants on the front bumpers screeched to an overly dramatic halt in front of the building. Reinhold Neumann got out from the lead car, took a last drag on his cigarette, and flicked the butt out onto the street. He walked up the steps, stopping below and to one side of Annika, as if in wait for someone. He made no effort to conceal his interest in her and stared approvingly. No doubt about it, she was a pretty girl. For a second, Neumann wished Maida were like that. Maida was pretty enough, but she didn't have the sense of purpose or confidence like this one. How many of the Dutch women here would be like that?

Annika looked back and caught his eye for a fraction of a second, then she turned away in anger. He smiled and tipped his Tyrolean hat. Two middle-aged German army officers deep in conversation emerged from the second car and walked up the stairs. One of them took a long look at Annika and smirked as he brushed past. Neumann followed them and called out loudly to them in German, "Gentlemen, if they're all that pretty, we're going to enjoy this war." They laughed as they went through the front door. Annika glared back at them and marched down the steps to her bicycle.

At home, she took a deep breath and telephoned Oscar. But as soon as he came on the line she began to sob. "The Germans have arrested Saul and Uncle Samuël, and our own police won't even tell me if they have him in custody, or where he is or how he is doing. I don't know what to do. I'm frightened."

Oscar was quiet for a second. "I don't know what to say, Annika, but you can't stay alone now. You have to come and stay with Nina and me."

"I can't go. If Saul is released, I have to be home, or if there is any word of his condition, I have to be here."

Oscar hesitated again before he spoke. He was doing his best to be precise but sympathetic. "I'll speak to your neighbours, Annika; if anything happens, they'll get word to us. But for now, you should be with us. Nina and I will be right over."

By the time Oscar arrived at her apartment, Annika had made up her mind. She wasn't leaving. "No, Oscar. It's very kind of you and Nina, but I belong here. Whatever it is, Saul hasn't done anything wrong and he'll be released shortly. I have to be here for him when he gets out."

Oscar and Nina exchanged glances. Oscar spoke softly, choosing his words carefully. "Annika, I understand completely how you feel, and I don't want to say anything to alarm you, but I think it would be wrong to underestimate the danger we're all in. The Germans have just conquered our country. They are in no mood to be nice to anyone, especially when they are in the process of imposing control on a newly conquered territory. I've heard that there have been a lot of arrests. All the diamond merchants have had their property seized. Politicians, newspaper editors... God knows who else has been rounded up."

Nina, who had been quiet up to this point, added, "And remember, Annika, in Germany the Nazis routinely arrest the entire families of political prisoners. We have to assume that Saul has been taken as some kind of political prisoner, or even as a hostage when they arrested your uncle. They're just as likely to come back and arrest you as well. It's best if you aren't living here, for a few days at least. You can't help Saul here."

Annika put her hand over her mouth and said nothing.

All that was three weeks ago now, and Annika had had no word of Saul since. She couldn't wait any more. There was no point sitting around waiting. She'd had enough. She was going back to the police station to demand Saul's release.

* * *

7 June 1940

WINSTON CHURCHILL WAS ANGRY, or at least he certainly appeared to be angry. It was often difficult to tell. He had an unlit cigar in his hand and reading glasses perched on the end of his nose. He was working on his speech to be given in the House of Commons in a week's time. He paced the floor of the dining room at Chequers, the prime minister's country house. Two expressionless middle-aged women in tweed skirts and jackets sat in opposite corners of the room with stenographer's pads on their laps. Churchill's private secretary suppressed a yawn. Sir John Peck was sitting at the long, polished mahogany table with a leather satchel of state papers by his side. Churchill's glass tumbler of single malt Scotch sat on the table in front of him. Peck noticed that tonight, like so many other nights, Churchill always had a drink at hand. Despite this, he rarely saw him drinking.

Churchill raised his head. He looked as if he were addressing some unseen audience roosting near the ceiling's decorative moulding. "'We do not win wars by staging courageous withdrawals. Wars are not won by displaying defiance in defeat. Victory demands aggression and offensive action. By all means, we shall justifiably and publicly extol the virtue of our gallant navy and merchant marine. We shall take courage and inspiration from the discipline and heroism of our army. But there is a hard-won lesson for those of us whom fate has selected to lead these heroic men. As valiant as the efforts of our fighting men have been at Dunkirk, they do not erase the stain of our nation's naïve lack of preparation nor the folly of strategic ineptitude.'" He stopped and paced back and forth like an animal gone stir crazy in a zoo. "No, strike that. Let's motivate and brace them, not criticize them. Strike all of that last piece; instead say, ah yes, say…" He looked about him dramatically. "'Death and sorrow will be the companions of our journey; hardship our garment; constancy and valour our only shield. We must be united, we must be undaunted, we must be inflexible.' Yes, that's much better."

Churchill began pacing back and forth again and then stopped abruptly, his back to the mullioned window. He glared down at his secretary and then glanced across at his assistants. "Yes, I much prefer that last phrase. The next line shall be, say… 'Our qualities and deeds must burn and glow through the gloom of Europe until they become the veritable beacon of its salvation.'" He took a step forward, lifted his head, thrust his jaw forward, and stared off into space. He looked as if he were about to weep.

Peck wondered how much of the prime minister's behaviour was simply theatre. Even if he was being theatrical, there was no question, the man was certainly persuasive, and the stream of his ideas flowed out from him in an unending and fully formed torrent. He could only guess where Churchill was going with all this tonight. As there had been the week before, a dozen impatient senior military officers and civil servants were fuming and pacing in the drawing rooms on the other side of the building. Many of them had been called up here for several nights in a row, but only a few had actually been given an audience with Churchill. Sir John Peck knew he had been pushing himself hard since he had been made prime minister, but he had also adopted the most perverse schedule. He rose at noon and worked through most days until five in the morning. It was almost as if he were deliberately trying to kill his government's senior leadership. The men loitering outside were forced to wait attendance on him and then head all the way back into downtown London to deal with their own staffs in the morning. The country may well have been encouraged by their belligerent new prime minister, but those who worked in Whitehall were finding that their superiors were almost all bad tempered these days.

"Where was I, Peck? Of course: 'For it is us, the members of this House, as well as the leaders of our British Dominions, who have been called upon to lead the world through this most perilous stage of history. We must be constantly vigilant and if we are to prevail against the most evil scourge the world has ever known, and prevail we will, then we must also brace ourselves for the prolonged conflict that will lead to the ultimate destruction of Mr. Hitler and his foul legions of acolytes.'" He put the cigar in his mouth and pretended to smoke it. "Yes, yes. That will do fine for now, as a first draft for an introduction. Have these typed up. I shall review and amend the drafts later tonight after I have been briefed for tomorrow's cabinet meeting. For now, send in the colonel managing the new resistance department. What's his name?"

"Colonel Harris, sir."

"Yes, of course, that's him. Send Harris in now."

The two stenographers rose and gave circumspect nods of their heads. As they closed the door behind them, Peck could hear the word being passed down the hallway. "The prime minister will see Colonel Harris."

A minute later there was a knock at the door and a footman announced gravely, "Colonel Harris, sir."

Harris stepped into the room dressed in his best barathea uniform. He looked fit and confident. His shoes glistened.

"Come in, come in. It's my pleasure, Colonel Harris. I have heard good things about you. I hear that you have been instrumental in drawing up the plans for an organization to resist Corporal Hitler's domination of Europe. Tell me, how far along have you come?"

Harris stammered for a second, "Th-the plans to establish the organization are virtually complete, sir. I have personally recruited our senior leadership. I have two training areas ready to begin operations. I have office space reserved in the Ministry of Economic Warfare. I have already recruited a smattering of potential saboteurs and I feel confident we can be ready to begin producing agents to operate clandestinely in a matter of months."

"Months? Can't you do it any faster? I want to hit the Nazi armies now."

Harris paused and looked steadily at the prime minister. "No sir. We have no equipment. No one has been trained. We have no vehicles, no staff, no instructors, and no budget. We have nothing but plans, a few foreign volunteers, and one trained agent I've earmarked to serve in our senior leadership. He's ready to go onto the continent to confirm and develop our standard operating procedures. We are very much in the early days. We've gone as far as we can without resources."

Churchill pretended to be absorbed in removing a shred of tobacco from his tongue. "Very shrewd of you to ensure that you have someone who will have some practical experience in all this. We shall be at this game for a very long time, I fear. Now, when you say 'we,' Harris, how many of you are there?"

"Full time, there are three of us, sir: myself, my second-in-command, and the agent who is going in this week. I have some Polish volun-

teers and a further half-dozen senior leaders whom I can call upon as
soon as I get the green light, and some funding."

Churchill made disapproving clucking sounds. "How long have
you been working on this?"

"Since war was declared, sir."

"Right. Well, things are going to change, Harris. We're under new
management. Well done. Get the Chief of the Imperial General Staff
in here. He's out there tonight, isn't he, Peck? Good, bring him in."

The call went down the hall for the CIGS and moments later Field
Marshall Sir John Dill stepped into the room. A frosty chill came over
the room—perhaps because the Chief of the Imperial General Staff
had heard that Churchill had taken to referring to the War Office's
behaviour as "Dilly dallying."

Field Marshall Dill looked every inch the marshall: tall, wiry, and
patrician. Churchill didn't greet him or waste a moment for formali-
ties.

"Field Marshall, your Colonel Harris here has been doing some
planning to set up an organization to establish a guerrilla network
in the German-occupied territories. I approve of this, but he has no
resources. That will change forthwith."

"Yes, Prime Minister. I'm aware of Colonel Harris's efforts. I hand-
picked him myself, but political constraints have thus far prevented
us from taking this project as far as we would have liked. I got this
topic on your agenda tonight in hopes that you will change that."

"Very good, Field Marshall. I intend to do just that. Ensure that
this project remains shrouded in secrecy, but make certain Harris's
organization gets whatever it is he needs. Give me a report on it in
three weeks. Now, Field Marshall Dill, there's another matter I want
to discuss. I want to hit the Germans and hit them hard. I want you
to develop a raiding force, one that will roar defiance at the enemy,
tie up his armies in protecting their coasts, and inspire the occupied
people's of Europe. I want—"

Churchill stopped in mid-sentence and looked over his reading
glasses. "That's all, Harris. And, Harris, thank you. Your efforts are
appreciated."

The prime minister turned back to his Chief of the Imperial General Staff and spoke only after Harris had left the room. "I mean this. Whatever his plans require, get it; but I want a new man leading this organization. If Harris hasn't been able to get more staff than that, I want someone else leading the organization. He is obviously a good man. He has imagination and drive, but not the political infighting skills this position needs. Get me someone else who can make this organization work. I'm sure he's a fine soldier, but we need more than just a good soldier for this job. Make him a brigadier and send him elsewhere... Now, my amphibious raiding force, what will it take for you to create a brigade of such troops over the next few months?"

10

RORY FERRALL LOOKED AT HIS WATCH for the third time in five minutes. He was leaning against a clerk's desk in the empty ground-floor office of a two-storey control tower beside one of the Royal Air Force's newest airfields, in Tempsford, Bedfordshire, forty-four miles north of London. The building reeked of stale cigarette smoke and what appeared to be the remains of a boiled cabbage someone had left on a hot plate at lunch. It certainly didn't look like much of a place from which to launch a military operation.

Tonight, Rory was feeling jaded, and more than once he wondered about why he was doing this. Was the operation being mounted because someone simply wanted to keep Churchill happy, as had been hinted at by one of his Polish friends? Since the German spring offensive, there had been four other false starts, and this was the second time he had actually made it as far as the airfield. There had been no explanation, no official reason given for the on-again, off-again status. But this morning he'd received a deliberately understated call from Ewen Crossley. "It's time, Rory, you're going in tonight. This time it's definite." Now that the British Expeditionary Force was safely evacuated from Dunkirk, the prime minister's senior commanders might well have been desperate to demonstrate that somehow the war effort was still in an aggressive posture.

There was a dead fly on the papers on the desk. He flicked it onto the floor. Whoever was running this office was a slob. There was no point trying to second-guess why they chose tonight to send him out. He knew he didn't have all the facts and he'd probably only get it wrong.

He opened the office door to let the evening breeze in. Out across the landing strip he could see the grove of trees beyond the eastern end of the runway. The trees assumed a sinister appearance as the sun dropped. The thought crossed Rory's mind that tonight's indistinct and forbidding shadows masked the true dimensions of the wood line. From here, you couldn't tell how deep the woods were. And for some reason, this broken silhouette of trees and shrubs evoked within him a premonition of hazard. The thought no sooner entered his mind than he began to scold himself for being foolish and letting himself fall prey to his Great War superstitions.

It was a bad habit he subconsciously lapsed into when he was under pressure or tired. He had never told anyone about his involuntary inclination to conjure the future from the familiar. On one level, he knew it was nothing more than a nervous trait that he had developed in the trenches: a perfectly normal reaction to the strain of living with the constant threat of imminent and violent death. There was no point in chiding himself about it. He knew it was absolute nonsense; but somewhere, deep in his psyche, he instinctively looked for signs indicating the future. It wasn't a good symptom. Old delusions were returning: omens and warnings, primaeval attempts to seek meaning and security in the commonplace. It was ridiculous. So why did he let these things colour his moods?

Foolish superstitions aside, he had to admit that he was worried. By the time the sun came up, he would be wandering around somewhere in Holland with two suitcases. If the contents of either were examined, he would in all probability be tortured and shot. He shook his head imperceptibly. Not only had he agreed to this mission, he had helped plan it; and looking at it now, less than two hours before his departure, it was about as close to being the most hare-brained scheme he could possibly imagine. Even back in his previous life as a police officer, the most dim-witted of the criminals he had arrested prepared themselves more thoroughly than the manner in which Harris, Crossley, and he had planned this operation.

He was to be flown in a Lysander airplane to Holland, where they would land at one of two pre-selected landing strips—well away, he hoped, from any German patrols. Once on the ground, he was to make his way to Amsterdam, where he was to contact Pieter van Meekeren, the brother of the Netherlands defence attaché to the United Kingdom. Apparently Pieter van Meekeren was a man who could be trusted and was unlikely to betray him to the Nazis. That was comforting. The two of them were then to establish the beginnings of a resistance movement, and once he was satisfied with his network, he was to radio back to England for a Lysander to pick him up at an improvised airstrip of his choosing.

How could he have ever let himself in for this mission? It was so loosely devised and so flimsily planned. In other circumstances it would have been laughable. He forced himself to look outside again. The treeline looked just as it should have on a spring evening. There was nothing in the least sinister about it. It was the kind of bushy, overgrown, romantic English hedgerow that Wordsworth and dozens of other poets had written about. It was probably teeming with rabbits and hedgehogs, squirrels and nightingales. It was peaceful and tranquil, not a portent of calamity. He wanted a cigarette. It had been years since he smoked, but now he wanted a cigarette.

Over at the end of the airfield, three men in blue coveralls opened a hangar door and pushed a Lysander airplane onto the runway. It was a strange-looking craft with large fixed landing gear, built as if some eccentric engineer had set out to make it look like a bird with a deformity. It had a single, massive, curved, gull-like wing running across the top of the fuselage. Rory smirked. It was an aircraft that wouldn't have qualified even for entry in a design contest. This particular Lysander was painted in camouflage colours, and in the sunset, with the long shadows trailing behind it, it looked as if a spotlight was shining on it. The ground crew pushed the aircraft along the tarmac; two of them were laughing about something.

Through the still of the evening Rory could hear the voice of one of the airmen. "Well, now that we've got old Winston as prime minister, maybe 'e intends to bring the fight to Jerry. And tonight this poor bloke's going to be Mr. Churchill's idea of a counterattack. You'd a thought he'd learned something after he cocked it up at Gallipoli." They all laughed again, and Rory had to remind himself once more about being superstitious.

A black sedan pulled up in front of the office and somebody in a dark suit climbed out from the back seat. He spoke briefly to the driver. The car drove off and Ewen Crossley strolled in. "Rory, they told me at the office that you'd already made your way up to Bedfordshire on your own. I'm sorry I didn't catch up with you earlier. I'd hoped to drive you out." He looked about the office and sniffed disdainfully. "Our newest service has something to learn about keeping things in order, it seems. They need a proper sergeant major here." He put his hands in his trouser pockets and rocked back on his heels. "How are you doing? I can only imagine what's going through your mind."

"Oh, nothing. The usual sort of opening night jitters, I suppose. Besides, if I don't like what I find, I can always call for someone to come and get me. Isn't that the plan?" They both laughed.

"Easy for me to say you've done this sort of thing before," Crossley said, "but I think it'll work out fine. My guess is that this game will get tougher the longer we play it." He lit a cigarette, shook the match with an exaggerated motion, and took a piece of tobacco off the tip of his tongue. "Colonel Geoffrey wanted to be here tonight, you know. Apparently with Mr. Churchill taking over as PM, things are really starting to heat up. I didn't get a chance to speak with the colonel, but he left a message sending his apologies. He's been called off somewhere. I can't imagine him not coming otherwise."

Rory said nothing.

Neither man spoke for a moment. Crossley exhaled a stream

of blue smoke. "Hell of a way to go to war, isn't it? No bands, no speeches, no troopship farewells." He flicked his cigarette into a tin ashtray on a crowded desk. "Well, let's go over everything one last time, shall we? Can we start with your papers?"

Crossley took a checklist from the pocket of his jacket. The two men spent the next ninety minutes doing a final recount of everything Rory carried, and then they rehearsed likely scenarios at checkpoints and police stops.

When they finished, Crossley lit another cigarette and walked to the doorway. With the sun down, the evening was turning cold. He could smell the chilly dampness of the dew falling over the clover fields surrounding the airfield. "You're certainly ready. Your story's credible. The only way I think you could be caught up at a checkstop is if you actually ran into a soldier who's run a seed and fertilizer business when he was in civilian life. And what's the chance of that?"

"Thanks," Rory said with a half-smile.

"No, I'm not saying it to make you feel good. If I thought you had a weakness, I'd tell you."

As Rory went to answer, one of the RAF ground crew stepped into the doorway. "Sirs, I think it's time our passenger boarded the aircraft." He was a young-looking airman, with gapped teeth, curly red hair, and a ready smile. "I think the weather's going to be perfect. The pilot's out at the plane now, and he tells me it's cloudy over the channel with broken cloud cover over your destination area. That's just what we want for you. If you'll come this way please, sir."

Rory picked up his two suitcases. Ewen lunged to carry the largest. "Let me take one."

Rory pulled away, "No. Thanks. This one's got the transmitter and batteries. It's heavy. I've got to get used to carrying it naturally. Might as well start now."

The moon was already rising in the east. At the Lysander, Rory could smell aviation fuel, rubber, and fresh paint. The pilot turned from his inspection of the plane and walked forward to meet them. He was a tall, thin man, with crooked teeth and a nose like a bird's beak. He held his leather helmet in his hand. Rory was surprised that a man of that height could even fit into the cockpit of one of these aircraft.

"Hello, sir. For tonight, call me Eric—no need for either of us to know one another's name. I'm your flight sergeant and pilot, and I fully expect that we'll have a pleasant and uneventful trip." Eric had an Irish accent and a cheerful and unconcerned manner about him. He might have been discussing plans to go for a quick pint at the pub.

"I reckon our flying distance will be just under two hundred and fifty miles, so if we keep to just under a hundred and thirty knots, that leaves us a shade under a hundred miles of fuel for manoeuvring should we meet up with any German aircraft who intend to give us trouble. If all goes well, you should be in the air for just over an hour and a half. When we approach the objective airfield, if I can, I'll make a loop to let you see the lay of the ground. If the intercom is working, well, I'll explain all this again in the air. If it's not working, I guess, sir, then this is your briefing."

Eric smiled and slapped the Lysander's propeller for effect. "When we hit the ground, I'll taxi to the far end of the strip, turn about, come to a full stop, and signal for you to get out. Don't get out unless you see me give the thumbs up. Once you see the thumbs up sign, return it. Then I'll unlock the cockpit cover. You pull it back and you push your bags out and climb out after them. Then lie flat on the ground. I'll count to four just to ensure you're clear of the aircraft, and then I'm off. I won't wait for anything. Once you're out, four seconds and I'm gone. So stay lying flat for your own safety. From the time I touch down until I take off again should be about one minute. It won't seem like much. Once I'm gone, you pick up your luggage and make for the nearest cover. After that, you're on your own."

Eric paused and looked intently at Rory. "When we bring you out, with the exception of you having three marker lights on the landing strip, it will be the same drill but in reverse. I know you've already heard this, but the review makes for a thorough insertion. We don't want any unnecessary drama."

Crossley looked slightly ashamed, almost as if he felt he should be going instead of Rory. "Well, I'll just say farewell and good luck here then, Rory." He put out his hand. "We'll see you back here in a couple of weeks or so." He forced a smile and turned back across the wet grass to his waiting car.

Rory climbed up on the fixed wheel stubs and onto the wheel cover and swung over onto the ladder attached permanently to the port side of the airplane. The design engineers couldn't have produced a more awkward means of getting into a plane if they'd tried.

The pilot handed his suitcases up to him. He grunted, struggling with the last one. "This one must be your radio. I've no idea how you're going to lug this thing around packed like this. For the life of me, I don't."

"I've thought of that," Rory said dryly. "I suppose I'll hide it out in the country and come back for it later once I have my bearings."

Rory climbed in the back and shoved the radio suitcase to one side. The earliest models of the Lysander had a bulkhead between the passenger seat and the pilot. It was a silly design. A passenger couldn't see the pilot. Back at the house in Norfolk, Rory had been briefed that the plane's rear seat was originally fitted for an observer and a gunner, but in this experimental configuration, all the weapons and ammunition had been stripped to make the plane lighter and give it greater range. Two people would make a tight fit. He fussed with his seat belt and strapped himself in while the pilot started the engine. He had flown so often in the North with the Mounted Police that he knew the knot in his stomach had nothing to do with any anxieties about flying. Rory could hear Eric fussing about forward of him. He struggled and found the leather flying helmet on the floor. He put it on and immediately heard Eric's voice.

"You hear me all right then, sir? If you do, just give me a pound on the bulkhead up. The microphone on your helmet doesn't work. Mine works fine, but I'll need this one if I have to talk back to the control tower. I hope not to have to talk to anyone until I'm back here later tonight to land. Are you okay back there?" Rory pounded the bulkhead once with his fist in confirmation.

"Good then, let's be off."

The engine revved up to a deafening roar, the red-haired airman pulled the chocks from the wheels, gave a thumbs up, and the Lysander eased forward onto the runway. Over by the control tower, Rory could see Ewen Crossley standing in the car's headlight and waving furiously. The Lysander turned abruptly and picked up speed; the landing strip rushed by and within seconds they were rising above the darkened landscape.

Eric's voice came over the intercom again. "These planes are as ugly as sin, sir, but you know, they're one of the most dependable aircraft ever built. As for our route, not to worry on that score. I switched my radio on a few minutes ago and the tower at the Gransden Lodge RAF Station tells me there's no sign of Jerry and we're going to have broken cloud from here to Holland. That's perfect."

Rory peered down, trying to make out the Bedfordshire countryside below them. He twisted in his seat and looked behind him to the west. There was only blackness. It was what he wanted to see. If any German fighters were about, he didn't want to be silhouetted against the last of the sunset.

They climbed for a few minutes with ragged streams of cloud rushing by them before hitting their cruising altitude. Rory looked down and could see the lights of farm buildings. He didn't think they could be very high.

After a few moments Eric was back on the intercom. "Those lights, the ones over on the port side, see them out there? That's Cambridge. Just had a large draft of university students in the RAF last week. They're off to Canada for their flight training. Me, I did mine in Scotland just before the war broke out and then went straight to fighters. Passed all my stick and rudder drills and I was top of the class in navigation, but my instructor thought I came close to blacking out in a steep dive on my last flight before I went solo. So, he sent me to Lysanders. Mad as hell at the time, but he could have put me on a desk, so things could be worse. Don't you worry, sir. If you think I'm blacking out, reach forward and give a good pounding on the bulkhead." Eric cackled into his microphone and Rory could imagine his shoulders heaving with laughter. A few minutes later, he could hear tuneless humming coming over the earphones. It was irritating, but he remembered men laughing at the simplest things in the trenches. He said nothing.

"That's the North Sea ahead now, sir. Shouldn't be anything for us to see for a while."

Eric continued his monotone snatches of song for several minutes.

Flying over the North Sea at night, there was no real sense of up or down. From the Lysander's rear seat, the only constant point of reference Rory could make out was the faint outline of his lap and knees and the cockpit glass above him. It was cold up here and he pulled his arms and legs in to conserve his body warmth. The cloud cover thinned and Rory thought that from time to time he could see stars. About thirty-five minutes out from England, Eric shouted over his microphone. "Look! At eleven o'clock! Do you see them?"

Rory looked up in the direction the pilot indicated, but he could see only black sky and cloud.

"Look, there's two formations of three. I think they're BF 110s. I can't tell. These damn clouds get in the way."

Rory strained his eyes in the darkness but could still see nothing. Thank God for the clouds. Suddenly, a dark shape well above them made a graceful diving motion.

Eric shouted into the microphone, "Shit! Shit! The bastard's seen us. Here we go." He wrenched the Lysander to the left and Rory lost sight of the sky above. There was a tearing sound as the wind shrieked over the Lysander's wings. His stomach flew up into his rib cage. They were hurtling towards the ocean and in a fraction of a second they were once again in cloud. Eric levelled off. His voice was steadier now. "Let's hope this cloud continues for a ways here. I think we lost him. My guess is he expected us to roll away from him but we were too tight and he overshot us. He'll be back looking for us, but if this cloud lasts for a few minutes he'll rejoin his mates."

Rory said nothing and did his best to control his breathing. For a passing second he thought that this deadly exhilaration must be commonplace if you were a minnow or any other small life form cowering in a three dimensional environment, exposed, and forever vulnerable to larger predators. The cloud cover seemed to be holding. Eric's voice came over the intercom. "If we can stay alive for another two or three minutes, we'll be past him. I'm hoping he won't stay that long out of his formation; they probably have something else they're up to."

Rory slipped back his coat sleeve and kept an eye on his watch. If they were discovered, he'd probably only be aware of it for a few seconds at most. He wondered if that was true; maybe they'd be alive and screaming all the way down until they hit the sea.

The clouds held for a further five or six minutes. Eric started his tuneless humming again. "Looks like we should be okay with that group, sir. I'm under orders not to break radio silence unless it's an emergency, and I didn't see any bombers with them so I don't think those six aircraft will be too much trouble."

They continued on course for several more minutes, then Eric said, "Hang on, sir, I'm going down to about three hundred feet. From here on in I'm keeping low so we can see outside this broken cloud. When I think we're a few minutes short of your objective area, I'll pop up to confirm our location."

This time the Lysander went into a controlled descent, and again Rory could hear the tearing sound as the wind rushed over the wing. When the aircraft levelled out, Rory could make out the ripples of the North Sea below them. Ahead of them faint patches of light punctuated their horizon.

"Those lights are towns and villages in Holland, sir. Shouldn't be too long now." Eric was cheerful again, as if nothing had happened. "Despite our little unplanned diversion, I calculate us to be about fifteen minutes out from your objective. My fuel looks good, so I should still be able to make it home as long as no damn Jerry bothers me, but that's my worry, not yours. Next problem is to find your landing strip."

Soon the lights of Holland were racing at them. There were fields and buildings and vehicles moving along roads. Rory could make out the blacker straight lengths of the canals, dividing the fields. The fields didn't look long enough to make a decent runway. His throat went dry.

"Right, that's Amsterdam dead ahead. You can see its lights. I'm taking us up a few hundred feet or so and I'm looking for the Amsterdam–Utrecht main rail line."

The Lysander's 905-horsepower engine made a high-pitched whine as they pulled upwards. As they gained altitude, Rory instinctively scanned the skies for German aircraft. The sky was clear but he got a good sense of the city's layout and its southern approach.

"Right, sir. I think I see it over to our left." Eric turned the Lysander south and after a few moments said, "Sir, I think your rail line is that dark patch to our left. Just up here beyond this next village is Hauwoud. Four miles east of that is a good patch of what should be dry pasture. That's your primary landing zone. I'll circle it once, so pay close attention. If it looks okay, that's where I'll put you down. If it's not good, I have another spot ten miles south, on slightly higher ground."

They powered on and made a sweep of what to Rory looked like a series of shadows: roads, ditches, and dykes. "It's pretty dark, but I think that's it on our port side. I'm going to go for this one. I'll be landing facing north. Amsterdam's straight on from the aircraft's nose about twenty miles from here. Hang on, sir."

The Lysander rose, and then went into an alarmingly steep dive, finally levelling out at what appeared to Rory to be no more than four or five feet above the ground. He thought they were flying level with a fence line off the aircraft's right wing. There was a hard series of teeth-rattling bounces and the Lysander was rushing over a rough field.

"We made it!" Eric shouted in his microphone. "Standby to deplane once I turn around at the other end of the pasture!" The sound of the propeller and the engine increased in intensity as the Lysander slowed down and slewed across the field. Eric pulled at a lever on the cockpit roof. "Pull back the cockpit," he shouted. "Take off your helmet and kick your luggage out. Once the luggage goes, I count to four. Good luck, sir. God be with you!"

Rory yanked the cockpit cover back. It didn't budge. He pulled again, straining his shoulder in the process. Eric shouted, "Wait, it's stuck," and wrenched at the lever above him. "Try it now." The glass canopy slid back. Rory yanked off the leather flying helmet and threw it between his knees. The first piece of luggage went out effortlessly but he had to heave and wrench at the radio, bouncing it off the aircraft's side. The engine noise was deafening. The blast of wind on his face was like stepping into a hurricane. He crawled up out of the aircraft and pivoted around on his belly searching for the boarding ladder with his legs. He scraped his stomach sliding down over the canopy rail and his feet flailed in the dark. Even before he got his footing the Lysander began to move forward.

The instant Rory was out, Eric reached up and slid the canopy back into place. Rory pushed himself away from the aircraft and fell heavily onto his knees on the wet earth. He flopped down flat into what felt like fresh mud. The Lysander pulled away in a roar. Outside the aircraft Rory felt exposed and was conscious of the unnatural smell of aviation fuel. His knees were soaking wet. The Lysander accelerated and pulled away, its sound diminishing. Rory watched those gull-like wings receding in the darkness. At last the plane lifted off from the field and was lost in the blackness. He lay on the wet earth, listening to the plane's drone diminishing in the night. Already he missed Eric's quirky Irish voice and his odd sense of humour.

He stood up and looked about him, inspecting the countryside with one eye, conscious that he was alone in the middle of the night somewhere in a strange and dangerous country. He was shaky and thirsty. Over to his right there was a lone tree and what appeared to be a thin line of scrub bushes and willows. To the north, he could see Amsterdam's glow on the horizon. There must have been a farmhouse nearby, but he couldn't see it. There appeared to be the roof line of some kind of barn or small outbuilding off to his left. This was about as nondescript a patch of the Dutch night as he could imagine.

How the hell did Eric ever find this place and land here? Rory was no pilot, but he knew enough to realize that this had been a stunning feat of navigation and flying. Thank God Eric, whoever he was, had failed as a fighter pilot.

Rory's shoulder ached. He gathered his two pieces of luggage and took a deep breath. The heaviest suitcase, the one with the radio, would go in the hedge over there. Somehow he'd come back for it later. Instinctively he reached down to brush off the mud from his knees. He put his hand to his nose and looked at the dark wet stains on his coat and trousers. They would dry off by morning, but there was no question that he was standing in a recently used cow pasture. It was time to move.

11

Rory had been walking for just over three hours and stopped to take a short break. As the night wore on, the air became damper, and in the hour just before dawn the dampness and chill went right through him. Rory shivered. He shrugged and flexed his muscles to keep warm. As he did so he noticed that Amsterdam's lights, which had been glowing just over the horizon, seemed to be much fainter. His arms ached from the weight of his suitcase. He could never get it so that he could carry the damn thing in a comfortable position and he found himself changing it from side to side every two minutes. It was much too heavy and he cursed himself for bringing weapons with him in the first place.

The whole mission was ill-conceived, and carrying hand grenades was just one of the ridiculous features of the plan. If he ever found himself in a situation where he could even envisage using hand grenades, he'd be as good as dead anyway. Better to save the last round in his pistol and shoot himself rather than surrender to the Nazis. But hand grenades? How would he conceal hand grenades? And if they were concealed, he'd never be able to get at them if he needed them. For the twentieth time that night he asked himself why he'd listened to Harris, who had never had any practical experience in this sort of thing before. He picked up the suitcase and resumed slogging towards the horizon.

Of course he knew the answer as far as the hand grenades went. He had deliberately chosen to humour Harris. Once he had agreed to accept a mission into occupied Europe, he was trapped. Many of the details would be beyond his control; and it was better to give in on some of the smaller points, ones that he could change later. The grenades were a compromise. He refused to budge on the more critical issues. He had insisted that he go in alone. Harris had wanted to send a half-trained backup man with him, a man who also didn't speak Dutch, or any language other than English. That would have been a disaster. No doubt the man Harris had selected was a capable fellow; in fact, when he met him he liked him, but an additional man who could only speak English had been one absurd addition too many. Two of them who didn't speak Dutch would have been fatally obvious. Fortunately, he won that argument, but now he was certain he had been right about the weaponry as well.

He stopped and put the suitcase down and wiped the sweat on his forehead. There was more than a faint glow to the sky in the east and he could see much farther into these fields than he could even just a few minutes ago. In that grey light he could faintly make out the outline of a pair of slow-turning windmills off to his right. It would be getting bright out in another twenty minutes or so. Somewhere in the field behind him, on the other side of the road, a pair of birds started their excited early morning chirping.

Over by the edge of the road was one of the drainage ditches that seemed to be everywhere in this country. It was filled with black water and looked deep. He stopped again, put the suitcase down, and stretched his arms above his head. His back ached. This was an ideal time and place to get rid of the grenades. He bent down and undid the leather strap around the suitcase. Just then he caught the sounds of a truck making its way up the road behind him. He refastened the strap and stood up. He couldn't make out what kind of a truck it was, but it was four hundred yards away, had its headlights on, and was moving steadily towards him. Whoever it was had obviously seen him.

* * *

IT WAS DAWN. On the maple-lined sidewalk outside Amsterdam's Central Police Station, early morning sunlight, long shadows, and a breeze wafting through the trees gave the impression of tranquil normalcy. It was quite a different atmosphere inside the cavernous red-brick building. Inside, the air was electric. The station's central briefing room had been filled to standing-room capacity for the last ten minutes as two shifts of Amsterdam's police waited for the beginning of this first "Combined Assembly of the Occupying Authorities and the Amsterdam Police Force."

To Reinhold Neumann, the apprehension in the room was a good sign. The large, high-ceilinged room hummed with scores of whispered conversations and the fidgeting and shuffling unease of two hundred tense and fretful men. Neumann had to restrain himself from smiling. He enjoyed the power, and looking out over the crowded room, he quietly exalted in the fact that not one man in the audience dared make eye contact with him. They weren't fools. Their anxiety was justified. They instinctively knew he was prepared to deal harshly with stragglers or anyone who chose not to show up this morning; but, as Neumann himself acknowledged, it would be much better if he didn't have to. Judging from the crowded benches and the dozens of men standing at the back of the room, it appeared that the problem of a reluctant police force wasn't going to be an issue.

Neumann thought it had been a good touch to schedule the briefing two hours before the normal shift change. It served two purposes. It told everybody that this was an exceptionally important meeting, and it also meant that both the incoming and outgoing shifts would be tired. Half of these men had to get out of bed two hours earlier than usual and the other half, the outgoing night shift, were tired anyway. A 5 a.m. briefing threw their schedules off, emphasized the need for caution, and telegraphed to everyone that momentous change was imminent. Neumann considered this kind of psychological advantage to be essential. If the courses in Berlin emphasized anything, it was the need for the police to create a sense of distance from, as well as an impression of indisputable authority over, their populations. You didn't want constant terror—that destroyed productivity—but perpetual intense anxiety instilled obedience and conformity.

Neumann raised his right hand and the room quickly went silent. He called out in German to the helmeted guards at the back, "One minute and then close the doors. Anyone who is late will not be admitted. We shall deal later with anyone foolish enough to have ignored our directions." This morning Neumann was dressed in his field-grey uniform. The Gestapo did not dress in the SS's black uniform, nor did they use SS ranks; instead they used army ranks. The Gestapo, when in uniform, dressed like the Wehrmacht; they liked to be nondescript and only their identity discs and armpit tattoos described them as SS. It was a subtle touch that increased the awe and fear in which they were held. Neumann liked that.

There was a time, not too long ago, when he enjoyed being dressed in plainclothes. Then, plainclothes had a certain cachet, as it meant he was no longer a plodding junior patrolman on the beat. But now, the more he wore his uniform, the more he liked it. It had a sense of the dramatic about it. The highly polished officers' jackboots, the Sam Browne belt, and the peaked forage cap gave exactly the right impression of power and menace. He nodded and the doors closed.

"Good morning. I am here this morning to advise you of the legal relationship that now exists between the German armed forces, the German security forces, and the people and government institutions of the Netherlands." He stopped and a tall intense-looking man in his early twenties with a bad complexion stood up and translated Neumann's words into Dutch. When he finished, he turned and looked up at Neumann. It was only then that Neumann noticed that his translator was wearing a swastika armband. Evidently, he was a member of the Dutch Nazi Party. Pleased, Neumann made a mental note to find out who had hired this fellow, and to get him to recruit more like this one as soon as possible.

"Let us be very clear about a number of things right from the outset." The translator was looking straight ahead, focused on some distant object on the far wall. In that large hall, the Dutchman's voice sounded like a feeble echo. "We have not asked for this war and we intend to bring it to a successful conclusion as quickly as possible… We are not at war with the Dutch people… Like you, we want to see an end to all hostilities and the resumption of a normal way of life… To that end, we shall not tolerate any attempts to resist the forces of the Third Reich … Anyone who disobeys this order, anyone who prolongs the conflict or resists the lawful authorities will be dealt with severely… You, as the Dutch police, will cooperate fully with all the forces of the Third Reich … An armistice has been signed by the Dutch government and lawful control of the state has been duly assumed by the forces of the Third Reich … This means that all police forces of the former Dutch Administration are now lawfully subject to the direction and disciplinary action of the forces of the Third Reich."

Neumann stopped speaking for a few moments and looked out at his audience. The room was unnaturally silent. "Be very clear about how serious we are to impose and maintain order and security in this land … We will not tolerate anyone who acts in a manner that in any way threatens the stability and security of the new state … This is particularly true of the Dutch police forces … You will be required to fulfil your duties, to maintain order just as you have in the past, and you will be required to implement the laws and directives of the Occupying Power… Any member of the police force who chooses to do otherwise will be considered to be a terrorist and will be dealt with accordingly."

Neumann paused again and stared out at his audience. This time every eye in the hall was riveted on him, but the room remained deathly quiet. After a long, slow half-minute he resumed. "As the senior German police officer, responsible for the coordination of police affairs for Central Amsterdam, I have three priorities: to maintain order in Amsterdam … to ensure a smooth transition to integrated police operations … and to ensure that the people of Amsterdam understand that their best course is to cooperate with the new order in Europe… Lastly, I can tell you that two Dutch policemen in this city have already been arrested … These men have been arrested for refusal to cooperate in a state of emergency… Their cases have been sent to Germany for disposition … I trust that there will be no more of this kind of irresponsible and criminal behaviour… We will all have to live together and we will start doing so now… Your duty is to stay on the job, working as you did before … You will all be receiving your orders from your lawful chain of command in due course."

Neumann nodded to the guards at the back who threw open the doors with a crash. He strode down the centre aisle and left the silent room with the metal cleats of his boot heels clicking on the polished linoleum.

* * *

SAUL WAS EXHAUSTED. His legs hurt, and over the last several hours he had developed a severe, steady headache, almost as if the top of his skull was too small to hold his brain. It wasn't his turn to sit down for another hour yet. There were fifty men crammed into a holding cell that in normal times was used for temporarily holding half a dozen prisoners before they were transported to court or to the municipal jail. Some time early the previous morning, at Saul's suggestion, the prisoners had agreed to give the older men a spot where they could sit down; the rest of them had to take turns, with four of them sitting for an hour at a time in one of the corners. When they weren't sitting, the remaining forty-odd men stood crammed together like passengers on a crowded bus. The lucky ones could lean against the walls and cell bars. The air was stuffy and hot, and the smell of urine coming from the corner that had been designated as a makeshift toilet was oppressive. Saul was beginning to feel nauseous.

Again, at Saul's suggestion, the night before they had all in turn identified themselves to the group. Starting at one end of the cell and working across, each had announced his name, occupation, and why he thought he had been arrested. There were several politicians, senior officers from the armed forces, numerous journalists, two junior policemen, union leaders, several Jewish businessmen. and a dozen individuals who had been rash enough to jeer at their German occupiers.

Saul had been adamant that Samuël be given one of the spots to sit down. That was yesterday. He wasn't sure now that he had the strength or the willpower if he had to make the same case again for his uncle. He was clammy, his legs had lost their feeling, his stomach was queasy, and he was becoming extremely irritable. On several occasions he felt he was on the point of passing out but he willed himself to hang on.

Later in the morning, the doors out in the hall were thrown open and several German soldiers in black and grey uniforms burst into the adjoining space beside the cell. Saul could only make out a few of them but he guessed there were a half-dozen uniformed men out there. One of them started to bark at them in German and someone off to the side who he could not see was doing a good job translating what he said into Dutch. At the sound of the Dutch voice, Saul felt a surge of anger. He began to mutter as the voice continued.

"I understand you men are finding things a little cramped here. Believe me, we intend to fix that. I've reviewed the list of who you are and we shall be discussing your futures." There was a hushed whisper and a rustling of paper. "First, let me say that—"

"Let us all go free," Saul shouted out hoarsely in German. "None of us have done anything to deserve this and there are men in here who are in serious distress."

One of the German voices shouted, "Silence. Who has interrupted the officer?" No one spoke for a moment. "If you don't give me a name all will be severely punished." The men beside Saul looked warily at him, but no one spoke. Saul licked his lips and said, "It was me. We only ask that we be treated decently."

"Remove him from this group. You who interrupted move forward." Where seconds before it seemed like there was no room in the cell, a path from the door to Saul emerged spontaneously. Saul took a deep breath and stepped forward, and as he walked towards the cell door he spoke again in a clear voice. "We only ask that you treat us humanely and with decency."

A voice in German snarled, "Get this clown out of here and on the first truck. The rest of you will be dealt with very shortly. Those of you whom we decide are unlikely to pose a threat to security will be released, but only after you have agreed not to break the peace or interfere in any way with the lawful conduct and governance of the German forces and the Dutch police."

As Saul reached the cell door, he faced several German soldiers. One was obviously an officer, a young man in his mid- to late twenties, dressed in a grey uniform, high black boots, and a forage cap. Saul looked down and swallowed hard.

"That was very foolish of you," the officer said in a level voice. "You obviously speak German. You should know we have no intention of allowing disrespect to turn into chaos." He turned to one of the guards. "This one goes on the truck now."

Saul was yanked forward by the arm and pushed towards the door. He had trouble making his legs respond. As he stumbled forward he could hear the officer. "We in the Third Reich want the Netherlands as a loyal and supportive ally. We have every intention of ensuring this country remains tranquil and prosperous. You people above all others must understand that. Of course, anyone who does not cooperate will be designated an enemy of the state and treated accordingly."

Saul had trouble walking steadily. As he approached the uniformed figures he put his arms out for balance lest he collapse. He was pushed to one side by a soldier with a rifle and then shoved through a doorway and prodded up a flight of stairs to an exterior courtyard. His head began to swim.

12

RORY'S HEART SANK. The truck coming down the country road was a large German military lorry. The canvas top over the cab was rolled back and he could see two coal-scuttle helmets in the front seat. As the truck drew closer and slowed to a halt, the soldier in the passenger seat stood up and levelled his rifle at Rory.

Raising his right hand in greeting, Rory did his best to look pleased and called out in German, "You have no idea how happy I am to see you gentlemen." As he spoke, three German soldiers who had been riding in the back stood up, curious to see what was going on and why they were stopping out here in the middle of nowhere.

The soldier with the rifle looked grim and threatening. "What are you doing out here at this time? Who are you? Keep your hands up where I can see them and approach the truck slowly."

"No need to be angry, my friend. I'm as German as you are. Or I soon will be. I'm a German businessman from Alsace. I was travelling to Amsterdam when the war started up. The trains all stopped weeks ago and I've been walking and hitching rides ever since. Last night, some farmer left me in the dark on this road. I guess it's been about ten or twenty kilometres back. I've been walking all night and I hope to get to Amsterdam this morning. Not any chance you could give an old German veteran a ride?" He was worried that his voice sounded shaky and it rattled him that the soldier with the rifle didn't smile back.

"Come over here, slowly."

Rory advanced unhurriedly, doing his best to maintain a convincing smile. "Not to worry, my friend. I have papers to prove that I'm who I say I am." His hands were raised above his head and he lowered his left hand slowly and patted the right breast pocket of his suit coat. He put his hands up again.

The soldier with the rifle stepped down from the lorry's cab and slung his rifle. Rory noticed from his badges that he was a Gefreiter from a supply battalion. He had an angry red scar running across his left cheek. "You pick a strange time to travel. Don't you know there's a war on?"

"That's the problem. The war wasn't on when I started out from Strasbourg. I was on my way to examine some new seed samples for barley in Amsterdam. I was halfway across France when all the trains there stopped. If I don't get to Amsterdam in the next day, the deal will be off, and I'll lose my job, war or no war." Rory slowly pulled out his billfold and began fishing through it for the relevant documents. "I walked to Maubeuge. They tried to stop me and everybody else at the Dutch border, but I paid a farmer to give me a ride across one of the farm roads. Since then I've had three really short lifts from drivers. Can you please take me to Amsterdam?"

"You're a French citizen. Why should we help you?"

"No, my friend, I'm German. My name is Martin Becker and I was born a German; and like the rest of us in Alsace and Lorraine, I lost my citizenship in 1918." Rory suddenly dropped the cheerful ingratiating tone and became forceful. "Like you, I fought for my country. In my time, I fought for three years for the Fatherland. I served for months and months in the trenches in 9th Landwehr Division. I was wounded, twice, and I have the scars to prove my allegiance."

Rory fished out his demobilization card. He noticed the three young soldiers smiling and nudging one another from the back of the truck. He nodded to them as if he were performing on a stage. He raised his voice. "The French never took this from me." He handed over his dog-eared military service card with his left hand. He held it out for a second, displaying the three remaining fingers on his hand so all could see. "The French took my fingers and one eye, but they never took away my allegiance to the Fatherland. When I went home to Strasbourg, I spent the next twenty-one years as a loyal German living in a part of French-occupied Germany. Like you, I'm glad to see things have finally started to change in Europe."

The German soldier smiled. "We are under very specific orders." His tone softened. "We can't give rides to civilians. I'm sorry. You're still twenty kilometres from Amsterdam. You can make it easily by mid-afternoon."

"Gefreiter," one of the soldiers in the back called out, "I think our orders were meant for Dutch civilians; this man is German, a veteran; he's one of us."

The Gefreiter bristled. "I'll make the decisions around here. When I want or need your opinion, I'll ask for it." The three soldiers stepped back and shrank out of sight. "I can't take you into Amsterdam, but I'll take an old German soldier as far as it's safe for me to do so. I'll drop you outside the city in a village where you can get a ride. Get in the back."

Rory smiled and whispered, "Thank you. I'm glad to see there's still a bond of comradeship between German soldiers; some things never change." The German driver and the Gefreiter were both smiling broadly. Rory picked up his suitcase, doing his best to make it appear lighter than it was. He walked around to the back of the truck. "I can go with you as far as the outskirts of Amsterdam, my friends. Thanks for your help." He swung his suitcase over the side and clambered in. The soldier nearest him was beaming and pulled the suitcase further back into the truck. "My God, sir, what do you carry in this? It weighs a ton."

Rory sat down heavily on the truck's bench and energetically drew the suitcase back in between his legs. "I bet it weighs a lot less than one of your packs." He reached out his right hand. "My name's Martin Becker. Thanks for your help. I was getting tired." He made a point of shaking hands with the other two as the truck lurched forward. "Tell me, gentlemen, what's the news about the war. All I know is that German troops are now deep into France and have occupied Paris, and that the Dutch and Belgians sued for peace a few weeks ago. What have you been hearing?"

* * *

OSCAR AND NINA left their house at nine. Despite Annika's promise that she'd stay inside, by ten past the hour she was pacing back and forth across the living room carpet, struggling with the notion of going back to the police station. She was convinced Saul was already lying dead somewhere and her imagination intensified her anxiety. The harrowing vision of Saul's unburied corpse staring sightless in a basement room made her more anxious than she could bear.

It wasn't anything that Oscar or Nina had said. It was what they didn't say. They had been the soul of kindness and common sense, but there was no point in trying to fool herself. Weeks ago, Saul had been arrested by the Nazis. He was a Jew and, in spite of all his other wonderful qualities, he was stubborn, aggressive, and volatile. A strong-willed, feisty Dutch Jew would merely provoke these people; and Saul, much to his disadvantage, had never been one to acquiesce or keep his opinion to himself in any kind of situation where principle was involved. It was, Annika thought with a flush of pride, what distinguished Saul from those of his peers who were merely successful. But there were two sides to that coin, and thinking about it made her frown. His temperament, the inability to hold his tongue, and his instinctive readiness to lash out at those he disliked, prevented him from ever rising in his firm. Now his obstinacy put both of them at risk. He had repeatedly ignored chances to get out of the Netherlands. Candour was a fine characteristic for travelling the moral high road, but as a practical approach to dealing with people like the Nazis it didn't help much in matters of survival.

No sooner had she expressed these thoughts to herself than she began to feel guilty. She didn't want to harbour negative feelings about her husband at a time like this. It was disloyal, and she told herself that imagining Saul was dead was a means of rationalizing away her obligation to do whatever she possibly could to secure his release. For the first time since his arrest, she acknowledged that she was torn between a deep-seated fear that she'd be arrested and her sense of duty to help Saul. She sat down and put her face in her hands. She didn't have to approach this like she was a donkey. There had to be a way in which she could do something while minimizing the risk to herself. Fear was not the same thing as cowardice.

Oscar and Nina were essentially telling her to do nothing, while her first instinct was to rush out and besiege the police and the Germans in an attempt to find Saul and get him released. But weeks had passed, and the more she thought about it, the more she realized that both these actions were wrong. She had to find out what had happened to Saul, and she had to protect herself while doing so. Doing nothing out of fear, or reacting on instinct and getting herself locked away, wasn't going to help anyone. Still, she had a sinking, inescapable feeling that being cautious was simply a means of justifying inaction.

Annika sat down and covered her mouth with a balled fist and stared intently at the floor, as if the power of her gaze would help her find a solution. She told herself repeatedly that guilt, anxiety, and apprehension were normal reactions, and that in spite of these she had to think through her situation. She couldn't stay here any longer. She had to find someone who could safely get the information for her. She didn't know anyone in the police station. That was the problem she first had to address. The more she thought about her predicament the more dispassionate and reasoned she became, and with this her confidence grew. She stood up and began to pace again, this time more slowly.

One thing was certain: she wasn't going to find a helpful policeman here in Oscar and Nina's house. She grabbed her purse and headed for the Central Train Station. There were always policemen on the beat in the Hoogstraat area of town and the ones you were likely to come across in that district almost certainly worked out of the Central Police Station, the station closest to Uncle Samuël's business. That was the most likely place Saul and Samuël would have been taken to. She would not be put off this time. She was determined to get information and then she would act. It was a beginning and that gave her energy.

Annika marched out of the house filled with resolve, but she began to tire within a few minutes. She hadn't been eating or sleeping properly for weeks and the strain was beginning to tell. By the time she reached the Uilenburger Canal, her legs went wobbly, her energy drained right out of her, and the confidence she had felt minutes before had evaporated. She walked over beside the canal and for a second she clutched onto the metal railing, pausing so she could get her breath. It was all madness. She should go back to Oscar and Nina's and sit tight. It would be the safe thing to do. What chance did she have against this massively organized evil? Who did she think she was to ever assume she could accomplish anything against such a monstrous organization? The German Army took Saul as part of a well-organized plan. There was no way she could oppose them. People on the street seemed to be going about their routine business. Life went on. Why should she presume to be different?

Annika pushed away from the railing. By the time she reached the corner at Verwerstraat she decided to turn back. There could be no shame in this. Oscar and Nina were right. Stay at their place. They were the ones who weren't under strain; they were thinking clearly. They'd probably already worked out their plan to get out of Holland and get to safety. Going forward was insane. Going back was the rational thing to do. She couldn't help Saul now. The stories that came out of Germany were true. They should have gone with Pauli and his family. She turned around, and just as she did so she caught sight of a policeman in his black uniform on the other side of the street. He was walking slowly towards her.

The policeman was in his mid-thirties, and quite short. For a second Annika thought he was lucky to be a policeman at that height, then dismissed the idea as malicious. His height had nothing to do with anything. The policeman was biting his lower lip as if he was deep in thought. Annika hesitated for a moment—and then, propelled by the shame of taking counsel of her fears, and drawing upon some newfound courage, which came from God knows where, she walked up to him.

"Excuse me. I need your help."

The policeman looked startled. It was obvious Annika had interrupted some private train of thought.

"I'm sorry? What did you say? Are you all right?"

"No. I'm not. I need help and I think you can help me."

"What—what's the matter?"

"My husband has been arrested by the Germans. I've heard nothing about him for three weeks. I think he was being held in the Central Police Station, but no one will tell me anything and I don't know what to do."

The policeman looked about him nervously. "Madam, you're not alone. I don't know the names of those who have been arrested, but even if we try to find out who they are, it puts us at risk." He took a deep breath. "It's hard to believe that this is happening. I've never had to deal with this kind of a problem before."

Annika stepped back and inhaled slowly and deliberately through her nose. In an instant she changed from being frightened and desperate to being composed and self-assured. Her confidence was infectious and the policeman looked at her expectantly.

"I'm sure you're right," she said. "None of us have ever dealt with anything like this, but I'm sure you're a Dutch patriot, and as one of our policemen, you're a man of honour. I'll tell you what I need you to do. Be discreet. When you go back to your station, find out what has happened to Saul Hammerstein and Samuël Van Zuiden. Find out where they are and how they're doing. Find out whatever other information you can get. I'll meet you this evening. What time are you off?"

The policeman nodded warily. He didn't seem to be taken off guard by these instructions from a stranger; it was almost as if he needed to be told what to do. He paused and then said, "I finish at four. I can meet you at five. Let me change into civilian clothes first."

"Yes, of course, that's a good idea. I'll meet you at five, then, at the

Keizersgracht Café. I see your badge number is 137, but if you can't make it and I have to contact you by another means, I need to know your name."

The policeman looked at her and then glanced up the street. His eyes narrowed. "I assume you must be who? Mrs. Hammerstein or Mrs. Van Zuiden? Perhaps it's better if you don't know my name at this point. I'll do what I can, madam, but I can't promise you anything. Now, I'm going to keep moving. I think it's better no one sees us. I'll do what I can."

* * *

RORY ESTIMATED that he had to keep up his chatter for at least a half-hour. That would give him enough time to get to the outskirts of Amsterdam and off this truck. He had to steer the conversation. They knew more than enough about him now. He smiled at the soldier next to him. "So, tell me what's going on with the war? The French seem to be in a complete state of collapse. Everyone I've talked to seems to think that the war is as good as over. Is that true?"

The young man beside him shrugged his shoulders and shifted to get more comfortable on the truck's wooden bench. Rory could see the man's eyes were bloodshot and his uniform was stained with mud and grease, but his leather ammunition pouches were in order, his boots had been brushed, he was freshly shaven, and his Mauser rifle was clean, its working parts glistening blue-black from a recent oiling. The young soldier looked across at his companions. "We don't get told much. At first we were supporting the drive into Holland, but for almost a month now we've been doing nothing but rear-area security activities. It's pretty dull. Some days we off-load supplies; we guarded Dutch prisoners for a few days, but most of the time we just drive endlessly around the countryside. None of us has had a shower or a full night's sleep since this started."

One of the men opposite, who had been restraining himself, interrupted excitedly. "Yes, that's true, but the Gefreiter read us a bulletin this morning. The British have completely run away, the French army's totally broken, and we've occupied Paris. It's almost all over now."

Rory stroked his chin. "I've heard that, in bits and pieces, mind you. I haven't heard any reliable news until now; but you know, you men have done something incredible. We fought for over four years and we never had success like this. We all owe you and the Führer a lot. Now I can be a German again." Rory smiled broadly at this observation, and then in a fatherly tone asked each of them where they came from, what they did in civilian life, and what they were going to do when the war ended.

The hometown conversations gradually ran out of steam. Rory could see that the three men with him were exhausted. When they weren't speaking, they slumped back as if trying to conserve their energy, and when they sat back, they had that faraway melancholy look in their eyes so characteristic of those suffering from deep fatigue. To a man they appeared on the verge of collapse. They seemed to be decent enough young men, hardworking, loyal, probably from good families, anxious to help a fellow countryman in distress, but completely oblivious to any sense of wrongdoing insofar as they had just invaded another country and helped in turning the world on its head. Rory thought these were good lads: honest, industrious, agreeable, and innocent enough within the realms of their own decisions. A lot of German men like these were going to die before Nazism was exterminated.

Rory shifted his weight and instinctively felt for his suitcase against his legs. He forced himself to smile and nodded his head at the soldiers. It was no time for him to get sentimental. He looked at his watch; they probably had another five minutes before they dropped him off. So far, they hadn't shown much curiosity about his background. "I think it's going to be another warm one today, boys," he said. "Much better than doing this patrolling in the rain though, eh? Rain, you should have seen the rain at Verdun. I am so glad for you and for Germany that this war isn't like the last one." Rory went on for a few minutes about the weather and how in his war so many good men died of pneumonia and how they used to get foot infec-

tions. He was deliberately boring. He tried engaging them in conversation about the quality of their boots and their food. They were
looking at him in a bored but tolerant way when the truck skidded
to a stop several hundred metres outside the tiny village of Nieukerk.

The Gefreiter got out and walked to the tailgate. "This is where
you get off, my friend. I don't think you want to be seen just yet with
the German army, but just to be safe, I was thinking that when you
get into Amsterdam you should register with the German military
police. Just as a precaution. I don't think there have been any attacks
against Germans, but it won't hurt for our security people to know
we have one of our own here."

"That's a very good idea. I'll do that, my friend. They might also
help me find a good place to stay, somewhere safe. Thank you. I'll go
see them this afternoon." Rory jumped from the truck and pulled his
suitcase off, doing his best to appear normal."

One of the soldiers shouted out, "Don't you go straining yourself
with that salesman's suitcase now."

Rory laughed and waved. "I can assure you, my suitcase is not
nearly as heavy as your pack, and I know. I've carried both. Thank
you for the ride, gentlemen; and thank you for what you have done
for the Fatherland."

The Gefreiter smiled and reached out his hand, giving Rory a
bone-crushing handshake. "Good luck. The trains are running again
now in Holland, but there's none out here. There's a bus that goes
through the village. It'll get you into downtown Amsterdam. We have
to go." He got back in the truck and the three men in the back waved
as they drove off.

Rory picked up his valise and walked briskly into town. The sun
was rising, and dressed in his trench coat and felt hat, he was hot and
sticky. He exhaled heavily; his head throbbed and his eye socket hurt
as it always did when he was under pressure. The encounter with
the German patrol had been a strain and he was unsure how it had
gone. He was still alive and on the loose, but he had hoped to avoid
revealing his cover for as long as possible. Now he had to assume
that German intelligence would know there was an Alsatian veteran

in the area. It was unlikely that the Gefreiter would report that he had disobeyed orders, but Rory had to assume they would be aware. Although nothing had been compromised, it was not a good start to this operation. He was no longer invisible and that was not good.

13

NEUMANN RUBBED HIS EYES. He needed sleep and some exercise, but he was pleased with himself and how things had been going so far. If they were ever to write a text book on how to occupy a country, this, he thought, would be the model to use.

Still, the work was taking its toll. Each day for weeks now he had been pushing himself relentlessly. It would be nice to have a day or two off, just to forget about the war. Getting a chance to go home was more than he was prepared to let himself imagine. Hope for too much, he thought, and you only make yourself dissatisfied, and there was too much to do to be dissatisfied. Dissatisfaction led to frustration and that led to sloppy work, and there'd be no sloppy work in his command. He was going to set the example on that point.

He pulled out a sheet of paper and began jotting notes on it. He'd write a letter to Maida later tonight. For now, he'd scribble down a few notes because by the time tonight rolled around he'd be too tired to write anything but gibberish and he wanted Maida and the children to be interested in his letter. What would he tell the children? This morning there were rabbits on the grass in the park at dawn, there were ducks swimming in the canals, and more starlings here in Amsterdam than in Vienna. He stopped writing and looked out the window over Amsterdam's red-tiled roofs and a swath of seventeenth-century, four- and five-storey buildings. He didn't know what to say to his own children. He hadn't seen them in months now. What would they be interested in? Not endless rubbish about birds and rabbits and the weather, or incessant questions about what they were doing and how they were feeling. Maida was another matter altogether. Her letters to him were so short they might as well have been telegrams. Everybody was fine, the children were healthy, and she signed them simply "Maida." It hurt—as it was intended to. What had he done to deserve this?

He'd think of something to write later in the day. He was tired and his thoughts were too much on his work. It would show in his letter home. He leaned back in his chair and called out towards the open door, "Hauptmann Ackerman, I want the breakdown of the Dutch arrests."

A fit-looking young officer in a grey uniform popped his head around the corner. "Sir?"

"Hauptmann Ackerman, I want your final report on the weekly arrest status. I want to review it and make whatever annotations will be necessary before I send it to headquarters."

"Yes, sir, I've done it," he said with his flat, gravelly voice, "but I thought you didn't want it before nine. I'll go get it."

Neumann sat back in his chair. He was pleased with himself. He had deliberately asked for the completed arrest disposition sheets at what he thought would have been an impossibly early hour just to keep his staff on their toes. And here Ackerman had it ready fifteen minutes early. The German police headquarters in The Hague was almost certainly not that efficient. He would make it a matter of pride that all reports arrive at the headquarters before those from The Hague. Third Reich police work in Amsterdam was going to be a textbook operation.

Ackerman reappeared at the door and came stiffly to attention before entering. "The first dozen prisoners have already left by truck for Neuengamme. Camp reception has been notified by telephone. Here is the list of those who have been dispatched, and on the back

is the list of those prisoners remaining in cells. I am prepared to discuss the backgrounds of those you think we should release, sir." Ackerman came to a relaxed position of attention and said nothing more.

Sometimes Neumann wondered if Hauptmann Ackerman wasn't
making fun of him with his overly correct behaviour. Then again, he
thought, that was probably a physical impossibility: his temperament
would never allow for anything quite so risky or inventive as poking
fun at a superior. He was one of those ambitious but careful young
men who live to work. He had a good analytical mind and a grasp for
detail that was often astonishing. He was dutiful, intense, and serious.
A man with a bland sense of humour, he never asked questions about
the person he was with or showed the slightest interest in things
beyond his immediate concern. He was an efficient bureaucrat if you
told him what to do. Neumann smiled at his insight; he was lucky he
had been born with such an ability to assess people. It served him
well. Ackerman however, without natural curiosity, was always going
to be a second-rate policeman, which was not a bad thing: Ackerman
was the perfect administrator.

"While I'm thinking about it, Ackerman, please have Rottenführer
Schmidt go out and get us some fresh coffee and rolls for our office.
Tell him to make sure that we have freshly brewed coffee and rolls
ready every morning by ten o'clock. Now, I see you have a dozen
names of those already sent to Neuengamme? This one, Hammerstein? With that name, is he a Jew?"

"Yes, Herr Major, and a troublesome one at that. He was arrested
with his uncle. I didn't send his uncle off. He's quiet enough; someone told me he's sick anyway. I thought he should be released—just
to let him go back to his people and let them know we mean business."

"Fine, fine," Neumann said dismissively, waving his hand. He
turned in his chair and looked out over the roofs of Amsterdam. It
really was a beautiful city. It had a pleasant Germanic feel to it. "Who
are the others?"

"Those two policemen who seemed a little surly; we've discussed
them. I told all the prisoners this morning that they've already been

shipped out. The army was supposed to transfer them last night and somehow they didn't. But I've made certain that there'll be no more transportation problems for prisoners."

"Fine. Ensure that whomever it was in the army who failed in this matter doesn't do it again. We want to keep on good terms with the army, but, you know what to do. What other sorts of people have you got on the list?"

Ackerman looked at his notes. "Three newspapermen, an anti-German politician, the owner of one of the local radio stations, and the other four are ..." He paused, checking his notes again. "Two writers, a retired army officer, a municipal politician, and a socialist labour leader. I can't remember which ones of this last group are which. I can match up the names for you if you like."

"No, no, the names don't matter, not to me anyway. Don't waste your time. I think these are fine for now, but make sure the names of those shipped to Neuengamme are published in the Dutch papers. There's been no real resistance here in Amsterdam since the ceasefire, so there's no point in being too harsh; it will simply breed unnecessary resentment. That may change, but I hope not. The sooner we get this city running as a productive territory for the Reich, the better. As for the rest, release the remainder under my signature—and Ackerman, don't forget to tell Rottenführer Schmidt about the coffee and rolls."

Neumann sat back in his chair and swivelled around to face Ackerman directly. "Schmidt, you know he's a good man to have around. He's smarter than he looks. In addition to being our driver, we should think of him as our quartermaster. He has a knack for knowing how to find things. He's a country boy at heart and he can be a cheeky scoundrel, so keep him on a short leash."

Ackerman was standing at attention again with his head bowed slightly forward. "Of course, sir."

Neumann thought he was wasting his breath. Ackerman didn't have the ability to recognize Schmidt's near insolent sense of humour. It was something he would never see, the same way some men are colour-blind.

"Oh, Ackerman, when you release the remaining prisoners, do it late tonight. Some time after midnight would be best. We have held them long enough. Just make sure there's no fanfare. No need to tell the press anything about those we have released. Send them home unexpectedly, in the dark. I want to send a very subtle message. Keep them off guard. We will deal with anyone who chooses to resist us, and we are prepared to be sensible with those who cooperate. As for the others, get them out of here as quickly as you can." Neumann picked up a pencil on his desk and toyed with it for a second. "You know both the Führer and Reichsführer Himmler believe the Dutch are racially more Aryan than the Germans? I've been led to believe that because of this they are particularly interested in how we handle this country. You do understand what the implications are for us of what I'm saying?"

"Completely, sir."

Neumann thought Ackerman may have lacked a sense of humour, but he was not a man wanting intelligence, ambition, or energy. He would be reliable in the future.

* * *

SAUL WAS UTTERLY MISERABLE. He was sitting alone, propping himself against the back wall of a heavy German army supply truck that was parked under a cluster of elm trees in the courtyard of the police barracks. Looking out beyond the tailgate from inside the truck, he could see two silent and grim-faced soldiers standing guard. Both men eyed him unsympathetically.

If the guards were trying to intimidate him, they were doing a good job of it. Saul thought they had an inhuman look about them. They had already smashed him in the back and the ribs with their rifle butts as they pushed and prodded him up from the basement and into the truck. Now he was left by himself, surrounded on three sides by a heavy curtain of pleasant-smelling thick green canvas. Saul tried to focus on the canvas rather than the guards. Its rich smell was the only enjoyable sensation he had experienced in the last two days, and he was grateful for it. It reminded him of a happier time, when he was a small boy camping with his family in a tent out in the country. Rather than look at the soldiers, he closed his eyes and inhaled. The relief was very brief. He opened his eyes and wondered what he had ever done to deserve this.

They left him there for some time. He was drained of energy and in pain from the beatings he had suffered. He had no idea how many days it had been since his arrest. They had taken his watch, and in the windowless basement of the police building the days ran together without any noticeable change.

Now that he had been moved to the truck, he was on his own, and for the first time since his arrest he was beginning to experience a kind of fear that he could not control. Fear overshadowed his pain. It started imperceptibly, a quickening of the heartbeat and rapid shallow breathing. His mouth went dry and his mind started to race, darting from the image of one horrifying possibility to the next, and all the while, there was a subconscious sensation that he was trapped and struggling unsuccessfully to break free. This kind of fear was all the more disturbing for him because Saul had never experienced terror like this in his life. He had been frightened and anxious before, but it was nothing like what he felt now. Never before had he endured anything like a prolonged mortal fear brought about by a very real, evil, and threatening presence. This new sensation was intense, beyond anything he had ever encountered. He could feel himself losing control. Involuntarily, he began to sob, great heaving spasms. He drew his knees up to his chest and covered his face with his hands. After a short time, the sobbing became less frequent and the new rhythm eventually forced him to breathe deeply; as he did so, his breath became more regular, and slowly, indiscernibly, he began to regain mastery of his thoughts. When he stopped sobbing, the two guards outside the truck looked impassively at one another but said nothing.

Saul put his head back and forced himself to be calm. He wanted to blow his nose but he had no handkerchief. After a while he became drowsy and his mind filled with more soothing images: home, Annika, and his life before this nightmare. By degrees he regained his composure. Even though his head throbbed and he was bruised in a half-dozen places, he could sense resolve and vigour returning. Courage began trickling and percolating back into his mind, like cool summer rainwater seeping through stone walls into a reservoir. As his mind calmed, he regained control of his emotions and began to reflect upon his situation.

Things were bleak, about as bleak as they could be; but thinking back on his time in the cage with the other men, Saul could see that he had already been an inspiration for the others. He took pride in that. They might break him physically, but in his mind he was going to stay focused and strong. Still, he was glad that no one but the guards had seen him crying. Strangely, he felt no shame in front of these louts with rifles and helmets. If they chose to observe how their victims responded to violent mistreatment, let them see it. He had done nothing to be ashamed of. Their presence here in front of an innocent and unarmed man was shameful. His tears were a physical reaction to something he had never before experienced. The progression of his emotions had been a natural evolution, and even in his pain and discomfort he knew there was no ignominy in this. He felt superior to the guards, but from now on he wasn't going to antagonize anybody.

Although it was less than an hour since he had been in the common cell with the others, he already felt dissociated from that period of torment. He had been one of those who had provided the group a sense of direction, and he had assisted in maintaining their dignity. He hadn't deliberately set out to take a leadership role, but his anger and sense of genuine righteous indignation imbued the men around him with a common purpose. And throughout the time they were together, their courage and determination to see each other through their ordeal with dignity and defiance never flagged. He had helped with that. It surprised him that he had found the strength to exert that kind of leadership. He had never thought of himself as a leader before. It wasn't that he accomplished much during that period, but he prevented his captors from exerting total control over them, and in doing that he had been instrumental in keeping the group's spirits up. That understanding gave him a surge of pride. He closed his eyes and breathed deeply. He was going to survive this ordeal. Somehow he would get home to Annika and lead a normal life again. He promised himself that.

A few minutes later, he could hear doors being opened and the shuffling and scraping of shoes on the stairwell. At the tailgate, uniformed guards prodded and pushed about a dozen unshaven and dejected-looking men into climbing into the back of the truck. In the background Saul could see men in Dutch police uniforms.

Saul grabbed at the truck's side and pulled himself to his feet. His side hurt and he moved in a crab-like motion to the back to help haul the others on board. Nobody amongst the prisoners spoke for some time.

After the tarp had been refastened from the outside, an anxious voice ventured, "Where do you think they're taking us?"

Saul spoke. "There are a lot of prison camps in Germany. I guess this time tomorrow we'll be in one of them. The challenge for each of us now will be keeping our spirits up. Getting through each day. We have to believe that we're going to get through this and get home."

Someone outside the truck smacked the tarpaulin and shouted in Dutch, "Silence. No one is permitted to speak." A few of the prisoners exchanged worried glances. The truck engine started up with a roar and Saul thought he could hear motorcycle engines revving outside the courtyard.

14

THE VILLAGE ON THE ROAD into Amsterdam turned out to be little more than a crossroads called Nieukerk. The place was a disappointment. Rory had expected something larger. He had imagined a community where he might not be so conspicuous—judging by the circle on the map, something with a town square and shops, a place that had some commercial bustle. From where he had been dropped off by the German patrol he could see Nieukerk's name on the yellow-and-black sign on the road up ahead. The place was small, insignificant. He could see the spire of a church rising from the tiny cluster of white- and green-shuttered buildings ahead of him. He didn't have to consult his map. He was still a good twenty kilometres from the city of Amsterdam. It was comforting to know roughly where he was, but he had no idea where to find the bus station the Gefreiter spoke of, or even if buses were running today. From back here, he could see nothing that remotely resembled a bus station.

There were a dozen buildings along the road and a few scattered farmhouses within sight. It was a clean and tidy little place, meticulously painted in uniform shades of white and green. Rory remembered reading about Dutch farms being painted in these traditional colours for hundreds of years, something about the availability of dyes made from local materials. From the looks of the place, Rory supposed the inhabitants would be fastidious, hard-working, and thrifty. Of course, there would be a lot more to them than that; but if forced to make a guess about their temperament, he reckoned that would be a good start. There were no signs in front of any of the buildings and the place was locked up as tightly as a vault. Rory walked on.

In the centre of the hamlet was a neatly painted two-storey building with a faded cardboard sign for Amstel beer in one of the front windows. He assumed that it was a pub, although he couldn't be sure—the curtains were tightly drawn, and this small sun-bleached sign in the corner of a recently washed window was the only indication of any sort of commercial activity in the village. Outside, there was a wooden bench painted green to match the building's shutters. Rory sat down and looked at his watch. It wasn't six o'clock yet and the sun was a scattering of orange splinters bursting from clouds on the eastern horizon.

Within a few minutes of sitting down, Rory noticed curtains on the opposite side of the street part ever so slightly and then close rapidly. A few seconds later, the sequence repeated itself. Shortly after, he could hear the ringing of an old-fashioned telephone in the building behind him. There was some anxious scurrying inside. The door opened and the bespectacled and unshaven face of a man in his early sixties peered out around a partially opened door.

"Ja?" the man shouted to someone still in the building. A torrent of incomprehensible angry Dutch followed from inside. The man, sensing that Rory meant no harm, moved outside. He was dressed in slippers, a pair of old tweed trousers held up by suspenders, and a collarless shirt. Clearly, the ringing phone had awakened him and he wasn't pleased.

Rory smiled and pointed at his watch, shrugged, and broke into French, enunciating slowly and deliberately. "I'm waiting for the bus. I've been walking all night. I'm very tired." He made a motion of wiping his brow and drooping his shoulders. He smiled again.

The Dutchman looked sternly at him and raised a finger, then disappeared back in the house, calling out something incomprehensible. Several moments later a sleepy young boy of about ten or eleven years of age appeared at the door. The older man prodded him forward.

Inwardly, Rory was cursing himself for ever having agreed to go on such a hare-brained mission. The boy spoke haltingly but with obvious politeness in French. "Sir, who are you?"

Rory replied slowly, making a great effort to pronounce his first name with an exaggerated French accent. "I am Martin Becker. I am from Alsace in France. I am travelling to Amsterdam. I have been walking all night. I was told I could catch a bus here." He paused and looked at the boy.

The boy smiled and cupped his hands to his mouth and began to laugh. He spoke hurriedly to the older man in Dutch and then said, "The bus for Amsterdam, it comes tomorrow, in the afternoon." The older man continued to glare at him.

"Can I get something to eat and a ride into Amsterdam? I am very tired."

Just then, a young woman, somewhere between sixteen and twenty-five, stepped out and said in perfectly clear, flowing French, "You don't sound like a Frenchman. Where are you from?" Her tone was confident and brazen. She was tall, with freckles, light brown hair, and delicate features, and she wore a summer frock. It was obvious why the old man had used the young boy as his interpreter. The old man scowled at the girl and there was an angry exchange in Dutch between them. The girl held her ground with quiet defiance. The boy was enjoying the fact that his sister was in trouble.

Rory let them talk for a few seconds and then interrupted. He could feel his pulse quickening. "I'm from Alsace. We speak French like Alsatians. Of course I'm French. I'm very tired. I have been walking all night and travelling for days. The war has stopped all the trains. I am a businessman and I have to be in Amsterdam today. I hope you can help me."

The young woman translated rapidly into Dutch, and without waiting for a reply from the older man, turned to Rory. "I think we can help you get a ride into town later this morning with Mr. Meertens.

You can get something to eat here in half an hour, but you will have to pay. My grandfather runs this house and it is also the village tavern."

Rory smiled and did his best to sound friendly. "You speak beautiful French. Where did you learn it?"

The young girl turned up her nose and looked away. "In school. In the Netherlands we learn other languages, not like the French." She slipped behind the older man and sashayed back into the house."

The older man frowned at him, raised his finger again in a "wait here" sign, and then shepherded the young boy into the house, closing the door with a slam. Rory was left sitting on the bench feeling foolish. He sighed heavily and hoped that the tavern keeper hadn't gone to phone the police. Across the street, he could see two sets of eyes peering out at him from opposite sides of a set of partly opened curtains. His arrival in Holland was far from inconspicuous and he had a hollow sensation in the pit of his stomach; this was not a good beginning.

* * *

THE JOURNEY FOR THE MEN in the truck lasted from mid-morning until just before dark. It was a dispiriting trip, passed in hopeless silence as the prisoners bounced and lurched around on the truck's steel floor. Once the convoy got going, Saul, in an attempt to keep their spirits up, did his best to engage the men nearest him in conversation. Several times he tried to get the men beside him to say something about how they felt, who they were, and what they thought they should do; but he soon grew tired of the effort. All he received in return were apprehensive looks and shrugged shoulders. Perhaps they thought he was a plant. From their appearance, though, he had a sense that nobody was thinking in those terms. They looked too exhausted and frightened to be considering that sort of possibility. The events of the past however many days they had been arrested had drained them of all emotion and energy. Most of them, without saying so, seemed to have given up. Even when the convoy stopped to refuel, few showed any interest in where they were or where they were headed. In their dejection, it was as if these men had already begun to abandon their futures. In doing so, their spirits retreated somewhere deep within, like a microbe that finds itself in a hostile environment and deliberately shuts down all indications of life as it retreats into a deep hibernation.

Saul pulled himself into his original spot by the back wall. He was just as tired, just as uncertain about the future; still, he didn't consider himself like the others. This wasn't some kind of arrogance, a trait that he had been accused of as long as he could remember. Nonetheless, he withdrew from the group, telling himself a dozen times that he had to make a conscious effort to hold himself together. He couldn't allow the despair of the other men to drag him down. He intuitively knew that becoming self-absorbed, however justified it might be, would be fatal. He sat propped against the back of the truck's cab, resting his head on his tucked-up knees. He vaguely sensed that he was teetering somewhere between blind fear and a state of rational self-preservation, but he could never be sure which of these two inner voices was talking to him.

During the trip, he drifted on and off into light sleep, but he woke whenever his neck and head snapped to one side. Despite a great need to sleep, he couldn't get into a position that allowed him more than a minute's respite. Periodically, he struggled to his feet and peered through the crack in the canvas and rope joints of the vehicle tarp. Both ahead of them and behind he could see Feldgendarmerie motorcycle escorts: a hostile, ominous apparition of men in sidecars, goggled faces, helmets, and machine pistols, motoring steadily across the Dutch and north German landscapes at a steady forty miles per hour. Their sinister little convoy passed through miles of red-brick housing estates and smoke-stained industrial complexes, as well as belts of idyllic-looking farmland with ripening grain fields and pastures full of fat sheep and cattle.

By early evening, the sky darkened and rain spattered heavily onto the canvas. The sound of the truck's tires changed from a steady droning to the rhythmic hum of water spraying against the vehicle's undersides. With the rain, the temperature dropped; and with the drop in temperature, Saul's mood changed again. Alone with his thoughts, Saul repeatedly wondered about Annika. She would be frantic with worry for him. He should have listened to her when she talked of leaving Europe. He should have agreed to going to South Africa with Pauli's family. He stared forward, frozen by guilt and self-condemnation. He began to think that this was all his fault. If he had not been so pig-headed about things, if he had been willing to listen to others, if he had kept his mouth shut when they arrested Samuël, if he had not attempted to be the prisoners' spokesman in jail, if he had only used his head, he could have prevented all this. As he stared at the floor of the truck, he couldn't escape the belief that the nightmare he was enduring was a problem of his own making.

And Annika, what was she doing now? He had made a bad situation worse for her, and somehow she would know that his capture was his fault. He had barged into a situation that he could only lose and in doing so he had put them all in danger. What had become of his uncle Samuël? What was to happen to him? Where were they going? Not knowing anything, not being told anything, being treated like he was completely inconsequential: it all increased his fear. If they had sentenced him to die, at least it would have given him some idea of what was going on, something concrete around which he could frame his thoughts and organize his thinking. It was terrifying. But of course that's what his captors wanted.

He put his head back and his breath came in a ragged shudder. His clothes were filthy, his hair was matted, and there was a rash on his unshaven face. He was itchy, and so hungry he trembled. His head ached. The floor of the truck had sand and grease on it, and every time he moved, it rubbed into his clothes. Saul was incredibly thirsty. The men on the motorcycles had pushed a single metal cup and a steel can of water at them at the first petrol stop and they all had a short drink then, but other than that there had been no food or water. Saul looked about him. None of the prisoners spoke and few of them showed much sign of anything. There was no spark of resistance, no defiance, and for a moment he felt contemptuous of his fellow captives. He was not like that. Then the self-recrimination returned. If he hadn't been so vain, obstinate and superior, he wouldn't be here.

This, he thought, was a hell of a place to have a revelation about his character. In other circumstances, his overbearing impulsiveness would have been amusing. Then it occurred to him that there was nothing at all wrong with the other prisoners. They were just in different stages of shock, and this too was part of the problem. He thought about the difficulties the others had experienced and how he had naturally looked at them in terms that made him feel superior. For a time it was almost as if he were outside himself looking in; and now, in the most dejected time of his life, he felt compelled to think through the implications of what this kind of thinking meant. Why was he condemning himself in these circumstances? He knew he wasn't thinking straight. He knew his ability to plan was limited and he resolved to be guided by one word: survival.

Just before dark, the truck slowed and stopped. Saul could hear the motorcyclists dismount: men stretching and laughing, voices of command. A truck door slammed, a gate swung open, a barrier was lifted, and the truck rolled forward onto gravel. Engines were turned off and a soldier jumped onto the tailgate and flipped the tarp onto the roof.

"Get out! Get out!" Voices in German.

The men climbed down from the truck, easing themselves onto the ground, looking about them with bewilderment, suspicion, and fear in their darting eyes.

A voice shouted at them again in German. "You are prisoners of the Third Reich and you are now at Neuengamme Satellite Camp Three. This is a small work camp. The camp runs a brick factory, and if you hope to stay alive here, you must work and prove your worth, every day. If you don't, we shall get rid of you in one way or another." The man speaking was in a black uniform with a Nazi armband on his shirt. He stopped and looked around him, then shouted to one of the guards. "These are the Dutchmen?"

"Yes, sir."

"Dutchmen," he grunted. "You speak languages. Which of you speaks German?"

The prisoners looked warily at each other. None of the others moved. Saul, sensing opportunity, raised his hand.

"Good, come forward, stand aside here," the man in the black uniform said, pointing to a spot just off to the left of him. "Translate what I've just said to the others."

Saul repeated the Nazi's instructions in a calm voice. He was quite certain most of the men in this group understood enough German to follow what had been said, but he said nothing about this.

"Tell them to get into two rows."

Saul did so and the prisoners shuffled into two rows.

The German barked again. "The first row goes to work on the canal. The second row goes to the brick factory." He turned and muttered something unintelligible to one of the motorcyclists, who fumbled in his breast pocket and handed over a sheet of folded paper. He read it for a minute. "Which one of you is Hammerstein, the Jew?"

Saul raised his hand.

The German made a contemptuous face. "Ha, so it's you. You go to the brick factory. You'll wear a yellow star. You'll get it at your quarters." He looked down at the paper again. "Which one of you is Landseer?"

One of the men in the canal line slowly raised his hand.

"You. So you are our communist. You get out of line and get over there with the Jew. You'll be in the brick factory as well." He flicked his head at the camp guards. "Take them away."

15

ANNIKA WAS SITTING at a table at the Keizersgracht Café. She had gone to some pains to make herself look presentable. She had carefully brushed her hair, and put on makeup and her navy blue dress. She didn't want to look too smart or as if she was on a date, but she wanted to present a credible image. There were not many others sitting at the outdoor café. As the occupation wore on, few people found themselves going out. There was an unnaturally subdued feeling in the city, as if most of the citizens had of their own accord gone into mourning. The other patrons of the café had an embarrassed and furtive look about them.

Annika had positioned herself outside at the very end table so that she could see north down the Vijzelstraat, which ran in the direction of the police station. It was, she reasoned, the most likely route for "Policeman 134," as she had come to think of him, to get here. She was surprised when she felt a tap on her arm and standing next to her in a neat, charcoal-grey wool suit and a trilby felt hat was the short policeman.

"Oh, you startled me. I expected you to come from that direction."

The policeman merely gave a thin smile. He spoke quietly. "I had no intention of coming straight from the police station. May I join you, madam?"

"Yes, of course, please do. Did you get any information for me?"

The policeman looked embarrassed and quickly put his finger to his lips as he pulled up his chair. He whispered, "You have to be much more discreet than that, I'm afraid. These are very dangerous times—I think more dangerous than either of us really appreciate. Yes, I have some information for you, but you must realize that we are both in serious danger. You, because you are the wife of Saul Hammerstein, and me, because I have nosed about and discovered information that the Germans want to be kept as a secret." He looked at her with a long, steady gaze. "You understand that you are in considerable danger, don't you?"

Annika was alarmed. For an instant her right hand flew up in front of her mouth. "Some friends told me that it's quite possible that the Germans might come and arrest me because they go after the families of those they consider political prisoners."

"I'm afraid your friends are right. They haven't done this yet. They're too busy consolidating other, higher-priority security issues. But they intend to put a very tight clamp on this country and all their occupied territories. You and the families of anyone who is deemed to be a potential threat to their regime will be quietly and swiftly removed."

"But what has Saul done? What have I done? Surely we're no threat to the German army!"

The policeman put his palm out abruptly to stop her from speaking further. He looked up and smiled. A waiter was standing off to one side of Annika, raising his eyebrows in an inquiring gesture.

"What can I get you?"

"Two coffees, please," the policeman said, "and bring me the bill with them. We are in a bit of a hurry. Thank you." When the waiter had moved away, he said to Annika, "We can't stay here and talk about this. This is much too obvious a spot. You have to realize that things have changed dramatically. I'm not being critical, but in the last few minutes you have twice been careless. It's not your fault. You're distressed and unused to this kind of behaviour. We'll finish our coffees and leave, and we will talk while we walk."

When the waiter arrived with the coffee, Annika and the policeman were talking about the weather and how it affected the gardens this year. The policeman was smoking and smiling broadly. "Thank you so much," he said. "We won't be staying long. We have a train to catch." He pushed a half-guilder note at the man. "Please keep the change."

The waiter left.

"Look as relaxed as you can, madam. We'll drink our coffee and then stroll out of here towards the train station, and then we will talk." He forced a smile and said in a louder voice. "Now tell me about everything you've done since we last met. What's it been, eighteen months? Two years?"

Annika smiled back and began a long story about how she had set up a small clothing store in The Hague and she was just down for a short time to see one of her suppliers. "The war hasn't really affected business, you know."

As they rose to leave, the policeman gallantly escorted her by the arm and whispered in her ear. "Well done. You're doing just fine."

They walked on for several minutes before they spoke. The sidewalks of the main streets were busy, and the policeman steered them towards the path that ran along the Herengracht Canal. They both turned and watched with blank faces as a German army truck with a section of unsmiling infantry in the back drove by. "They're everywhere now," the policeman said. "I'm afraid we are also going to have to be very careful what we say and to whom. Things have changed dramatically and they're going to get a lot worse."

They walked towards the railing as if they were two lovers out for a stroll and intent on watching the family of ducks swimming happily in front of them. The policeman leaned forward and lit a cigarette.

"I'm sorry that I don't have better news for you. Your husband was moved to Germany some time ago, along with a dozen others."

"What does that mean? Will he be brought to trial or released some day? How long will they keep him? They can't just go on like this without anybody knowing anything. I've never heard of anything like this before."

"I'm afraid that none of us have. Believe me, this is causing the police force tremendous problems. But as for your husband, we don't know where they have taken him. Before all this happened, we used to hear reports about people disappearing in Germany. Anyone who ran afoul of the Nazis was arrested and simply disappeared. There would only be a trial when it was convenient for them to do so. I'm afraid that this is what's happened to your husband and the twelve other men with him." The policeman stared out at the black water of the canal. "I wish I could tell you something more than this, something to give you some hope, but I'm afraid I can't. I heard this morning that the Germans even have a name for it—it's a policy now, 'Night and Fog.' People disappear into the night and fog and they're never heard of again."

Annika put her fist in front of her mouth and sobbed, but only for a second. She stopped and looked out over the water, visibly gathering her composure. She stood tall and took several breaths. "I've been afraid that this was the worst thing that could happen. I've been preparing myself for the worst. I've told myself for the last two weeks that this is the most likely outcome. We should have gone to South Africa with the Herschels. We should have left a long time ago. How stupid we were. Poor Saul. Do you suppose he's alive? Have they tortured him?"

"I think he may still be alive. I don't think they wanted any information from him, so, no, I don't think they've tortured him, although it's likely they've been treated roughly. From what I can gather, he was arrested along with his uncle. The two of them kicked up a fuss when the Nazis confiscated everything at your uncle's diamond business. Neither of them was wanted for any political reason or for offering resistance. They just behaved defiantly. It's what the Germans are calling a 'manner disrespectful to the authorities.'"

He paused and cleared his throat. "Your husband interrupted one of the chief Gestapo officers here in the Netherlands when he was addressing Dutch prisoners. That's why he was sent to a labour camp."

The policeman stopped and looked intensely at Annika. "But, you know, that makes you vulnerable as well. It will be much harder

on him because he is a Jew. The Germans have accurate Dutch cen-
sus data on everyone in the country. Apparently traitors and German
spies passed on this information before the invasion. They know
the names and addresses of every Jew, and everyone is in their little
black book." He shook his head slowly and they both stopped talking as a group of cyclists pedalled past them. The policeman nodded
in greeting as they went by. "Dutch Nazis were waiting when they
arrived, and they've already provided them with more information
than you can imagine."

"What happened to Uncle Samuël?"

"He's all right." The policeman stopped himself. "Well, no, he's
not all right. I gather he's a sick man. The period of detention hasn't
been easy, but he'll survive this. He got roughed up a bit because he
was a Jew, but they have nothing further against him, yet. Like all the
others who were dragged in, they'll be released tonight. I think that
the Nazis see this as being magnanimous. From what I hear, they
eventually want the Netherlands to be incorporated into Greater
Germany. That doesn't mean your uncle Samuël or any other Jew
will be safe. There's already talk about the Germans rounding up all
the Jews and shipping them out someplace else. I'm not surprised.
Look at how they've isolated the Jews in Germany."

Annika's voice was quiet but deliberate. "I'm glad Uncle Samuël is
all right. Is there any more information that you can get about Saul?"

"I'll get whatever information I can, but you must remember, the
Nazis are deliberately conducting a campaign of terrorizing our population. It's their means of keeping us in line and ensuring we comply
with what they want."

"How did you get this information? How do I know you aren't
some kind of a spy?" Annika looked both angry and bewildered.

"I suppose you don't. You just have to trust me. But if I was working for the Nazis, I'd have simply arrested you by now and hauled
you in. Our new German bosses would give me a good chit for that."
He turned back and leaned against the rail, looking out at the street
as if he had something difficult to say. "I've been thinking about it
before I came here. You already know my police badge number and

I know your name. I've told you enough to have me carted off and sent to prison in Germany, so you might as well know my name. I'm Henrick Schulyer." He put out his hand and Annika shook it. Her hand was cold and limp.

"Thank you," she said. "You didn't have to help me; I'm very grateful for that."

Schulyer nodded. "I feel we have to do something, and you have already suffered a great deal. When you asked for help, I felt obliged. But as for you, I think you have a degree of safety just now. The Germans aren't well organized yet. They will be soon. For now, you aren't a high priority for them; you have no intelligence value. They just don't like who you are."

Annika looked down at the pavement. "I suppose you're right. I'm sorry, that was rude of me. I should have thought of that for myself."

"No. You have other things on your mind. Besides, you should be suspicious of everybody now. There are people here collaborating with Germans: some from fear and others because they think they can gain something; and of course, we've had our own Dutch Nazi Party." Schulyer fumbled about in his pockets and got himself another cigarette. As he lit it he said, "Things are changing here quickly, and if you're going to survive you have to be able to anticipate what the threats will be." He shook out the match. "Before, we took trust for granted; not now. Be very careful who you trust. You can already see it at the police station. Before, we were a team of men working towards a common cause. Now we're not sure of anything any more. Nobody trusts anybody else. It happened in one day, like someone throwing an electrical switch. If we don't go to work and do as the Nazis say, we'll be hauled off to a labour camp. We've already had policemen disappear. Nobody knows what to do or who to talk to, so they simply do as they've been told. It's probably going to be the same everywhere else."

"So why are you helping me and how'd you get this information about Saul?"

"When I saw you this morning, I had just come out of a meeting with one of my supervisors, a man I thought I could trust, but now he pretends nothing is wrong and that we should all be willing and obedient servants to the Nazis. I can never be like that." He took a deep drag on his cigarette. He was obviously worried. "I can tell you the invasion and the German occupation has stunned all of us. After the Germans told us we are now working for them, I didn't know what to do. I don't want to cooperate with these people. You were in trouble, you needed help, and so I thought that the least I could do was to get you some information. It made me feel like I was doing something. Besides, like I said, things are going to get worse. This isn't a time to sit on the fence."

"How did you find out about Saul if they aren't telling anyone what's happening?"

"The Germans are smart. They know they won't be able to run their occupied countries profitably unless they get assistance from the local authorities. There are a few senior members of the department who have access to the Nazi lists. I made a point of going to see one of them this morning after we met. When he was out of the office I read the list on his desk. I'm not certain he didn't know exactly what I was up to. I don't normally work with him. It was as if he deliberately left the office to allow me to see the document. We're not all caving in."

Schulyer paused and looked out at the street. He was measuring his words. "You can't tell anyone about this meeting or that you know Saul has been deported. If the Nazis knew, they could trace the leak back to my source and he would be a dead man."

Annika nodded.

"Do you have a family?"

"No, we have no children. My parents are dead. I have a cousin living in The Hague. Saul has family."

"As far as they're concerned, you know nothing. Your uncle will be able to provide some information. I'm very sorry. I wish there was something more that I could do or say about your husband."

"You've been a great help. But I just can't believe this is happening—it seems so unreal. And you say it's going to get worse? How could it be worse than this?" Annika felt hollow and sick. She was sure that Saul, if he wasn't already dead, would be murdered soon. She wanted to scream but she willed herself to think. "There must be something we can do. We can't just sit around like cattle waiting to be slaughtered!"

"What are you suggesting?"

"I don't know exactly, but there must be others like us who want to resist these people."

Schulyer sighed. "All of us left it much too late. But I agree with you. I don't know what to do either—I'm thinking that if we create a network of like-minded people we may be able to at least help some of those who are threatened by the Nazis."

Annika's voice was breaking. "What could we possibly do? I heard this morning on the radio that a German soldier was killed yesterday in Maastricht and twenty hostages were rounded up and shot. We can't do anything against that!"

"No. We've lost the war militarily. You're right. Violence is futile now, but I'm sure as hell not willing to join them; if you are completely passive in this and do nothing, then sooner or later you become a part of them." Schulyer pushed himself back from the handrail and stared at the ground. He began pushing a small pebble around with his shoe. "When I went to get the information about Saul this morning I learned something else."

"What?"

"One of the first things the Germans are planning is to institute a system of identity cards for every member of the population. Everyone will have to carry an identity card with them wherever they go. It's going to be one of their principal ways of controlling the population. The process is to start in a matter of days. They intend to have a file on everybody."

"I don't follow you. How does this involve me, or you?"

Schulyer looked out over the canal and grasped the metal handrail tightly. He was weighing his words carefully. "I'm going to volunteer to join the administrative section of the traffic department. They handle the issuing and control of driver's licences."

Annika looked puzzled.

"Let me explain. It won't involve anyone but me immediately. But I've been thinking about what I've heard over the last few days. If someone is deeply involved in the identity section, that person will have the chance to influence who gets what identity card; and in the future, that will be important, believe me. The Germans plan on developing a Dutch identity card system that will be built upon the current driver's licence administration. I'm sure that by volunteering now I can secure a minor but valuable position early on. If the Germans don't know who's who, we can influence who gets identity cards and hopefully protect people from them."

Schulyer looked uncertain. "I'm not sure just now what we'll do, but being able to change people's identities will be essential to any kind of resistance effort. That's why I've confided in you. I'm going to need others to help me at some stage." He stopped talking and started pushing the pebble around again with his shoe. "I don't know what it's going to involve, but it won't be easy. Can I count on you some time in the future to be a part of my network?"

Annika didn't hesitate. "Yes, of course. Of course! What do you want me to do?"

"Nothing, for now."

* * *

Rory estimated Mr. Meertens was about the same age as himself, somewhere in his late thirties to mid-forties. He was a strongly built man, with glasses, a head of thick fair hair, and a serious face. He wore a short blue coat, and if he'd had a peaked cap, wooden clogs, and a clay pipe in his mouth, Rory thought he would have been a perfect match for a storybook Dutch farmer. This morning he was taking his truck with a dozen large wheels of cheese into Amsterdam. He spoke no French, but from school and contacts in his cheese business he had more than a smattering of German. Mr. Meertens was a shrewd merchant. As he explained, he was only charging Rory two-thirds what it would have cost him to take tomorrow's bus into town.

Almost as soon as Meertens had the money in his hand, he seemed to switch from being grim-faced to cheerful. Thankfully, he was an individual who had little interest in the people he was with, and so he asked no personal questions. For Rory, this was a blessing. He didn't need to elaborate when he explained that he was a French Alsatian. He'd been forced to learn German at school before the Great War and he was at a loss to know what was going to happen to the provinces of Alsace and Lorraine now that the Germans had invaded and his home was once again changing ownership. Would all the French-speaking Alsatians have to move to France? It was all very troubling.

Mr. Meertens was anxious to talk about his cheese business and didn't seem in the least bit suspicious of the cover story. He was, however, intrigued by the business implications of Becker's situation. "So, Mr. Becker, what will you do if you find new kinds of seeds and fertilizers? How will you ship them back to Alsace, and will there still be a market for these kinds of things with the war on? Can farmers pay for this kind of thing in this economy? The reason I ask is that I'm already having problems getting my cheese shipped to Germany."

Rory shrugged his shoulders. "I don't know. Perhaps once I get to Amsterdam I'll send a letter or telegram to my company and ask them these questions. I hope that things won't change too much. If there's too much disruption, I'll lose my job."

"Isn't that the problem, though? Nobody knows what all this means for the people at the bottom like you and me. I hope soon that there can be a peace conference and we can go back to living like we did before. All this war, fighting and killing—what is it for? It's so stupid. It never solves anything anyway."

Rory nodded in agreement. "Yes, you're right. We just want to live our lives in peace." They drove on in silence for a few minutes, and when they rounded the edge of a thick grove of birches and willow trees, Rory pointed out the window. "Look out there."

Off in the field to the right of the road was a small, tented German army camp.

Meertens slowed his truck and put his head forward to see better. "This wasn't here two days ago."

"No, it's probably the last of the German army moving in from the east." Rory said. "It looks to me like they don't plan to stay here long, though. They look like they're getting ready to go somewhere." From inside the truck at least, it appeared as if this column was getting itself organized to go back on the road. In the distance, troops were pulling tents down and loading equipment onto wagons. Ahead, next to the road, a German field artillery battery and its horse-drawn supply echelon were shaking out into their order of march.

"They have beautiful animals though, don't they, Mr. Becker?"

"Yes they do," Rory said absently. He was in no mood for disagreement, but he couldn't help but think how the two men differed in their perceptions. Meertens saw an army camp whose most important feature was its sleek, well-tended wagon horses, and he saw a motorized, eight-gun, medium artillery battery with a much slower horse-drawn echelon. Off to the east he could see tents and trucks with antennas, which looked like something large enough to be at least a co-located regimental headquarters. There would be a lot of other units not far off from here, and the supported infantry and armoured units must be only a few miles south of them, somewhere back in the direction he had come from. He wondered if last night the Lysander had unwittingly put him in the middle of a division on the move. If that was the case, he was luckier than he had any right to be.

From the side of the road, a bored-looking soldier who didn't look old enough to shave made a sign for them to halt and waved them over to the side of the road. He spoke in German and asked who they were, where they were going, and what was in the truck. Meertens answered in German, "We are from Nieukerk and I'm just going to take my cheese to market in town, like I do three times a week."

Two other soldiers with their weapons slung over their shoulders walked over to the roadside to watch. The soldier who had stopped them nodded at Meertens and wandered around to the back of the truck, pulled open the door, and looked in. Rory's heart raced. His suitcase was beside a stack of heavy, circular, cloth-covered wheels of cheese. The soldier looked sideways as if he was considering calling over a superior, but he closed the door and slapped the side of the van. He slung his rifle over his shoulder. "Go on, quickly. This road will soon have military priority and there will be no civilian traffic until after one o'clock."

Rory couldn't help but notice the soldiers had small black-and-green shields with a stylized castle stencilled on the side of their helmets.

They drove on in silence for a few minutes. Meertens was the first to speak. "Maybe it was for the best that there wasn't a lot of fighting in this war. Can you imagine what it would have been like if all our homes and our farms and towns had been destroyed?"

"I can't imagine. I was just a private soldier in the army in the last war. I was wounded very early, within days of going to the front; it was horrible. I guess I was lucky."

Neither man spoke again for some time, and as they drew into the outskirts of Amsterdam, Meertens said, "I can take you into the centre of town. It's a bit out of my way, but you can find a place to stay near there. Over by the Westerstraat area, near the market, there are lots of boarding houses, and from there you will be able to walk anywhere you want to go."

Rory was impressed by Amsterdam on his first drive through it. He had been briefed on the town back in England and he had read pre-war travel brochures; but when you were here you realized that the city really did merge old-world charm and dignity with an industrious temperament. Well-dressed cyclists flowed silently and serenely up and down its broad avenues; there wasn't a lot of motor traffic, and horse-drawn wagons were everywhere. The city was clean. Narrow townhouses and large trees lined the streets; every three or four blocks were broad canals. The city retained the look and feel of the days when the known world was much smaller and Amsterdam had been at the centre of the world's trade. It was the kind of place that given different circumstances Rory would love to have returned to as a tourist.

Mr. Meertens let Rory off on a busy corner. "Just down that street you'll find several good boarding houses. They're not too expensive and you can make a deal to get your evening meal. Don't let them overcharge you because you're a foreigner. Be firm. Good luck." He held out his hand and they shook firmly.

Rory smiled at him. "Many thanks. You've been a great help. It's been my pleasure. I certainly hope we meet again some time." As he smiled, he thought Mr. Meertens was a peaceful and law-abiding man; but he was also unimaginative and self-absorbed. He was a man who did what he was told and he would probably hand him over to the Gestapo at the slightest threat. The ride and the conversation had been a practical lesson in trust and the sort of upright citizen who was to be avoided. "Many thanks again, sir. Good luck with your cheese business."

Rory put his suitcase down and tightened his tie. That was the heart of his problem. He was here now but what kind of people would he be able to trust? Hopefully his contact, the retired Dutch army officer, would be able to help him with that problem. He straightened his hat, picked up his suitcase, and began to walk.

* * *

Rottenführer Dieter Schmidt blushed and stammered as he spoke to the woman behind the counter in the patisserie. He hadn't expected this kind of reception. The stout, fair-haired woman stood defiantly, hands on her hips, jaw jutting forward, eyes narrowed. Schmidt and his partner had been under orders not to go out alone, but he had left the other uniformed policeman outside the shop so he would not intimidate the store clerks. The woman wiped her hands on her dark blue apron. Her face didn't change.

"We have done nothing wrong. Why are you here?"

Her husband, a dark young man with a thick but neatly clipped moustache, was in the back room and he stepped forward, closing the door behind him. Schmidt could hear the muffled sounds of small children's voices from behind the door. The man with the moustache stepped in front of his wife.

"What can we do for you?" the man asked. His wife continued to glare at Schmidt with as much warmth as if he had just tried to molest one of her children.

"I'm very sorry to intrude, sir, but I have to buy some coffee and rolls for my superiors. I don't want a lot, perhaps a half-dozen of the fresh butter rolls in the glass over there and five hundred grams of freshly ground coffee, please."

The woman spoke stiffly. "We don't speak German." She remained rigid.

Her husband leaned forward and said quietly, "We speak a little German. I can serve you this one time, but you must understand that we are running short of coffee. Supplies are low all over the city, and we would ask that you go elsewhere the next time. We have only enough for our regular customers." He took a deep breath and swallowed. He looked steadily at Schmidt. "Besides, we have family in Rotterdam and we have had relatives killed by your bombing."

Schmidt said nothing at first. He had never been in a situation like this. He had done his best to be polite. He understood how they felt, but this was awkward. Neumann would never tolerate something as simple as this refusal.

"I understand. I'm very sorry, but I have been ordered to come here every morning. I have no choice in this. Whatever supplies you have, you must sell to us. We will pay the regular price, but I can't go back and tell my officer that you have refused us service. For what it is worth, I have children of my own in Germany. I just want to go home and see them again. Please don't make things difficult for all of us."

The woman muttered something in Dutch and her husband patted her hand. She turned away in disgust and went into the back room, closing the door forcefully behind her.

The man behind the counter put the rolls in a bag and measured out the coffee carefully. When he handed the package over to Schmidt, he saw that Schmidt had handed over a five-guilder note. It was much more than the purchase was worth.

"Please, this one time, keep the change," Schmidt said.

The shopkeeper shook his head and handed back several coins and a folded bill. "No. Absolutely not. Please go."

As he left the store, Schmidt saw the man drawing the curtains and locking the door behind him. He flipped the cardboard "Open" sign over. The two men locked eyes for a second and the shopkeeper pulled a curtain over the glass door.

Schmidt's face burned and he felt numb. Never in his life had he been snubbed like that. He was thinking slowly, as if he had just been given an electric shock. He remained beside the door for a few seconds as his counterpart walked back down the street to join him.

"So, Dieter, how did it go?"

"They don't like us, but I've got newly promoted Herr Oberstleutnant Neumann his rolls and coffee."

"You seem upset, Dieter. You're much too nice a guy. This shouldn't surprise you. You know what they told us: a small percentage of the Dutch like us, most hate us, and another small percentage are indifferent but quite prepared to work with us. Eventually they'll all come around to like us, but next time I'll go and get the coffee. They'll understand what they are dealing with if they want to be rude."

Schmidt chewed on his lower lip. "No. I think it's best that in the future we have these morning rolls and coffee delivered. We'll go back this afternoon and I will speak to him."

Forty minutes later, Schmidt stood stiffly at Neumann's office door; he had his heels together and held before him a silver tray with a silver coffee service in his hand. "Sir, your morning coffee as ordered."

"Very good, Schmidt. Did you have any trouble getting this?" Schmidt merely shook his head and gave a feeble smile.

Neumann looked at Schmidt quizzically. "You don't like it here, do you, Schmidt? No surprise. You and I both know that many of the Dutch don't like us, but I hope that you don't behave too softly towards them. I sometimes think you have too much of the village constable in you to be really effective at occupation work. Here a policeman requires a completely unemotional approach to his work. If we aren't ruthless, we'll never succeed, and success demands diligent consistency in our approach to the local population. We can't have some people dealing with the locals in a correct manner and others being too kind-hearted. You know that, don't you, Schmidt? If they don't like us, they should fear us." Neumann was leaning forward. Schmidt had never seen him quite this intense before.

Then, as if he were releasing himself from an exercise, Neumann leaned back from his desk. "And now, Schmidt, I have a report on my desk that there is a rumour going about that the trade unions are planning a strike, some sort of a non-violent policy of disobedience to the German forces. That won't happen here in Amsterdam, Schmidt. Things will run as normal here. Now, how does this news about a strike involve you?"

Neumann didn't wait for an answer. "It's nonsense, Schmidt. Now, something of interest for you. Now that I'm an Oberstleutnant, the army has found us a new house. It's one that they have requisitioned for us. You will be moving with me. You will have a good-sized room of your own at the back of the house, and we will stay there for the duration of our posting in the Netherlands."

Neumann stopped and looked at Schmidt, who merely nodded, "Yes, sir."

"We move out in three days time. I want you to ensure that all my things are prepared and that we have adequate staff to man our house. In addition to being my driver, orderly, and personal bodyguard, I want you to hire and oversee the Dutch staff that will be working with us. We will have a housemaid, a gardener, a cook, and a porter. Make sure the people you hire are qualified, dependable, and loyal. Anyone in our new staff who thinks of participating in a strike or a work slowdown will be dealt with. I want you to be the person at the house who makes sure everything runs smoothly. I don't have time for that. I have a list of contacts here that you should deal with. They'll help you get us suitably qualified and motivated people."

Neumann pushed back in his chair, stood up, stretched. He turned to Schmidt and chuckled. "I'm sure you'll do a good job; I'd hate to lose you by seeing you posted into the army."

Schmidt smiled. Neumann was a menace. Schmidt forced himself to keep smiling as he stepped back from the desk. He retreated the way someone backs away from a venomous snake. At the door, he clicked his heels and ducked his head in an informal salute.

As he went down the hall, Schmidt thought to himself that Neumann didn't really seem to understand the purpose of laughter or joy. He lived to work, and even when he tried to be amusing, he confused it with being threatening and grim.

* * *

ANNIKA WALKED AWAY from her meeting with Henrick Schulyer thinking it strange that though she was about to join a conspiracy against the Nazis, she felt amazingly tranquil and composed. She didn't know what to make of this change, especially since all day she had been a grief-stricken bundle of nerves. Though pleased with herself for taking some kind of action, she felt no joy. The pleasure was more a symptom of relief. Annika knew she was anguished about Saul, but she felt distant from all that now. His imprisonment and possible death left her feeling wretched and exhausted. But now she had a sense of purpose that for the time being seemed to dominate all her other emotions. Perhaps, she thought, this was what life was like in the eye of the storm; maybe she was simply passing through to another period of turbulence.

So much had happened in the last few days it was difficult to say how she felt about anything. Perhaps Schulyer's vague plans of resisting the Germans merely provided a veneer that covered her turmoil, a means of sweeping things under the carpet. After all, she had no idea of what they were going to be doing. He had only mentioned something hazy about false identification and that was little enough to go on. As she thought about her predicament, she became angry. The Germans had taken her husband for no reason. For all she knew, he was dead. That's what everyone had been hinting at. She didn't like thinking about the possibility of Saul's death; but equally, she wasn't prepared to sit around and have someone destroy her life without striking back. It wasn't in her nature. Who were these people to ruin so many lives with impunity?

As she walked forward along the Kerkstraat, she was oblivious to the people walking and cycling around her. She put her head down and clutched her handbag close to her side. This new calmness allowed her to see things more clearly. There appeared to be three broad options open to her: she could stay and wait for the hammer to come crashing down on her a second time; she could run and do her best to escape with Oscar and Nina; or she could stay and fight. Not that she imagined herself for a minute as some kind of Joan of Arc, rallying brave Dutch troops to drive out the invader. But there had to be something she could do, something she could contribute, no matter how small, to fight these people; and Schulyer, as vague as his ideas were, offered a possibility that involved action.

She stopped walking and for a moment considered what capture would mean at the hands of these people: certain death. She was no martyr; then again, what if she was going to be arrested and hauled off simply because she was married to Saul? In that case, she would likely die a slow, exhausting death in a labour camp. It wasn't just her imagination. Oscar and Nina had both spoken of it and so had Henrick Schulyer. Really, then, she didn't have three options, just two: flee; or stay, go incognito, and do what she could to fight.

It was now clear that no matter what happened, she could no longer go on living her old life as Annika Hammerstein. That was all in her past now. She started walking slowly again, doing her best to remain focused, to think this through logically; so much depended on it.

Fleeing Holland wasn't such a bad option. She could escape and still resist by helping the British. Perhaps she could make her way to Britain, or some other place that continued to hold out against the Germans. She could wait there for Saul. And perhaps she could get word to him that she was safe; that would be a huge relief to him in prison—if he was still alive. She didn't have to stay here. It never occurred to her that she would have trouble getting out of Holland. She could speak German and French well enough, she'd studied English in secondary school, and she'd been to Britain once before. Somehow she could make her way across Belgium and France and into Spain, and from there go somewhere else. There was no question that the escape itself posed a whole new set of problems, but they were problems she felt confident she could do something about.

On the other hand, she had already committed herself to helping Henrick Schulyer. True, she hadn't agreed to any particular kind of help. Perhaps she could be of more value to him abroad. What she knew for certain was that she could no longer stay at home, living her old life. That was gone. She had to go somewhere else and start anew. She didn't know where; but as of today she could no longer be Annika Hammerstein.

As she walked, she caught sight of her reflection in a ground floor window of a house beside her. The face looking back at her was thin and drawn. She wouldn't have recognized herself if it was a photograph. She could stay with Oscar and Nina tonight, and it was probably safe to go back one last time to her old flat, just to collect her things, and then she would go to the bank and withdraw all their savings in cash. If she did that, then she could decide what to do tomorrow.

At the Reguliers Canal, she stopped again and, leaning against the guard rail, looked over at the line of houseboats moored alongside the opposite bank. These little self-contained floating homes could simply cast away their mooring lines and leave. They could go almost anywhere in Holland and find a place to stay. As she stared out at the line of boats bobbing gently on their mooring lines, a plan began to take form in her mind. She stuck her jaw out and straightened herself. She'd made her decision. She turned left onto the cobblestone path beside the canal and picked up her pace heading back to her old flat.

16

SAUL WAS SO WEAK from the effects of dehydration and not having eaten in more than forty-eight hours that his first night at the Neuengamme prison camp passed in a haze. He and five other prisoners were marched away to their quarters shortly after they were assigned to the "Brick Factory." Despite his pledge to keep his spirits up, he was worn out, tired to his very marrow, and longed to simply fall down. Each second he felt like he was two steps away from total collapse, and every minute was a conscious struggle not to let himself faint away on the spot.

When the six-man column set off, Saul was walking behind two prison guards. Although he was tired, he watched the two guards closely. It was obvious that they knew the Dutchmen were fatigued, but they purposely set off at a good clip. Saul also noticed the way the two of them carried their riding crops and instantly realized that from here on in, being next to one of these men with their pistols and whips was not a smart place to be. He promised himself that in future he would fall-in to the middle of any lineup.

Up ahead, one of the guards snapped at them to walk faster, and then just as abruptly, with a wave of his riding crop, he halted the little file of prisoners. He called out something indistinct and motioned for the prisoners to wait until another guard, one with a large, vicious-looking dog, caught up with them. The dog handler was walking towards them at a right angle, about two hundred metres away, strolling between two lines of cheaply made wooden huts. Saul noticed that the huts were roofed with torn bits of tarpaper and were probably not much good at keeping the rain out. There were no lights in them. The huts themselves were little more than windbreaks. He had seen much more inviting-looking tool sheds.

Saul studied the guard with the dog as he approached. He was baby-faced, with ruddy cheeks, and unlike the man at the head of the column, he had a perpetual smirk on his face. He wore a black shirt and trousers with high, black, cavalry-style boots and a black peaked cap with a shiny brim, which he wore at a rakish angle. His cap had a death's head cloth badge sewn on it. He stopped and looked down one of the rows of huts. He was in no hurry, and smoked a cigarette, obviously enjoying the moment. Except for the massive dog and the uniform, he could have passed for a man out for a leisurely evening stroll.

His dog, on the other hand, looked anything but calm. It was lunging and straining at its leash, growling, barking, and snapping at something unseen in the dusk. Saul had never seen such a vicious animal. It looked like a mongrel German shepherd, with its long, coarse, black fur and pale brown streaks on its withers and forelegs. For a second he wondered what you had to do to train a dog to be that savage. Who in their right mind would ever breed such an animal? Then he chided himself for being so stupid. The answer was standing in front of him at the other end of the dog's leash.

When the guard with the dog stopped three metres away, the guard at the head of the column slapped his leg with his riding crop and shouted, "You, Jew, tell your friends that our little pet here is named Fluffy." All three guards laughed at this. "Fluffy and friends just like her are on patrol every night. Once prisoners are led into their quarters it is a capital offence to be caught outside them. You don't want Fluffy to catch you. Shall I pick one of you for a demonstration?" Saul translated the gist of what the guard said.

One of the men in the line behind Saul began to whimper softly.

"No? No demonstration? You are wise, and tonight we are feeling kind, so perhaps Fluffy will stay on her leash. Look down this row of huts." He paused to allow Saul to translate. "Beyond the huts you see a high wire fence with search lights. Anyone approaching that fence at any time of the day or night will be shot. Those are all the rules I'm going to give you tonight. This is your hut behind you on the left. There are other prisoners in it. They can tell you the other camp rules. They are very simple. Do what you are told and you will stay alive. Disobey the rules and you will die. Translate that."

Saul translated. The guard looked at him. "Good. Tell your men they have fifteen seconds to get inside that hut and close the door or we will let Fluffy go for a run."

Inside the hut it was dark. Saul could hear men moving around. The newcomers stood by the doorway trying to accustom their eyes to the gloom. The building smelled like a pigsty that hadn't been cleaned for a month. Saul shouted in hoarse German, "We are six Dutch-men who have just arrived. We are very tired, hungry, and we need your help." Then he paused. He hoped his greeting didn't sound too abrupt or inane, but it was the best he could do. There was a stirring in the dark. Someone came forward, a man about five-foot six. He had thick glasses and was dressed in ill-fitting striped prison clothes.

"My name is Wendell Bloch. We haven't got much here, but what we have, we'll share with you. Tell your men there are empty bunks over by the far wall. We have a can of water in the far corner, and here by the door there is a bucket that serves as a toilet. Be careful you don't spill it."

Saul's eyes were growing accustomed to the light. There were two small windows at each end of the hut and what appeared to be broad double bunks in two rows down the building's length.

"The rules are simple," Bloch continued. "Each of us has a bunk. They will give you prison clothes in the morning and take away your own clothes. Don't get caught keeping your civilian clothes or trying to hide them. It is against the rules and disobeying a rule results in death. We have had two men from this hut shot in the last three months." Saul translated this into Dutch.

Bloch spoke without emotion. "This is a work camp. We work and try to stay alive. We get two meals a day: bread and soup at 6 a.m. and bread and soup at 7 p.m. We figure we get just over twelve hundred calories a day. Some days we get a little more bread than others. Not often." Bloch paused again to let Saul speak. "The work in the brick factory is hard and the conditions are bad. You cannot complain and you must not get sick. Those who get sick go to what they call the infirmary, and they are never heard from again."

One of the Dutchmen behind Saul called out in heavily accented German, "Does anyone ever get out of here?"

"Not so far. This camp is less than two years old and there are many men in the other huts who have been here since it opened. We hope that eventually, after several years, we will be released; but no one has ever been told how long his sentence is for. You live for each day and stay alive for the chance of freedom some time in the future."

Saul translated. The last thing Bloch said was, "The guards have their rules. We have just a couple: everyone helps one another; everyone stays as clean as possible; everyone shares in cleaning the hut, and that includes taking out the bedpans in the morning; and no one hoards food or takes more than their share. I wish there was more than this that I could tell you, but I can't. The best thing you can do now is get as much rest as you can until morning."

By the time Bloch finished speaking, Saul found that his eyes had accustomed fully to the light in the hut. He could see bearded faces with hollow eyes staring out at him from the bunks. The bunks themselves were just two levels of rough boards hammered between flimsy upright posts. Each bunk was wide enough to hold two men, and each man was wrapped in a thin blanket that looked like some kind of heavy sackcloth.

Saul found an empty bunk near the centre of the room. There was a man lying watching him beside the empty bunk. Another man was trying to sleep on the bunk across the aisle. Over by the wall there were several empty bunks. He considered it wiser to choose one in the middle of a group than to be left on the fringes by a wall. He thought of the guard with the riding crop and reminded himself that safety was going to be found in numbers.

"Is this free?"

The man beside him grunted in a deep voice, "Yeah, the last man who had it went to the infirmary last week. You can have it."

Saul slumped down and stretched out. He was glad it was a warm night. He closed his eyes. The hard wooden bunk suddenly seemed like paradise. His head swam and within minutes he was asleep.

When Saul awoke he was covered in one of the brown sackcloth blankets. All the regular prisoners were up and shuffling towards the door. Only a few men muttered in low tones to one another. There was a lineup for the bucket that passed as a toilet. Saul's bunkmate was up, trying to stretch some life into a body that had lain on a wooden crib all night.

"You slept soundly. You were snoring for most of the night. Wendell Bloch redistributed blankets so that each of the newcomers got one. He runs a good prison block; that's why we elected him as our mayor." He made parenthetical motions over the word mayor and grinned. "My name's Derek Heltriger." He thrust a slender hand forward.

Saul sat up and shook it. "I'm Saul Hammerstein. I'm from Amsterdam." His throat was dry and his head ached.

"With a name like that from Amsterdam, I guess you're Jewish then?" Heltriger said. "That won't help you here, although in one way or another, most of us in the brick factory are on the Nazi shit list, so you're not alone. We've got some Jews, a few Gypsies, we had a homosexual here in the prison block until last week; there's a writer over there, and we even have one poor gullible soul who tried to resist being conscripted into the armed forces. We like to think of the brickyard men as the better class of prisoner. You're in good company." Heltriger chuckled and then started to cough.

"What did you do to be sent here?"

"Not much." He tried to suppress his cough. "I travelled to Den-

mark as part of my job. I sell, or used to sell, German medical equipment. While I was in Denmark, I attended an anti-Nazi rally in
Copenhagen. Just wanted to see what was going on, really. When I
came home to Munich, I was accused of conspiring against the Third
Reich. Someone had seen me, or someone was watching me. They
had a photograph of me in a crowd. I didn't try to hide it; I told them
I went just out of curiosity, but no luck. Things got worse after the
police went through my bookshelf at home and found some banned
titles. Now, here I am, a certified enemy of the state. And you?"

"Nothing." Saul stared forward at the edge of the bunk. "I asked
them to let my uncle go when the German Army arrested him—they
were stealing the contents of his diamond cutting business. Then, in
prison, I heckled an officer and demanded to be released."

"Whooh! Don't go getting uppity here, my Jewish friend. Keep
your head down and your mouth shut, or you'll get a bullet in the
back of the head. You got off lucky. Try that in the Neuengamme
brickyard and your prison mates will have extra soup and a blanket that night. The guards here shoot Jews and queers for sport. It
doesn't take much to provoke them, believe me."

"You seem like you're in goods spirits for living here."

"Don't believe it. You've got to put on an act. I tell myself this is
just temporary. You've got to treat this as normal. How else can you
survive? The day I start feeling sorry for myself, I'll be dead."

"Do you really think the Nazis will let any of us out of here?"

"What else can I believe? I've been here a year and I'm still alive. I
plan on walking out that gate some day a rehabilitated man. The only
way to do it is to keep your spirits up, every day, every hour, every
minute. The ones who start feeling weepy and depressed are dead in
a month. Believe me, I've seen it."

* * *

THE WOMAN WHO ANSWERED the doorbell at the boarding house had
her hair in a cloth cap. She was late middle-aged, stout, wore a green
apron, and came to the door with a broom in one hand and a dust

cloth in the other. Her eyes were red and it looked as if she had been crying. She stood in the doorway and stared at Rory suspiciously.

"A room? Do you have a room for a few days?" Rory's Dutch was near the point of exhaustion. He tried to smile. "I'm from France. Do you speak French?" He pointed to her window, which had a "Room to Let" sign in it. He smiled hopefully.

The woman nodded and motioned for him to come in. Rory picked up his suitcase and followed her inside. The house was large, larger than it looked from the street, with airy, high-ceilinged rooms. The walls had dark prints of flowers, and the tables and the backs of the chairs were carefully protected with thick lace doilies. Against the far wall there was an upright piano with a half-dozen family photographs on it, one of a smiling young man in a military uniform. Rory stepped into the parlour. The room gave the impression of being a formal sitting room. It had a high Victorian feel to it, the kind of place where three or four times a year upright Dutch families entertained unsmiling visitors with tea and biscuits. Rory guessed that the remainder of the time the room was probably kept in a state of sanitized readiness. It was a good thing he was travelling in a coat, tie, and hat, because as boarding houses went, this one was probably only interested in the most respectable lodgers.

The woman led Rory through the parlour and dining room and into the kitchen. There were five other people sitting at the kitchen table—three men and two young women. They all looked red-eyed and devastated, as if consoling one another over terrible news. Rory had a sinking feeling that he was intruding on something very private and tragic, and immediately wished he had found another house. The older woman spoke for several seconds in rapid Dutch and one of the men stood up and offered his hand. He spoke in fluent French. "My mother tells me you're looking for a room, is that correct?"

"Yes, perhaps for a few days, or a week, until I can find a small apartment of my own. I'm French, from Alsace, and I've been sent here to do some work by my company. If this is a bad time, I can come back."

"No, please follow me."

The man led him up four and a half flights of narrow stairs. Rory did his best not to bang his suitcase against the walls. At the top of the last landing the man opened a door and said, "This is the room we have available. It's twenty guilders a week, which includes breakfast and supper. Breakfast is at seven and supper is at six-thirty. Guests can only be entertained in the parlour between seven-thirty and nine in the evening on weekdays. Payment for the first week is in advance. There's a toilet and bathtub across the hall. Right now, you're the only guest up here so you don't have to share the bathroom with anybody." He stopped and looked uncomfortable for a few seconds. "I should tell you, so you know, my family is in mourning today. We just received word today that my youngest brother died."

"I'm very sorry to hear that. That's terrible."

"Yes, it was a great shock. He was serving in the army; he was listed as missing in action on the second day of the invasion. We thought he was all right and had been taken prisoner. But today we received word that this information was wrong; he had been severely wounded and the records were mixed up. Yesterday he died of his wounds. My mother was advised of this only two hours ago. It's a great shock for all of us. Please, come forward and look at the room."

Rory squeezed past the man. The room was a good size. It had a tiny clothes closet, a single bed, an empty bookshelf, a small dresser, a bedside table with a large wooden radio on it, and inside the alcove of a dormer on the sloping ceiling was a small writing desk. The dormer window provided a view of a small connecting canal and the tops of massive maple trees.

"This will be fine. Thank you. Can I ask you to please give your family my condolences?"

"Thank you. You'll understand if we don't have supper tonight."

"Perfectly. Again, I'm very sorry."

"Here is the room key; the front door key is on the dresser." The man nodded and closed the door quietly behind him.

Rory sat on the bed and took off his shoes. His feet ached. He thought of the shattered family downstairs sitting around the kitchen table. How often had they all sat around that table in happier times?

Sunday mornings, birthdays, Christmases, thousands of school days, tears and laughter, disappointments and triumphs. Now there was one who would forever be missing. He exhaled heavily. There would be more scenes like that before this war was over. Who knew how many more—hundreds of thousands, probably millions. It was hard to imagine. Then, for a second, he felt a pang of guilt for thinking that if his cover were blown, this family would be unlikely to turn him over to the Nazis.

Rory slept for two hours and awoke with sunlight streaming onto his face. He was hungry. He washed and shaved and stepped outside to find a place to eat. After eating, he wanted to conduct his initial survey of the city.

The sleep left Rory feeling invigorated, positive, and confident. It was one of those glorious early days of summer, with brilliant sunshine and towering fluffy clouds floating above the city. As he walked through Amsterdam's western, tree-lined neighbourhoods, he was forced to remind himself that this was a country at war, one that was just entering the earliest stages of what was almost certainly going to be a brutal and exploitive occupation. Despite this, in the middle of June 1940, Amsterdam was, on the surface at least, a charming place. It had picturesque canals and distinctively Dutch, human-sized architecture, with buildings that weren't designed to overwhelm you. Rory walked for several minutes through sun-dappled streets bordered by high, narrow houses, and then turned along a tranquil canal lined with boats. Many of the canal boats looked like they were homes, either of the many working barge families Rory could see along the canals or of the smattering of artistic-looking eccentrics who also populated the area.

Despite the circumstances, Rory felt an affinity for life in Amsterdam. Even with the city in the grip of a hostile foreign occupation, there was something relaxed and unhurried in the feel of its streets. There was a kind of reassurance in being in a place that valued different perspectives on life. Walking through the streets, he thought

that what really distinguished Amsterdam from so many other cities was not only its prosperity, but that it had escaped the industrial
character of so many other large commercial centres. It was a city
that was, superficially at least, still reflective of a more settled time
and a more deliberate pace of life. As a city, it somehow appeared to
retain the temperament and the rhythms of life before the introduction of the steam engine. That was quite a feat. But, he reminded
himself, appearances were deceiving. And whatever its appearances
at present, Amsterdam, Rory felt certain, was about to change. Given
what he knew of the Nazis, he was sure that they would soon jolt the
city into the most violent and anguished period of its history.

He emerged at a large square across from the main train station,
and as if to underscore his thoughts, Rory noticed two German army
motorcycle teams and a half-dozen Feldgendarmerie with rifles slung
over their shoulders, in front of the station's main doors. He wasn't
certain exactly where he was going. Today, apart from getting something to eat, he was just trying to familiarize himself with his new
surroundings. He wanted to understand how the city was laid out,
where the German patrols were, and get a feel for where he could
blend in and where he could not. He picked up his pace. He didn't
want to appear different from the Dutch pedestrians around him, all
of whom seemed to be, at least in the area of the train station, walking
with a greater sense of purpose in their step.

Looking at the faces that passed by, he noticed that nobody
smiled or looked in the least bit cheerful. They could be forgiven if
today they looked serious and distant. German vehicle patrols were
everywhere in the town centre, as were German officers. The officers strolled about the shopping areas in small clusters, hands behind
their backs, clutching leather gloves, dressed in their walking-out
uniforms with forage caps and highly polished jackboots. They acted
as if they were on holiday and looked as if they had just stepped off a
bus. Rory tried not to stare at them; but he couldn't help notice that
although they wandered through the shopping districts like tourists,
they all wore automatic pistols. None of them seemed entirely com-

fortable as they glanced with tentative curiosity at the Dutch civilians. These sightseeing and innocuous-looking officers contrasted with the mobile patrols. Out on the streets, every few minutes, lorry loads of heavily armed motorized infantry roared up and down at high speed, glaring distrustfully at the civilian pedestrians.

Rory felt detached from all this. He was walking amongst his enemies in a foreign country and didn't feel at risk or threatened. For a moment he allowed himself to believe the operation was going well. After all, this might turn out to be a fairly routine mission: a quick insertion, make his contacts, and then get out without anyone being the wiser. But something deep inside told him not to become smug, not to be mesmerized by appearances or lulled into a false sense of security. He knew the Germans. He was part German himself; he had spent summers in Germany when he was a child. He spoke their language and read their books. He'd fought them and lived amongst them and spied against them; and if they were anything, they were efficient. And the most dangerous mistake to make about the German Army was to underestimate it.

He walked on for a few minutes, stopping and looking in a shop window, pretending to be interested in a display of shoes. He bent down to tie his shoe lace and glanced behind him. As he stood up, he checked the other side of the street. Nothing was out of the ordinary. He walked on and decided to continue for another twenty minutes until he found a spot for his first meal, somewhere where the enemy wasn't quite so evident. He didn't want to find himself making polite conversation with a pair of German officers. He turned south, heading away from the main shopping area in search of a small café or restaurant.

After twenty minutes he found a likely looking place, the Brasserie Waarden. It was a nondescript little restaurant in a side street; and better still, it was empty, the kind of place where working men might take their lunch or stop for a quick drink on their way home. It certainly wasn't fashionable, and that was fine. The place didn't have much charm and it was unlikely a German soldier would ever want to stop here. When the waiter took his order, he didn't seem at all put out by Rory's French, but in the end they both wound up deciding what he would eat by pointing to items on the menu.

The meal, when it finally came, was a rubbery pork cutlet, boiled potatoes, and steamed vegetables, which made Rory wonder if the Brasserie Waarden ran a secondary business catering for a hospital. Not that it mattered: the food was nourishing, and more importantly, nobody seemed to take any notice of him. The waiter had no trouble understanding his request for coffee, bringing it smartly, and wiping his hands on his apron as if making a subconscious display of his desire for this lone customer to leave so he could close up shop.

Rory smiled at the waiter and sat back with his coffee. With his successful entry into Holland, a few hours sleep, and a meal, it was hard not to feel a certain sense of satisfaction. After so many months of waiting and hanging about, he was at last established in Holland. For now, he had a reasonably safe place to stay. Tomorrow he would do a quick reconnaissance of the neighbourhood of his contact, retired Lieutenant Colonel Pieter Van Meekeren. Then he was going to spend the day improving his alibi by checking out the agricultural exchange and Amsterdam's only seed company. This would be a reasonably safe means of getting some credible background detail to spin out to the Germans in the event of an interrogation that was more comprehensive than a simple examination of papers at a checkpoint.

Rory steepled his hands in front of his face and stared out the window into the darkening street. In the next phase, things would become considerably more hazardous. This would be the first time he had to reveal his true identity and he wasn't prepared to take Geoffrey Harris's word for it that the Germans hadn't penetrated his new organization. Harris was probably a good man, but he was being a touch naïve or insincere if he expected him to believe that only a half-dozen trusted people knew about the insertion of an agent into Holland. A special aircraft had been used; ground crew involved; flight plans filed. The new Polish radio had been issued, and large sums of Dutch currency. The Prime Minister's Office had sanctioned the operation. The very fact that the British had already lost their complete intelligence network in Holland would have alerted the Germans to the likelihood of an early attempt to rebuild it. And once this new organization started deploying agents, if only to prevent future fiascos, there would have to be some kind of coordination with the established intelligence agencies. For all he knew, Van Meekeren himself might have been alerted. If you plotted out all the possible individuals who had knowledge about this mission and could leak key information, they almost certainly ran in the dozens. Now was not the time to rush things.

Rory sipped his coffee. There was no point in making his plans too complicated. It would be like trying to work out all the moves in a chess game in advance. For now, he needed to think out the details of the next few steps as well as mull over the broad options for the remainder of the mission.

Clearly the next steps were to develop his cover story, reconnoitre Lieutenant Colonel Van Meekeren, and then make contact. When he was satisfied that he could safely establish contact, he'd probably have to convince Van Meekeren of his authenticity; and that by itself might be a problem. He'd then have to come to a decision on the man. He might or might not be someone who could be trusted; but for now, it looked as if he didn't have much choice.

After meeting Van Meekeren, he would still have several sticky issues to resolve. He had to retrieve his wireless telegraph and make contact with his control station, and then he had to get himself back to England. Rory signalled the waiter for the bill. It was certainly much too early to become self-satisfied with his success to date. The potential for disaster was still huge.

17

DIETER SCHMIDT WAS WAITING outside the police headquarters beside the car. For the third time in as many minutes he smoothed imaginary wrinkles in his uniform and straightened his wedge cap. The Opel was running; last night he had fuelled it at the police petrol pumps. The Oberstleutnant's Gestapo pennant was flying from the front bumper and the car had been washed and polished just yesterday afternoon. He was certain Ackerman wouldn't be able to find fault this time.

When Oberstleutnant Neumann and Hauptmann Ackerman came down the steps, Schmidt forced a broad smile and crashed to attention giving a crisp salute. "Good morning, gentlemen. I trust that you slept well last night. Where would you like me to take you this morning?"

Neumann returned the salute uninterestedly. "We're going to the army's field security headquarters at Aalsmer. Are you sure you know the route?"

Schmidt nodded cheerfully. "But of course, sir," and with a flourish opened the rear door for Neumann. "I double-checked the directions and I have a map."

"Good, we can't be late. You'll make us look like fools if we are." Neumann climbed inside, motioning Ackerman to go round the car.

"Now, Ackerman, today it's my intention to show the army that the SS and particularly we in the Gestapo have things under control here at Amsterdam headquarters. It's important for two reasons: one, we don't want the army nosing around in SS police business; and two, we have to stake out our territory. There's a lot riding on this for the future of how things will operate in the Reich."

"What sort of things are you referring to, Herr Oberstleutnant?"

"To start with, I've heard from phone calls to Berlin that the army is already claiming the right to administer all conquered territories. Their thinking is that the territories are under martial law so they are responsible."

"And how do we in Amsterdam fit into this, sir?"

"A good question, Ackerman. Today we'll assume that SS administration of the territories is a foregone conclusion. We'll be helpful, but we will operate in purely an advisory and liaison role. In territorial administration, the army is there to support us. All command decisions regarding territorial administration are an SS responsibility. If you have to answer any questions at the conference, I want you to frame all your responses in such a manner so that we are perceived as wishing to be helpful, while stressing that our hands are tied and we must coordinate all policy decisions with our own chain of command."

Neumann rifled through his briefcase. "Now, just to confirm, I'll run over with you the topics for our presentation on police administration." He flipped through a series of manila files. "Right, here it is. First off, our three most important initial activities and actions we have already undertaken. One: Sealing and monitoring of all internal borders. We want to be able to have a good long look at anyone trying to escape Holland. These people will be of interest to us. As of today, surveillance at all border crossings and transport nodes will be complete. Two: Creation of the Amsterdam subdivision of the Gestapo identification bureau. Everyone in the country is to be given an identity card. Amsterdam is going to be the first major occupied city to implement this policy. Planning is complete for that and I expect the setup and organization of that activity to begin today. The entire task should be completed within a month. And the third point: Handling of dissidents and saboteurs. This is important. The army will help us, but we direct operations in the occupied areas. We need army manpower and resources for this last one."

Neumann pulled a red file from his briefcase. "In Amsterdam, we have already captured several key dissidents. As a result, we have had no incidents of sabotage or resistance. We intend to round up a second and much larger group of dissidents later this week. We'll need at least one motorized infantry battalion to continue to support us in this role for another two weeks. I'll need them for cordons and snap roadblocks as well. I'll also need a Feldgendarmerie platoon for prisoner handling and control. The important thing to note here, Ackerman, is that population control is our responsibility." Neumann paused and smiled as if he was letting his subordinate in on a secret. "Now, for that, when we get to additional army resources, I'll need to have an army wireless direction-finding platoon permanently attached to us, as well as a signals telephone line platoon for establishing control of internal communications in the Amsterdam area. I want radio and telephone surveillance up and working in Amsterdam within the week."

"Do you think that the army will just give us these resources, Herr Oberstleutnant? They'll kick and scream."

"Let them. I've already got the request cleared through SS headquarters in Berlin. So if they refuse, be reasonable with them, act calmly, and we'll quietly advise them that we think orders will be coming down shortly to attach these troops to us. Oh, that reminds me—make a note—you have to find living quarters and cooks for the signals troops when we get back. If the army asks, tell them that it's in hand."

Neumann looked up from his papers. "Rottenführer Schmidt, is that a picture of your wife and children you have pinned on the sun visor?"

"Yes, sir." Schmidt looked up at the rear-view mirror and beamed at Neumann. "This picture was taken at my mother's house two weeks before I left Austria. It was on the day of my oldest daughter's first communion."

"Schmidt, it doesn't belong in an SS vehicle any more than it does pinned on your uniform. Get rid of it."

Neumann returned to his briefcase. "Now, Ackerman, with regard to dissidents, I want you to ensure we start the second round of arrests within the next three days. We should have our infantry battalion attached to us by then. We'll probably only keep them for a week at most. The army will claim they'll be needed in France. The signals troops we'll be keeping for quite a bit longer."

Neumann looked out the window. "Oh, speaking of France, did you hear the news this morning? France is probably going to sue for an armistice with us today. I read it in the morning bulletins. The Führer is going to Paris tomorrow."

Neumann chuckled at this and Ackerman gave a thin smile.

"Regarding the next wave of arrests, Herr Obersteutnant," Ackerman said, "I've already taken the liberty of preparing a list for you of the names of those I think we should pick up in that activity. I've had talks with our Dutch National Socialist friends. They've been very helpful. With their help, I've drafted up a more comprehensive breakdown of dissidents, and we'll also bring in any potentially dangerous family members and key co-workers from our first priority list. I assume for the wider list you will want us to do the same thing again: screen them all, hold the low-value ones for forty-eight hours, and ship the higher-value arrests to labour camps."

"What are you trying to do, Ackerman? Are you angling for my job? Every day, you second-guess me."

The Hauptmann pulled back.

"I'm joking, Ackerman. Don't look upset. I'm just joking."

* * *

By the morning of the third day at Neuengamme, Saul was beginning to doubt whether or not he had the constitution to survive life in the camp. The food was sickening and every time he moved he had sharp pains in his stomach and abdomen. He lay in his bunk and looked at the bedraggled lineup for the morning's ration of bread and soup. They were all as wretched as he was. Every man had some kind of rasping cough as well as a fungal skin infection that left large, round, itchy splotches on the prisoners' legs. This morning, Saul had discovered that he hadn't escaped that either. He would have loved a shower. It was one of the things that would make his life immeasurably better. He closed his eyes; a nice hot shower would wash away his problems.

"Saul, get up." It was Derek Heltriger speaking. He was bent over and leaning across the wooden slats of the bunk. "You can't miss breakfast. Not once. Now get up."

Saul stared at him and rubbed his eyes. "I suppose you're right."

"Of course I'm right. The food's terrible but it's the only nourishment you're going to get, so you get up and you eat every day, twice a day. You eat to survive. There's no point lying there feeling sorry for yourself."

Saul sat up stiffly and dragged himself into line. He scratched at his forearms and grimaced. Heltriger was right: ignore the aches and pains; ignore the anger and frustration; focus on staying alive and getting out of here. He looked at the other prisoners. They all looked the same now. Two days ago they had taken away his clothes and issued him red-striped prisoners' clothing. The only difference with Saul's prison uniform was that he was forced to wear a yellow Star of David pinned on his left breast. He was as unshaven and as grubby as the others.

One of the prisoners standing behind a large metal tub shoved a tin bowl of thin vegetable soup at him and pointed at a bucket of sliced bread crusts. Wendell Bloch stood beside the man dishing out the cold soup. Bloch was there at every meal so he could monitor the distribution of breakfast. "We only get three pieces each this morning. I'm afraid that's all."

Saul looked up in dismay. They were usually given four or five slices of bread at each meal. This was a new low. He shrugged and didn't say anything. He trusted Wendell.

Later that morning, in the brick depot, Saul struggled with a small, flat wheelbarrow loaded with bricks. It was heavy and swerved erratically on its single metal wheel. In the last three hours he had made endless trips from the cooling area near the kilns over to the loading docks. It seemed that each day had become more difficult as some additional hardship made life more painful. Now his hands had raw blisters and he found himself trying to control the wheelbarrow with his unblistered fingers. He was trying not to think of the pain as he rounded the corner to the connecting hallway when across the room he saw a prisoner rolling back and forth on the floorboards clutching his foot in silent agony. It was his bunkmate Heltriger. He made a hissing sound with his breath through clenched teeth.

"What's the matter?" asked Saul. "You can't let the guards see you down on the floor here."

"I tripped on this load. I don't know what happened. I slipped on something." Heltriger grimaced. "The bricks tipped off and I've smashed my foot. It hurts like hell."

Saul grabbed him by the arm. "Get up, for God's sakes, get up. The guards are coming. I'll help you." The two men struggled to their feet and Saul bent over, hastily stacking bricks onto Heltriger's wheelbarrow.

Seconds later, one of the guards ambled by with his thumbs stuck in his belt. The two prisoners breathed a sigh of relief. This guard was the most reasonable of the bunch. Not that he actually ever said or did anything that was reasonable, it was just that his face was always blank and he rarely shouted. The prisoners had nicknamed him "Poker Face." Poker Face was unusual in that Saul had never seen him snarl or strike out at anyone. Despite this, he looked disturbingly content in his work.

"What's going on here? Why are these bricks on the floor?"

Saul answered. "There must have been a rock or something on the floor, sir. The wheelbarrow's tipped over. We'll get it cleaned up and things will be fine."

"Do it quickly. If you don't make your quota this morning, I'll cut the rations for your whole hut tonight. Come on, come on, we haven't got all day." Poker Face tapped the truncheon on his belt. "I don't want to have to use this, you know. I will if I need to, but if you want to stay alive, you have to meet your quota." He took a few steps and turned around. "It's up to you; if you haven't met your quota by noon, there'll be short rations for everybody tonight."

Saul loaded some of the bricks onto Heltriger's wheelbarrow and piled his own precariously high with the remainder. "How many bricks were you trying to take? This is crazy! No wonder you had an accident."

"It's my fault," Heltriger gasped. "We didn't make our count last night. That's why we had short rations this morning. We've been falling behind. Some of the others aren't keeping up. They're tired." Heltriger was limping painfully but he managed to push his wheelbarrow forward.

Saul looked exasperated. "We'll never make it this way. The only way to get our quota is to have more deliveries, not more bricks per delivery. That's the only way."

Heltriger gasped with the pain of every step. "I think I might have broken one of the bones in my foot."

The two men finished the delivery to the brick stacks. At the loading dock Saul said, "I'm going on ahead. I'll tell the others about your accident. We'll speed up the deliveries for the next hour or so. We can make it. Just hold on, just a few more hours. The swelling will go down. Just keep going, but slowly. We'll get it done."

Saul pushed his cart away, and to every prisoner he met, he said, "Heltriger's hurt. We have to catch up for his loads by noon or they'll cut the rations again. Just two hours—we've got to step it up."

Miraculously, by noon the loading dock was filled to capacity. The men from Saul's hut stood in a dejected group around the bricks stacked neatly in several dozen piles a metre and a half deep and a metre high. Their faces were grimy and sweaty.

Poker Face shook his head in admiration. "Very good. I didn't think you'd make it. You see what you can accomplish when you put your minds to it. Now we have both met our quotas. Now you'll get a little wait as the train won't be here for another hour." It was the first time Saul had seen the man smile, but there was no joy in his expression.

The men at the loading dock sat down where they were. They sprawled out on the floor using as little energy as possible. Saul walked over to where Heltriger nursed his foot. His face was grey and drawn.

"You made it through the morning. Keep going a few more hours. The swelling will go down tonight. We can cover for you. It'll start to get better. Just hold on for a few more hours. You've done brilliantly."

Heltriger nodded. He looked ashamed of himself. "Thanks. I'll try. I'm sorry."

Saul clapped him on the arm. "You made sure I ate this morning. We look after one another."

The men on the loading crew had rested for just under an hour when the morning's train announced its arrival with bursts of steam and a shunting and crashing of cars.

They needed no instructions. When the freight car was pushed to the loading deck, the doors were shoved open and a narrow wooden ramp was laid between the freight car and the loading dock. The men formed a chain and began passing bricks across the gap, loading the car in smaller but equally neat stacks a metre high and a metre square.

By five o'clock the work was complete. Poker Face seemed to appear as if on cue, strolling along with his thumbs in his belt. He looked down the rows of loaded rail cars. "You're done. You go back to full rations tonight. That wasn't so hard now, was it?" He looked at Bloch. "Take them back to your hut. You're done for the day. You're lucky. There are no more bricks at the kilns. But there will be lots tomorrow," he said with a grin.

As the men turned and walked to go back to the hut, Saul put his arm around Heltriger's shoulder to give him support. "Here. Lean on me. Take the weight off your foot."

"What are you two doing?" Poker Face bellowed. "We don't allow men to hug one another here."

Saul turned. "This man's hurt his foot. I'm helping him, that's all."

Poker Face's cheeks went red. "You filthy little piece of shit. Don't talk back to me! We don't keep queers here and we certainly don't keep Jewish queers. You keep your hands to yourself."

"Sir, I wasn't doing anything wrong." Saul spoke slowly doing his utmost to keep the anger out of his voice. He could feel his ears burn.

"I said don't talk back to me. Especially you. You never talk back to me." Poker Face walked forward and jabbed hard at the yellow Star of David on Saul's chest. "You never talk back to me or any other guard!"

The other men all began to step backwards. Saul's face went crimson. "No, sir. I was only helping this man. He was injured."

Poker Face kicked Saul in the leg and reached for his truncheon. "You never talk back." He screamed and took a breath as if trying to control himself. His hand moved away from his truncheon. "Stand up, stand up." He flipped the top off his holster and pulled out his pistol. "Do your friends want to see what happens when a prisoner disobeys orders and talks back?"

Saul raised his hands. "Sir, believe me, I never meant anything …"

"Shut up!" Poker Face flourished his pistol and fired once.

Saul collapsed, a large crimson stain spreading where his head hit the floorboards.

* * *

GOING BACK TO HER APARTMENT was an odd sensation for Annika. She approached the old building with a degree of apprehension. What had once been a place of welcoming sanctuary now seemed remote and cold. Today she felt detached from the place, as if this had been a house she had lived in years before and whose memories had now become hazy and tenuous. She stood momentarily on the street and looked up at their windows.

The apartment that she and Saul had shared occupied half the space of a complete floor in a merchant warehouse. The building's huge windows had been the openings from which sacks of grain and bulky merchandise could be hoisted up. For two hundred years, the old warehouse had been used to store wares transported from Holland's colonies. Sixty years ago, the building had been converted to apartments. That was a time when the streets were filled with horses, and when it was apparent that Amsterdam was never again going to be one of the world's most important ports. The building had been witness to more than a few changes since then. And now, Annika thought dejectedly, it was changing again. The apartment in the old building was no longer the safe haven she had once enjoyed with Saul.

Now she felt like an animal sniffing around poisoned bait planted outside its lair. But this was ridiculous. This was her place. She had every right to be here. She tucked her handbag under arm and strode up the stairs. As she opened the building's front door, she thought she heard a window above her close.

On the second floor, Annika again felt a chill of unease sweep over her. It had to be her nerves. She went inside and quickly pushed the door closed behind her. Everything looked normal. The plants needed watering and the rooms had that close, locked up air; other than that, things were fine. She opened the hall cupboard and took out a suitcase and hurried into the bedroom. She began quickly packing her things when for no apparent reason she stopped and turned about. Behind her, standing in the bedroom doorway, was Mrs. Britt Roeme, the old widow from across the hall.

Annika gasped. "Britt, you startled me. How did you get in?"

"The door was unlocked. You left it slightly ajar when you came back. I just wanted to check that everything was all right," Mrs. Roeme said. She stared at Annika as if waiting some sort of response.

"Yes, well, you certainly scared me."

Mrs. Roeme was a lonely soul. It was difficult making conversation with her. Annika often wondered if she'd had some kind of a stroke. She always looked slightly deranged. Her hair hung to the side in long wisps and she spoke as if she were having difficulty framing her sentences. She rarely seemed interested in making conversation.

"I heard that Saul has been arrested by the Germans. Is this true?"

"Yes. Yes, they took him away some time ago. I've been staying with some friends."

"You know the German police were around here again this morning asking about you. They told me I had to tell them the next time I saw you."

Annika began to feel weak at the knees. "Britt, neither Saul nor I have done anything wrong. You have to believe that."

"Why did they take him away? Why do they want you? They told me I have to tell them when you come back."

Annika smiled at her. "Of course, you can call them tomorrow morning. I'll be back then and we can both talk to the police. Would you like that? But in the meantime why don't you join me for a nice cup of tea and you can tell me what the police wanted to know."

Mrs. Roeme didn't respond to this offer. Annika led her by the hand to the kitchen and sat her down at the small table in the corner. She put the kettle on the gas stove and got down a plate of sugar biscuits. "Now, while that's boiling, you tell me everything the police said to you. I need you to help me get Saul out of jail. He hasn't done anything wrong."

Mrs. Roeme looked disdainfully at the plate of sugar cookies and began to tug at her hair. After a few moments she said, "They didn't say much. They weren't very nice. They said I would be in a lot of trouble if I didn't report to them when you got back. Then they went and knocked on some other doors and said the same thing to the other people."

"Well, you've done the right thing, Britt. We can tell the police about this tomorrow and we'll both be here to meet them then."

Mrs. Roeme tilted her head to one side and picked up a cookie. "Okay," she said, and her voice had a far away quality to it. She hung her head to one side and when Annika turned around to get sugar from the pantry she whispered inaudibly, "But when you were coming up the stairs, I phoned the number they gave me and told them you were here."

Annika turned about and said with a flourish, "There now, I do have some sugar here after all. I know you like your tea sweet, don't you, Mrs. Roeme?"

* * *

"HELLO, MADAM, I'm looking for Lieutenant Colonel Van Meekeren. Is he in?" Rory Ferrall asked in French.

The woman at the doorway of the Amsterdam townhouse was in her late fifties, tall, blonde, and dressed in a two-piece wool suit. She wore pearls and spoke with authority in flawless but deliberate French. "You're not German?"

"No, ma'am."

She stared at him for a moment and then said, "Several weeks ago my husband was arrested by the Germans. I haven't heard anything from him or about him since. Why do you want him?"

"I'm from Alsace. I'm here on business and a friend of mine told me that your husband would be able to supply me with some information."

She looked him up and down and bit her lower lip. She took a deep breath, was about to speak, stopped herself, and then said, "Come in."

Rory took off his hat and stepped inside. The vestibule smelled of furniture polish. There were original oil landscape paintings on the wall, and in the living room he could see dark furniture and thick Persian carpets. The rooms could have graced the pages of a designer's catalogue.

Mrs. Van Meekeren looked tired. She took a deep breath and studied Rory for a moment. She looked him in the eye and spoke with defiance and authority. "You realize that my husband is a vocal critic of these Nazi invaders. Do you still want to speak with him?"

Rory looked impassive. "Yes, madam, that's correct."

"What kind of business are you in?"

"I'm in the seed and grain sales business, madam." He looked about him, listening and searching for signs of anyone else in the house. "I've been working here since the war broke out, and before that—" He looked about with an exaggerated sense of caution. "Before that, I was in London." He stopped and stared directly into her eyes, searching for any rapid shift in her vision or signs of agitation.

"London? I think you should come in and take a seat in the living room. We should talk."

Rory followed her into the living room and sat in a large comfortable armchair opposite her.

"How do you know that I'm Pieter's wife?"

"I don't, but you match the description given to me by Pieter's brother, and you're here in his house."

"You know Pieter's brother?"

"We've met, briefly. I'm sorry to hear about your husband. I didn't know he had been arrested."

"Yes, it was a shock to both of us. They came early one morning. I haven't heard anything of him since. Some of the others who were arrested in those first days have been released, but not my husband. I have no idea where he is." She looked away as if she had suddenly chosen to study the painting on the wall beside her. She seemed to be losing her confidence.

"There's not much I can say to be of comfort to you at a time like this, madam. I only hope he comes back to you safely and soon."

Mrs. Van Meekeren looked back at Rory. "Thank you. Somehow I get the feeling you are being polite. Do you know much about these people? The Nazis?"

"Yes. I can't say much, but I've made it my business to know them these last few years. But you shouldn't stay here. If they've arrested your husband, they may well come back for you later. That's generally how they operate. They usually go after families, to make an example of them. It's unfortunately a very effective way of imposing control on the rest of the population."

Mrs. Van Meekeren bit her lip. "This is all so unbelievable."

Rory fiddled with his hat and stood up. "I'm sorry to intrude, ma'am." He looked down at his shoes and spoke quietly. "Do you know anyone else who shared your husband's opinions of the Nazis that I might be able to talk to?"

"My husband was not very popular for a while. He spoke too openly about the Nazis. Even some of his friends said he was far too harsh, that it wasn't wise to stir them up by berating them. Well, look what it got him. My husband was unfortunately a bit of a loner; so no, I don't personally know any of those who shared his hatred of the Nazis. But if I were you, I would go searching among the relatives of those who were arrested along with him."

Rory perked up at this suggestion. His face showed the sense of welcome discovery on hearing an unexpected and useful new idea. "Anyone in particular that you would suggest? I don't know many people here in Amsterdam."

"The only name I recognized when the list of those arrested was printed in the paper the other day was Saul Hammerstein. He used to play chess with my husband. I have met him only briefly, once or twice over the years. They were in a club. I don't know if he was released or not."

Rory pulled out a small pad and a pen and scribbled down the name.

Mrs. Van Meekeren smiled and stood to see him to the door. "For a seed salesman, you seem a lot like a policeman to me, Mr. ...?"

"You are very observant and you've been very helpful, Mrs. Van Meekeren. I hope you get your husband back soon. I should go now. Thank you." Rory forced a smile, shook her hand, and turned for the door.

As Rory stepped onto the cobblestoned sidewalk from the front steps, Mrs. Van Meekeren spoke from the doorway. "I might take your advice. I have a brother-in-law living in town. I might go and stay with his family for a few weeks or so. If you need any further help from me and I'm not here, contact him."

Rory smiled and tugged at the brim of his hat. "Thank you, Mrs. Van Meekeren, I may just do that." He took a step down the street and turned about. "Madam, I can't emphasize it enough. If your husband was one of the first ones arrested, I think you really should get away from here for a few weeks." He locked eyes with her for a moment and Mrs. Van Meekeren gave a noncommittal nod.

Three blocks away, at the Prinsengracht Canal, Rory stopped walking and leaned against the black steel railing. Mrs. Van Meekeren was certainly an impressive woman. She was probably quite intelligent; she was undoubtedly loyal; she made decisions quickly; and she had the courage to take a risk. Beyond all that, she seemed like a genuinely nice person. Rory clasped his hands on the canal railing and fastened his gaze on a leaf floating in the black water. Despite all her qualities, she was an unlikely candidate for his network. Her husband had been arrested, and if the Gestapo did come after her, as was quite probable, it would only take them a matter of hours to extract whatever useful information she possessed.

The thought of Mrs. Van Meekeren being tortured by Gestapo thugs was sickening. He pushed his hat back on his head and shifted his gaze to the houseboats moored against the canal's far bank. She was almost certainly on the Gestapo's wanted list. It would probably only be a matter of time until they got around to picking her up and that would be a terrible end to a gracious lady. He hoped that she chose to follow his advice.

Rory felt a twinge of guilt. Maybe there was something more he could have done to alert her to the danger she was in. Mrs. Van Meekeren had been helpful; she'd provided him a name for another possible contact. But strangely, it felt like he was using her. He'd had no idea that her husband had been arrested. How could he have known? Mrs. Van Meekeren had provided him valuable information, and now, he had to forget about her. If there was any kind of justice, the Gestapo might just choose to leave her alone.

There was a telephone book at the rooming house. Rory remembered seeing it perched on the shelf at the bottom of the hallway telephone stand. He doubted that there would be many listings under Saul Hammerstein. He pulled his hat down on his forehead and silently reprimanded himself. Dutchmen never wore their hats pushed back off their foreheads. Nobody in Europe did; it was much too casual a gesture for a man on the street here in the Old World. It was the kind of inconsequential thing some Europeans scoffed at Americans for—like putting your hands in your pockets, or chewing gum—and when you told them you were Canadian, they shrugged cheerily as if to say, "Oh well, that's all right then." It was still the kind of involuntary habit that could get you killed.

The rooming house was quiet when Rory returned. The telephone book was tattered and frayed but concealed in an efficient-looking leather cover. It was dated 1936 and listed three Hammersteins. There was only one S Hammerstein. Rory consulted his map. The address was just over a mile away. He slipped out the front door. The boarding house was quiet and nobody seemed to be home. He wondered if today was the young soldier's funeral. He hadn't really talked with anyone since he had arrived.

18

RORY WALKED BRISKLY past the Hammersteins' address. They lived in a beautiful old building. Whoever Mr. Saul Hammerstein was, he and his wife had probably enjoyed a wonderful life together. The war had changed all that. Now, in all likelihood—if he was still alive—he was being worked to death in some nightmarish camp, clinging to whatever shreds of dignity he could find.

There was nothing unusual about the apartment building and it didn't appear that anyone was watching the place; at least from the street, there was nobody in evidence. A hundred yards down the road, Rory made a show of pulling a paper from his coat and checking the street number. He turned and went back to the Hammersteins' building.

He climbed the stairs and on the third floor knocked firmly on Annika's door. His heart was racing and he forced himself to breathe slowly, to keep his wits about him, to remain calm.

Feet shuffled around inside and seconds later a stout woman with bad skin, in her late sixties, peeped out at him from behind a half-closed door. She was smiling and there was something child-like about her. She said something incomprehensible in Dutch. Rory forced a smile and answered in French. "Is Mrs. Hammerstein at home, please?"

The older woman smiled and opened the door. Rory couldn't

understand a word she was saying. She made a sweeping gesture for him to come in.

Rory stepped inside and removed his hat. "Madam Hammerstein?"

A younger woman's voice called out something in Dutch from a room down the hall and the older woman began nervously twisting her hair. Again she muttered something unintelligible. She looked as if she were trying to ingratiate herself with him. She smiled.

Rory raised his voice. "I'm looking for a Mrs. Hammerstein."

A younger woman entered the room. She was a petite blonde, well dressed, but with dark rings beneath intelligent blue eyes. She spoke quietly in clear French but with obvious reserve. "My neighbour, Mrs. Roeme, wants to know if you are from the police. I'm sorry, she only speaks Dutch."

"No, madam, I'm not from the police. I was hoping you could help me. I believe we have some things we should talk about."

The older woman was furiously plaiting her hair. She spoke again, looking at Annika. Annika looked startled. Her face went white.

"Mrs. Roeme thinks you are from the police. She says she called you and that you were on your way."

Rory looked back and forth between Mrs. Roeme and Annika. He didn't understand what was going on, but there was obviously something very wrong with this conversation.

"Mrs. Roeme lives across the hall," Annika said.

"Madam, I'm not from the police, please believe me, but could we please go for a walk? I have to speak to you in private."

Both Rory and Annika looked at Mrs. Roeme, who shrugged her shoulders and made a sheepish face. She muttered something incoherent in Dutch.

"Tell her we're going out for an hour; if the police come, we will be here at four and we'll be happy to meet with them then."

Annika looked hesitant and was about to speak.

"Mrs. Hammerstein, the Germans may already be on their way, in which case you will be thrown into one of their concentration camps and never heard from again. This is your last chance."

Annika's expression changed from someone torn by indecision and worry into that of a woman determined to survive. She scooped up her coat and took a felt hat from the hall cupboard. She spoke quietly in rapid Dutch to Mrs. Roeme, who went tamely into the kitchen and sat down on one of the chairs.

Out on the street, Rory took Annika by the arm and hurried her along. A block away she stopped and said, "You just can't push me along like this. Who are you? Why did you come to my apartment? I just can't run off like this. It's crazy."

"I'll tell you everything when we're a long way from here. Don't stop now. If the Germans realize that we left a few moments ago, they'll send out vehicle patrols and arrest every couple they come across within a mile of here, so please, keep walking."

A few moments later, as they turned the corner onto Damsestraat, they could hear behind them the twin alternating tones of a police siren. The siren grew in intensity and stopped.

"They're probably at your apartment building now."

They clattered on down the cobblestoned sidewalk. Two minutes later a bus approached on the opposite side of the street.

"We're getting on that bus. It doesn't matter where it's going." Rory stepped out into the middle of the street holding Annika by the arm. He stopped in the path of the oncoming traffic and waved, forcing the bus to halt. The driver muttered angrily, making a frustrated open-handed gesture as he opened the front door. Rory couldn't understand what he was saying, but it was obvious the bus stop was nowhere near here. He gave a conciliatory wave and forced a smile, stepping back to let Annika on. Annika said something in a sweet voice; the driver smiled with sympathetic understanding and sat back in his seat. Annika fished in her purse and gave the driver several coins. She tilted her head, directing Rory to move back. Rory nodded appreciatively to the driver, who made a disdainful face as he passed.

When they were seated, Rory whispered, "What did you tell him?"

"I said my mother was very sick and we had to get home in time to see her before she died."

"Fair enough," Rory said. "That would explain me smiling stupidly at him."

Annika gave a thin smile. "Who are you? What's going on here?"

Rory spoke quietly. "Let's talk when we get off the bus." He pointed out the window as a pair of German army motorcycles with sidecars sped past, heading in the direction they had come from. Annika turned away as if she was bored by the sight of them. The bus moved forward and accelerated.

There were few people on the bus and no one seemed particularly interested in them. Annika looked out the window as if this was just another monotonous day, as if the two of them had done this trip a thousand times. Rory was impressed with her poise and self-confidence. It was all he could do to keep from staring at her. She was obviously tired and under a great strain, but he found her almost irresistibly attractive. "I hope this bus takes us somewhere busy. We can talk then, preferably at an outdoor café or in a crowded street."

"We're headed downtown. I'll tell you when we should get off." They passed the rest of the trip in silence.

As the bus approached the Stadhouderskade shopping district, Annika nudged Rory. He stood up and leaned over her to pull the stop cord and in doing so caught the faintest whiff of her perfume. She was, without a doubt, an incredibly desirable woman.

They left the bus by the back door and hurried quickly along the busy sidewalks. "Where can we go away from the bus stop, some place where we would be a part of the scenery?" Rory asked. "The Germans may have radio-controlled cars and they've probably already figured out that we're no longer in their vicinity."

Annika nodded. "We'll go through the Nieuwenfaal department store. There's a door on the main street and a small café and bar overlooking the Amstel River Canal. Follow me."

Seated at a small table in the shade of a linden tree at the back of the patio, Rory and Annika watched a small barge loaded with wooden barrels motor down the canal as the waiter brought two small beers.

Annika thanked him. When he was gone, Rory leaned forward, toying with the ashtray, and said, "I'm here in Holland on a special kind of trip." He paused, as much for dramatic effect as it was to organize his thoughts. "I went to a Pieter Van Meekeren's house this morning. Unfortunately, he's been arrested and no one has heard anything of him. I spoke to his wife. I asked her if she could recommend to me anyone who shared Mr. Van Meekeren's views of the Nazis." Rory looked up at Annika. Her face was stern but her eyes were intently focused on him. "I'm sorry, did you know Pieter Van Meekeren?"

"Not well." Her voice was as crisp as cut glass. "He played chess with Saul, my husband. His wife told you to come and see me?"

"No, she suggested that if I was looking to make contacts with similarly minded people as Pieter Van Meekeren, I should talk to members of the families who have had someone arrested. She gave me a newspaper with the names and I looked Saul Hammerstein up in the phone book. That's how I ended up at your door."

Annika stared at Rory for a long time. The silence was uncomfortable. "I think I know some things about you already. My guess is that you're probably a Canadian working for the British and you expect me to help you. Is that right?"

Rory sat back and inhaled sharply. He collected himself and then leaned forward, and then he said in a slow and deliberate voice, "What would make you think that?"

Annika looked frosty. "I put two and two together, Mr. Martin Becker, if that's your real name, which I doubt. For one thing, your accent isn't at all like anything I've ever heard before in Europe, and when we left my apartment you spoke of the Germans arresting every couple within a mile. Only the English-speaking countries still talk in terms of miles, Mr. Becker. Those of us in Europe measure distance in kilometres. Your French is good, and I hope you take no offence, but some of the words you use have an unusual pronunciation. It's certainly not European French. I was just guessing as to whether or not you're Canadian, because frankly, I'm not familiar with Canadian French. But I think your expression proved me right. I'd also guess that French isn't your mother tongue."

Rory took a long sip of his beer and put his glass down carefully. He decided not to make the obvious and fatuous remark that she was a regular Sherlock Holmes.

Annika continued. "I know what you're thinking, Mr. Becker." She didn't make eye contact with him. "I'm a musician who has studied modern languages. I'm not clairvoyant. I have a well-trained ear. The rest was straightforward."

"Mrs. Hammerstein, please, let's discuss your situation. If we agree that we have a common position from which to go forward, then we'll both put our cards on the table. Is that fair?"

"It seems I don't have any cards left to put on the table, Mr. Becker. The Germans are looking for me now. They're not looking for you."

"Perhaps not now, but Mrs. Roeme will have told them that a Frenchman left with you. They have my description. We won't be on their most wanted list, but they'll be keeping an eye out for both of us. As you're finding out, they're thorough and efficient."

Annika swirled the beer in her glass. "Things don't look very promising. My husband's in a prison camp. The police are looking for me and it won't be long before they catch up with me. A single woman in Amsterdam, I don't have any money; I don't even have my clothes." Annika looked despondent.

"I think we can help each other then. You need cover and shelter and a means of escaping, and I need contacts. I can probably help you, and you can certainly help me." Rory folded his hands on the table, doing his best to look trustworthy and non-threatening.

"This is so unreal. It's as if I'm living in a bad dream." Annika looked out over the canal. In the late afternoon sunshine, two little girls in pigtails and summer frocks skipped along the canal's cobblestoned sidewalk. Across the canal, a strongly built barge woman was hanging out her laundry along the railings surrounding the stern of her houseboat. "It looks so normal, but this is really a terrible time to be alive." Annika's eyes were moist and she turned away from Rory.

Rory didn't speak for a few moments, and then said, "It's going to get a lot worse, I'm afraid. Much worse. The Nazis have been allowed to become so strong that it will take an unprecedented effort to destroy them. We intend to destroy the Nazis, Mrs. Hammerstein. We need people to help us, and I'll need someone who knows the Dutch people and the city of Amsterdam in particular to help me. I can't make any guarantees just now, but will you work with me?"

* * *

"THIS IS A VERY PROMISING start that you've made, Chief Superintendent. I'm impressed, because I'm sure that these are difficult times for you; but you know, you've made a wise decision." Reinhold Neumann stood up from his desk and clasped his hands behind his back. It was a posture he had seen army officers adopt and he thought it gave one a sense of dignity and authority. "I know that there has been some foolish talk about starting a resistance to the German presence in Holland, but believe me, it would only hurt your country."

Chief Superintendent Van Noorden sat stiffly in the red leather armchair that had once been in his office down the hall. He was one of those officers who didn't like the Nazis; and to tell the truth, since the invasion, the senior ranks of the Amsterdam police force had been badly split. There were those officers who had for many years openly supported the Nazis because they viewed the German Nazi Party as Europe's bulwark against the communists. Now the invasion was an embarrassment to most of them; but there were some in the senior ranks of the police force who had managed to shift their allegiances without too much loss of sleep. Chief Superintendent Van Noorden was clearly distressed by the new regime and the way some officers had adapted to it. He showed it in every vein on his red face.

At the best of times, Van Noorden was never a very strong conversationalist. In fact, when he was a sergeant, the police on the beat nicknamed him The Sphinx. This afternoon, he didn't reply to Neumann but instead shifted his weight. The old leather cushions squeaked under him as if calling attention to his discomfort. Neumann smiled. Not only was Van Noorden uncomfortable, but he was much older and senior in rank to Neumann. It was an incident in which the victim was suffering a loss of dignity and Neumann derived a certain pleasure from this.

"You seem to be having trouble making conversation tonight, chief superintendent. Please have a cigarette. I insist."

"This is not easy for me, Oberstleutnant Neumann," Van Noorden said as he reached and took a cigarette from the box that Neumann pushed towards him from the top of his desk. "You have left me no choice but to cooperate with you, and we feel that—" He swallowed and looked up defensively. "Well, some people feel that working with the Germans is treason."

"No." Neumann spoke softly. "No, I appreciate what you are saying, but working with us is the right thing to do for your country. That is not treason." He gestured magnanimously with both hands and then took a deep drag on his cigarette. "You are saving lives and contributing to peace and good order. We can't tolerate resistance and we would have to act harshly. You can appreciate that. It's much better to cooperate; it saves lives in the long run. In fact, I think it's the only moral choice you can make."

The chief superintendent said nothing.

"Well, let's forget morality for now, shall we? I asked you here to review some things. But first I want to thank you for the cooperation we have had from your police force today. I know that has been in no small part due to your leadership. I know you will keep up the good work."

Van Noorden didn't know what to say. He certainly didn't want Neumann to think he was a willing accomplice in the way the Nazis were running things in Amsterdam. He put his cigarette to his lips and inhaled deeply, as if the more smoke he put into his lungs the more it would soothe his tortured conscience.

"Today we pulled in almost everybody on our list of those who might be a risk to the German occupation forces. But almost everybody isn't enough, Van Noorden. There are still a few people outstanding, and you will help us find them. Also, I regret to say that we have had some incidents, incidents that are minor in themselves—things like slogans painted on walls, refusals to serve German

troops in shops. By themselves, these aren't a big problem." Neumann waved his right hand as if to dismiss the seriousness of slogans
painted on walls. "But we can't let that sort of thing happen. They
lead to more open and violent forms of opposition. You and I both
know that, and we won't let it continue. And you, Van Noorden, will
stop it. Because if it doesn't stop, I have orders to send you and your
family to Germany to serve in a labour camp." Neumann paused to
let this threat sink in.

Van Noorden stared straight ahead.

"Chief Superintendent Van Noorden, I sincerely don't want to see
that happen, and I wish these orders had never come to me. I would
like us to be friends some day. Germany and Holland will share a
long and glorious future together. That's an historical inevitability.
We are of one racial type; we share the same blood lines. So let's start
our relationship on the right foot." Neumann handed a typed piece
of flimsy paper to Van Noorden. "Here are the names I want brought
in by the end of the week. Please see that they are all accounted for.
That will be all for now."

* * *

THE EARLY EVENING TRAFFIC in downtown Amsterdam was lighter
than he had hoped and that wasn't good. Busy streets provided better
cover than half-empty ones. Rory looked at his watch and frowned.
He'd arranged to meet Annika three blocks from the Central Train
Station, and he didn't relish the idea of walking around hauling his
suitcase with him in hopes that she would eventually show up. At
this time of the evening, sweating and struggling around Amsterdam's streets, he felt he'd be too obvious. Luggage advertised him as
an outsider to everyone who saw him.

Perhaps it wasn't such a good idea teaming up with Annika. He
certainly didn't know her well and bringing her in on this operation
had been an impulsive act. He hadn't really given it much thought.
Nonetheless, what he had seen of her so far showed that she could
be counted on to fight against the Nazis. And there was no ques-

tion, she had an incisive mind; besides, she knew Amsterdam, and she certainly seemed bold enough. Despite all this, there could be a thousand other things about her that could prove to be disastrous. She could be neurotic, unreliable, a bad judge of character. For all he knew, she could be hearing voices. She could have any one of a thousand character failings that would make her unsuitable. He hadn't done any vetting of her and hadn't even spent much time in her company; and now, he was angry at himself for having buyer's remorse at making a deal with her.

There was no going back now, though. He had already moved out of the rooming house. That was the only prudent thing to do. Mrs. Roeme would almost certainly have given his description to the police, and as a matter of routine the German police would eventually check every hotel and rooming house in Amsterdam. So, if he hadn't moved out, it would just be a matter of time until he found himself trying to survive a Gestapo interrogation. He reassured himself for the tenth time that he hadn't done anything foolish.

He looked at his watch again and cursed himself. Why not admit it? Would he have made the offer to team up with her if she looked like Mrs. Roeme? Errors of judgment inspired by a pretty face were the single most common—and most preventable—mistake people made in this line of business. He saw it almost every week in one form or another in his police work. How stupid could you be? He had once made a similar mistake years ago. It wasn't as potentially serious but you'd think he'd have learned. He looked up and down the street. There was no fool like an old fool. No question about it, Annika had brains, she was cool under pressure, and most importantly, she was the only person he had come across that he could possibly enlist as an ally. Rory was getting angry with himself and felt flushed. His thoughts wandered. It was amateurish of them to send him over with only one contact and no fallback. Harris had forced him into this predicament. Then he chided himself for blaming Harris for everything. He had to be the one in control of things now. Fatalism and self-pity made you less effective. He was responsible for making his own decisions with whatever information was at hand. Harris was doing the best he could without any resources. Lack of preparation for the war wasn't his fault. Who he chose as an accomplice was up to him. No one else could make that decision; and truth be told, he wouldn't have allowed anyone else to make that decision for him.

Even putting his judgment aside, there was another aspect to all this. There was no escaping it: she was beautiful, and in this kind of work, a beautiful woman was a liability. Espionage, police under-cover work, private detective investigations, clandestine intelligence work—they all required grey nonentities, people who, if they sat next to you on the bus, you couldn't remember five minutes later. The kind of people you did not want were those you had to restrain your-self from staring at when they walked into a room.

Rory forced himself not to look at his watch again. If he looked anxious, he'd just draw further attention to himself. He took a deep breath and tried to look relaxed and calm.

"I was watching you from the bus stop by the corner over there." Annika's voice came from behind Rory and it surprised him.

"You startled me. I was beginning to wonder if you were going to show up after all."

"No, I got here several minutes early," Annika said. She was carry-ing a folded newspaper under her arm. "When I made the arrange-ment for us to meet here, I knew I could observe this meeting place without being seen from over by the corner, by the newsstand." She pointed with her newspaper to the street corner behind her. "There's a bus stop there for several routes, and I could stand by the news-stand waiting without drawing attention."

Rory forced a smile. "Where shall we go? Let's not stand around here any longer." He was doing his best to sound cheerful.

"Before we go any further with this, I want to talk some more, Mr. Becker."

Rory pursed his lips and nodded. "Of course. I'd do the same if I were you. Where do you suggest?"

"A block over, there's another café we can sit inside, and it's not too far to carry your suitcase."

Rory snuck an involuntary peek at his watch as he picked up his suitcase. Annika was just about five minutes late—exactly the same timing he'd have used if he'd been in her shoes. It was good trade-craft to leave an uncertain contact waiting under discreet observation. It could prevent you from falling into a trap. It was amazing, he thought, just how much of an aptitude Annika seemed to have for this kind of work. He shifted his grip on the suitcase and struggled to keep up beside her as she clipped along the cobblestoned sidewalk in her high-heeled shoes. Perhaps Annika read police and spy novels as a hobby.

At the De Graf Café, Rory was tempted to order a beer but his better judgment prevailed and he settled for coffee. "You caught me off guard when you came from behind on the street."

Annika looked directly at him. He could see that she was appraising him and assessing her situation carefully. "I just wanted to make certain you weren't in league with anyone else. I was watching to see what you'd do if I didn't show. There was nobody else with you, so I thought that when it looked like you were ready to leave, I'd approach you, but only if you were genuinely alone."

"That's very good. Did you think of that?"

Annika looked suspicious and hostile. "Yes. Yes, why do you ask? Do you think I can't think things out for myself?"

"No. I'm sure you can. I've seen evidence of your reasoning ability. It's very impressive. It's also a standard procedure for this kind of operation. I just wondered if you'd had some kind of police training."

Annika looked down and blushed. "No. No I haven't." She looked embarrassed by the compliment. "I'm sorry I spoke sharply. I don't know who to trust any more and you've already saved me once. You must think I'm ungrateful. I'm sorry."

She sounded genuine, Rory thought. "Not at all. I'm glad you're free. I'm happy to have helped. Besides, we have the same enemy."

"Do you know anything about my husband?"

"Nothing at all, nothing more than what I've told you, I'm afraid. I

got his name from a newspaper article and your address from a telephone book."

Annika said nothing. Saul's disappearance was consuming her.
Rory looked down. "I'm very sorry about your husband, Mrs. Hammerstein. How long ago did they arrest him?"

"It's been a few weeks now. I've heard nothing. He was arrested
along with his uncle. His uncle was released, but I've had no word
about Saul." Rapidly switching out of French, Annika said, "I can
speak English. I studied music in London one summer and I read
modern languages as a minor at university. I read English every day
for practice. There are more books available in English. If you are
more comfortable, we can speak English."

"That's impressive. You're fluent in English, Dutch, French, and
German; but I think when we're in public we should speak in French
or German."

For a moment there was silence. Rory began toying with the sugar
spoon. "I can't expect you to take everything on trust and you've
already figured out much of my background. For your own sake and
for the sake of the war effort, I can't tell you everything, but I'll tell
you what I can."

Annika nodded, her eyes fixed on Rory.

"You certainly surprised me at how quickly you identified me.
You're correct so far. I learned my French in Canada and I've come
here from London. I arrived here not long ago, shortly after the fall
of Holland. I'm here to establish the beginnings of a resistance. I'm
not staying here for long and I need someone to help me develop a
range of contacts. The single point of contact I was supposed to meet
has been rounded up by the Gestapo." He paused, stopping himself
from blurting out that he didn't expect anyone would ever see him
alive again.

Annika clenched her fist and put her hands to her mouth. Her
blue eyes burned with intensity.

"I'm sure you've already figured out most of this, but now that
you've had a few hours to think things through . . ." Rory found him-

self becoming embarrassed, as if his lack of a contact was a personal shortcoming. "I need your help. Are you still prepared to work with me?"

"I think I know someone who can help us."

* * *

NEUMANN DRAPED HIS TRENCH COAT over his arm and adjusted his forage cap. He liked wearing it off to one side, tilted at just a slight angle. Some of the more swashbuckling Luftwaffe pilots he'd seen in newsreels wore their caps like that and it certainly gave the impression that you weren't a rule-bound administrator flogging a desk. The coat was a good idea; it might be cool tonight and there was no point standing around shivering for nothing.

It was good to get out of the office and see for himself what was going on. It would be a long time until they would be able to completely trust the Dutch police, but things were moving along in the right direction. This was to be Van Noorden's last raid of the night, and Neumann had promised himself that he was going to be there to watch it. Leadership meant demonstrating that you weren't afraid to roll up your sleeves and pitch in with the men when it was required, even if it meant putting in a fourteen- or fifteen-hour day. When this was over, he'd go back to his desk, but you had to be seen sharing in the hard work. Besides, he wanted to see how things were going now that Chief Superintendent Van Noorden had been working for a few days with his integrated Gestapo and Dutch police team. One of the Gestapo NCOs who worked as a part of the liaison team had written a glowing report on how the Dutch police were cooperating with the Nazis.

Out at the car, Dieter Schmidt was putting the police pennant in place. Neumann thought he was putting on weight. He'd speak to him later; it wouldn't do to have an overweight driver. It would make Neumann look indulgent and lenient.

"Good evening, sir." Schmidt clicked his heels and saluted. That was another problem. Neumann couldn't remember Schmidt ever giving a fascist salute. He was supposed to be in the SS, not some conscripted yokel in the army.

"Where would you like me to take you tonight, sir?"

"Out to the Weesperstraat area. We're going to observe the last roundup from Chief Superintendent Van Noorden's list tonight. When we link up with them, just tuck the car in at the back of his column. I want to keep a low profile."

Schmidt hummed away to himself as he drove. That damn humming always irritated Neumann, but not tonight. Tonight he wasn't really bothered by it. In fact, he was much more focused and less irritable than he'd been in months. There were two reasons for his good humour. First, he realized that he had grown to like his work. He was good at running the police in an occupied country. Doing your job well, earning the gratitude of your superiors, enjoying the deference of your staff: that was fulfilling. And fulfilling work made you feel at ease with yourself. Secondly, only this afternoon he had acknowledged to himself that he had grown accustomed to being estranged from Maida. It wasn't so bad. She had been a problem. He didn't understand her on-again, off-again behaviour, but he had stopped worrying about it; and now, he had just mentally let her go. He was no longer ashamed of her distance. He was prepared to deal with her on his terms. She was the one who had to worry about things now. The very thought gave him confidence. He certainly wouldn't admit it to anyone, but Maida's airs about her social status had always made him feel deferential and indebted to her. He'd always been secretly afraid that if something went wrong between them, she could not only hurt him emotionally but also ruin him professionally. Here in Amsterdam, however, that was no longer the case. He was succeeding entirely on his merits. Soon Maida was going to be the one who had to toe the line.

Schmidt pulled the car up behind a line of three idling police sedans and Neumann got out. Van Noorden and a plainclothes Gestapo officer came up to greet him. "Good evening, Oberstleutnant," Van Noorden greeted him stiffly. "One more to go tonight.

We've had very good success so far today. We've found eighty per cent of those we are looking for. Some, I fear, have gone into hiding, but Holland is a small country and they can't hide for long."

"Who is last on your list, chief superintendent?" Neumann stuck out his jaw and rocked back on his heels. He didn't look at Van Noorden when he spoke to him.

"A Jewish couple, Herr Oberstleutnant. They are good friends of one of the Jewish activists we locked up some time back. He's a damned lawyer, so he won't be missed." He chuckled at his own wit and squinted at the paper in front of him.

Neumann wondered if Van Noorden had started to drink. He looked red in the face and there was something about his movements that looked slightly exaggerated.

"It doesn't say here what she does, though." Van Noorden snorted. "Look! They even have a Dutch name. These two have been actively complaining about the registration of Jews and Roma, and it says here that they've made preparations to escape to France. Well, Oscar and Nina Van Sittart can do their complaining from a jail cell tonight." Chief Superintendent Van Noorden put the arrest sheet back into his leather folder. "Are you ready, Herr Oberstleutnant?"

19

AT TEN PAST SEVEN, Rory and Annika stood at the doorstep of an apartment block in the Westerveldtstraat section of Amsterdam. The building, sandwiched between a bakery and what appeared to be a retail store for plumbing supplies, was clean and seemed in good repair. Rory noticed that two of the apartments had plants in the windows—always a sign of a minimum level of domesticity and order.

The woman who answered the doorbell was in her forties, stout, red-faced, and wearing an apron and head scarf cut from the same floral-patterned cloth. Annika spoke to her in rapid Dutch for several minutes, then she turned to Rory, speaking in French. "She speaks only Dutch and a little German. She tells me that she has a small partly furnished apartment. It was her brother's, but he's been in the Dutch East Indies and won't be back for a long time. She wants far too much money for it and she wants us to show identification to prove that we are who we say we are. She doesn't want to get in trouble with the police, especially not now."

"Tell her we will pay a month's rent in advance but that when we came back to Holland the police kept your identification and we expect to get it back later this week."

Annika nodded, turned to the landlady, and spoke in rapid-fire Dutch. To Rory, the conversation didn't sound like it was going well, but the two women abruptly broke into smiles and laughter and shook hands.

"We're on the top floor," Annika said in French. "If you show her your identification and pay thirty guilders in cash, everything will be fine. She thinks you're my husband and that we are going back to Alsace in a month. She's invited us to come down and have some soup with her. I agreed."

Rory fumbled in the breast pocket of his suit coat and pulled out his Alsatian identification. The landlady laughed and pushed his cards back at him as if she never really meant to look at them. They were friends; it was just a formality. She chuckled and said something in Dutch to Annika and they all laughed together.

The apartment was wallpapered in a very old, yellow-tiled pattern. There was a cramped front room with a sink and stove, cupboards, a small table and two chairs, a tiny bedroom with a double bed and an armoire. In the back was a sink, toilet, and shower. Rory noticed approvingly that the frosted window beside the shower opened to a metal fire-escape at the rear of the building. Annika walked to the bedroom doorway. Looking down at the double bed, she said in English in a flat detached voice, "It looks like there's no choice, Mr. Becker; if we are to appear as man and wife we'll have to sleep in the same bed. We'll both stay on our own side."

Given her circumstances, Rory chose not to make a joke of the situation. "Fine," he said matter-of-factly, and then added, changing the subject, "but I think that before we go downstairs for soup and the first test of our new relationship we should agree to a common story for our background. We've been married for nine years. We got married on July 1 in Alsace. You were still a student. We have no children. I'm in the seed sales business, you like to travel with me, and we've been stranded by the invasion. And one thing, if you're now Mrs. Becker, you shouldn't answer to Annika. What should I call you?" He softened his tone. "It's better cover if you change your Christian name."

Annika looked away. For a moment she became distant and thoughtful. Her past and her identity was rapidly being chiselled and slashed away. A stranger was gradually assuming her character. The transformation was an unwelcome waypoint in creating her new persona, and although on an intuitive level she understood and acknowledged what was happening, now, for the first time, she was forced to accept that these changes in her life were irreversible. "Call me Marika. It's my middle name. I'll remember it when I'm frightened," she said briskly. She forced a weak smile and spoke in French. "I don't know about you, Martin, but I'm hungry. Let's go downstairs for a short while then, shall we?" She tucked and tidied her hair in the reflection from the kitchen window. "Good luck."

* * *

JUST AFTER SEVEN the next evening, Annika strolled through the Jordaan fruit and vegetable market. She clutched a paper bag full of wrapped slices of brisket, flour, fresh bread, leeks, potatoes, and cheese. Tomorrow, she'd make a potage for dinner. She was lucky because it was already getting harder to find some things in the market. Life in the Netherlands was becoming more difficult for everybody, and Annika did not look out of place nosing and rummaging about in the stalls, searching for ingredients they had once taken for granted. In the last twenty minutes, she'd almost convinced herself that shopping was her real reason for coming this evening. She was doing her best to play her role in this new life as efficiently as possible. But who was she fooling? It was easier to lose herself in the moment than to think about the perverse calamity her life had become in the last weeks.

Earlier in the day, she had phoned Henrick Schulyer and arranged to meet him here under a guise of a chance encounter. She'd be out shopping and he would come down the street from the east. She stopped and looked in a store window, as if she were really interested in the collection of aluminium pots, brushes, and brooms offered for sale. Saul used to be forever on the lookout for bargains of any sort.

It was one of his endearing qualities but it meant they accumulated closets full of junk.

She sighed heavily. In her heart, she had known for weeks now that she'd never see him again. Somehow, though, she felt that if she even began to acknowledge that he was dead she was being disloyal to him. In some distant way, she owed him the hope of life; but was she only deceiving herself? Several people had already told her in the gentlest of ways that he wasn't coming back.

Every one of the policemen she had met had been embarrassed and evasive when speaking about him. Martin Becker, whatever his real name was, said it in his expression. And Oscar and Nina never said anything directly, but the certainty of his death hung over them like a ghost that no one wanted to acknowledge. She wondered where Oscar and Nina were. She had tried to phone several times from a pay phone earlier that afternoon and gotten no answer. Maybe they had already left for France and onwards to freedom in Spain. But surely they would have contacted her first. If they did leave, perhaps they wanted absolute secrecy and they had sent her a letter. In that case, it would arrive tomorrow—and if it did, it would lie unopened in her letter box at the old apartment. She took a step sideways and fastened her attention on a stack of detergent boxes in the window's corner. There was no point worrying herself with imaginings.

An hour before, there had been a light shower and tiny puddles remained in the seams of the cobblestoned road. Off to the north, there was a faint rainbow. Annika felt a distant thrill on seeing it. If the rainbow had been the sort that she imagined existed when she was a child, then the end of this one would have been hovering right now over the Royal Palace. When she was very small, she used to chase down Amsterdam's streets hoping to find the pot of gold waiting at the rainbow's end. Back then, she thought rainbows had a real start and end point. She smiled as she remembered how disappointed she'd been when she found the rainbow kept moving away until finally it disappeared altogether. What a long time ago that was. In those days, her biggest worries were whether or not she had to eat her liver and onions, or how late she could stay up.

Tonight, the air in the market was fresh with the smell of summer rain. There were few people about. Tired farmers and their wives were busy packing up their carts with unsold produce, pulling down their awnings, and collapsing their tables. Having made their final sales of the day, they were now preparing to go back to their farms, do their chores, and go to bed. Annika imagined they followed a routine that lasted from the day they were old enough to help out around the farm until they died. She had never envied farmers before, but now their lives looked so reassuringly sedate, so safe.

There was nothing sedate about her life now. Saul had been brutally taken from her and everything seemed as if she was trapped in a terrifying nightmare. But even in acknowledging the outlandish nature of her life and her desire to respect Saul's memory, she felt guilty. It was a confusing emotion. She had done nothing wrong. And even though she had no proof Saul was dead, increasingly over the last few days she realized that she now thought of Saul in the past tense. Hope had drained out of her, and accepting this lack of hope as decent and normal behaviour was more than she could manage. It was as if somehow her lack of faith in his survival had something to do with his death. As well as the emotional turmoil she felt, she knew that her feelings about her life and her future were confused, and confusion was not a sentiment that Annika bore patiently.

The very thought of losing Saul hurt with a pain that came close to crushing her spirit. At the same time, she found the prospect of sharing an adventure and an apartment with Martin Becker exhilarating; and because this situation masked and interrupted her feelings of loss, she couldn't help but feel that she was cheap and treacherous. She'd done nothing disloyal to Saul. Over the years, she had never even imagined the possibility of it. But there was no getting around it: she was stirred by aspects of this whole crazy encounter and the dangers that went with this extraordinary life she'd been thrown into.

She walked on, looking at shop windows without seeing their contents. She had passed last night sharing a bed with Martin Becker. How ridiculous it was; of course nothing happened; but in addition to a sense of unwelcome excitement, she felt shame and embarrassment. They had both lain on their sides of the bed, frozen with the awkwardness at being forced into intimacy in such circumstances. She was certain that she fell asleep before him, and when she awoke from a light and restless sleep, she slipped out of bed long before he opened his eyes. There was an excitement to it, but it wasn't the kind of excitement she would have ever wanted. It was bizarre and dream-like, as if she were caught in a recurring and embarrassing nightmare and couldn't wake up. And she recognized the truth that, against her will and her sense of decency, she was attracted to this man. She wondered if there was something wrong with her. Was she simply callous, shallow, and selfish? She reassured herself that all she was doing was putting one foot ahead of the other and doing her best to think things through.

Most of the market stalls had shut down now and the last of the shopkeepers was bringing his wares inside before locking up. She continued walking, oblivious to the lack of anything to look at, thoughts swirling through her mind. She looked up from the store window and saw Henrick Schulyer walking briskly towards her.

Schulyer looked genuinely surprised and delighted to meet Annika. He tipped his hat and smiled, and the two began walking in the direction she had come from. "How wonderful to see you," Schulyer said. In a lower voice he added, "Please, walk along with me. I don't think anyone's following us or watching, but let's walk away from here for a distance just to be sure."

Annika nodded. Only days ago, this obsessive and suspicious behaviour would have seemed utterly ridiculous to her; now it seemed practical and normal. "Thanks for coming, Henrick. I was at my apartment the other day and I met someone I think you should talk to."

"I do want to meet this person, Annika, but before we do that, you should know that what we were afraid of before has now come true. You're on the Nazi's wanted list. The list was circulated this afternoon. I saw it. Like I thought, it includes the close relatives of all those picked up and shipped off in the first wave of arrests. I'm delighted to see you alive and free, but you're definitely on the list. I can't tell you how much danger you're in. I could be arrested simply for talking to you."

Annika looked off as if she were window shopping and spoke without emotion. "I know. I've already escaped an arrest attempt. I'm on the run now."

The two of them walked to the bus stop from where she had observed Rory. They stopped and joined a small crowd and made small talk, waiting as if they expected their bus to arrive at any moment. Rory walked past them a few minutes later. Their eyes didn't meet. When he had walked a further fifty metres and crossed the street, they both turned and followed him. Annika said, "We've agreed to meet in the café around the corner."

"Your friend seems to understand how to spot a tail. Are you sure he's not working for the Germans?"

"If he was, why would he be interested in any information I could give him? I'm a musician and the wife of a commercial lawyer who's in prison. I'm not Mata Hari."

Rory was sitting at a small table in the back corner. He stood as they arrived. "Mr. Schulyer speaks some German," Annika said, "but you'll have to speak slowly."

They sat down. Annika and Henrick Schulyer chatted in Dutch while the waiter brought coffee. When the waiter was gone, Rory spoke in German. "I'm from London. I'm here to help establish a resistance movement. We'll be back and we'll need patriotic Dutch men and women to help us when the time comes."

"How can you prove that you are who you say you are?" Schulyer asked.

"I haven't brought any identification, if that's what you want. I'm not going to ask you to do anything just now. I'm simply looking to find several men and women that I can use to begin a resistance network. Annika tells me you're in the police?"

Schulyer looked sceptical. "Yes, I am."

Annika spoke rapidly in Dutch and Schulyer nodded approvingly.

"Annika speaks highly of you. Apparently you whisked her away from the arrest team. That certainly helps."

Rory smiled. "I didn't do much, but thank you. Annika also tells me that you're trying to get into the police identification bureau?"

Schulyer nodded again.

"Would you be able to get identification cards made for someone whose identity we wanted to change?"

"I probably could. I haven't been transferred yet, but it looks likely that will happen in the next week or so."

"Excellent. When the German identification system is fielded, we'll need copies of all their cards, good impressions of their stamps, and a description of their process—how they go about determining who gets what card, that sort of thing."

Schulyer looked thoughtful. "Yes, I think I'll be able to do that. Is that all you want me to do?"

"For now, yes. You've made a wise move, but you can't do anything that will draw attention to yourself. If you're a trusted member of the police force, you'll be invaluable in providing the kinds of things that I've just described to you, not in fighting. Keep your eyes open for future contacts, but don't try to establish your own cell or associate with any other resistance group. It will be too dangerous. If the only person you know of in the network is your contact, and the Germans capture you, they can only destroy one link. I'm afraid this will be a very lonely and difficult task for you."

Schulyer was silent for a few moments and then said, "I know it's going to be hard, but I want to do it anyway. I have to; it's the right thing." He lit a cigarette and shook the match vigorously. "Will you continue to be my contact, or someone else?"

"No." Rory leaned forward. "I'll be replaced. The person who replaces me will identify himself or herself, and when they do, they'll use the word 'cornerstone' at least twice in their introduction to you. That will be your initial means of authenticating them."

Annika listened to the conversation carefully, saying nothing, watching the reactions of the two men with tight-lipped concentration.

Schulyer looked stern and suspicious. He looked over at Annika and bit his lower lip.

"Is something the matter?" asked Rory.

"Yes. I'll work with you, no question of that. But there's something I've been avoiding speaking about until now. Something I don't want to say." He turned to Annika and spoke slowly in hushed tones in Dutch. They spoke back and forth for over a minute.

Annika went white and put her hand to her mouth. Silent tears welled in her eyes and streamed down her cheeks. She pulled away from the table and faced away from the two men.

Schulyer reached out and rested his hand on her back in a consoling gesture. "I'm afraid I've had some very bad news for Annika. Her husband was killed in a German labour camp. I found out today from a document the Germans were circulating internally. To make matters worse, they're still looking for her." He sighed and shifted his weight in the chair. "I had more bad news as well. Yesterday, her best friends were arrested and shipped off to Germany." He looked sheepish and stared at the table. "I didn't know how else I could tell her. It seems so harsh."

Rory put his hand on the table and spoke in English. "Annika, I'm so sorry."

Schulyer looked embarrassed and muttered in German, "I don't think I did a very good job of telling her."

"Henrick," Rory said, "nothing you could say will make it any better. Annika, is there any place that you can go for a few days? Some place where you could have some privacy, with people you trust?"

She didn't answer for a moment, and then shaking her head, said, "No. I don't think there's anywhere I can go that would be safe. I think we should carry on with what we've started. This is not a surprise. I've been expecting this for several weeks." She sniffled and sat up straight. "I want to hit back at them now."

* * *

THE JUNIOR OFFICERS were in a huddle around the piano in the corner of the headquarters mess, singing "Lili Marlene" at the top of their lungs. They had been there for two hours already and it was the third time they had sung the tune in the last ten minutes. The room was blue with cigarette smoke, and fifty other police and army officers were holding shouted conversations above their singing. To Neumann, it seemed he was the only one in the room who wasn't enjoying himself. He didn't like to drink like the others. They made fools of themselves when they drank. Could you imagine what they'd have thought if someone filmed any one of these men in the room tonight and they could watch it the next day? Shouting and singing and laughing—at what? They sang like donkeys in heat, their jokes were ridiculous, their conversations were inane, and they shouted themselves hoarse.

He had been nursing a glass of sekt for the last hour. That was how officers should drink, not like these oafs who swilled beer and wine as if they were the village cow at a trough. Still, it would have been nice to have a friend to talk to in the mess. A sober, intelligent, quiet conversation would be pleasant for a change. The general commanding the Amsterdam military district had given a specific order that, without exception, all officers in the area were to attend the mess tonight to raise morale and reinforce a sense of comradeship. Neumann wouldn't have come if it wasn't obligatory. Why should he come to something like this? His work was more interesting—and valuable.

He'd joined in a game of cards with a group of junior officers earlier in the evening, but even though they were the same age as he, they were a closed group and he didn't warm to any of them. Despite the fact that he was wearing a grey uniform, they all knew he was the senior Gestapo officer in Amsterdam and it was obvious they were wary of him. For them, it was like playing some strange game with a cobra. Nobody ever wanted to upset him. They joked and taunted one another, but with him they were serious and deferential. Weren't they smart enough to realize this was insulting to him? He played

their foolish game of whist for an hour and then excused himself
from the group. Now he stood alone at the end of the bar looking out
at everyone else enjoying themselves.

"Herr Oberstleutnant, your drink needs refilling and you don't
look like you're having any fun tonight." The voice was husky and
feminine and belonged to the Dutch woman behind the bar. She
was in her mid-thirties, had brown, permed hair, and was a bit heavy.
Neumann thought she looked pretty—she certainly exuded an air of
voluptuous sensuality.

"Does it look like I'm bored?" Neumann asked, turning his attention to her.

He had certainly noticed her—who wouldn't—but he'd never
paid her or any other women in Holland serious attention until now.
He noticed that she wasn't wearing a wedding ring and he forced a
smile. Then without thinking about it, he blurted out, "I'm very hungry. Perhaps if you're free you would go with me to have dinner after
this is over? We could have a more interesting conversation than this."
He waved his arm at the crowd and no one in particular.

Why not? Maida hadn't written him for two weeks now, and
besides, it would do him good to get out and talk to someone other
than the police and soldiers he saw day in and day out. This woman
behind the bar had an intelligent-looking face and she was quite
pretty; that was probably how she got the job. He shouldn't really
fraternize with Dutch civilian employees, but who was going to
report him? The file would come to his desk anyway; and besides,
it was an open secret that several senior army officers had already
found themselves Dutch girls as company. Some of those girls were
even working as private secretaries in the headquarters.

As he looked at her, the thought crossed his mind that for the
same reason the captains were deferential to him, women would be
reluctant to turn him down. There were definitely certain advantages
to being feared.

The woman behind the bar smiled and blushed. "Well, it will be
late and I really should go home."

"Oh, come on now, you're not married, are you?" She shook her head. "Good. Then you can show me the good restaurants that are open. We'll choose one and we can get ourselves a decent meal. My car will be waiting at the front door of the mess at eleven."

"Okay," she said with a quiet smile.

He smirked at her, pushed himself away from the bar, and slipped out the back door. He could go to the office and review some of the files that had arrived earlier in the evening.

The lights in the upstairs hallway of the police headquarters were darkened. Neumann slipped into his office and flicked on his desk lamp. He opened his safe and pulled a stack of files out of the in-box he had locked away several hours before. He sorted through the files, searching for something to catch his interest. Although he wanted to work, he was restless, and it was hard to keep focused on any one file. As he sifted through the pile, he cradled the phone on his shoulder and ordered the duty NCO to have his car and driver at the front of the garrison headquarters mess at eleven.

At the bottom of the stack was a secret file folder from Gestapo headquarters: "The Netherlands." It was the only interesting one in the group. All the other files were administrative summaries and routine reports of who had been arrested and where tomorrow's search would be conducted for those still on the wanted list. The Gestapo file contained a single message form with a simple, typed, two-paragraph memorandum from the chief of the Gestapo in the Netherlands. He was convening a planning session for next Tuesday in The Hague. The meeting was to be a small session of senior police officers, who would examine methods of improving security measures in Holland. There was going to be a presentation by the Director of Reich Field Security from Berlin, as well as a special guest presentation by the second-in-command of the Gestapo in France. Those senior Gestapo officers from Holland wishing to speak at the conference were advised to table their agenda topics no later than seven tomorrow evening.

Neumann sat back and put his hands on his head. He swivelled around in his chair and looked out over the courtyard of the police barracks. The poplar trees over by the perimeter wall swayed in the breeze. It felt like the barometer was falling again. Even after the downpour late this afternoon, there might be more rain tonight. He hoped the weather would clear before the meeting next week. If he wanted to be clever, he thought he should have something useful to say at the security conference, something that would make him stand out from the herd.

"Oberstleutnant Neumann." The voice was deep and authoritative. "You are working late. What keeps you at your desk when all the officers from the headquarters are enjoying themselves in the mess?"

Neumann swivelled about in his chair. "Oh, Mein General, you startled me." He stood up and came to attention. The general smiled and waved for him to sit but was obviously anxious to get an answer to his question.

"I was down at your party, but I just nipped up here for a moment to jot down some ideas I had regarding the security conference for next week. These days, if I don't write things down I forget them."

The general was a man in his fifties, short and dark with a square face and the powerful, thick-set features of a prize-fighter. He laughed. "I know how that feels, Neumann, but you're still a young man." He beamed. "But, that's why I ordered a party in the mess tonight. Don't work too long at putting those ideas together." He turned to go and spun back on his heel. His eyes weren't smiling. "Oh, and Neumann, you know I'll be interested in seeing what it is you have thought of that has taken a senior officer away from the party I ordered. Good night."

Neumann sat down slowly and again turned his chair around. He could see a pair of sentries with flashlights and coal-scuttle helmets on their rounds walking across the courtyard. What the hell was he going to table for the agenda for next week's meeting that would pacify the man whose order he had just disobeyed? He cursed quietly to himself, wishing he had a more productive imagination.

20

NEUMANN THOUGHT THAT AT TIMES it could be irritating having Rottenführer Dieter Schmidt as his driver. On his most intrusive days, he was a pious little prig, and on his best days, he was just a whisker away from being insufferable. Schmidt hadn't said anything tonight, but Neumann could see that he was scandalized by this outing with a Dutch woman. Schmidt had always been asking after Maida and the children, and even long after Neumann had made it clear that Schmidt's interest in his family life was unwelcome, Schmidt would follow up with some pathetic comment about his own children. He invariably looked hurt when it was obvious that Neumann wasn't going to be drawn into the conversation. Tonight Schmidt kept peering in the rear-view mirror to get a better look at Laurina. It was making both Neumann and his date uncomfortable.

"Keep your eyes on the road, Schmidt. I don't want to speak again." You would think he was dealing with a small child. Why did he have to have the most unsophisticated police driver in the entire Third Reich? Turning to Laurina, he said as cheerfully as he could, "So tell me, what restaurant have you chosen for us tonight? You know, I've been working so hard these last few weeks, I need a little time away just to unwind."

"What sort of place would you like to go to?" Laurina purred in a child-like voice. Neumann liked her little-girl affectation; it made her seem sexy and provocative. She was quite unlike Maida, who when you thought about it was a straightforward, middle-class Austrian girl. She was pretty enough, but she had no real sense of the exotic or glamorous. That's probably why she was getting bored with her life. It was a good thing she was going to stay in Vienna. Besides, Maida's withdrawal from him was a kind of disloyalty. She had been the first to be unfaithful.

"I want you to choose," Neumann said. "I want to see something. Show me something different here in Amsterdam."

Laurina tilted her head to one side. "Oh, there are lots of places that are different in Amsterdam. But I think you don't want something too different." She laughed. "You want something fun. The Hoorn Club is quite good, I hear. It's open very late, and a friend of mine tells me that there are a lot of German officers there now with their Dutch friends."

Neumann did his best to appear relaxed. He wasn't very good at this sort of thing. He didn't want to appear like he was inexperienced with women, but he'd only really known Maida, and their relationship had never been anything like this. There had been no tinge of guilt or illicit excitement to it. "So tell me about yourself. What did you do before you started working at the German officer's club?"

Laurina looked out the window. She seemed ill at ease with the question. "I used to work as a waitress at the Burgemeester Restaurant. I saw the ad for the officer's club in the paper and I thought they'd pay more money. They did, and so here I am."

"And have you always lived in Amsterdam?"

"No, I used to live in Amersfoot, but I was married then. I have an eight-year-old boy to raise, and he has a serious medical condition. He has problems with his lungs, and the doctor's bills are expensive. I haven't seen my husband for four years now."

Schmidt's eyes began darting back and forth from the road to the rear-view mirror, and this time he had a worried look on his face. Neumann chose to ignore him.

"That's too bad. I'm sure that your husband, whoever he was, has never done any better for himself than the day when he met you."

He looked out the window and back at Laurina. "Now, tell me what you do when you aren't working." Neumann was beginning to relax. After all, this kind of conversation wasn't much different than a simple interrogation. All you had to do was be sympathetic, ask the right questions, and let your suspect do the talking. They usually said more than they wanted to, especially if you showed kindness and understanding with them.

The restaurant turned out to be a smoky supper club, located above a store. It had a jazz quartet that was playing an insufferable kind of American Negro music. Neumann agreed with the Nazis about music: jazz was decadent. You couldn't dance to it, you couldn't sing along with it, it had no real form, and it represented a lack of discipline and order. He wasn't alone in these thoughts. There were a dozen other German officers in the club with their friends, and eventually an infantry Major got up and shouted at the manager to have the band play something more appropriate to the occasion. The music changed to American popular music from the 1930s. Neumann wasn't certain if he liked it or not, but Laurina seemed to enjoy it. She tried to get him on the dance floor to do a foxtrot. Neumann refused. "No, no. Wait until there is something closer to a waltz; that I can dance to."

Laurina finally got Neumann onto the dance floor but only after she had coaxed him to have several glasses of champagne. Over the orchestra, Neumann shouted, "I don't dance very well, you know, and I certainly don't drink this much normally."

"Oh, don't be so modest. You're a natural, and besides, you should get out and have some fun some time. You're light on your feet and you have a great sense of timing."

Despite Neumann's natural talents, however, it became clear after the first two dances that his mind wasn't on dancing and they found themselves sitting again at their table. By one in the morning, Laurina had finished the better part of a bottle of Moët et Chandon champagne. The wine produced its intended effect, and the fears and suspicions she'd felt earlier in the evening seemed to have evaporated. She moved her chair closer to him and did her best to cuddle. "What's bothering you? A few moments ago you were having such a good time. Now you look worried."

"Oh, it's nothing. I was just thinking about work, that's all."

"Work, work, work! That's all you Germans do! What could be so important? The war is almost over now; and besides, it's late on Saturday night. Why don't you laugh like the others?"

Neumann had no one to talk to, Laurina was attentive, and what the hell, it wasn't as if it was a secret. He put his arm around her. "Well, you know, I have to come up with a topic for a conference next week, and I have no idea what I'm supposed to say. The general is expecting something clever from me and I have nothing new to say." Neumann looked frustrated and forlorn. His uniform collar was undone and his normal sense of aloofness and formality had vanished.

Laurina was serious for a moment. "So what are the biggest problems facing you? The fighting has stopped. We all have to live together now. I don't see your problem. What do you think your problems are?"

"Well, for one thing, we don't know who our enemies are. They all look the same. Once the war is over, nobody wears a uniform."

Laurina burst out laughing and spilled some of her champagne over the table. "That's easy: give your enemies badges to wear so you know who they are." Laurina giggled and had to steady herself. "Make them wear badges saying 'I'm an enemy of the Third Reich.'" She poked him playfully, laughing at her wit.

"That's a brilliant idea." Neumann sat up and put his drink down. "Laurina, you're on to something there. We'll make different categories of people wear badges just like in the camps. The Jews, gypsies. It will be so easy to identify them on the street. Control will be no problem; they'll have to wear a badge. You're brilliant."

Laurina stopped laughing and put her drink down. "Reinhold, maybe it's time I should go home. I was only joking."

* * *

"ANNIKA, BEFORE WE GO much further, I have to go out to the country. There's something I have to get."

Annika looked up from her breakfast. She had been thinking quietly and munching slowly on a piece of toast. She took a sip of coffee. "What's that?"

"I have to go and retrieve my radio set. When I came here, I was travelling through the country and I had to hide it. It's heavy and cumbersome, and I thought it would give me away. I can't put off getting it much longer. I have to establish communications with London."

Annika put her cup down. "I was expecting that sooner or later you'd have to do something like this."

Rory said nothing for a few moments. Annika looked at him as if expecting a reply. "You know I haven't told you things for reasons of security. I'm sorry. I'm not concealing anything from you to be difficult. I realize that you're in as much danger as I am."

"I understand." She said it quietly and sincerely. Her tone made Rory feel self-conscious but not uncomfortable. It was almost as if she was trying to be accommodating. Once again, despite the distance created by her grief, Rory felt an irrepressible attraction to her. He remained impassive, wondering for a moment if Annika felt the same way. He knew that he was emotionally drained and was misinterpreting things, that he had to be on his guard. He watched her as she stared out the window. Annika looked tired, but despite her situation, she was also remarkably composed.

Rory had been uncertain how to proceed with things once they heard of Saul's death. He needed Annika's assistance, and he knew that he couldn't manage without her. Now he reckoned he had two options: to express his condolences, then press on and get down to work right away; or to tread softly, give Annika space to grieve and time to come to grips with her situation gradually, and only then resume work on the network. As they sat there over their coffee, he tried to put his situation into sensible perspective. Annika provided him a fairly straightforward moral dilemma: should he do his duty and get on with his larger mission, or should he slow down, increase the risk, and give Annika a decent interval to mourn her husband?

He couldn't spend much time waiting for others to deal with private tragedies. That was how things were. He had a serious job to do, and there was far more at stake than the sentiments of a few individuals. But he knew that finding the right balance between the exigencies of war and the needs of peoples' lives wasn't as simple as balancing an equation. There was no set of rules you could follow. Instead, he decided to steer a middle course. He'd be gentle and polite, give Annika as much space as she needed, but try to keep them both focused on his larger mission. He said nothing about his concerns.

Annika hadn't complained. Since they had left the café two days before, she'd been withdrawn and dignified. He admired her composure and self-control. She carried herself with grace and poise; and against his will, he found himself constantly thinking about her.

Yesterday, shortly after breakfast, he had left the apartment, leaving her to as much privacy as he could manage. He had spent most of the day walking about the city.

He needed time to think about things as well. There was no concealing it from himself: Annika infatuated him. He thought about her constantly, and in his imaginings, he pictured her back in London and Canada with him—in his wilder moments, he was even assessing how he could rescue her from this situation. He'd never expected this to happen. Before coming here, he had assumed he would come to Holland, make a series of connections, and scoot back to London to make his report. His personal life would resume once the mission was over. But yesterday, instead of observing the movements of the German army and the Dutch police and assessing the mood of the population, he spent most of his time staring into canals or coffee cups thinking about Annika.

He hardly even knew her. But now he knew he was vulnerable, and he had wilfully, although unconsciously, avoided thinking about that vulnerability. Strong men didn't acknowledge that kind of weakness. The unspoken expectation was that he was rugged enough to get by on his own resources; and God knows, he'd done that for long enough. He had kept himself busy since Ruth's death, throwing himself into his work in the Mounted Police, then leaving Canada and taking on this new role. Now it was all a blur. All he'd managed to do was to insulate himself from reality and the task of getting on with his life. That life was catching up with him now. He was obsessed by this poor, grieving woman.

For all he knew, she probably hadn't given him a second thought, other than that he had been involuntarily dropped into her life She certainly had her own mind, and she would more than likely solve her own problems in her own way. She'd already proven herself to be that sort of woman. She was bright and capable.

Rory shifted in his chair and got up to pour himself a second cup of coffee from the pot on the stove.

Annika put her cup down. "Why don't I go with you to get the radio? I can help provide you cover and you'll almost certainly need someone to speak Dutch for you."

Annika went out at ten that morning to buy new clothing and replace some of the essentials that she had been doing without since she fled her apartment. Living out of her purse for the last several days left her feeling seedy, and she hoped that a few hours of shopping would do something to raise her spirits. In the end, her shopping expedition proved to be nerve wracking. No sooner had she left the apartment than she was gripped by the fear that someone might recognize her. She did her best to reassure herself. She normally avoided shopping. It wasn't something that gave her pleasure anyway, so it was doubtful any of the shop assistants would recognize her. And it was unlikely any of her friends or acquaintances who had jobs and families would be out shopping on a weekday morning.

All that may have been true, but her stomach was still in a knot. She told herself this was a new life. It had a whole new range of stresses and strains, and from here on in things were going to be much more tense. Pressure was something she was going to have to live with.

After buying some new nondescript skirts and sweaters, a felt hat, and a new pair of shoes, Annika went to the Dorland Hair Salon over on Nieuwendijk Street. Although it was a bit out of the way, it had the advantage that she had never been there before. An hour later, she emerged with a shorter cut—a chic new perm—and her bright blonde hair was dyed a light auburn colour. She liked the new style. She'd never coloured her hair before, but there was no question it suited her. Out on the street, she involuntarily stopped to look at her reflection in a shop window and was immediately stabbed by grief and guilt. She instinctively wondered if Saul would have liked it—and then almost simultaneously hoped Martin Becker would approve. For a moment, the twin thoughts paralyzed her; and although Annika understood the confused nature of her distress, on a deeper level she was stung by her emotions.

She walked on, trying to think things through, hoping somehow she'd reason her way out of her sorrow and guilt. And although Annika knew she couldn't come up with any answers that would restore her old life, the more she thought about it, the more her spirits began to rise. Considering the circumstances that the two of them now found themselves in, it could have been much worse. Martin was easy enough to get along with. He seemed fair and sensible, quick-witted and decent; and, above all, he provided her the best chance of survival.

She stopped at the street corner and took a quick glance around her. There was nothing unusual. She turned at the corner, crossed the street, and continued on her way. Since meeting Martin, she hadn't seen anything to dislike about the man. He'd been discreet and sensitive about her circumstances, and he had a generous nature. That morning, he'd readily agreed that she had to get some new things. Annika thought that his concern wasn't just a practical fear for the mission's success. He seemed genuinely concerned for her. They were in vigorous agreement that going back to her apartment to get her things was too dangerous. She had no doubt he was who he said he was. After all, her trust was based on practical evidence: he had got her away from the apartment in time to prevent her from being captured. There was instinct too: from what she could see, he was a gracious individual. He certainly seemed competent and decisive, and she trusted his judgment and his motives. She dismissed the notion from her mind that her attitude towards him was in any way influenced by the fact that he was also ruggedly good looking.

After the hairdresser's, Annika strolled through Damrak Square on her way to buy their tickets. Both the square and the central train station were busy, and there was no sign of unusual police or military activity. For a second it seemed as if there wasn't a war on. Trains shunted back and forth with puffs of steam, loudspeakers announced imminent departures and arrivals, and porters steered luggage around busy travellers. However, there was one thing out of place: amongst the crowds were armed German soldiers travelling to and from leave. The German soldiers looked like young Dutch conscripts going on furlough—except that most of those young Dutch conscripts were now wasting idly in German prison camps. It amazed her how quickly the appearance of normalcy reasserted itself. But when she looked closely, she noticed nobody amongst these Dutch travellers was smiling.

As soon as she closed the door to the apartment, Annika launched immediately into business. She spoke quietly. "I've got us two train tickets. It doesn't look as if they're watching the train station. The town nearest your landing field with train service is Hauwoud. We'll go there tonight and stay in the hotel. I can rent you a bicycle at the hotel. I've already telephoned them from the train station, and the bicycle shouldn't be a problem. You can pick up your case in the dark and we'll return tomorrow."

Rory looked amused. "That's great. Wonderful. Thank you. You've changed your hair. It suits you."

Annika dodged the compliment. "I had to; at least now I won't fit the description that Mrs. Roeme probably gave to the police. I've also got us a map of the area we'll be going to."

Rory was impressed that Annika had thought to pick up a map.

It was more than he had the night he landed. Back in England, they couldn't find a genuine Dutch map, and carrying anything else would have exposed his identity. His briefings had been conducted on an old Royal Air Force flight planning map that he had to leave behind.

Annika was anxious to discuss their trip into the countryside and she paced the room. "You'll have about a seven-kilometre cycle from the hotel to where your case is. If all goes well, you should be able to get there and back and find the case in the dark in an hour or two. I'd be surprised if there are many Germans about in Hauwoud, but the local police may be a concern. The weather tonight will be clear. That should help you find your case, but I don't think it will be a problem if someone sees you on the road. You'll just be a travelling Alsatian salesman out late at night."

At three o'clock, Rory packed his suitcase. Annika watched him remove his Webley revolver and the two hand grenades. "You travel as if you mean business."

"It wasn't my idea to bring so many weapons. I thought I'd be safer without them."

Annika looked serious for a moment. "I think you should bring the pistol. If we get caught, I'd rather die fighting than at the hands of some guard in a German camp."

"Yes, that's what London thought too. But once you're caught in a checkpoint with a weapon you're finished. You can't bluff your way out. But if you feel better about the pistol, I'll bring it. The grenades stay here, though."

At four o'clock they left the apartment together.

* * *

IT HAD BEEN THE LAST STRAW. Neumann was thoroughly sick of Rottenführer Dieter Schmidt. As of this morning, he was transferring him back to regular duties. He hadn't said or done anything, but this morning, when they passed in the parking lot, Schmidt had saluted and then turned his back on him without saying a word. He acted wounded, and affected a distant and superior attitude, as if he had been let down. It angered Neumann. The army could charge a man with dumb insolence. The army believed a man didn't have to say something to be insolent. But charging Rottenführer Schmidt wasn't the route to take. Neumann didn't want Schmidt saying anything about Laurina. There was no point in being embarrassed by that clown. But from here on in, Schmidt was going to find that his life had gotten a little harder.

No, Neumann would never explain his reasons to anybody for transferring Schmidt. He didn't even want to admit that this lumbering yokel from an Austrian backwater could make him feel uneasy about himself. Better to just get rid of him now. He had outlived his usefulness. There were several ways of doing it.

Neumann stared at his desk pad as he considered this problem. Schmidt actually personified an aspect of the new society they were building. When you thought about it, his relationship with Schmidt was just one example of how the Third Reich functioned. In a closed hierarchy like the Reich's, leaders exercised power that gave them almost complete control over the lives of their subordinates; and if those leaders didn't like you, or you were no longer useful, one way or another you were disposed of. That was life. The strong ruled the weak everywhere you looked. Hadn't there been some English scientist who'd proven the theory of survival of the fittest? It made sense.

Neumann pressed the buzzer next to his desk. The buzzer was an old system that had been in place since God knows when. The Dutch police must have installed it at the end of the last century. It had old, fuzzy, brown wiring and cumbersome-looking push buttons, but it was a piece of communications equipment that the modern world could use. Neumann liked the idea of pushing a button and having someone scurry in to attend to you—it was much more direct than a telephone; and most importantly, it had the unmistakable aura of command about it.

Hauptmann Ackerman hurried in, straightening his tunic. "Yes, Herr Oberstleutnant?"

"Ackerman, I've been looking at the reports from the arrest teams. I don't think we are making satisfactory progress here. What do you think?"

"Herr Oberstleutnant?" Ackerman took a deep breath, sensing a trap in his supervisor's manner. "The teams have been following your instructions implicitly. Is there something wrong?"

"Yes, of course something's wrong. We haven't made any more arrests since our last big sweep. All those who evaded us last week are still on the loose. Don't you think that's a problem?"

"Of course, Herr Oberstleutnant. What did you have mind?"

"I want you to look at how we are using our joint Dutch and German teams, and in addition to raiding houses and work places, I want you to start a series of snap roadblocks. I want the train terminals watched. I want the bus terminals watched. I want anyone who moves in this city to come under our scrutiny."

"Sir, the police are almost at the limit of their manpower resources now. We have been running joint patrols night and day; and, respectfully, Herr Oberstleutnant, things have been quiet not only in Amsterdam but right across the Netherlands."

"What would you do if you were a Dutchman, Ackerman, or better still, what would you do if you were an Englishman?"

"Sir? I don't understand." Ackerman pushed his glasses back up off his nose.

"No, well, let me tell you something. If I were an Englishman, I'd want to get a resistance going in Holland and Denmark, Norway, Poland, and France. That's not just me talking. This fat old fool Churchill has already started talking that way in public. Of course you read the intelligence bulletins, and so that means that you can bet he has already got agents into our areas. Since the English have already been stupid enough to lose all of their agents here before the invasion, you can bet your boots, Ackerman, they are doing something about it. I think there are agents here in Holland, and I want to find them. But we won't find them unless we step up the pressure."

Hauptmann Ackerman licked his lips. He was on thin ice. "Sir, what did you have in mind?"

"Create more joint patrols. Get some army troops to help fill out their ranks, and use them to seal areas. Now that the fighting is over, we've had artillery and engineers sitting about on their asses doing nothing for weeks. We'll get them working for us. Also, I want you to increase the number of hours our own police and the Dutch are working. Don't be soft-hearted when you make your plans. To show you how serious I am in this, I want you to reassign my personal driver permanently to checkpoint duties. You and I will set the example, Ackerman. From now on, you and I will have to share a driver. Squeeze the organization for more men until we get results. Draw up the plans for my signature. I want them on my desk by tomorrow. Oh, by the way, I'm going to use your driver today. I have to go to the Reich security director's conference in The Hague. I'll be back tonight." Neumann stood up. He was smiling. He pulled his tunic down and straightened his collar. "But first I have to go see the general."

Ackerman stepped backwards and came to attention. "Certainly, Herr Oberstleutnant. I'll warn my driver." Not only had his one evening off this week been ruined, but Neumann wasn't going to share a driver. He'd just lost his.

21

THEY SET OUT FROM THE APARTMENT at four, walked three blocks,
and took the No. 7 bus to Damrak Square. Rory carried a half-empty
leather suitcase with their overnight things. He had the Webley
revolver firmly tucked in the rear of his waistband. Not for the first
time in his life did he think that this was a ridiculously sized hand-
gun for the modern world. It was uncomfortable, but it was secure;
and with his suit, coat, and hat on, he looked like a peaceful traveller
setting off with his wife.

They were in the train station at ten to five. A few police and
army patrols were in evidence, racing up and down the streets. At
the train station itself there was no sign of heightened security, just
as Annika had told him. Rory noticed, however, that armed German
troops had taken to using the Dutch train system as part of their routine administrative travel. None of the other travellers seemed to pay
the German soldiers much attention, and for their part, the soldiers
seemed remarkably uninterested in their fellow travellers. Rory and
Annika got on the Hauwoud train on Platform 4 and found a four-
person compartment occupied by two older Dutch women. The
women looked up at them, obviously unhappy that they had chosen to fill their section when others were empty. Rory had picked
this one rather than have the possibility of German soldiers joining
them. Annika didn't question the choice and seemed to understand

the reasoning without need of an explanation. She smiled at the two ladies and sat down. As far as they could see, no German troops had got on the train.

The train lurched forward a few times and was soon underway. Rory occupied himself staring out the window. Annika spoke in French, "We should be about fifty minutes to Hauwoud, darling." She turned to the Dutch women and said, "My husband is French; he doesn't speak much Dutch. Makes things a little difficult sometimes. Still, that's hardly something to complain about at a time like this, is it? This war has been such a strain on all of us." The two Dutch women smiled sympathetically.

At Hauwoud, Annika touched Rory's hand. She nodded cheerfully to the older women and wished them a good day. They left the train and descended onto the station platform.

"The hotel is only a few minutes walk from here," Annika said as she steered him in the right direction. They set off and she looped her arm inside Rory's. They walked along comfortably as if they were a trusting and happy couple. Neither spoke but Rory liked the feeling. Despite the strain of what they were embarking upon, he felt remarkably little anxiety. There was an easy, natural swing to their stride; and for the first time since they met, he thought they felt truly comfortable in one another's presence.

Their room was comfortably furnished: a large double bed, an armoire, and a pair of good-sized armchairs. None of the furniture matched. In front of the gas fire was a vase with dried wild flowers. Annika took an appreciative look at the room, and as she began to store their things, she said, "I love these old country hotels. They have such character."

A few minutes later, their things put away, they began to go over the plans. "I'll go down in a few minutes to arrange for your bicycle," Annika said. "Do you think we'd be too obvious if we went downstairs and ordered a drink in the lounge?"

"No, I'd like that." Their eyes met briefly. There was no romance in the action. They were both appraising one another to see how enthusiastically the other reacted to the prospect of a drink.

"I know what you're thinking," Annika said with a sad smile. "I rarely drink much." She forced a laugh. "Besides, I get headaches. I thought we should look normal, and I'd like to relax just a bit. The past few days have been a strain."

"You're doing marvellously. I can't imagine how you do it."

They went down to the lounge and seated themselves at a table in the corner. A distant radio was playing classical music. Rory ordered a beer and Annika ordered sherry.

"I think I should head out to get the radio just before dark. I'd guess from your map that it's twenty or thirty minutes from here. I suppose it might look a little suspicious if I go out empty-handed and come back with a suitcase."

Annika smiled. "No. I thought of that. When I arranged for the bicycle, I told the man at the desk that you were a seed salesman and that you'd be out tonight on a call. I said that most of your clients are farmers and that they sometimes kept you drinking with them late at night. I asked if they would please leave the front door unlocked. They shouldn't notice anything."

Once again Rory was impressed. They shared their drinks and talked quietly about the weather and how long the German occupation might last. Annika steered the conversation away from any mention of Saul. It wasn't that she wanted to forget him; now she was deliberately trying to put him in the past. She was afraid that if she didn't, she would be unable to think clearly or make decisions when it was required of her. Things had gone so quickly and her life had changed so irrevocably that she almost subconsciously hoped that she could achieve a sense of normalcy by putting him out of mind.

At dinner, they had a table by the window. They were the only diners for much of the time until a local couple in their late forties came in and seated themselves across the room. For most of the meal they spoke quietly of their plans for the next days.

"I'd like to see a number of people in different organizations," Rory said. "I don't think we want to focus on people who were influential in peacetime. I'm afraid they'd be too obvious. They'd only get themselves caught. We should concentrate on people you wouldn't normally expect to be leaders."

"I think I'd like to go with you when you meet them. I could help."

Rory looked thoughtful for a moment before he answered. "That's probably a good idea. I suspect that if we're lucky and we choose our cell wisely, we could be finished this in a couple days time."

"Then you're leaving?"

"Yes." There was an uncomfortable pause. "I could probably get you out of the country, you know. There's nothing here for you now. Are you interested?"

Annika's eyes flashed with enthusiasm but she spoke in a restrained voice. "Yes, if you could do that, that would be best."

"There's one problem. I haven't told you much, but I came in here on a specially designed airplane, one that can land on rough fields. I left my radio near the field where I landed. I didn't come in via France, which is what I let on, for security reasons. The plane can land in a cow pasture at night and can get to and from England on a single tank of fuel. I think it can take both of us on the return trip, but I'll have to clear it with London. There may be issues with how much fuel it has."

Annika's face remained impassive.

Rory leaned forward. "I can't make any promises, but if they allow it, and if it can only take one passenger, I'll put you on it and I'll return at a later time."

"You don't have to do that."

"I know, but you could be very valuable to us; and besides, you're an unofficial part of the organization now."

At that moment a boisterous family of seven came into the dining room and seated themselves beside them. Annika and Rory smiled at the newcomers and continued their meal in silence.

Rory left their room at nine. He went downstairs and found the bicycle. It was the only one in the rack at the side of the hotel. Thoughtfully, the hotel owner had left a trouser clip hanging on the handlebars. Rory fastened the clip around the bottom of his right trouser leg, gave the bicycle a good shake to test for any rattles, and was off. The air was cool and the town was washed in the golden light of a midsummer sunset. Out past the train station, he could hear the lowing of cattle. His pulse quickened as he cycled past the neat green-and-white-painted village houses and into the grassy farmland. As he remembered, the fields were neatly separated by ditches filled with black, stagnant water. Off in the distance, several fields over, he could see a large white windmill, its massive arms slowly turning in the faint breeze. He didn't remember seeing it the night he landed. For a few seconds he feared he was on the wrong road, but a mile later, the road turned from tarmac to hard-packed fine gravel, and the reassuring steady grinding sound the bicycle tires made over the stony surface had a calming effect on him. The road he had walked on that night was made of the same hard-packed gravel, and as he cycled along, he could remember the sound of it crunching underfoot just before he had been given a ride by the German troops. The only person he met along the way was a man out walking his dog. The man was seventy years old, dressed in tweed trousers, an old shirt, suspenders, and a flat cap. He was swinging his walking stick in a manner that told everyone he was both determined and cheerful. They both waved and smiled at one another as they passed.

Rory continued pedalling across the flat Dutch landscape. By 9:20 he reached the landing field. As the sun was still several minutes from setting, he continued cycling to the northeast. Tonight the road was empty. Well before ten, he turned about and went back without incident to the hedged field where Eric had deposited him on that first night. It seemed like he had been in Holland for a long time.

There was no one to be seen as he wheeled his bicycle off the road, unlatched the gate, and stepped into the field. The night air was invigorating. A sliver of a crescent moon was rising in the east, crickets were singing, and the grass was wet underfoot. Although the light was different, the field looked familiar. He could see the roof lines of the outbuildings that he remembered, and tonight he could also see, off in the distance, the farmhouse. He walked along the hedge, trying to recall just how far down he'd been when he hid the suitcase.

The hedge had grown up around an old three-strand wire fence. It was about six feet high and three feet wide. Its lower edge was overgrown with long grass, cowslip, brambles, and Queen Anne's lace, but then again, every field within a hundred miles of here probably looked the same and had identical vegetation. He got down on his knees and began to feel inside the hedge for the straight leather edges of a large suitcase. His hands were scratched by brambles and the sharp edges of branches.

Without the radio, he'd be forced to try to escape southward through occupied Belgium, down past Paris, and through Vichy France. It wasn't an appealing prospect. There were borders and frontiers and any number of chances of being caught. His pulse quickened. He needed this damn piece of equipment. He groped feverishly with his hands. This had to be the place he'd left it. He stood up and surveyed the hedge line. He must be close to it. He was sure he had left it about thirty feet from the gateway. He got up, moved twenty feet over to the left, and got back on his hands and knees. It couldn't be this far down. Could some farmer or child have discovered it? He began probing faster. As his search dragged on, his breathing became heavier. He suddenly noticed that he was oblivious to everything around him. He stopped and listened and then looked around behind him. There was nothing.

He continued searching frantically with his hands until he was almost at the corner of the field. He knew the suitcase couldn't be down this far. What was he doing wasting time here? Suddenly his hands hit wet leather. He pulled the suitcase out of the hedge. The branches and the leather made a loud scratching noise as he yanked the case from its hiding place.

He peered round the hedge before venturing out. The road was clear and he wheeled his bicycle back onto the gravel surface. He felt clammy with sweat and realized that he must have been more nervous than he thought. Closing the gate behind him, he noticed

that the latch on the post was new and had been screwed in with
oversize screws about as far up the gate as was possible. It was an
awkward-looking job. He wondered why the farmer had done it that
way, as everything else around here looked so neat and methodical.
He would want to remember that detail when he came back, especially if the night was dark or he had trouble identifying this particular field under pressure.

Finding the suitcase so far down the hedge had rattled him. He
began to doubt himself. How could he have gotten a detail like that
wrong? Was he really mentally cut out for this kind of work?

He strapped the suitcase to the parcel frame over the back wheel
and cycled back to town. There was no one behind the desk when
he came in.

Annika was walking back and forth in the middle of the room, one
hand on her hip and one hand on her mouth. She turned to face
him, and for a fraction of a moment, he was mesmerized by her. She
was slender and striking, energetic, but faintly vulnerable. Her soft
auburn hair and delicate features contrasted sharply with the fierce
blue of her eyes. Rory was enthralled by her and turned away as soon
as he realized he was staring at her.

As if in response, Annika took a step backward. Rory sensed the
move was deliberate. It embarrassed him and he felt oafish. But she
looked relieved he was back. "Thank God. I was worried you'd been
caught. I didn't think you'd be so long."

"I'm sorry. No, I'm safe. I wanted to wait until it was good and dark
before I went looking, and then I had trouble finding it. It gave me a
hell of a scare. This thing is soaked as well. I hope it works. It looks
as if the rain and the dew have got to it." He deliberately didn't look
at Annika as he spoke. He threw the wet suitcase over the arm of one
of the chairs and unhooked the soggy leather belts fastening it.

"It looks dry enough inside."

Seconds later he had a wire antenna dangling from the window
with the headset on and the telegraph keypad set up. He hand-

cranked the battery charger for several minutes and then from his billfold pulled out a one-page handwritten letter. On a separate sheet of paper, he scribbled down a sentence from the letter and pencilled in the alphabet beneath the sentence. Then he began tapping. He stopped and listened. His face looked worried. Again he repeated the sequence, deliberately keying each letter as if the clarity of his Morse code would influence the reception at the other end. He listened, broke into a wide grin, then started scribbling. Again he tapped out a brief message and listened. He tapped out a closing sentence and exhaled loudly.

"Thank God! It works. They're listening."

"What did you tell them?"

"Nothing much. I identified myself. Said I had problems setting up, but I was in location, ready to begin my task, and would get back to them soon at the same time. They monitor the radio every night between seven and two in the morning. Annika, we're in business."

Annika didn't say anything; she simply smiled.

"I think I'd like a drink," Rory said. "This calls for a celebration."

"You deserve one. I'll go downstairs. What'll it be?

"Brandy."

"I could use one too. You know, for the first time it feels like we're actually doing something."

While Annika was downstairs Rory repacked the suitcase. They had to have better batteries than the heavy steel-and-lead ones attached to this set. He made a mental note that in the future when they sent agents into mainland Europe they needed radios smaller and lighter than this ridiculously cumbersome, experimental set that he had been issued. The radio wasn't the only problem. There was still the ungainly Webley revolver. Neither was of much value to a spy.

There were probably dozens of other lessons to be learned from his foray into Holland. Soon he'd have to sit down and think them through before he forgot them. The more he thought about it, the more convinced he was that he could do a lot to make future agents more effective—not just in the areas of equipment and techniques, but also with things that he still needed time to think through fully, such as understanding the psychology of an agent at different stages of the operation—when the low points hit, how to keep going, and what signs to watch for when you felt isolated and hopeless.

Of course he was kidding himself. His mind wasn't really on the job. He was obsessed with Annika. He wasn't really thinking about much of anything else, not radio batteries or revolvers or espionage psychology; none of it engaged his mind for more than a few fleeting seconds and this bothered him. This was not the time to become obsessed by having some kind of juvenile crush on this woman. Puppy love under these circumstances would probably be fatal. He yanked forcefully at the leather straps on the suitcase.

22

ANNIKA RETURNED WITH two balloon glasses of brandy and they sat in the armchairs looking at the dried flowers. Rory raised his glass. "Here's to a successful mission and a successful partnership, Mrs. Becker." Then he added in a lower voice, "I only wish it was in happier circumstances." He paused. "We'll hit them so it hurts, Annika. They won't get away with what they've done."

Annika lifted her glass. She didn't look at him and spoke in a voice devoid of emotion. "I'll drink to that."

They were silent for what seemed a long time, both intensely conscious of the other, both aware of the extraordinarily intimate circumstances forced upon them. Annika was the first to speak. "It's funny how a few days ago we were total strangers; and now, even though we don't really know one another, we're forced to trust and depend on each other completely."

"I'm grateful you agreed to help me. With Colonel Van Meekeren gone, I'd no idea what I was going to do. It was an incredible stroke of luck that I found you."

"I'm the one who should be thankful. You saved me from the Gestapo."

"Lucky timing." Rory stopped and focused on the fireplace. He wished there were a flame there instead of dried flowers. The conversation would have been easier if there were a fire to watch. The dance and glimmer of firelight would have made perfect punctuation, the flickering of the flames filling in the gaps when words faltered.

"You've had no opportunity to talk at all about your husband. I know when my wife died I should have talked to someone. I didn't for a long time and I think I made it worse for myself."

Annika shifted in her chair and curled her legs up under her. "I didn't know you had a wife, or that she'd died. When was that?"

"It seems like a long time ago now, but it was just last April. We were in Winnipeg. She'd been sick for a little while. I knew it was coming, but it all happened quickly at the end."

"Was that why you joined the war effort again?"

Rory didn't say anything but looked over at her.

"I'm sorry," Annika said. "I just assumed that your hand and your eye were the result of a wound from the last war."

"You're right on both counts. I was wounded in the last war. And yes, when my wife died I joined up when I was asked. I probably wouldn't have gone if they hadn't asked me. I suppose once she died I needed a sense of purpose. We had no children. I had to do something for the future." He swirled the brandy in his glass. "It worked out well for me. I needed a cause, and luckily this was one I believed in. I often wonder where it's all going to end. What about you?"

Annika tilted her head to one side and sighed. "It's all been so fast. Once Saul was arrested, I almost went mad with worry. I wasn't thinking clearly, but from the outset I think I knew he was dead. I just couldn't bring myself to admit it. Even now, it only seems half-real that he's gone. I suppose I should have tried harder to convince him to leave. He could be very obstinate, you know. He was a good man; but once the Nazis took over... In retrospect, I should have known they'd take him. Saul was stubborn and uncompromising and some kind of a collision was inevitable—but we were all naïve. I should have been more insistent about leaving. I was as much at fault."

Annika looked down at the floor for a moment. "We thought being Dutch we'd escape this. People tried to tell us. We had some other friends who got away. We should have gone with them. What were we thinking?" She shook her head slowly from side to side.

"Now Saul is dead, and I've lost everything. You know, before all this happened I thought my life was dull, that things hadn't worked out for us. It's so hard to believe. It's all happened so fast. I never thought of it before, but sometimes life is best when it's dull and predictable."

Neither of them spoke for a while. The air was charged like an electrical storm building on a mountain. They could both feel it. Like a barometer dropping, they could sense the mood shifting from intimate and mellow to a pleasurable and restrained intensity. Annika reached over and for a second touched the back of his hand. She smiled. "I'm very sorry. I know this may be awkward for you, but I can't think of a nicer person to be with in this predicament. If I have to be grateful for anything, I'm grateful for that." She put her drink down and frowned. "I suppose that sounds disloyal of me."

"No. It's not." Rory stared at his brandy as if he was struggling with what he was about to say. "I know what you're saying. I feel the same way. The only difference between you and me is that I've had more time to come to grips with all this. Having time to heal makes a big difference."

"What's the saying ... ? 'Time heals what reason cannot'," Annika said pensively.

"Seneca. I had a teacher in high school, a priest, a strange old bird. He made us translate something from Seneca every week. Every test, there was always a translation question from Seneca."

"You have a classical education?"

"Yes. Some people have told me I wasted it. I went into the army after university, and after the war I joined the police. I never understood why some people believe certain professions are unsuited to a liberal education."

"You like being a policeman?"

"I did. I liked being around different kinds of people. I liked the drama, I liked the fact that it was something useful; and I suppose I liked that I spent a lot of time in the North. I loved being in the northern woods. What about you? What did you do?"

"I was a musician and a lecturer. It's funny to say it in the past tense, but I play the violin and I teach music and I lecture on symphonic composition. Do you have any hobbies?"

"A couple, I suppose. I read a lot of ancient history. I'm a bit of a classicist, as you call it, and I ... I paint, or I used to paint. I haven't done any painting since my wife got sick."

"What do you paint?"

"Landscapes and portraits mostly. For some reason, I could never do hands very well. I never understood it. I've often wondered if it was some sort of psychological block. I can do faces reasonably well, though. Maybe when the war's over I can try hands again." They both laughed.

"What medium do you like to paint with the most?"

"Oils—mostly bright colours. I don't think I could paint in pastels or water colours if I tried. It's not in me."

"I'd like to see your paintings someday."

"There are a lot of them sitting in an attic in Winnipeg. I'd like to hear your music, maybe when we get to England. I can paint again and you can play for me. What else do you do?"

Annika smiled and shrugged. "Oh, that's about it. Music's my hobby and my work. I really do want to see your paintings some day. You know, I think it's time I went to bed. She put her glass down and touched his hand again. "And I think it's best that you follow me only when you're sure I'm sleeping."

Rory looked wistfully at his drink and thought the better of making a smart comment. Instead, he said, "Like with so many other things, you're right. Good night, Annika."

Annika got up and left him. Rory forced himself not to look at her when she walked by. He remained seated, trying to think through his situation, but it all seemed an incoherent muddle at this stage.

It was almost an hour later before he could be sure her rhythmic breathing meant she was asleep. Carefully he lay down, fully dressed, on the bed beside her, and later in the night, when it was cold, he slipped under the covers. Without waking, she rolled into him.

* * *

"YES PLEASE, SIR. Please open your baggage for me. Thank you."
Dieter Schmidt stood nearly half a head taller than all those around
him. His police forage cap and his eagle eyes stood out above the
small crush of people in line at the train station. Beside him were
two helmeted soldiers and a uniformed Dutch Nazi. The people in
line were frightened. Passengers seemed to shrink away from them
as they shuffled forward, as if those travellers with their suitcases and
parcels had to make their way through a defile where they might be
infected with the plague.

Schmidt was directing a hasty checkpoint at the Amsterdam Central Train Station. The two soldiers with him were from the Amsterdam garrison, and the new special Dutch constable was a local man
who had been a member of the Dutch Nazi Party. They all seemed to
be enjoying their task, except for Dieter Schmidt. Schmidt certainly
didn't let on that he wasn't completely satisfied in his work. He had
a job to do and he did it to the best of his ability. That's how he had
been raised and trained and that was how he behaved. As for the soldiers, checkpoint duty was more interesting than riding about all day
in the back of a truck or standing around for hours at a time as part
of a roadblock. This morning, they were enjoying the startled reactions of the travellers, not to mention having the opportunity to look
inside people's cases. It was amazing: people carried the strangest
things in their luggage. Schmidt didn't care what people carried. He
didn't like the idea of rooting through people's private possessions.
It just didn't feel right. But if that's what he was ordered to do, he
would do it thoroughly.

"What do you have there? Open your bag fully, madam. What is
that you are bringing with you? Bread loaves? Why are you carrying
bread in your suitcase?"

He didn't wait for an answer from an elderly farm lady in a scarf.
"You, Gefreiter, stick your bayonet into that bread. Go ahead, check
it."

The young soldier beside Schmidt pulled his bayonet from his
belt and pierced the old woman's bread lengthwise, leaving an oily

streak on the soft brown crust. "Okay, move along now, keep moving. Thank you." The woman howled as she saw her bread being ruined. Schmidt waved her on and the Dutchman translated. "We are sorry to inconvenience you, madam, but we have our orders to check everyone and everything that comes off these trains. Now, show me your identification. No? No identification, please wait over there, madam." One of the soldiers clamped on to the woman's arm and escorted her to a cordoned area where a dozen Dutch citizens stood forlornly beside a truck awaiting further interrogation and confirmation of their identity.

Schmidt was pleased that he had been reassigned. He'd never really liked Oberstleutnant Neumann, and the longer he'd worked with him the more he came to detest him. He had worked with many senior officers in the past, but they had all treated him with a degree of friendliness and respect. Neumann was different. With Neumann, you had to be careful around him, even when he was pleasant. He was sneaky and forever ending all his conversations with an abrupt order, as if he had a need to reinforce the fact that he was the one in charge. And never mind about his Dutch girlfriend. Schmidt was a policeman, not—what was the phrase Neumann had used before— "a Hamburg pimp." Being reassigned to general police work was a much more honest kind of employment. Last night he wrote his wife to tell her how pleased he was that he was relocated. Not that he ever dared complain about his old job. If the censor caught that, he could be in real trouble. This job was much better. He worked for a decent supervisor, and now, just maybe, he might get a furlough and have a chance to get home to see his family. Who knew, maybe even before Christmas.

As the last of the train's occupants cleared the checkpoint, Rottenführer Dieter Schmidt pulled a rope and closed the access to Track 4. Turning to the Dutchman and the remaining soldier, he said, "I'll be back here in one hour. You are to remain here with at least two of you guarding this platform. One of you can take a break. When the second soldier returns, you can spell one another off, but there must be two of you on duty at all times."

"But Rottenführer Schmidt," protested the younger of the two soldiers, "the train is empty now. Why do we have to guard an empty platform? Why don't we come back when the next train leaves?"

Schmidt looked frustrated but he spoke patiently. "You don't know the train is empty, you only know that those who got off are all through your checkpoint. People could be hiding and waiting for you to go away. No, we have been ordered to guard this checkpoint, we will guard this checkpoint at all hours."

Schmidt turned and walked away. He needed some breakfast. He'd be back early just to make sure those men obeyed his orders. Maybe in addition to some breakfast he could find some postcards and souvenirs to mail to his wife and his daughters. His children would like that. He looked at his watch. He had time.

* * *

WHEN RORY AWOKE, Annika was already up and dressed. At the best of times, he was never very alert in his first few minutes of rising. Today was no exception. He sat up, looked about him groggily, stretched, and lay back. Annika scolded him from the bathroom. "Come on, get up. We should get downstairs and have breakfast before we get the nine o'clock train for Amsterdam. It's included in the price for the room."

When he arrived downstairs after shaving and dressing, Annika was sitting at the same table they had shared the night before. She looked up from reading a Dutch newspaper. "There's not much in it, I'm afraid. Paper is getting scarce because of the naval blockade of the continental ports and the Nazis decide what news is going to be in our papers anyway. I wouldn't be surprised if we saw our newspapers disappear soon."

"I'm sure you're right."

Rory said little during breakfast while Annika studied almost every word of the paper's four pages. She tossed the paper aside with a flourish. "There's nothing in here: a few ads, municipal events, and German war news. For what it's worth, it appears that the Germans are getting ready for a huge air campaign against the British and they've started sinking merchant ships with their U-boats. Of course, they say they've inflicted heavy losses in both the air and the sea."

"I suppose they would say that. What's happening in France?'"

"Nothing good. Marshall Petain has signed a peace treaty with the Germans and broken off relations with Britain. The Germans are consolidating their occupation of the northern half of France. Hitler has been to Paris and the Nazis had a massive parade."

"We should keep tabs on that part of the world, because if for some reason we can't link up with our plane, we may have to get out of here via France and Spain."

"Do you think there'll be a problem?'"

"I don't expect one, but I like to have a second plan up my sleeve if something ever goes wrong."

They finished breakfast in silence, paid for their room, and walked together to the train station. When they were in public, Annika briefly attempted to link her arm in Rory's, but the radio was heavy and it was awkward for him to carry it and at the same time appear composed. Annika cheerfully took the lighter suitcase from him, and except for this perfunctory display of affection, they were both focused on appearing to be a travelling seed salesman and his wife.

The train rolled into the Hauwoud station at precisely nine. Rory thought that whatever else may have happened to the Dutch, they had obviously managed to keep their trains running punctually. The conductor waved them on to the second coach, explaining in rapid Dutch that there was no room in the first car. They followed a half-dozen others into the second coach, only to find that they had to share it with twenty other people. Rory and Annika had to sit opposite each other. There was no sign of police or German soldiers. Several children chattered animatedly, while much more serious-looking groups of businessmen and country women who were going into town for their shopping stared out the windows. All the adults seemed focused on their own thoughts. It was obviously a busy run. At least, Rory thought, there was a measure of safety in the number of other travellers on the train this morning. He kept the radio by his legs. The suitcase was still damp from its sojourn in the hedge and he could smell the wet leather.

When the train pulled into Amsterdam's Central Station the children rushed for the door. Rory indicated to Annika with a flick of his eyes that they should follow them. She smiled reassuringly at him and stepped into the aisle. She had to wait for a few moments at the door for the children to get off, but when she reached the bottom stair of the carriage she stepped back in horror. "Martin! There's a police checkpoint at the end of the platform!"

Rory was being jostled from behind by anxious children and adults. He stepped down and took a quick glance at the group of soldiers ahead of them. He could see the tall German policeman standing between a pair of soldiers and a Dutch police auxiliary. They were busy rifling through the luggage of the travellers on the first car. The line ahead of them grew worried and restless. People started shuffling and whispering to one another.

"Martin, what shall we do?" Annika's voice was tense and she looked around searching for a place to run. At the other end of the train, a soldier was standing on the concrete quay with his rifle slung over his shoulder.

"Stick close to me. Speak only in German. Let's go!" Rory stepped off the train and moved briskly around the queue of nervous Dutch travellers. He headed straight towards the checkpoint, making eye contact with Dieter Schmidt. He raised his hand as if beckoning a taxi. "Rottenführer, Rottenführer!" he shouted in a loud, angry voice. Turning to Annika, he commanded, "Follow me!" He snapped his fingers impatiently and raised his suitcase. "Rottenführer, I'm here and I have the radio you're searching for." He and Annika pushed to the front of the line.

Dieter Schmidt looked down at this total stranger in the fedora and dark suit holding up a heavy piece of luggage.

"Why have you let these people in front of us and why is your car not ready and standing by for us? What the hell's going on?" His tone was livid. Dieter Schmidt looked confused.

"I'm Obersturmbannführer Büchner from Counter Intelligence. I was told up the line that the message had been passed. Now, don't gawk at me like a fool. I have the radio. Where's your car? We have to get this to the counter intelligence cell at headquarters now. We need to broadcast to England using this before ten-thirty. Don't you be the one that makes us miss our timings."

Dieter Schmidt's jaw dropped. He had heard nothing about having to meet a senior SS officer. Rory stepped closer to him and whispered, "And don't look like such an ass, especially when you are in front of army troops. Get your car!"

"Yes, Obersturmbannführer, at once. Please follow me." Schmidt turned to the soldiers. "Do as you've been told. I will be back in twenty minutes."

Rory snapped at him. "Come on, quickly! We caught them red-handed with their codes and we have to send a message before the code expires."

Dieter Schmidt broke into a jog. "The car's parked, just here by the curb, Obersturmbannführer."

There was a black unmarked Audi sedan parked beside a German army truck. Beside it was a motorcycle and sidecar with two helmeted soldiers lounging and smoking cigarettes in the morning sunshine. They would have been the detail that provided security for the vehicles and any prisoners the checkpoint might catch. Rory looked at them disdainfully. The two soldiers stood up and threw away their unfinished cigarettes. They looked anxious as the trio approached.

Schmidt was breathless. "Salute! He's an Obersturmbannführer!"

They crashed to attention as Dieter jumped in the car and started the engine. Rory turned to Annika. "Get in the front." Rory climbed in the back with the suitcase across his lap and shouted at Dieter Schmidt, "To police headquarters as fast as you can! Now, go!" The two soldiers in the sidecar looked nervous and jumped on the motorcycle to provide the Obersturmbannführer security. As they were kicking the motorcycle into life, Rory rolled down the window and shouted, "Stay here, you fools. Secure the truck!" They stopped and watched as the Audi lurched away from the curb.

"Hurry, Rottenführer, God damn it! Can't you drive?"

"Yes sir, we'll be there in five minutes. I'm going as fast as we can."

Schmidt loved the adrenalin rush of fast driving. He pulled away from the station and drove like a madman, weaving in and out of traffic and leaning on the horn. "I'm sorry, sir, but this car does not have a siren!" At Spuistraat, he cut across the traffic and cornered onto Heerenstraat, screeching the tires and careening into a red metal mail box, sending it rolling down the sidewalk. Schmidt was grinning from ear to ear. Seconds later they crossed the bridge over the canal and passed into a residential area. The side streets were lined with four-storey houses and maple trees. Rory shouted, "Stop, stop! Turn here, now. Turn and stop."

"No, sir, we go straight."

"I said turn here and stop! Quickly!"

Dieter Schmidt shrugged his massive shoulders and spun the car around into the road beside the Kings Canal. He smashed down on the brakes, bringing the car to a violent stop and throwing Annika up against the windscreen. With the car at a complete stop, Dieter Schmidt twisted about to protest, and as he turned Rory rapidly squeezed off two rounds through his forehead. The noise in the car was ear splitting. Annika screamed in horror. Schmidt's lifeless body was thrown back against the car door and the steering wheel. His dead foot slipped off the clutch and the car rammed into the canal's guard rail. Schmidt's elbow landed on the horn which started to blare. Rory reached over and tugged him backwards. "Annika, follow me."

He wrenched open the back door, hauled the suitcase out, and pulled Annika's door open. She was staring aghast at Schmidt's still body, eyes staring sightlessly at the car roof.

"Come on. Come on."

She sprang to life and jumped out, dragging the smaller suitcase with her.

"Forget that. Let's go!"

The two of them scrambled down the side street and disappeared around the corner heading away from the canal. A minute later a handful of curious bystanders surrounded the car and peered through the Audi's windows. Nobody quite knew what to make of it. There was a small teddy bear by the gear shift. A clutch of postcards and a photograph stuck in the sun visor dripped with blood and brains. One of the crowd, a woman who a second before had simply been morbidly curious, realized what had happened. She saw the uniform and screamed out that the dead driver was a German policeman. In seconds the street was deserted.

* * *

"WHAT DO YOU MEAN, Rottenführer Schmidt's dead? I saw him just last night." The voice at the other end of the telephone line was patiently trying to explain to a not very attentive Oberstleutnant Neumann that his driver had been shot a short time ago.

"He's not my driver any more, but no matter. A German police officer has been shot, is that what you are saying? By whom? Where? When did this happen?" The voice at the end of the telephone started to recite the details again. When he was finished, Neumann spoke quietly. "Have a platoon of our motorized infantry mobile reserve made ready. I want them waiting here with an extra three trucks at police headquarters in five minutes. Get me a car in the main courtyard and send Hauptmann Ackerman here immediately." He put down the phone. Rottenführer Schmidt was a very unlucky man, but more importantly, this was the first violent sign of resistance here in Amsterdam.

Reinhold Neumann had been expecting something like this for some time now. He expected violent resistance sooner or later, and he had already made up his mind how he would deal with it. Hauptmann Ackerman showed up at the doorway.

"Sir, you sent for me?"

"Yes. One of our policemen has been found dead in his car downtown. I don't know the details. I'm going to go down personally to see what happened. I have ordered the army's mobile reserve to assemble immediately and I will take them with me. I expect the reserve will be back here within the hour. They will have rounded up seventy Dutch adult males and they will bring them here with them. Take twenty into the back courtyard and shoot them immediately. The remaining fifty are to be sent to Germany to labour camps. Release the names and the reason for this to the Dutch newspapers before six tonight."

Neumann pursed his lips. "You know what to do. I want my orders carried out as soon as possible." Neumann looked at Ackerman and raised his eyebrows. "You understand?"

Hauptmann Ackerman's mouth went dry. "Yes, Herr Oberstleutnant."

"Good. I'll be back in an hour. Prepare an incident report for my signature. I want it sent out only after all the necessary punitive actions have been taken. I want that report wired to SS and police headquarters in The Hague before they hear about this from anyone else. So don't waste any time."

When Ackerman left, Neumann picked up his leather pocket notebook. He made a quick phone call. "Yes, Oberstleutnant Neumann here. Advise Mrs. Laurina Ordelmans that she has been given a new job. She currently works as a bartender in the officer's mess. Tell her she will report later this afternoon to the police secretarial pool. Tell her to report to me first at—" He looked at his calendar. "At 13:15 sharp."

He hung up the phone. From outside, he could hear the roar of powerful diesel engines and the swish of tires on fine gravel. A platoon of infantry soldiers from the standby reserve were hanging on to the side skirts of their Opel trucks as the column sped into the courtyard.

Neumann stepped out of the back of his car and casually returned the salute of the soldier standing guard over the scene where Schmidt had been killed. He walked up and peered in the passenger side-window. Rottenführer Schmidt's body lay untouched. Neumann could clearly see the bullet entrance wounds: one slightly left

and above the bridge of the nose and the other above the left eye.
Schmidt's face had turned an unnatural grey colour and there was
a streak of blood drying on the driver's window. Flies were buzzing
about Schmidt's nose. Neumann turned away and made a face.

An SS Scharführer came up and saluted him. Around his throat
he was wearing the chain plates of the Feldgendarmerie. "We got
here immediately, Herr Oberstleutnant. We have touched nothing,
but the driver would appear to have been shot from within his vehicle and from the back seat. The only bullet holes in the car are exit
holes on the driver's side."

Neumann merely nodded and said, "Thank you." The sight of
Schmidt lying dead with flies buzzing around him made him queasy.
For a second he had a pang of remorse. He hadn't treated Schmidt
very well. No matter. That was life. There were more important
things to attend to. He turned to the Scharführer. "He used to be my
driver. We won't allow this. Bring the infantry platoon leader here."

The Scharführer saluted and said, "I'm sorry to hear that, sir." He
doubled back to the line of waiting trucks.

Seconds later, a young Leutnant from the army and the SS Scharführer stood before Neumann. "Take your platoon and round up
seventy men between the ages of sixteen and sixty," Neumann
ordered. "I don't care where you get them, but men from around
here would be better. Bring them back to the police barracks and
report to Hauptmann Ackerman. I'll meet you there."

Driving back to the police barracks, Neumann looked out the
window of his car. It all looked so normal: people on the streets going
about their business—shopping, running a thousand errands, moth-
ers pushing prams, people fussing over the flowers in their window
boxes. He stopped himself from becoming maudlin. Schmidt was
dead. It was his duty to see that he didn't die in vain. He would pacify
this town and it would be peaceful on his terms. He massaged the
bridge of his nose in a pinching motion. He was tired. He decided
to cancel his meeting with Laurina. She could come tomorrow. After
seeing the flies buzzing over Schmidt's corpse, he didn't feel romantic.

23

"THE QUESTION NOW, Annika, is can we stay here?"

They had been back in the apartment for just a few minutes. Rory paced the floor and Annika sat on the bed. She had her hands clenched tightly on her lap, and was staring at the floor. Rory looked at her with sympathy.

"I know what you're going through and I think I know how you feel." Rory put his hands in his pockets and shrugged. He lowered his voice. "I did what I thought was right at the time. Now is not the time to worry about whether or not this was morally correct. We've got to leave matters of conscience for later. Right now, we're still dealing with our own survival. If they had caught us, think about what would be happening to you and me. It would have been extremely unpleasant and painful; and we'd both be dead in a matter of hours."

"I know that," Annika said sharply. She turned her head away. In a softer voice she said, "I'm sorry. I just can't help but think what's going to happen now. Not to us, but to the others the Germans will take revenge on."

"I thought that one through before I came over here. Was killing that German policeman worth the deaths of however many reprisals they may take? Would your life and my life be worth it? Is what we're doing worth it? I had to think those questions through before I accepted this job." He looked at her expectantly. "The answer to the first two questions is 'no.' We are insignificant. The answer to the third question is yes. I believe that what we are doing is not only worth it, but also essential. The Nazis won't be defeated by us being nice or trying to reason with them."

"I never expected this kind of thing. I don't know what I expected."

"Getting your country back is going to mean that a lot of innocent people are going to die. Our problem is keeping those deaths to a minimum. If we were killed this morning, other people would have to come back here and replace us, and they'd probably have to go through all this again, or something a lot like it. It's our duty to stay alive, to keep operating. We have to have a resistance movement if we're going to destroy the Nazis."

"I don't know if I'm up to this sort of thing. All I feel now is a total sense of revulsion."

Rory walked over to her and put his hand on her shoulder. "You're allowed that. It shows you're human."

A few seconds later Annika said, "I noticed in the car that he had a little stuffed bear. He was probably going to send that to his child somewhere." She willed herself not to cry.

"I didn't see that detail, but even if I had, I would have shot him anyway." Rory stopped. He didn't want to sound tactless or cavalier about killing another man. "I'm sorry, Annika. I know, I shot and killed an unsuspecting Nazi policeman this morning. I didn't like it, but if I had to, I'd do it again. Unless we acted promptly and violently, he was driving us to certain death. When I saw him in the train station, I knew in an instant he had us boxed in. It was him or us. And frankly, I'm glad he's dead now and we're alive." Rory had to keep his voice from rising. In a whispered voice he said, "Besides, it was probably someone like him who killed Saul. It will be someone like him who will shoot innocent Dutchmen in reprisal."

In response, Annika drew in a long shuddering breath. She said nothing.

Rory walked away and began to pace again. "The real problem is the one you've already mentioned: the innocent people who we know are going to be killed in reprisal. Could we have done something about them? We didn't know the train stations were being watched. They weren't yesterday; they weren't this morning when we got on. We did what we thought was best. There was no other way to get the radio."

Annika stood up and walked to the window. The late morning sunlight on the street had shortened the shadows. Everything looked brighter and harsher. She remembered reading in English that photographers called these harsher conditions "flat light." She thought it was a good metaphor for her life—harsh, unappealing, and exposed. She turned. "You're right. What you are saying is right. But I still find it hard and I don't like it."

Annika put her hand to her mouth and then snapped her fingers. "Wait! Maybe we can still do something now. What if—what if we let it be known that the Dutch didn't do it, that you and I were British? The Germans might not kill Dutchmen if an Englishman killed one of their policemen."

Rory said nothing but tilted his head sideways as if weighing her words. "Perhaps you're on to something." He looked cautious. "They might still do reprisals, but it's worth a chance. It doesn't make their problem any easier." He didn't say it, but the thought crossed his mind that it would also make the next step of their job a lot easier. Persuading people to join a resistance group was going to be a lot harder if the Germans had just slaughtered large numbers of innocent Dutchmen for resistance activities.

Rory sat down on one of the kitchen chairs and began drumming his fingers. "It's worth a try." He stood up and started pacing again. "We can't go out together for a while. Our descriptions are going to be all over Holland soon. We should phone the police and the newspapers from a pay telephone and tell them, but we have to do it now. Then we have to move. Too many people have seen us here, and if your plan doesn't work and there are reprisal killings, there's a good chance we may be reported."

"Where do we go now?"

"I don't know. I don't know the city well enough. I'm hoping you can think of somewhere. Someplace we could use as an operating base. If you find one, you'll have to make the arrangements; and once you've got a place, we should go there separately. We can't be seen together for a while. It'll be much too dangerous."

"I think I may know of a place." Annika rubbed her forehead. "Let me think about it. We have a few hours." She stood up and grabbed her purse. "There's a café several blocks from here. It has a pay telephone outside it. I'm going there now. When I get back, we can talk about what we do next."

* * *

As a rule, Neumann didn't go to interrogations. They were frequently upsetting, and that took his mind off the larger task of cracking a case. He would make an exception if there was some vital piece of information that he needed and no one else was likely to extract it, but confessions, denunciations, and the messy pre-trial work he usually left to others. Today was different, though, and this afternoon he was getting restless. He was considering going downstairs to see for himself how things were going when one of the shift supervisors came crashing to attention at his door.

"I have some information for you, Herr Oberstleutnant."

"Good. Call in Hauptmann Ackerman. I want him to hear this as well." A few moments later Ackerman appeared at his office door, trim and efficient looking, notebook and pen in hand.

"Now, what is it you have to tell us, Untersturmführer?"

"Sir, we have talked to all the guards who were on duty this morning, and we rounded up several of the passengers from the railway car as well as the train's conductor. We've traced back the murderers' movements to last night. It was definitely a man and a woman. The man was tall, in his early to mid-forties, medium build. There are several reports that he has something wrong with one of his eyes; and he may or may not be missing some fingers. He speaks excellent German. The woman was in her thirties, auburn hair, clear complexion, quite pretty, small build. The people from the train said she spoke perfect Dutch. The man was claiming to have captured a radio and ordered Rottenführer Schmidt to take him to police head-quarters."

Reinhold Neumann sat back and slowly tapped a pencil against his closed lips. "Go on, there must be more. So far, so good. If he looks anything like what you've described, we'll eventually catch him. That's good news."

"We've traced him back to a hotel at Hauwoud. He and the woman went there last night. She told the desk clerk that he was a seed sales-man and might be out late visiting farmers. No one was sure, but he might have gone somewhere on a bicycle last night. This morn-ing they both returned to Amsterdam on the morning train. Nobody could think of anything unusual about them as a couple. Very quiet, very normal."

Neumann smiled at the Untersturmführer. He liked this man. He always had a cheerful way about him. He always brought good news. He was a likeable sort, always ready with a quick answer, and he seemed to be the kind of man who got things done without a lot of fuss. "Is that it, Untersturmführer?

"No, sir. I don't know how much I believe in this last piece of infor-mation, but some hours ago we had a telephone call, which we could not trace, but a woman is claiming that the people who murdered Rottenführer Schmidt were British agents."

Neumann laughed and pushed himself away from the desk. He threw his pencil up in the air and caught it, and then swivelled back and forth in his chair. He grinned. "Yes, I don't doubt that's what they're saying. That's good. Someone is thinking. They're trying to prevent any reprisals. Well, I think that's too late, isn't it, Hauptmann Ackerman?

"Yes, sir, and as you directed, the message has gone to headquar-ters in The Hague. You should know that they phoned to say the Oberführer was pleased that you took such decisive and prompt action."

"Well, if Rottenführer Schmidt's death was to mean anything, it was that this sort of thing will not happen again. There will be no resistance in the Netherlands. Thank you, Untersturmführer. But you know, the question that remains unanswered in all this is why did this couple go to Hauwoud last night and then return to Amsterdam the very next day? From what I understand, Hauwoud's not the kind of place where you go to see the sights. Maybe his base is in Hauwoud. You know, I think he really was carrying a radio. Maybe he got it from someone in Hauwoud? Nobody looked inside his luggage, did they? And poor old Schmidt did exactly what he was told to do by someone claiming to be an Obersturmbannführer from counter-intelligence. My guess, in fact, is that this man probably is a British agent. We don't know who she is."

"She spoke very good Dutch, sir."

"She could be Dutch." Neumann wagged his pencil back and forth. "And she could be an Englishwoman who speaks good Dutch. Who knows? What's her connection to Hauwoud?" He tapped his pencil on his day book for emphasis. "But my first instinct was right. If you throw up enough checkpoints, you will eventually interrupt terrorists when they are moving from one point to another. It's like catching spawning fish when they swim upstream. This time we caught one, but he got away. He's dangerous, this one, and so we have to catch him again." He swivelled in his chair and looked out at the courtyard away from his small audience. "I suspect that he's trying to build a resistance cell—not that I have any inside information or clever powers of deduction. Only, we all know the British foolishly lost all their agents and contacts in the Netherlands not so long ago. They have to rebuild; they have to do it quickly; and this man with the funny eye and missing fingers is probably doing that while we speak. Now we have a description. We have to go out and capture this man.

"Put out a bulletin that describes these people, run it on all the radio stations and in the newspapers. In the meantime, we'll stop every male between thirty and fifty, and if there's anyone in this group with the slightest thing funny about his eyes, bring him in for further questioning. Oh, and Hauptmann, offer a reward. How much if we capture this one? Five hundred guilders? That should do it. Let's see if we get any more leads. Good work, Untersturmführer. That's all for now, gentlemen."

* * *

THE CRAWL SPACE under the rafters was a likely place to hide the suitcase, and with luck, it might not occur to the Germans that Rory would ever think of leaving the radio behind. Taking the suitcase and the radio meant he would have to carry it to wherever Annika chose as a safe place for them to move to—and that would almost certainly be risky. He'd be much too obvious lugging a suitcase across town. By now the Germans and Dutch police would be stopping any male on the street with a suitcase.

Rory was standing on a chair with his head and shoulders inside the crawl space above their apartment. He could probably put it over in the corner farthest from the ventilation slats—that way it wouldn't leave any tracks in the dust and it would be harder to see. He stooped down and pulled the attic cover closed.

Annika had been gone for three hours. Rory was beginning to wonder if she'd been picked up by the police while she was out. He should never have let her go. The police would have both their descriptions. Still, it made more sense for her to go out: there were a lot of women in Amsterdam who could answer to her description, but a lot fewer men who looked like he did. His eye gave him away every time. People often couldn't describe what it was about him. They would just say there was something odd about one of his eyes. In a picture, it looked normal, but in person, one eye didn't move. No doubt about it: he would have been spotted. He sat on the edge of the bed and waited.

Forty minutes later Rory turned on the apartment's big Blaupunkt radio. It was a massive thing, one of the early sets produced in the 1920s, that came in a large wooden case. What a status symbol they used to be. He fiddled with the dial, tuning it carefully until he finally got a station, but it was a serious-sounding male voice speaking in Dutch, which he couldn't understand. He turned it off. The radio wasn't a good idea: music might mask the sound of anyone approaching their apartment. He looked at his watch. Annika should have been back by now.

He went to his suitcase and took out the Webley and the two grenades. He put them all on the dining room table beneath a tea towel. He felt sick thinking about it. If Annika had been arrested, she'd certainly break under interrogation. Everybody did. And the Gestapo would have had no compunction about torturing her until she talked. They were good at that sort of thing. It wouldn't take them long, and that was no slight against Annika.

He didn't want to think about the possibility of Annika being picked up. He wondered if he would be worrying about her in the same way if she wasn't so beautiful and she hadn't totally mesmerized him. Then he started questioning himself again for letting her go out. He certainly couldn't have made the call to the police, nor could he find another safe place for them to move to. He looked at his watch. If she hadn't been arrested, how much time could they safely remain in this apartment? There was no way of knowing. Rory didn't want to stay here for more than a few more hours at most. Wanted bulletins would be circulating by now, and it would only be a matter of time before someone advised the police that a man and woman matching their description were seen going in and out of this apartment.

He stood up and went to the front window. From three feet back he looked out on the street. It was deserted. He stood further back. He could still see from here and it was less likely anyone could see him. He got one of the chairs from the dining set and placed it where he could view the approaches to the front of the house, and then waited.

Two hours went by. He looked at his watch and decided that if Annika hadn't returned by six he'd have to leave. He took the suitcase with the Morse transceiver and lugged it up through the attic cover. At 5:30, he put on his suit jacket and got his hat. The Webley sat on the table beside him. He looked down at it. It was the same ungainly weapon he'd used in the trenches. He'd killed at least one man at close range with one of these revolvers before he'd been wounded. It didn't seem that long ago.

And now, twenty years later, in a new war, he'd shot another man with the same sort of weapon. In the trenches, he'd shot an armed man who was trying to kill him. This morning, he shot a man driving a car, a man who had a teddy bear for his child. He didn't want to think about the morality of that. There would be time later for the whole range of bad dreams, imaginings, self-condemnations, and vindications. He knew in his guts he'd had no choice. What he did was justifiable. He'd think it through another time—when he had a clearer head and a better opportunity to concentrate. Now he had to think about survival. But it was hard to focus. He was angry at those responsible for making him do all this again. How had the world's leaders let things go so far off course after all the suffering and slaughter they'd endured in the Great War? Of course he knew the answers to all those questions. What was it Aristotle said? "We give up leisure in order that we may have leisure, just as we go to war in order that we may have peace." He'd thought about that quotation often enough over the years.

It wasn't the time to be philosophical, though. There were practical decisions to make. How long could he wait for Annika? He looked at his watch. She had to have run into some kind of trouble. She wouldn't knowingly stay away this long. He told himself again that he'd have to leave at six and that was only ten minutes away. He feared he'd let her go to her death. There was probably something else he should have done. He could have prevented this. He could have acted instead of her. He licked his lips. No, there really wasn't any option. He did the right thing.

He tidied the apartment, not that there was much to straighten up. He put fifteen guilders on the table to pay for the rent and pocketed the keys to the front door and the apartment. The landlady would have spares and someday soon he'd be back. It was six o'clock. There was no sign of Annika in the street. He had to assume that the worst had already happened. His feet were like lead. It was time to go. He got up and then sat down. He'd give her a few more minutes, and if she didn't come in the next hour he had the Webley.

* * *

NEUMANN ENJOYED THE FOOD the mess served here in Holland. Although nobody would say so, it was much better than what they'd been used to in Germany. And of course, what made things even better was that, as an SS Oberstleutnant in the police, he had much more status in the mess here in Amsterdam than he'd had in a regular police barracks in Germany. Ordinary meal times like this were a good example. If he chose to sit by himself, as he did this evening, he could think about things and not be forced into making the stupid chit-chat that passed for conversation amongst the rest of the officers. Fortunately, now people were even more wary of him. When you enjoyed making people anxious, you didn't mind sitting alone. After today, it was certainly evident that most of the other officers were wary of him. In the hallways and here in the mess, few of them would look him in the eye, although to be fair, this afternoon a handful of them were unusually cheery around him. It was intriguing the effect shooting a few prisoners had on people.

Tonight he sat alone, off to the side of the head table, indulging in a rare glass of wine with his meal. It was a Dutch chicken dish in a cream sauce and he could easily have had a second helping, but not tonight. He was already getting a little tight around the waistband in his uniform trousers, and lately, he knew he wasn't quite as sharp at the end of the day as he should be. He was working too hard. In addition to cutting back on rich foods, he should be getting more exercise. But how could someone of his rank do that here? He couldn't go for a walk. Some of the army officers here in the Amsterdam headquarters went out riding in the country, which in his view was an affected bit of snobbery. Neumann had grown up in a modern city in the twentieth century where equestrian sports were practised only by the wealthy bourgeoisie attempting to flaunt some sort of genteel association with the country.

He took another sip of his wine and looked about him. It was time to relax. There was no point in getting worked up about his upbringing and background. After all, today had been a good day. So why should he be upset? He'd got a "well done" from the Brigadeführer in The Hague, and that didn't go unnoticed by the army general here in Amsterdam who had been so miffed when he slipped out of his party. There was also the matter of his suggestion of making the entire population carry identification cards—and of course special badges for the Jews. That may not have been original, but it was almost certainly going to be implemented across the Netherlands; and once again, it earned him praise in the SS chain of command. He could also be proud of his new scheme of drastically increasing the number of searches and checkpoints. Hadn't they already identified a British agent in Amsterdam as a result? He knew there were people in both the army and the SS who'd made snide comments about him being too enthusiastic, but his keenness had paid off and it would be noticed higher up. Of course, it was too bad about Rottenführer Dieter Schmidt. Perhaps he should do something in his memory. What the hell, he'd drink a toast. He motioned for the mess waiter to refill his wine glass.

He sighed and pushed his plate away from him. It was too bad, but there was no denying it: he'd long ago identified Schmidt as a weak link. He should never have been allowed in the SS. Ah well, he was no longer a problem. In fact, looked at in the right way, Neumann felt it was probably a good thing. He raised his glass and sipped his wine, then let out a relaxed sigh. Yes, things had worked out well for him this week.

Only one thing puzzled him: the letter from Maida that came in this afternoon's post. Maida's letter came from nowhere. One day she was frosty and cruel, and the next she was conciliatory, optimistic, full of stories about the children, and asking when he was going to get a furlough. What was he to think? One thing was certain: her little episode of petulance had changed things. Before he came to

Holland, Maida had held the upper hand in their relationship. No question about that. Even a few days ago, he would have done anything for her. But her silence and her distance had worried at him for weeks—and then he met Laurina. He took a long sip of his wine. Not that he was in love with Laurina—far from it—but Laurina had shown him that, if he chose to, he could succeed with other women. This was the last time Maida would humiliate him. The party didn't approve of womanizers, but if you were discreet, people turned a blind eye. And as of tonight, there would be other women; of that he was certain.

* * *

IT WAS LONG PAST SIX. The shadows on the sidewalk outside were growing longer, and in the surrounding streets the background din of traffic noise had faded. Rory was still agonizing over whether he should stay or go when a door slammed and the sound of deliberate and steady footsteps reverberated in the stairwell. He stood, picked up the Webley, and hooking one of the grenades onto his belt, slid off to one side and crouched low so that he had a clear shot along the wall by the apartment door. The steps stopped outside and the door opened slowly. Rory levelled the Webley, taking up the first pressure on the trigger. Annika stepped into the room loaded down with bags and blankets. She kicked the door closed behind her.

Her face was drawn and troubled. She was wearing wire frame glasses, an old blue cleaning smock, and flat shoes; her hair was wrapped in a handkerchief, and in one hand she carried a large cloth shopping bag and in the other arm she cradled what appeared to be a baby in a light blue blanket.

Rory put the Webley down. "Thank God, it's you."

She looked at the grenade on his belt without expression and put her cloth shopping bag down on the table. Her face was drained and fatigued and her lip trembled.

Rory put the Webley down and grabbed her by the arms. "I was worried that they'd got you out on the street. What do you have there?"

"It's a doll. I went out and made the phone call, and while I was in the café, I could see that the police were patrolling the streets. In the time I was in the café I saw two people being stopped: one was a couple about our age, and the other was a man in his forties. We've stirred up a hornets' nest." She dropped her blanket and doll and pulled off her glasses. She stood in the centre of the room looking utterly drained. She massaged her eyes.

"I went straight to Nieuwendijk Street, to a rag and bone shop, and bought the doll and blanket to use as a decoy. I bought these old clothes and some for you as well, so we would look different. While I was in the market, I heard the news from one of the merchants there. The Germans shot twenty men this morning and shipped a further fifty off to a labour camp in Germany in reprisal for killing that driver. They just rounded them up off the streets downtown and put them on trucks. The bodies were left for the families to retrieve." She put her hand over her mouth.

"It's been announced on the radio and it's been in all the papers. Our descriptions are included. It's savage beyond comprehension. It's the only thing people are talking about out there. My God, Martin, we're living in a nightmare." She shuddered and was on the verge of tears. "I took so long, I couldn't help it. I never expected to be this long but I couldn't move openly. I didn't know if you'd still be here. You should have gone." She started to cry, huge silent tears rolling down her cheeks.

Rory drew her close and put his arms around her. "You've astonished me every moment I've known you. I didn't know if you'd been arrested or not, but I wasn't leaving with you still out there. I should have gone instead of you."

She nestled her head in his shoulder and shook her head. "No, we were right. You'll be too obvious. They have your description; mine's much more general. Before I left the market, I slipped behind one of the stalls and put this clothing on. With the baby blanket and glasses, I'm invisible—the police just walked past me. They stopped others.

"I walked to the Prinsengracht Canal and waited at one of the canal boats. There's a woman I knew, Wiesja—she lives there. I helped her years ago. She had a drinking problem and her husband left her. She had quite a past. It was very sad and very ugly. Anyway, she's been recovered for several years, and after she recovered, she took over running her brother's small canal barge. She lives on it. I've known her since we were in school and I helped her a bit during the bad times. She's given us the use of her houseboat to live on for as long as we want, she says. No questions asked. In the next day or so she's going to move out to the country to live with her mother, who is sick. She told her neighbours there would be a couple visiting from abroad and we'd probably stay for two weeks. Apparently they're good people and don't suspect anything about this morning. She told them we're German Jews hiding from the Nazis, and they're sympathetic." She fished in her purse and pulled out a key on a brass chain.

"That's wonderful," said Rory.

"That's not all." Annika sighed heavily. "She's given us her small boat as well. It has a little outboard engine. That's how she gets around the canals on routine business. Once I thought it was safe, I came here as far as I could using the outboard. I tied up by the Rozengracht bridge and walked the last few blocks. The police are out on all the main streets. When I came here, a policeman on one of the bridges into town even waved at me."

"Annika, you're brilliant."

"No. I'm lucky. When I was in the rag and bone market I remembered my friend Wiesja. The last time I saw her was about two months before the invasion. She was shopping there and we went for tea. I knew she'd help me. She's very kindly and completely trustworthy."

"Does she suspect that we had anything to do with this morning?"

"She didn't ask any questions, but she's very bright. So yes, I think so. When she saw me with the auburn hair she almost certainly put two and two together. She told me how terrible it was, but she hates the Germans. She was outraged by them attacking us in the first place and by what they did to Rotterdam. I told her that they killed Saul and they were looking for me as well. We both cried. She also knew Oscar and Nina Van Sittart, not well, but she had met them with me once years ago when she was getting better."

"Would she volunteer to join our movement?"

"I never thought of that, but I'd be almost certain she would if we asked her." The tone of Annika's voice changed abruptly. She was vacillating between being in control and a flood of emotions. "Martin, I'm so glad you were here when I got back. I couldn't walk through the town and I was frightened that you would have given up, thinking you had to go because I'd been captured."

Rory pulled her closer. "I thought you were captured." He put his head down and closed his eyes. "I'd made up my mind that if you weren't back by six, I'd have to accept that they'd caught you and leave. But when the time came, I couldn't go without you."

Annika said nothing. She didn't try to break away from his embrace. She put her head on his shoulder and they stood there in the middle of the room holding one another.

Rory finally stepped back. "We still can't stay here. I've hidden the radio in the attic. We'll keep the keys and come back some time to get it. It's too dangerous now. I'll wear the clothes you bought. Give me directions to the outboard, and I'll follow ten minutes after you and meet you at the boat."

Five minutes later, Annika had the blue blanket and the doll in her arms and started out the door. At the top of the stairs, she stopped without speaking and turned, put her hand on Rory's lapel, and kissed him on the cheek. "Please, don't be long."

24

LOOKING AT HIMSELF in the mirror, Rory was quite pleased with his new look. Annika had done well buying his clothes. The flat cap was a touch large, but the workman's jacket and cotton trousers fit well, and they were sufficiently worn to look authentic. He was satisfied that he could pass for a Dutch working man. Annika was proving to be more resourceful and capable than he could have imagined. Considering the strain she had been under for the last few weeks, buying old clothes and developing a simple disguise was clever work. Would he have been up to that kind of quick-witted action so soon after Ruth's death? He could only admire Annika's resilience. He bundled his suit, shirt, tie, fedora, and shaving kit into a neat ball and tied it into a pack. The fedora might be a bit crushed, but it was a good quality soft felt, and with luck it would rebound back into something presentable. Anyway, he didn't expect that he'd be walking around Amsterdam in his seed salesman clothes any more. That character was dead.

He took a last look up at the access panel to the attic when he turned out the light in the main room. There were no telltale dust or dirt streaks to indicate anyone had recently been ferreting around up there.

The outboard was moored six blocks away. Outside, Rory tucked the bundle of clothes under his arm and set off at a brisk pace through the commercial section. In the space of a few blocks, the city changed from a down-at-heel commercial district to one made up of the more sedate, tree-lined streets and narrow four- and five-storey houses owned by affluent merchants of Amsterdam's canal district. Both sections of the city were empty. Rory made a mental note that this time of the evening would probably be the best to return for his radio. The half-hour just after dusk was still early enough not to look conspicuous and few people were on the streets.

At the canal, as she had promised, Annika was sitting patiently in the stern of a small boat. From a distance, with her glasses and shapeless coat, she didn't look like the same woman. She gave a small wave and a relieved smile as he approached. The boat was moored between two old canal barges, with the bow bobbing six inches away from the canal's concrete wall. To steady himself, Rory grabbed a mooring line from one of the canal barges and did a quick two-step onto the boat, taking a seat in the bow. The boat rocked in the black water. Even though the water in the canal appeared still, the air smelled clean and fresh.

"You didn't have any problems?" Annika spoke in a whisper.

"No, not a soul out tonight but me. Shall we go?"

"Yes, but you and I have to change our positions. It won't look right if I'm sitting in the stern, running the outboard and holding a baby at the same time. I'll direct you where to go."

Rory saw the good sense in this and they set off with the engine purring, looking like a hard-working family heading home after a day of ferrying goods across town.

The boat was about fifteen feet long, constructed of wood, and had bench seats and stainless steel keyhole screws at regular intervals along the side for securing a large canvas tarpaulin that was stowed neatly forward in the bow. A shallow puddle of dark rainwater washed around in the stern section. Rory bent over and scooped at it with a tin bailing can as they made way. They travelled just slightly faster than a glide. Annika had warned him that it was against the law to have any kind of a wake.

They chugged along through a series of brick-lined canals, and within minutes, in the dim light, Rory lost his sense of direction. Annika seemed to know exactly where they were. They passed two other boats chugging off somewhere into the night. In both cases, the occupants of the oncoming boats waved enthusiastically. Rory noticed that people walking along the canals and on bridges also waved at them excitedly; in turn, they smiled and returned their greetings. He wondered about this. It all seemed a little forced. Perhaps for the residents of Amsterdam, who had been stunned by the violent rule of the Third Reich, the sight of people going about their business in canal boats must have been a reassuring and subconscious symbol of normalcy.

"Our barge is just up here, the third on the left." Annika pointed to a freshly painted blue-and-white canal boat. It was bigger than most, about sixty feet long, with a thirty-foot, single-storey cabin at the stern. Lights burned in the cabin's three portholes. Annika directed Rory to bring the outboard up so they could tie alongside. As they glided into position, a heavy-set woman with her hair tied in a bun emerged from the cabin. She didn't speak as she deftly lashed the bow and stern of the outboard to its parent vessel.

"We'll talk inside," Annika said as she handed over the blanket. The woman took it carefully and disappeared into the cabin.

Inside, Annika took off her glasses and rubbed her eyes. "Wiesja, this is Martin Becker, the man I told you about," she said in English.

Wiesja was a big, strong-looking woman. It was hard to tell her age. She looked Rory up and down. When she finished her appraisal, she smiled, showing a mouth dominated by a gold front tooth. Her English was almost unaccented. "Welcome to my home, Mr. Becker. Annika speaks highly of you. You two must be tired and hungry. You've had an eventful day and I've made some supper for you."

Rory glanced about the cabin. It had been recently painted and was spotless. There were blue-and-white curtains alongside the portholes. The furniture was tasteful and scaled to the room's size. Along one bulkhead was a table with a small vase of fresh-cut flowers and two chairs. The bulkhead was lined with a bookcase of four shelves, filled with volumes in Dutch and English. In a corner was a pair of red leather barrel chairs, and in between them, a small mahogany table with a miniature brass oil lamp. Along the bulkhead behind him, there was a sink, an icebox, and a stove. Through the passageway in the stern, Rory could make out a double berth covered in a blue-and-white bedspread. The place was functional, tidy, and stylish. Rory's first assessment of the cabin was that its owner probably had an organized mind and a simple sense of elegance. Something about the place was reassuring.

Annika flopped into one of the barrel chairs. "Wiesja, you have no idea how grateful I am to be here tonight."

Wiesja smiled. "You have no idea how grateful I am to be able to repay any kind of a favour to you, Annika. Now, let's eat."

Wiesja proceeded to serve a simple meal of beef stew accompanied by a fresh salad and cheese. The conversation at dinner was strained, as Wiesja steered away from any questions as to why Rory was here or what he was doing with Annika.

When they had finished eating, it was Annika who provided the answers. Laying down her knife and fork, she said directly, "Wiesja, Martin has been sent here to organize a resistance movement. We want you to work with us and establish a cell of your own." She looked over at Rory. "I didn't think there was any point in being coy. Wiesja knows me well enough to understand that we are up to something more than just being on the run from the Germans." Turning to Wiesja again she said, "Wiesja, you should know how Martin and I came to be here. Martin was following up with the families of men who had been arrested by the Gestapo. He was looking for someone to help him who wouldn't betray him to the Germans. His primary contact was arrested at the same time as Saul. When he came to my apartment, he realized I was in danger and he got me out minutes before the Gestapo arrived to take me. I've decided to work with him." She looked self-assured and glanced over at Rory as if he should confirm any omitted details.

Rory smiled. "I suppose I would have taken a bit longer to get around to asking you, Wiesja, but Annika's right." He shifted his weight and looked from Annika and back to Wiesja. "Wiesja, please

understand that we are at the very beginning of organizing any resistance at this stage. We've only begun to sort ourselves out. All I'm
looking to do just now is establish a cadre of trustworthy volunteers
from whom we can begin to develop a serious resistance movement
when the time is right."

Wiesja sat back. "I certainly want to see my country freed, Martin,
but what do you have in mind for me? What do you want me to do?"

"Initially, nothing. Now, I'm guessing, but from what I've seen in
the past few days, any kind of violent resistance without the imminent prospect of being liberated militarily is only going to result in
the deaths of a disproportionate number of Dutch citizens. That's
the Nazis' tactic for maintaining order and it's not going to change.
So, my guess is that your tasks would initially be limited to more passive things."

"What sort of things?"

"Well, I'm not entirely sure just now, but I would think things like
helping us organize here in Amsterdam, doing some reconnaissance,
keeping us advised of what German troops are based in Holland,
keeping the spirit of Dutch pride alive—perhaps some propaganda
tasks, passing information along for us to other cells, maybe even
helping key people escape from the Nazis."

"Do you think there's a chance there will be a guerrilla war here,
Martin?" Wiesja asked.

"Frankly, from what I've seen of your countryside and your cities, there isn't much scope for fighting a guerrilla war—and sporadic
resistance is, for now, out of the question. That may change over
time."

The table was silent.

"Wiesja, if you need some time to think this over, I'll understand."

"No, I'll help. I want to help my country, but I'm still not sure what
you see in me. Don't you want someone who has more influence?
I'm a barge woman."

"That's what makes you valuable. You'll be less likely to be suspected; and besides, you can move around the city without raising
suspicion. There will be tremendous advantages in that. And from

what I hear, you're courageous, intelligent, and reliable. That's what we want, not social status or influence. Influential people who are highly visible will make poor resistance leaders. They'll be too easily identified and eliminated. We need steady people we can rely on, people who can operate under the noses of the Germans. I think Annika's right: you would be perfect."

"You are very flattering, Martin. I'll help in any way I can. I don't have much family. My mother lives in the country now. I don't have a lot to lose."

"Wiesja, I'm sure you recognize the dangers involved in this. I admire your courage."

They talked for an hour longer. Rory managed to pull back from the conversation while Annika and Wiesja spoke of the future and who might be of value to them in their resistance movement. They switched back and forth from English to Dutch. At one point, Rory suspected that they were talking about him killing the German driver and the reprisals that followed. That episode only seemed to harden their resolve to do something about fighting back. Both women appeared to have wasted no time in adopting the resistance as their own project, which Rory thought was only reasonable. It was after all their country, and they had suffered the most at the hands of the German invader.

Watching Annika, Rory thought that somehow she had changed. It was almost as if the events of the last few days had been an enforced metamorphism. She had, in some way, reconciled herself with her bereavement, and moved on from her grief to immerse herself in playing her part in this new and highly dangerous endeavour. There was also something alluring and hypnotic in her ingenuity and her unhesitating acceptance of the risks.

The conversation drifted around to tomorrow's plans, and Annika and Wiesja launched into another animated discussion in Dutch. When their conversation paused, Rory asked Annika, "Have you two come up with any ideas as to who we should approach to develop the network? We really should get moving on this tomorrow."

"I think I've got the names of two good people we should talk to.

But if you don't mind, Wiesja, I'd like to discuss this with Martin tomorrow and get his approval." Looking to Martin, as if seeking his consent, and then to Wiesja, she said, "Unfortunately, as Martin has advised, when we choose them, we won't be able to confirm with you who they are or who will be in their cells. It'll be the same when you create your own cell: you won't know any of the people in the cells that your immediate contacts create. That way, if the Germans capture you and torture information from you, you can limit the number of people you reveal."

Wiesja nodded, accepting this gruesome truth as if the two of them had been discussing a shopping trip. She rose from her chair saying, "Well, it's bed time for me." She stopped and looked around her with a trace of a smile. "I don't want to be rude or intrusive, but how shall we prepare the sleeping arrangements tonight?"

Annika laughed and looked mischievously at Rory. "I should stay with you tonight, Wiesja. Martin and I have been partners in the resistance only!"

Rory smiled and said, "Of course. I'll bed down here on the floor, that's not a problem." He shrugged and laughed, but inwardly he wished Annika had phrased it differently.

In the morning, Rory was up before the other two. He had spent an uncomfortable night on the floor. He wasn't sure if his failure to sleep through the night was because of the oak floorboards, the prospect of meeting new contacts that day, or because Annika's impulsive behaviour on leaving the apartment had left him further fixated on this woman. The sun wasn't yet above the horizon, and the dawn's light was still grey and delicate. He dressed hurriedly and sat in one of the barrel chairs looking out the porthole window. There was a fine mist lingering on the canal. A family of brown ducks paddled soundlessly past in the black water.

The street opposite him looked idyllic. Mature hardwood trees created a leafy canopy over the road. On one side of the street was a line of tightly packed, narrow, brick townhouses. Rory guessed that they were probably three or four hundred years old. He noticed that on each one, jutting out toward the street, there was a sturdy stylized wooden arm just below the roof's peak. He studied this odd architectural detail, then realized it wasn't just a fanciful design embellishment. Any house that narrow needed a hoist to raise furniture to the top floors. The residents would then swing the items through the large open window frames. The stairs in such long, tall houses would have been too narrow for anything but one person to go up and down. The Dutch really were an ingenious people, Rory thought.

On the near side of the street and at the outer edge of the treed canopy was the canal. It was lined with houseboats, all of which swayed and creaked on their moorings, rising and falling almost imperceptibly on some invisible swell. Most of the boats he could see were much like Wiesja's: clean, and painted in green and white, or bright blue and white. They had small, carefully tended container gardens with geraniums and petunias in full bloom. He looked out thoughtfully at the scene in front of him. This kind of cityscape was at the other end of his aesthetic spectrum from what he knew at home. He loved the rugged splendour of the lakes and woods of the Canadian Shield; but he equally appreciated the magnificence and serenity of a skilfully planned cityscape. Someday he'd like to come back and paint this scene; and perhaps by painting it, he could capture it perpetually in his mind. This morning, as the mist drifted in front of him, he wondered why he wanted to paint the things he admired. There must have been a natural impulse to do it. Perhaps it helped him to understand what made them so attractive and by capturing their images on canvas he could relive that moment of insight forever.

"I thought I heard you get up." Annika was standing beside him, barefoot and in one of Wiesja's oversized dressing gowns. Her hair was tousled. She pulled the housecoat around her shoulders and smiled in a peaceful sort of way. She looked sleepy and extremely sexy. She sat down in the chair opposite him and curled her feet under her.

"It's beautiful, isn't it?" he said, motioning to the view out the window.

She smiled in agreement. "Would you like to paint it?"

"Funny you should ask that. I was just thinking how I'd paint that scene."

"I thought you were thinking about painting. I was watching you for a little while before I spoke." She looked down at the table, and after a few moments her eyes became focused on something distant. "How long do you think we have here until the Germans catch us?"

"Hard to say, but the sooner we get our work done, the safer we'll be. If we can recruit someone each day, just have them agree to setting up their own networks with the kind of understanding that Wiesja agreed to last night, then I think we can do our job in the next three or four days. If not, we'll be longer. After that, we'll have to wait and see how soon we can get a plane to get us out."

"So I guess that means it's up to me to find us some good contacts." Annika looked wistful.

"I think Wiesja can help in that too. Also Henrick Schulyer. We have two other good people to work with. It's not all on your shoulders and it's far from hopeless."

"What if we're caught? What if someone betrays us?"

"Then we will all probably die screaming in a basement somewhere here in Amsterdam ... but Annika, I'm planning on you and me being successful."

* * *

"ACKERMAN, THE PROBLEM with using members of the Dutch National Socialist Movement to root out members of a resistance cell is that they're distrusted by most of the society."

Hauptmann Ackerman raised his hand. He could see Neumann was in another one of his impatient moods. "Please hear me out, Herr Oberstleutnant. Yes, of course, we both agree that using these men in most roles is going to backfire on us. I know the average Dutchman wouldn't trust them with their cat, let alone provide them with information on life or death issues about resistance members."

"You are confusing me. What are you suggesting, Ackerman?"

Reinhold Neumann walked to his office window and sat on the window ledge. He began drumming his fingers.

"I think we have to use the Dutchmen in the same way the British will probably use their agents," Ackerman explained. "Put them in undercover roles and infiltrate them into Dutch resistance cells. Let them gain their confidence; and then, when we're sure that we've discovered enough of them, we simply round them up."

Reinhold Neumann stopped drumming his fingers. It was an act of the will not to roll his eyes. "That takes a long time. We can try it, but not today. I want something that will pay faster dividends. I want to make examples of anyone helping the resistance. We started to do this yesterday: get the message out that fighting the Germans, resisting us in any way, is suicidal."

"Herr Oberstleutnant?"

"Who do we know that may be hiding these people who are still at large? Pull them in. Do it very publicly." Neumann waved his arm for emphasis. "We'll shoot a few if we have to, but we need to send the message that resistance is suicidal and cooperation with us will ensure that you lead a long and peaceful life. It's that simple."

"So what should be our next move, Herr Oberstleutnant?"

"I think we want to take two approaches to this problem. This is where your Dutch Nazis come in, Ackerman. Have some of your teams sit down with them. Get them to give you the names of the people they think are the next ones down in the chain of anti-German attitudes."

Ackerman had his notebook out and was scribbling furiously.

"Be careful that they don't just give you the names of people they dislike. Verify each one. Just like you, I don't trust most of these people. Between you and me, most of them have some kind of problem, and if we pull in the wrong people, we'll waste our time and, what's worse, we'll make the Dutch think we don't know what we are doing; and that is the opposite of what we want to achieve. If every week or two we pull in a dozen or so legitimate malcontents, we'll soon get the word out that any sort of resistance is pointless. But I also want you to think through what we should do to reward those who cooperate with us. That's important. Think about it, Ackerman. Then come back and see me."

"I'll get back to you tonight, Herr Oberstleutnant."

"Oh, and Ackerman, don't let up on the snap checkpoints. Look at where we've been putting them up in the last few days, and except for the train station and main roads, move the rest of them around to catch the unwary. We'll catch these people when they least expect it."

* * *

"HAROLD, DID WE HEAR anything from Rory Ferrall last night?"

Ewen Crossley stood in the doorway of Harold Thornton's office in the Baker Street headquarters. His face was drawn and he had circles under his eyes.

Thornton looked expressionless and shook his head. "We've only had the one transmission, the night before last, and that was just to tell us he's in location and he'll be getting back to us."

"Let me know, will you, when you next hear from him. People a long way up the line are interested in finding out how this mission's going."

"Of course, you'll be the first to know, but what do you mean? You think the prime minister is waiting for his report?" Thornton sat back and began drumming the fingers of one hand on his desk top and rubbed his lower lip with the other hand.

"No, not yet. I don't think we have routine visibility quite that high just now, but certainly at cabinet level I think there's interest. People want to know the feasibility of this kind of warfare. And eventually, Churchill's going to want a detailed report—which will include Ferrall's mission. Churchill is very keen to see this kind of thing grow. As he's said before, he wants to set 'Europe ablaze.'"

"Are you worried about Ferrall?"

"Oh, yes, no question of it. We sent him off into the dark. He's the first to go. What he's doing is dangerous. We just don't know how dangerous, and we've left him to fend for himself. I certainly want to see him come back alive. Besides, we'll want to debrief him thoroughly when he gets back."

"Do you really believe there's any kind of future in this sort of thing?"

"Certainly. It's not going to win the war by itself, but at the very least it'll give occupied nations the impression that we haven't given up. At best, it'll tie down and demoralize large numbers of German troops. I think this kind of warfare is going to grow larger than anything you and I would have guessed even a week ago. I suspect that after this initial expansion that you're working on, we'll continue to grow. Right now, we've been talking about getting ready to send fifty or sixty agents into occupied Europe. In the next year or so, we'll probably want to boost that into the hundreds, and who knows after that, perhaps even thousands. So, if Ferrall is successful, we'll want to know why."

* * *

ANNIKA STOOD AMONGST the produce stalls at the Jordaan market. She was wearing an old cloche hat, her shoulders drooped, and with both hands she clutched a cloth shopping bag to her chest. She timed her arrival so she wouldn't be earlier than three or four minutes before the hour. Drifting through stands that sold fresh peppers, tomatoes, and cherries, she watched the north end of the street for Henrick Schulyer's approach. The glasses she wore were a weak prescription and they strained her eyes, which made her face look pinched and drawn. She could still see reasonably well at a distance, as long as she knew what she was looking for.

She picked up an apple from a wooden bushel basket and saw Henrick turn into the market. He was wearing a dark suit and had his hands in his pockets. He ambled along whistling, looking for all the world like he was carefree and simply enjoying an idle morning's stroll. Annika thought he was overdoing it and that he stood out from the remainder of the Dutch population, all of whom had a gloomy and hunted look about them. She turned so that he could see her as he approached. Henrick smiled at the stall owners and looked around him, obviously searching for someone; but as he drew near the apple stall, he looked through her and walked past. Annika's heart raced. She studied the street behind him but could see nothing or anyone unusual. Twenty metres on, Henrick slowed down, looked at his watch, and became interested in a stall selling green beans and carrots.

Annika walked to the stalls on the other side of the street and slowly worked her way towards Henrick Schulyer. When she got a few feet from him, she spoke quietly. "Is something wrong?"

Henrick Schulyer turned rapidly. "Annika?"

She frowned. "Yes, of course."

Henrick quickly regained his composure and allowed himself a slight grin. "Walk with me. That's very good, I didn't recognize you, or expect you with glasses, dark hair, and everything else."

"Shall we go and meet up with Martin Becker?"

"That's not a good idea." He steered her away by the arm towards a stall selling handmade hope chests and wooden bassinets. "When I heard the descriptions of the suspects in the shooting yesterday, I knew it was you. Now the Germans are searching high and low for a man with something wrong with one of his eyes and missing fingers. You aren't such a problem any more. I didn't even recognize you and I was looking for you. But Martin Becker, if he stays around here, he's a dead man."

"What shall we do?"

"Keep Becker hidden indoors until he leaves. The first policeman that sees him will arrest him, and he'll die a horrible death."

Annika stooped down and looked at the carved headboard of a wooden cradle. Her fingers ran along the engraved and varnished surface. "We have to develop contacts for resistance cells before we leave. We can't go yet. We hope to have about nine cells in operation before we go."

For a second Henrick's face contorted, as if he were doing a calculation in his head. "You're going with him?"

"Yes. He said he'd—" She stopped herself. "He said he'd take me out of the country to work with the British." She hoped she didn't sound like she was hiding something.

Henrick looked around them and up and down the street. He licked his lips. "That's probably good. If you've no other alternative character that you can take on here in the Netherlands, then you have to get out. They are very organized, and it'll only be a matter of time until they catch you, despite your aptitude for disguises. So you'll be working for the British?"

"Yes. I hope to. If they'll have me. Henrick, can you create two or three cells?"

"Yes. I won't tell you who, but I already have one other group that I know I can expand, and I know some others that I trust enough for this kind of thing. I intend to expand and create a small underground movement."

"I still think Martin will have to talk to you. Can you go and meet him, then?"

"No. I can't emphasize enough what danger he's in. He shouldn't be on the streets. His description is in all the papers and it's being broadcast continually on the radio. The Germans certainly aren't saying it after shooting Dutch hostages, but the word in the police department is they think he's a British agent. There's a reward for him, and you."

"So, if we can't have you meet Martin, we'll have to create a means of contacting you." Annika paused again and looked pensive. "We may not see one another again before we leave. I suggest that the way you recognize a legitimate contact is that he or she will use the words ..." Again she hesitated and looked about her. She stood up. "The contact will say, 'Annika told me that you have a handmade wooden cradle for sale.'"

Henrick thought about that for a second. "Okay," he said. "Tell Becker that I've got the job in the identification bureau. It's too early for me to do anything with it yet. I'd like to hear what support we can get from him and what he needs from me. I've been thinking about this." He picked up a small ornamental box. "I think I should be very careful about which identities I create. I don't expect that there will be anything anybody will be able to do for us for a while, but I look forward to hearing from you whenever you get someone permanently on the ground here. We'll talk then."

"If we can, we'll try to contact you before we leave, but if I don't see you, good luck and thanks."

Annika turned and walked away. Henrick Schulyer strolled over to the next stall and bought a small bag of cherries before returning to work.

Annika took an indirect route from the market, making several turns and backtracking on herself to see if she was being followed, then she boarded an oncoming bus and rode it for several blocks back past the market. When she got off, she was on Beursstraat, near the city's centre. She walked with a purposeful stride until she came to the Onderdonk department store. She turned into the store, stopping occasionally to browse, once at a stand selling women's scarves and later in the women's hat section, where she made use of its mirrors. She squinted down the aisles to see if anyone was ducking out of sight when she turned around. There was nothing. She left through the Warmoestraat door.

She got back to the canal boat at around eleven. Rory was sitting in one of the red leather chairs. "Wiesja's gone to her mother's in the country," he said. "I had quite a chat with her while you were gone. How did it go with Henrick Schulyer?"

Annika removed her glasses and massaged her eyes. "Henrick thinks it's too dangerous for you to meet him—for that matter, he thinks it's too dangerous for you to even go out at all. Your description is still being broadcast all over the country, and apparently they've mounted quite a search for you. Henrick thinks they believe you are a British spy."

Rory frowned but said nothing.

"Henrick has started to develop his own network. He intends to have at least three other cells reporting to him. I told him that he could identify a friendly agent from the greeting, 'Annika told me that you have a handmade wooden cradle for sale.'"

"That's very good. Wiesja spoke to me about creating a couple of cells as well. She's going to put one together out in the country, which will be good, as we may be able to use that as a reception team when we start to insert agents. She's putting another one together here in the city. It'll probably be based on some contacts she has with the people that work in the canal boats over by the dockyards."

"That's five cells. How many more do you think we need?"

"There's no set number. I came up with the number nine. They wanted me to come in here and assess the situation, to figure out how we should approach these kinds of operations. We could go back now, but I want to leave with nine cells in place." He paused and looked Annika square in the eyes. "Do you think we can get them?"

"If you're asking me, I'd like to go now. The police have your description, Martin. Your presence poses a risk. But if you want nine cells, we should get to work and get them." She took a deep breath. "What else did Wiesja say?"

"Not much. She tried to get information from me about who I am and where I come from, that kind of thing. But I was evasive."

"Did she say anything about me?"

"She thinks the world of you. She thinks you're the most capable person she's ever met and she doesn't want to see you get hurt." He stopped short of blurting out that he felt the same way.

Annika didn't say anything for a moment. "Martin, I've never wanted to hurt anyone before, but I'm prepared to take risks now. I'm going to fight." Then she added in a dejected voice, "I've a feeling it'll be a long while until I can be a musician again."

"Perhaps when you get to England you can play in an orchestra again."

"Martin, when I get to England I intend to volunteer to fight." She said it gently. "These people have taken everything from me and they're in the process of destroying my country. I have no choice."

Rory didn't say anything. He'd hoped Annika would settle down as a refugee. If she were in one place, he'd have a better chance of seeing more of her. He didn't want her coming back here to play this game of Russian roulette.

"If you are determined to stay here, then I think I should meet two other people this afternoon," Annika said. "And then we should get the radio. We can't stay here for much longer. We don't have a safe house here to hide up in."

Rory held up his hand in protest. "Not so fast. I appreciate your enthusiasm, but this is my operation. I'm going to go with you. I've got to meet these people, Annika."

She looked sympathetic. "Martin, you know the risks." She didn't want to sound condescending. "What are the chances that someone will see you and link you with the bulletins that are being broadcast?" Annika knew he was much too bright not to have figured this out and thought that he was struggling with his pride. He was probably worried she was usurping control of his mission, and then there was the unreasonable male issue of his courage. He didn't want to look like he was staying here where it was safe. There was little point in arguing this one.

"I've thought of that," Rory said. "The other side of this is that we stand a better chance of convincing your contacts that we're genuine and that we mean business if we're together. If I go along with you, we'll be a lot more convincing."

In her heart Annika thought it was a bad idea, but he did have a point. "I suppose if we both go together, we can wrap things up faster here."

"Exactly. We'll have a quick lunch and with any luck we can meet both contacts this afternoon."

Bram Piet te Lintum was an athletic-looking man with a receding hairline and a blond beard. He was in his early thirties but looked a decade younger. His office was a mess, with stacks of books and papers on every available surface. In one of the far corners was a pile of climbing ropes and an ice axe. On the walls were black-and-white photos of peaks that could have been the French or Swiss

Alps. Beside his climbing gear was a musical case that looked like it might have contained a French horn. His desk was littered with sheet music, on which hastily scribbled notations had been pencilled in and erased repeatedly. He was friendly but looked sceptical.

"Annika, you know the Student Union is almost completely against the Nazis." The door was closed and they spoke in hushed tones in English. "But you're also well aware that we've had a number of pro-Nazi students here in the university. These people have a lot more influence now that the Germans are running things. People are frightened of the little bastards." Bram extended his hands over his head and stretched. "You know they are probably a danger to you. We've had a couple of our students arrested already. Nobody has heard from them since. I'm sorry to say it, but my guess is that most of the students and faculty have probably been completely cowed by the Germans. Most people just want to survive this." He looked down at his desk for a moment. "But I guess we could do something. I don't know what." He shrugged and spread his arms out. "I'd like to help, but I don't know what you have in mind."

"Nothing much at this stage." Rory spoke quietly and outlined his early plans for the resistance.

Bram looked at Rory closely and a wave of recognition flooded over his face. "Are you ... ?"

Rory nodded in agreement. "Yes. That was us. We had no choice, believe me. And we didn't know the Germans would react with that kind of reprisal killing. Because they've adopted such a tactic, it means that any resistance in the future is going to have to be passive in nature."

Bram leaned forward. He was utterly absorbed in this conversation. "I suppose it's easy to make recriminations, but you didn't kill them, the Germans did."

Rory shifted in his seat. "Thank you, that's what we believe. But realistically, I think a lot of Dutchmen won't see it that way."

Bram looked thoughtful. "I think we are going to have to convince some of the people around here of the morality of any kind of resistance. Mr. Becker, I see five kinds of people that you'll find here. First,

there are those who understand the need and justification for fighting—in whatever form it takes. They're out there, and to get them
to join they only need to understand that there is an organized and
viable resistance. They have to be certain that they're not going to be
killed needlessly."

He sat back and toyed with the pencil on his desk. "Then there's
a second group: they will have a genuine concern that what they're
doing is morally right. You may or may not have to convince them,
because you can probably get sufficient, good-quality volunteers
from the first group. And in the third group are those who will always
hide behind the morality issue as a sanctimonious means of justifying doing nothing and saving their skin. In the fourth group, which
is probably miniscule, are the true pacifists, genuinely gentle people who, as an article of faith, don't believe in fighting under any
circumstances. The pacifist group is so small as to be insignificant."
Bram threw his pencil on the desk. His face was bitter. "And in the
last group are the Dutch Nazis and sympathizers. I think we should
concentrate on eliminating as many of them as we can if we can't kill
Germans."

"Do you think you can raise a cell from the first group?"

Bram stood up and ran his hand across his blond beard. "Right
off? I can probably get a dozen students and others I know who
could come in and start cells. When do you want me to start?"

"Thanks. A dozen would be too many. It would put you at risk.
Besides, I think there's value in staying small for now. We can grow
later. We'll probably want to be careful as to who we think we can
trust. I think, initially, we'll need help just getting organized: safe
houses, identities, communication networks, passing information,
that sort of thing."

Bram cracked his knuckles. He was hanging on every word.

"Don't try too much too early. This is going to be a long occupation. It will be years before any armies are ready to re-occupy the
Netherlands." Rory stood up and reached over and offered his hand.
"There's not much more I can tell you. We'll be in touch. Someone
will contact you. I don't know when, but when they do they'll say this

to you: 'Annika tells me you have some rare sheet music for sale.' If they don't say that, be confused and irate."

Outside the building, Annika smiled. "Bram will be good; he looks disorganized but he's brilliant and has a lot of common sense."

Rory smirked. "Brilliant we can get lots of; common sense and courage are the unusual virtues." And then he added as an after-thought, "And you've got all three. I've been very lucky meeting you."

Annika didn't reply. She looped her arm inside his and tugged him forward. They walked together to their next meeting.

* * *

THE ARMY MAJOR sitting in Reinhold Neumann's office looked dis-tinctly uncomfortable. Neumann stared icily at him from behind his desk and then turned his head away to think. It was a difficult prob-lem. The English couldn't set up any kind of a resistance that would seriously hurt the German occupation forces in the Netherlands. But at the same time, Reinhold Neumann wanted a system in place that eliminated all possible sources of resistance—whether they were a mortal threat to them or not. Unfortunately, getting such a system would change the very nature of what they hoped to establish in the Netherlands.

Neumann steepled his fingers and swivelled in his chair. He said to the Major, "You know, we've got to think our way through this problem." Then he turned away again, leaving the officer in front of him to stew. It was obvious to Neumann that they couldn't go on arresting Dutchmen forever and throwing them into labour camps. They had to get the Dutch on side. The Dutch eventually had to work willingly for the Reich if Germany ever intended to maximize profitability in the occupied lands. It was surprising how many of the senior officers in the army, the SS, and the Nazi Party didn't under-stand this last concept. Slaves and labour camps weren't a very effi-cient way of running things. But then, the Nazi leadership had always been more focused on inflicting punishment on their enemies than actually creating something. Neumann sat up in his chair. He knew that kind of thinking was heresy. For a second he thought about this and what it meant for his relationship to the Third Reich. He smiled. He was never going to change the world anyway, so why should he get worked up about it? He swivelled his chair forward.

The man sitting before him was Major Sachs of the army signals corps, a bright enough fellow in a purely technical sense. "So, I see, Major Sachs, you have created a very impressive plan for me that shows how you have divided up Amsterdam into zones. And you tell me you can use your radio direction-finding equipment in these zones to identify all radio broadcasts originating in each zone. Let's look at the map."

The two men walked over to the map of Amsterdam. Neumann said, "What you're proposing would give us good coverage of the area, but I need something a lot more specific than that. Think now— where would you put your radio if you were a spy trying to set up a resistance network?"

Major Sachs put his hand to his chin. "I'd keep the radio, Herr Oberstleutnant, somewhere near where I lived. I'd position it so that getting to and from it wouldn't be a big problem."

"Yes." Neumann looked encouraging. "Go on."

"But I wouldn't use the radio too often, Herr Oberstleutnant."

"Exactly! So the problem is an intuitive one, not a deductive one. You have to figure out where they intend to live and thus we can't use a long mathematical process of elimination like you have suggested."

"Yes, Herr Oberstleutnant." The Major's voice sounded not only suspicious but just a touch sullen.

Neumann ignored that. "The problem I have is finding out where he lives. And I think I only have a few days to do that, because if I were him, I'd do what I have to do and then get out of here, if that option were open to me. So, where do you think he would choose to live, Major?"

"I know where I would live, sir. Right in here." He made a circular motion with his hand over the four square kilometres closest to the harbour and Amsterdam's Central Train Station.

"And why would you choose that area?"

"Well, Herr Oberstleutnant, you say that he may not know the city and that all his previous contacts have been eliminated. Well, if you don't know a place, you would probably start in the centre and work out, not start at an edge and work inwards. That's too haphazard."

Neumann was about to speak, but the Major held up his hand. "And if it were me, sir, I would look for my potential contacts in the resistance in the places closest to the key institutions. Not that I'd necessarily choose key people to run the resistance, because you would catch them quickly. And I'd also live near a good bus line."

"Why a bus line?"

"Because I don't imagine this fellow has a car and you almost caught him once getting off a train. He's dependant on public transportation. He needs to get around and I would guess that if he's in Amsterdam he's taking one of the buses."

* * *

THEY STOOD BESIDE the bicycle rack outside the main library. Annika reached into her handbag. "I borrowed this from the tool bag on Wiesja's boat. I had a feeling it would be useful. We've quite a distance to go for our next meeting." Surreptitiously, she pulled out a pair of heavy-duty pliers with a wire-cutting edge, and winked at Rory. "These two look nice." She pointed to two nondescript-looking bicycles and whispered, "Could you please cut the chains? I don't think I'm strong enough."

Within a minute, the two of them joined the swarms of cyclists criss-crossing Amsterdam's flat streets. Annika led the way, while Rory, with flat cap pulled down over his eyebrows, pedalled a few yards behind.

The crowds of cyclists thinned the farther they got from the centre of town. Rory increased the distance between the two of them. Without having previously discussed this, Annika seemed to understand exactly what it was Rory was thinking. When she turned a corner, she slowed down long enough for him to see where she had gone.

Annika glided to a stop in front of a large brick building with newspapers and handbills taped inside the front windows. The sidewalk had been freshly scrubbed and terra cotta pots of geraniums dripped from a recent watering. Inside, the sound was deafening. The room smelled of fresh ink and oil. A printing press hammered out copies of a coloured leaflet. When Rory arrived, Annika was waiting behind the counter with a man wearing an ink-splattered apron. He was in his mid-thirties, wore horn-rimmed glasses, and had a tightly wound look about him. As soon as he closed the door, she motioned for Rory to come with them.

They went into a back office, where prices and sample handbills decorated the walls. The man gestured for Rory and Annika to be seated. He spoke to Annika in Dutch.

"Annika, I was so sorry to hear about Saul being arrested. Have you heard news from him?"

Annika lowered her head. "I've heard that Saul was killed while he was in captivity."

The printer hammered his fist onto his desk and his voice rose, "No! How can they do this? Saul! What did he do? We can't stand by like this!"

"That's why I'm here, Gerard." Annika was poised. Her voice was composed and without emotion.

Gerard looked puzzled.

Annika continued. "Gerard, if you don't mind, we will speak in German. I would like you to meet Mr. Becker. He has come here from London and he wants you to work with him and his organization in resisting the Germans."

Gerard looked at Rory and then at Annika. His face was sceptical.

"Let me explain." Annika recounted the story of her meeting Rory, and over the next twenty minutes, they described their intentions to build a network.

Gerard was enthusiastic. "Never mind. I know the right people and we will assassinate German leaders." He punched one hand into the palm of the other. "I've got contacts who would be happy to fight and kill Germans."

Rory looked at Annika. "Gerard lost several relatives when they bombed Rotterdam," she said quietly. To Gerard she said, "I appreciate how you feel, but you must understand, we will have to be disciplined. Killing Germans at this stage of the war will only result in the deaths of Dutchmen."

"How long do you think we'll put up with this? We have to strike back, just for our own pride. We can't let them blackmail us into not resisting."

"I don't know how long it will be. It may be years. My guess is that it will be a very long time, but in the meantime we have to prepare ourselves. We will have to be disciplined. Can you do this?"

Gerard looked flustered. "Yes, but I think we could choose our targets carefully. We could—"

Rory waved his hand and interrupted him. "The more important your target, the more Dutchmen will be killed. It's not worth it. Gerard, if your actions end up in the deaths and deportations of hundreds of Dutch citizens, we will have the population against us. And, yes, they can blackmail us for a little while. Your resistance will have to be measured, but we will eventually kill lots of Germans, believe me."

Annika looked directly at the owner of the printing shop. "Gerard, if you want to be in on this, you have to give us your word that you'll restrict your activities to what we've discussed. We have to go soon."

Gerard looked cornered. "Yes. I'll follow your advice. When do I start?"

"Begin recruiting your network now," Rory said. "We'll contact you. Someone will eventually meet you and they will say to you, 'Annika tells me that you have antique maps and books for sale.' When you hear that, you know we are back on the ground to help with the resistance."

Annika was the first to leave the shop. Rory waited a minute before he left. While waiting to leave, he smiled at Katelijn, a morose-looking middle-aged woman who mopped the floor beside the printing press. She shrugged her shoulders ever so slightly. Katelijn had ink on her face and looked like she carried the world's sorrows in her soul. She stood up and watched Rory leave. When he had cycled away, she laid her mop aside. Katelijn glanced at Gerard's office door. It was still closed. She picked up the phone and dialled. "I'd like to talk to someone about the reward for the spy…"

Katelijn wasn't sure it was the right man, but as she told the police officer, the man spoke German and had something wrong with one of his eyes. As she waited for the arrival of the police, Katelijn thought about what she would do with the reward. She could certainly use the five hundred guilders, and getting the money would certainly please her husband—so would her helping to catch a spy. Her husband had been a sympathizer of both the German and Dutch Nazi parties for years, and only last night he had railed away to her about the need for all Dutch citizens to support the Nazis. Yes, today was her lucky day.

25

THE OPERATIONS ROOM telephoned Hauptmann Ackerman informing him that there had been a possible sighting of "the man with the bad eye." It was a name the Dutch police were using to refer to the most wanted man in Amsterdam. Ackerman wasn't sure if the Dutch had made up some kind of private joke about the "evil eye" and were using it as a subtle means of mocking the Germans. He had always been sensitive to people taunting him about not having a sense of humour, so he chose to treat the call as being entirely legitimate. A few minutes after the phone call, the duty officer from the operations room downstairs deferentially handed a slip of paper to Ackerman listing the time and place of the sighting. Ackerman turned the notice over in his hand as if it were something distasteful. "And of course you have sent someone out to check on this?"

"We certainly have, sir. We despatched a car immediately, and as soon as we have another car available, we'll send that one out as well. There were no police operating in the area at the time of the report." The duty officer remained standing at attention in front of Hauptmann Ackerman.

Ackerman nodded in agreement. "Fine, I'll notify Oberstleutnant Neumann." He waved his hand to dismiss the police officer.

Notifying Oberstleutnant Neumann wasn't a task he was keen on doing. Neumann had taken his driver as a guard and had gone

off for the afternoon to Laurina's apartment with orders only to be
disturbed if "something serious came up." The problem with Neumann was knowing what he considered to be serious. There had
already been several sightings of "the man with the bad eye," and all
of them had proven to be false. He had a gut feeling that this sighting
was probably no different. He'd take his chances. He wasn't going
to phone Neumann. Ackerman was beginning to think that offering such a rich reward for information leading to his arrest was not
a clever idea.

* * *

Before they left the university, Rory and Annika agreed to take a
different return route from the one they had used to get to Gerard's.
It would be much slower, but it had the benefit of avoiding most of
the main roads. It was a wise and a fortunate decision. The Dutch
police arrived at Gerard's print shop six minutes after Rory left; and
driving at speed along the main roads, none of them saw anyone
matching his description on a bicycle.

At the sight of two black-uniformed Dutch police standing in the
doorway to his office, Gerard sat up and suppressed the urge to
look taken aback. He did his best to control his emotions, sat back,
opened his arms and smiled.

"Good afternoon, gentlemen. To what do I owe the pleasure of
your visit?"

The policemen rattled off Rory's description and said they had
received reports that a man answering to that description had been
here.

"There was indeed a man here, but his eyes looked normal to me.
He also had his wife, a little mouse of a woman, she was with him
too. He was asking about quotes for getting a handbill made up to
advertise the sale of machine tools. He had his nerve. He practically
wanted me to do it for free."

Gerard looked at both policemen. Their faces were expressionless. He waved his hands and pretended to be angry. "He wouldn't leave his name or number and he said he was getting quotes from various printers, so if I wanted his business I'd better give him the lowest price. Can you imagine that? I think the little prick was trying to intimidate me. There was no discussion of any terrorist connection. I certainly didn't see anything wrong with his eyes. His brain maybe, but not his eyes." Gerard made a face and shook his head.

The two policemen looked at one another and one of them rolled his eyes.

"If he comes back, I'll call you. But this man was no terrorist. He wasn't smart enough. He was just a dull, plodding, self-important, pain in the ass. I hope you catch him. Bring him in and smack him around for me for wasting my time."

The police laughed and turned to go. As he walked back to the front door, one of them gave Katelijn a wink. "You didn't get rich this time."

Gerard closed the door behind them and turned to Katelijn. She looked humiliated and broke eye contact.

"You know, someone actually thought that guy who was in here trying to get me to print his machine tools handbill was a terrorist. What a waste of time. He was the cheapest man I've met in years." He rubbed his chin. "How are you doing anyway, Katelijn? You look a bit tired these days. Are you feeling well?" He smiled at her. Who would have thought that after working here all these years, the silly old bat would have pulled a stunt like that? Katelijn was definitely going to be a hazard. Just to be safe, he'd wait until next week to tell her that since the German invasion the slowdown in business was killing him. It was unfortunate, but he'd have to be doing the cleaning around here himself.

* * *

RORY AND ANNIKA reached the canal boat at just after four. They carried the bikes aboard and left them under one of the tarpaulins that were stowed forward. Inside the cabin, they crumpled into the bucket chairs.

"I wish there was something to drink in this boat," Rory said, looking about the cabin. "Annika, you've done brilliantly. I don't know what I would have done without you. I think we've made enough contacts now. We can go back. We've achieved what we set out to do."

"So, tonight—should we get the radio?"

"I'd rather stay here and just take it easy for a few days," Rory said with a smile, "but you're right, we should try and get the radio back from the apartment, make our calls to London, and get out of here as soon as we can."

"I agree. You know, maybe I'm being too suspicious, but did you see that lady at Gerard's, the one cleaning the floors? She scowled at me when I went out. I don't trust her."

"I don't trust anyone around here. With one huge exception of course."

Annika smiled.

They left the houseboat at eleven. Rory transferred one of the bicycles into the runabout and covered it with the canvas sheet stowed in the bow. The sky was cloudless, with a bright crescent moon. Looking at the canal and the surrounding city bathed in light, he thought if he had a choice he wouldn't attempt burglary on a night that was quite so bright; but then again, over the years he'd known successful thieves who'd been more daring. So tonight wouldn't be an impossibility. An intermittent breeze rippled the canal's surface, and despite being July, it was chilly on the water. When they had been underway for ten minutes, Annika began to shiver. She shifted closer to Rory as he steered. Twenty minutes after leaving the houseboat, she squeezed his arm motioning for him to manoeuvre the boat into a landing.

As he got up to get his bicycle, she gave his arm another gentle squeeze. "Good luck. I'll wait here until five o'clock, and then I'll wait at the houseboat, but don't be too long."

"Thanks. I'll be as quick as I can. Don't wait here a minute past five. If something goes wrong, I'll meet you later in the day. I'll be fine." He manhandled the bike onto the roadway beside the canal. "See you."

Rory pedalled uneventfully to the apartment building. No one was out at this hour. When he got to their old building, he saw lights burning at the back in one of the downstairs rooms. He cycled around the block. There was no one around and the only sound he could hear was the rubbery, grinding sound of his bicycle's tires on the pavement. The buildings on either side of the apartment were in darkness. In the shadows, he could make out a bicycle rack near the back of the bakery next to the apartment block. He glided into the driveway, dismounted, and put the bike in the rack. Looking around him, he could see nothing to indicate anyone had seen him. He stepped into the shadows behind the bakery and stood beside the wooden fence. From a standing position, he could see the lights shining from the apartment building. He put his back against the fence and slid down into a crouch. From this position, he couldn't see the lighted windows of the apartment building, but he could still make out the glow on the fence and brick walls.

After a few minutes, his legs began to ache, and he shifted farther down into a sitting position. His watch indicated it was midnight. The minutes crept by with glacial slowness. He sat in the dark, listening and watching. A block away, a vehicle drove past, and for a few moments he could see the looming and receding sweep of its lights casting a rapid succession of angular shadows on the bakery wall. Ten minutes later, the lights in the apartment building went out. Rory looked at his watch. Ruth had given it to him on the last Christmas she was alive. She was just starting to get sick then. It was hard to make out the time. The watch's luminescence had always faded quickly. Maybe it had been some kind of omen?

As he sat there in the dark, his mind raced. Rory was impatient, and thoughts rushed in and out of his head as if he were lying awake at night unable to sleep. What would he do if the landlady and her husband were still up? How would he try to explain things if they interrupted him? If they barged in on him, should he brandish the Webley at them? Probably, but he'd never use it. For most of his worries he didn't have pat answers. He'd play things as they happened.

Then he started thinking about Annika. His thoughts about her were an order of magnitude greater in their intensity than they were about what he was supposed to be doing tonight; and when he thought about her, he ended up focusing almost exclusively on his insecurities and his fears rather than on anything positive or rational. Was he misconstruing Annika's actions? He'd done that before with women a long time ago and he'd felt foolish after. He knew that he was so lonely that he hadn't been thinking straight about women for a long time now. Was Annika in some kind of rebound situation from losing Saul? She had to be.

He thought about her in Wiesja's oversized dressing gown with her feet curled up beneath her, how she smiled and how the light played in her hair. He imagined the tantalizing curve of her breast beneath her blouse. And he could still feel the warm touch of her thigh against him from their trip here in the runabout. So many images and sensations of her flooded his mind. He could still feel her warm beside him and he could sense her fragrance from the nights when they shared the same bed. The reminiscence was immediate and it stirred him. He wanted her in a desperate way. Just thinking about her, he could feel that most of his mind was shutting down and he was running on primeval instinct. That wasn't so unusual. It was normal, except that in these circumstances it was also dangerous and could be fatal.

What an insane time this had been. He had been vacillating between obsession and pretended indifference, as if there was nothing arousing about sharing a bed with a beautiful woman and being forced to act like nothing was going on. It had been torture for him. Did she know that? He wondered if she felt the same way. Maybe she didn't, maybe she did. After all, Annika had proven to be good at pretending to be someone she wasn't. She was a natural at playing a complicated and dangerous game. In the short time he'd known her, there wasn't a situation she hadn't been able to think her way through. But then again, did he really know her? He started through the same cycle of obsession and questioning followed by self-censure and all the while he looked at his watch.

He waited until just before one o'clock and then stood up. His legs were stiff and his back was cold. He flexed the muscles in his arms and did three slow, deep knee bends to get the blood flowing in his legs again. He wiggled his toes and walked to the front of the bakery, keeping to the shadows and close to the wall.

The street was quiet. His heart pounded. He could feel his pulse quickening and his breathing becoming shallow. He stopped. He couldn't go in there without being in complete control. Misgivings engulfed him. Why the hell did he get involved in this line of work? He wasn't cut out for it. He never had been. He wasn't a comic book hero who did this sort of thing without so much as a second thought. Now he'd killed a man at close range without thinking about it. He had been responsible for the deaths of twenty innocent men and the imprisonment of another fifty in labour camps. He wanted to shut all that out of his mind. Had he become some kind of monster? Was he insensitive to the most basic kinds of human decency?

He'd done more than his share of dangerous and brutal things in his lifetime, and all of it was pushing against the grain of his nature. He stopped, slowed his breathing, and looked up. He had to think about getting the radio out safely. Getting in and getting out undetected: those were the only things that were important to him. Right now, it was his only motive for living. The rising anger and dread passed. His breathing and pulse slowed. In a few moments he became refocused on the task at hand.

He pulled the keys out of his pocket and took a series of deep breaths. He headed for the front door. His footsteps made no sound as he went up the concrete steps. The front door was locked. He fumbled with the keys and when the door swung open it creaked loudly. He imagined the landlady sitting upright in bed in her nightgown and curlers clutching at her husband and demanding to know, "What was that sound?" He padded past their apartment and up the wooden stairs, which were quieter than he remembered. Then he thought, what if, in the time he and Annika had been gone, someone else had moved into the apartment? Too late for that now.

.   At the top of the stairs it was pitch black. It would take five or six minutes to adjust to this darkness and there was no time for that. He felt for the keyhole, and with his left hand on the hole in the metal face plate, he fingered the key ring in his right hand. It was a large, old-fashioned key from the previous century and it made a solid clicking sound in the oak door.

The door handle went down soundlessly and the door swung open quietly. He stepped in. The light was better in the apartment. Something was piled against the far wall and some of the shapes in the room looked different than he remembered. He couldn't risk turning on a light. Soundlessly he moved one of the dining room chairs under the attic hatchway. He had just stepped up on it when he heard the unmistakable sound of a man sleeping fitfully in the other room. He froze for a minute. The man snored intermittently and tossed and turned for a few seconds, then his breathing continued in a series of regular wheezes and gasps.

He shifted the hatch cover over as gently as he could, wincing as it made a grating sound sliding over the wooden cross beams. When he released the cover, he let it down as lightly and as slowly as possible, but it still made a heavy clunking noise. He stopped and listened. Nothing. The man continued sleeping noisily. Rory put his head through the opening. Inside the attic was a stifling blackness, impenetrable as a sealed tomb. He could see nothing. He reached forward and felt for the leather handle. It was there, exactly as he remembered. He gave a slight tug. The suitcase refused to move. With his arms fully outstretched and standing on tip toes, he made a tremendous effort and lifted the suitcase so that only the back edge trailed on the cross beams. He pulled it slowly, making a scraping noise. For a split second he considered his options and then gave a firm jerk. The suitcase bumped against the frame of the hatch cover and he lowered it through the opening. Stepping off the chair, he heard the sleeping man turn. The snoring stopped and there were muttered words that sounded like a challenge in Dutch.

Rory turned for the door and headed downstairs. He could hear the man in the apartment call out. At first the voice sounded bewildered but it soon turned angry. The suitcase was heavier than he remembered and he banged it on the wall as he clattered down the stairs. Outside, he took his time and strapped the case firmly onto the rack over the bicycle's back tire. He tried to force himself to breathe slowly, to get the straps on properly. Having the radio fall off a hundred feet away would be disastrous. A light went on downstairs as he mounted the bike. He began pedalling frantically. As he rounded the corner, he took a quick glance behind him and noticed the light over the front steps coming on and the silhouette of a man standing outside.

The most direct route back to the canal was down two side streets and onto Van Houweningenstraat to the feeder canal where Annika had the runabout tied. If he was chased, taking the more travelled street would be too obvious. Something deep in Rory's instinct told him to stay away from the main road. He cycled past the turnoff that would have taken him to Annika and the canal, and pedalled away through the back streets.

***

ACKERMAN WAS EXHAUSTED when they woke him. Too many days without a break: working for eight hours a day in his office and then spending his nights in the operations room, or going out and inspecting the Dutch police at all hours; coordinating the search for terrorists; filling in for his Oberstleutnant while he was off visiting his Dutch girlfriend; and attending to the administration of the SS police services in Amsterdam. It was all taking its toll.

Someone had opened his door and was speaking from the hallway. All he could see was a darkened profile. "Sir, we have had a report of a burglary at the house where we believe the English terrorist and his girlfriend were staying."

Ackerman struggled into a sitting position in his bed. "How long ago?" He squinted in the light and grabbed his glasses.

"The call just came in, sir. I have taken the liberty of dispatching police and the full company of our motorized infantry reserve."

Ackerman rubbed his hand over an unshaven face. "Good. That was exactly the right thing to do." These Dutch duty officers were finally getting the message. Drag your feet in any matter related to security and you'll find yourself in a labour camp. It was simple and it worked. "Has anyone alerted Oberstleutnant Neumann?"

"No, sir, we thought we would leave that for you to do once you have made an assessment of the situation."

"Again you did the right thing. So what exactly happened tonight?" He got out of bed and threw on a dressing gown.

"Sir, we got a call two minutes ago from the woman who rented the apartment to people who matched the terrorists' descriptions. Well, sir, she phoned us after hearing the descriptions broadcast on the radio; and when we questioned her the first time, we left her strict instructions to advise us of anything she might have forgotten or failed to tell us or anything that turned up."

"Yes, yes, go on." Ackerman didn't want to hear any self-serving padding.

"Well, just a few minutes ago this woman phoned. She said that a burglar had been in the apartment that the terrorists were believed to have used. She didn't tell us earlier, but she never got the keys back from them. She thinks he came back using the keys. No doors or windows were forced."

Ackerman looked unresponsive. "So? Maybe this was just a routine burglary. These people pick locks for a living." Although, to be fair, he thought that there hadn't been too much of that activity since the occupation. "Anything else?"

"Yes, sir. Nothing of value was stolen. The burglar went straight to the attic and probably took something that was hidden there. He left the attic hatchway open when he ran away."

Ackerman's face lit up. "The radio! It had to be his radio. He had to hide it because any man carrying a suitcase on the street would be stopped immediately. It's him. It's got to be him. Phone Oberstleutnant Neumann. Have the entire reserve battalion called out and sent to seal off all the streets in the area within a two-kilometre radius and get me a car immediately."

* * *

RORY STOPPED HIS BIKE in the middle of a narrow cobblestoned street. It was crowded with buildings on both sides. On the ground floors were small shop fronts. From where he was, he could see a women's clothing store, a butcher's, a confectionary, and a pharmacy. Upstairs were apartments. The area had window boxes of flowers; it was neater and had a prouder, more formal appearance than did the area of their old apartment.

Something was wrong. Whatever instinct had told him to avoid the most direct route to the canal was right. From the road next to the canal, he could hear the sound of a pair of cars racing down the main route. And within a minute, off in the distance, he could hear heavy engines revving at speed. At this time of night, this was a bad sign. He pursed his lips and swore to himself.

Across the street was a lane leading to the rear of the row of buildings. He wheeled the bicycle down the lane. Behind the buildings were more flower boxes alongside neatly ordered trash barrels and wooden packing crates. There was the inevitable row of bicycles in a metal rack. Several of the houses had large wooden staircases. A truck roared in the street he had just left. It stopped and he could hear a tailgate banging and the sound of steel-shod jackboots scrambling over cobblestones. Orders were shouted. He put the bike in the nearest rack, removed the suitcase, and looked up at the line of back stairways. One was as good as the other.

He chose the middle one and ran up. At the first landing, he tried the door. It was unlocked. He stepped inside, finding himself in a tidy, darkened kitchen. Through a lace curtain, over the backdoor's window, he could see a pair of helmeted German soldiers with rifles. They flashed lights up and down the lane and shouted something unintelligible. They went back the way they came. Rory took a deep breath and exhaled noisily.

He was startled by the voice behind him. A man in pyjamas was standing in the doorway holding a bone-handled carving knife in front of him. He was saying something in Dutch. Behind the man, Rory could make out his wife in her night gown. Nobody spoke. Rory swallowed hard and put his suitcase down. He raised his hands in a surrendering motion and jerked his head towards the lane. He spoke in English. "I'm from London. The Germans are chasing me. I need your help."

The man looked at him and then back at his wife.

Rory spoke this time in French. "I need your help, I'm from London." He breathed heavily. He was beginning to become frantic. "The Germans are chasing me." He put his hands down and his shoulders sagged.

"I speak English, a little," the man said. He still held the knife in front of him and his wife appeared to be trembling.

"I need your help. Please."

The man looked at Rory and a flicker of recognition grew across his face. "You? You are the person who killed the German policeman?"

Rory felt defeated. For a second all he could think of was that he hoped that at least Annika would get away from this. He swallowed. "Yes. I had to. There was no choice."

The man lowered the carving knife. He looked serious but nodded obligingly. His eyes never left Rory, but the menace in his voice was gone. "Come, come with me." Rory picked up his suitcase and followed him.

His wife stepped back to make room. As Rory passed her, she grabbed his hand and gave it a good luck squeeze. Her face had changed from angry and belligerent to apprehensive.

The apartment block Rory thought he had stepped into turned out to be a narrow house built over a shop. The man led him up a constricted staircase, past a floor with two bedrooms, and into a tiny bedroom on the fourth floor. The moon had moved steadily into the western sky and only a sliver of light illuminated the room. It was hard to see, but Rory could make out that there was someone sleeping in the bed. The Dutchman motioned for Rory to put the suitcase in a cupboard. "It is safe there," he said in a hushed voice.

Inside the closet, Rory could see heavy winter coats hanging, and beneath them, on the floor, was the family's leather suitcase. He moved the family suitcase over and placed his beside it, closest to the wall. He closed the door. The man pointed at the sleeping figure in the bed and whispered, "My father-in-law, he is very sick. You go under the bed. He will always sleep."

It'll be a tight fit, Rory thought. He had to wriggle and twist himself to get under, and he could feel the boards supporting the mattress pressing against his shoulders. He lay on his stomach. His feet were at the head of the bed with his face wedged so he was facing the room. The lace fringe from the bed clothes hung down just off the floor, preventing him from seeing much beyond the bottom two inches of the room. He could hear the man leave the room. The sound of his footsteps receded as he went down the short flights of stairs in his bare feet.

Rory lay there. He could feel his pulse beating in his temples and in his wrists. The room smelled of floor wax. The Webley in his waistband was jammed between his hip bone and the bed supports. Again he thought that it wasn't a great weapon for carrying concealed. The raised foresight cut sharply into his hip. If he was here for a long time it would be extremely uncomfortable. The old man in the bed was breathing regularly, but Rory thought he sounded raspy and shallow. The breaths came too quickly. Periodically, the man would cough gently in his sleep and then mutter a few incomprehensible but painful-sounding phrases. The longer Rory listened, the more he realized that there was something gruesome about the man's breathing, as if each set of breaths between his mutterings was part of a final, inexorable, downward cycle. Rory blinked as he looked out at the wall across the room; the old man inches above him was probably in a heartbreakingly slow process of dying from some kind of dementia.

Outside, he could hear the movement of heavy trucks and occasionally people shouting in what sounded like indistinct German. Rory wondered what had become of Annika sitting by the main road in the runabout. How would she ever explain her purpose in being at the side of the canal in someone else's boat in the middle of the night? He should never have involved her in this filthy business. She'd suffered enough and hadn't deserved any of this. He should have left her the Webley; at least she would have gone down fighting. There was an all-too-familiar sinking feeling in his stomach. Once again he had put her in an impossibly dangerous situation, and he could now only hope the Germans didn't catch her.

Rory couldn't move his arm to see his watch, but he guessed that it had been ten or fifteen minutes since his arrival when he heard the hammering on one of the doors down the street. He couldn't make out if the hammering and shouting was coming from the street level or from one of the rear landings. He could hear shouting in German and screams of terror in Dutch. Outside, he could hear a heavy truck's engine revving as it moved down the street at a snail's pace. There were more shouts in German. From a distance away, he heard the sound of muffled small arms fire. What the hell were they doing? He couldn't believe they were shooting hostages on the street. They would have had no real proof that they were even searching for him at this stage. Could they have possibly shot innocent Dutch civilians simply because they were in the search area? Did someone get angry and shout back at them?

The engine noises receded and increased, and ten minutes later he heard the same pattern of shouting followed by muffled shooting. It was alarming for him, lying immobilized in this ridiculously helpless state under a stranger's bed. The man and woman downstairs were remarkable people. He was grateful that these two strangers had not simply come up and turned him out on the street. Whoever they were, they owed him nothing; yet without questioning him or his reasons for fleeing the Germans, they hid him. Rory thought it was this spontaneous kind of courage that was the supreme test of character. There was no forethought or consideration in doing the

right thing despite certain peril to oneself. It was the kind of courage Rory saw ordinary people display every day when he was in the
trenches. Oddly, he thought, it was not encountered nearly as frequently in everyday situations, when the stakes were much lower.

Rory tried to shift his position but he was locked in at the heels,
hips, shoulders, and head. He gave up any attempt at making himself
comfortable. The old man above him continued sleeping in his painful and laboured state of unconsciousness.

It was probably forty minutes or an hour after he hid under the
bed that Rory heard the pounding on the door below him. The Germans had been going methodically from house to house. There was
no mistaking it this time. They were downstairs. There was muffled
banging, and the crashing of things being thrown aside, and then the
sound of small arms fire from inside the building. There were about
a dozen shots—too many for an execution. There was more banging, bumping, shouting, and children crying. A minute later, Rory
could hear the voice of the man of the house speaking in worried
Dutch. There were shouted German voices. Doors slammed, something crashed to the floor and broke, and then he heard the sound
of gunfire again. It was across the street or next door. For a second
there was a silence.

And then it seemed everything was happening in slow motion.
Steel cleats on the toes and heels of jackboots thundered on the
wooden stairs. A floor below him, they roused a sleeping child who
immediately began to cry. Rory could hear the sound of clothes
being shoved aside in the closet below. Then the boots banged and
crunched upstairs. The woman shrieked. The door was pushed
open and several people came into the room. The woman howled
again and sobbed. It didn't sound like an act. Rory could feel another
body on the bed. The woman's feet were by the head of the bed. By
the door he could see two pairs of jackboots and he could hear the
laboured breathing of the soldiers who had been running up and
down stairs for the last hour. The whole bed began to rock gently.
The woman was cradling the old man and through her sobs she
rocked him in a slow soothing motion. The jackboots headed to the

closet and pushed the coats around. Then they turned around and went out the door heading upstairs.

It was well past dawn when the Germans left the street. The birds were up, singing and whistling away, oblivious of the drama and the terror that had gone on while they slept. The light in the room steadily turned from shades of dark blue and black, to grey, to bright sunlight. Rory could hear the German trucks revving, the sound of NCOs ordering their troops to mount up, boots clambering on the steel floors of truck beds, tailgates clanging, and then it stopped. They had left. His body relaxed; and once again the street became quiet.

Some time later, the man and his wife came back into the room. They closed the door. The woman sat on the edge of the bed saying something softly in Dutch to the old man. Rory couldn't hear a reply. The man got down on one knee and looked at Rory under the bed. "The children do not know you are here. They should not know. You must stay here until tonight. When it is dark and the children are asleep, then you can go."

The household's morning routine went on as usual. Early in the morning, ignoring the strange man under the bed and like a well-trained hospital orderly, the woman came in and sponge-bathed the old man and changed his pyjamas. Then she briskly changed the bed linen. Later, two children came to the door when it was time to feed the old man. The woman shooed the children away in Dutch. Rory could hear the clatter of a spoon and a bowl. The old man seemed to be awake for a short period and he muttered things, but it didn't sound like a real conversation.

Later, the woman came and knelt beside the bed. "I think you can come out for a few minutes." Rory edged his way to the side of the bed. His legs and arms were frozen and his body felt as numb as if he had been buried in a snow bank overnight. His bladder and back hurt and his head ached.

In the daylight, the woman looked the soul of a hard-working Dutch housewife. She was probably in her mid-thirties, but today looked much older. Her light brown hair was tied up in a neat bun and she wore a blue apron over a plain grey dress. She had dark circles under pale blue eyes.

"I can only say thank you," Rory whispered.

She nodded. "I don't know what you are doing, but if you are their enemy, you are our friend. Please hurry. Go to the bathroom downstairs. The children are out. I will bring some food and then you must go back under the bed until tonight."

Rory followed her downstairs. On his first steps, his numb legs almost gave way beneath him and he clutched the handrail with two insensitive and unresponsive hands. He went to the toilet and washed his face. In the mirror, the rim of his left eye socket was red and angry, and he had the stubble of three days growth of beard. He bathed the area around his glass eye gently with cold water. It was as refreshing and invigorating a sensation as he had ever felt. He splashed water on his hands and massaged his scalp and then he splashed more on his face. When he looked again in the mirror, he noticed for the first time that there were very definite patches of grey on his chin. He stared warily at himself as if he were looking at someone he hadn't seen in decades; the face looked like a man he vaguely recognized, but it had a strange and forbidding appearance. It was not the time, however, to ponder the meaning of grey in his beard.

When he opened the door, the woman was standing on the upper landing with a tray. "Come. The children are outside playing. I do not know when they will be back in our house."

Perched on the edge of the bed beside the old man's feet, Rory ate some bread and cheese and a bowl of hot vegetable soup. The woman stood over him. "These are terrible times. I am glad my father can not know what is happening. I worry about what the world will be like for my children. That is why we are helping you."

Rory nodded. "You are very brave. I can't thank you enough."

He felt foolish. He should have had something more profound, more meaningful to say, but he didn't and continued to eat.

"Tonight my husband will drive you away. It will be too dangerous for you to go on your bicycle. That is your bicycle in our rack?"

"Yes," he said, and then looked at her with his mouth half open. "I am here from London to organize a resistance movement to the Germans. Can I contact you or your husband later to help us?"

The woman looked down. "What do you want us to do?"

Rory liked her. There was something direct and practical—a quiet confident intelligence about her. He thought of Annika and wondered if this was a characteristic of Dutch women. "You will have to do very little at first. We can't resist the Germans now by fighting here in Holland. They will only kill more hostages. But we need people we can trust, who we can use as contacts, for passing messages and getting information. I know you have a family and it will be hard, but even if you just help us find others like you."

"You can talk to my husband. He is in the shop downstairs, but I think so, yes. You must hide now."

He wedged himself back under the bed. This time he moved the Webley and positioned his wrist so he could see his watch. The Dutch woman thoughtfully pushed a small pillow under the bed. "I don't think you can come out until the children are asleep."

Time crawled by. Rory spent the day alternately dozing and flexing his muscles. Every minute he was awake his thoughts meandered back to Annika. The odds had to be that she was caught. It was probable someone had reported that they had been seen at the apartment after the shooting, and last night the people in the apartment had obviously called the police. When the police heard about the open attic hatch cover they had to know it was him. That was the only explanation for such an intensive search mounted so quickly. Now they would have almost certainly caught Annika. If so, she'd be dead now, or worse. The cycle of guilt and blame started again.

He tried to sleep. He was grateful for the thin decorative pillow, but remorse and shame and numb limbs prevented him from ever really drifting off. Throughout the day, he could hear the sounds of the street and the house. The woman checked in on her father every half-hour. She fed him in the evening, and Rory thought he could hear dinner being served and then the children getting ready for bed.

He was hungry and thirsty. Again his bladder hurt, and his legs and arms were so numb he had given up trying to flex them.

At nine it was almost dark, and the man was kneeling beside the bed. "You can get up now."

He helped Rory extricate himself from under the bed and smiled at him. "You have had a long day. You should not go downstairs until it's time for you to leave. You never know who is watching."

After Rory had gone to the bathroom, the man brought him a plate of food and a glass of cool beer. It was the most satisfying drink he could remember. "My wife tells me you are organizing a resistance movement?"

The two of them took a liking to one another and discussed what Rory hoped to accomplish. The man who introduced himself as Piet de Jong readily agreed that he would create a cell; and in turn Rory told him that someone would eventually contact him, declaring, "Annika tells me you are looking to buy a new bed."

Piet owned the pharmacy on the street. It had been doing quite well until the war restricted cross-border trade. Now, many things he sold were hard to come by. And today the Germans had made a mess of his pharmacy. They knocked over cupboards filled with his chemicals and medicines. He grew angry thinking about it. "These bastards know how to terrify us. Rather than get down and search each of our shallow little crawl spaces in the foundation, they have one man watch us in the room and then they shoot through the floors. I think they are looking to see how we react if someone really was hiding there."

In the lane behind the house, Piet loaded Rory's bicycle into the back of a small delivery van. Rory thanked his wife. There was no ceremony or emotion. She smiled, gave him a little hug, and wished him well. They drove away. Twenty minutes later Piet dropped Rory off three blocks from the canal. A light rain was falling. Rory got on his bicycle as he watched the tail lights of Piet's small van round the corner of the cobblestoned streets.

26

"OF COURSE HE'S OPERATING somewhere in Amsterdam." Neumann gestured in frustration with his hand while he spoke on the phone. "We know he killed one of our police officers. We have had at least two positive identifications of him and we suspect that he has a radio with which he is in contact with London."

Neumann listened patiently and then interrupted. "Listen, I want the radio intercept unit down here and I want it tonight. If I don't get it, I will make a report to the effect that your army signals corps is withholding critical services from the SS and the Gestapo at a crucial time. We asked for your help in pacifying the country when you were not otherwise employed and you refused."

He rubbed his hand across his mouth. "I don't care if it's raining tonight. I want the direction-finding troops deployed and on the streets within the hour."

Hauptmann Ackerman stood cheerfully at attention beside Neumann's desk. He smiled as his superior tore into the army Leutnant. Like every other policeman, he thought the army was sitting about doing nothing since the fighting stopped. It was good that now they had to get out to support them, and even better that they had to do it in the rain.

"That's fine. I want you to provide coverage of the boxed area due west of the train station, north to the harbour, east of the Amstel

River, and south to the Stadhouderskade roadway. He's in that box. Are there any questions? Good. Call me when your teams are in location and operating." He hung up the phone.

"Hauptmann Ackerman, don't stand there grinning like a fool." Neumann was smiling. "Get the army reserve company on two minutes notice to move. Have the complete four companies of reserve infantry ready on twenty minutes notice to move. We have our British friend somewhere in this area, I'm certain of it."

"What if he has left, Oberstleutnant? He probably knows we're searching for him."

"He hasn't left. He went back to retrieve his radio last night, and he got it. That means he has a message to send and he'll probably be on the air tonight. He hasn't finished doing what he set out to do. When he goes on the air, we'll catch him. We should have half a dozen listening posts and two of the new mobile direction finders out this evening. If he goes on the air, we'll catch him this time."

Ackerman clicked his heels, grabbed his papers from the desk, and gave a quick Nazi salute. It was his way of showing enthusiasm. It was a mindless gesture, and it irritated Neumann—although he used it himself often enough. It was an excellent means of cultivating favour with his superiors. There was a practical aspect to it as well. It forced your superiors to agree with you at the conclusion of a meeting. It was even more effective if you looked them in the eye and gave a convincing "Heil Hitler" as you clicked your heels. Nobody was foolish enough to disagree with that. It guaranteed ending things on a positive note. He was training Ackerman too well.

Neumann took a cigarette from the wooden box on his desk and lit it with his Zippo lighter. The Zippo was one of those American inventions that he admired: simple and reliable. It was a shame the rest of the world wasn't designed that way. He shrugged and gave an involuntary sigh. There wasn't much to do now but wait. He had foolishly left Laurina's last night and gone out to the search area. He only ended up wasting his time waiting around for nothing. Tonight he would wait here in the office. They had radios and phones here.

He inhaled deeply and sat down, drumming the fingers of his left hand on his desk. He was on edge, and it wasn't just catching this spy that made him that way. The women in his life had a lot to do with it. Maida had sent him several letters in the last few weeks. Now she seemed to have rekindled her enthusiasm for him. Perhaps she had heard something through her family. Was she feeling threatened now that she had estranged herself from a rising star in the Gestapo? Was there another promotion in the offing? Who had she been talking to? The Reich security office was expanding and so far he had done quite well. Maybe Oberst Scheidler had said something to her or to a member of her family back in Vienna. Maida didn't want to join him a month ago; she could stay put for a while longer.

Laurina was a problem too. She had been useful. She had given him confidence around women. He had never considered himself a womanizer, and he hadn't been; however, he had always secretly wanted to be a lady's man, someone who was sophisticated and self-assured. This was his first affair. He could do much better than her, though: someone younger and prettier and more fun. He certainly wasn't in love with Laurina. Once he caught this spy, he'd find himself a new friend, either here in Amsterdam, or in Berlin—if he could get there in the next few months.

$$* * *$$

THE STREETS WERE EMPTY. When the van turned the corner, as if on cue the wind picked up and the rain lashed down in torrential sheets. In the few minutes it took to pedal to the canal, Rory was soaked to the skin.

The boat was in darkness. He looked about him with a sinking feeling in his stomach. There was no sign of the runabout. He dragged the bicycle onto the front deck, put it under the tarp, then lugged the suitcase to the front door. It was locked. He swore aloud and shook the handle violently. He pulled at it a second time and swore again. There was no point in getting rattled now; shaking the door handle longer wasn't going to unlock it.

He looked closely at the lock. It was an old model. He could probably pick it. He'd learned how to pick locks one winter from a fellow Mountie, a man with a suspiciously wide range of criminal expertise—but he'd never had to pick one in a driving storm before. As he looked about him for some kind of a stiff wire, something moved beside one of the portholes inside the boat. It was only a flash but there was no question: someone was lurking inside. He yanked the Webley from his waistband and with two hands trained it on the spot beside the door. He called out, but there was no reply. He was about to fire a round through the cabin wall and sprint away when Annika's voice called out, "Martin. Martin? Is that you?"

"Annika? You're here! It's me! Let me in!"

The lock clicked and the door swung open. As he stepped in, Annika threw her arms around him and murmured, "Thank God!"

He kicked the door shut without letting go of her. They stood for several seconds clasped together. Rory closed his eyes. The warm contour of Annika's body pressing against him was a pleasure he thought he'd never experience. He luxuriated in the moment. He looked down at her. Warm rainwater streamed off his face and onto Annika's forehead and cheek. He pushed aside a strand of her hair. "I was certain the Germans got you last night," he said. "How did you manage to get away?"

"I thought they got you. I stayed as long as I could, but when I heard the police and the soldiers, and then the shooting, I thought you'd been boxed in and captured. I felt like I was deserting you, but once the cordon was in place, I knew you could never make the rendezvous. So I untied the boat and just pushed it off." Annika had to take a breath; she was on the verge of tears. "They were watching inside the cordon. I drifted to the far side of the canal, tied up the boat and just stayed there, hidden under the tarp until well into the morning. They never searched the far side. An hour after they left, I simply motored back here. I tied the runabout a hundred metres from here in case anyone recognized it from last night. I'm so glad you got out."

Annika's face was drawn and pale. The tension of the last several days was etched around her eyes. It pained Rory to see the strain, but he delighted in her obvious joy that he was back. He continued to hold her, and while they stood there in the dark cabin, the story of his last twenty-four hours bubbled up out of him. When he finished, Annika rested her head on his shoulder and held him close. She said nothing for a long time.

He pulled himself away, and looking out at the rain falling into the canal, said in a flat voice, "We should send London a message. The sooner we contact them, the sooner we can get out of here."

Annika drew the curtains on each of the portholes and lit a candle so they could see without attracting attention from outside. Rory took the radio from the suitcase and set it up next to the door. He ran the wire aerial outside along the deck, cranked the batteries, and was about to put the headset on when he stopped suddenly. "I've got to take my time preparing this one. I need to draft the message so that I won't spend any more time than I have to broadcasting. I don't want a lot of chatter back and forth with questions. I don't trust London's radio operators. They're not well trained, and I don't know how fast the Germans can get a fix on a strange transmission. My guess is they know we have a radio, and they'll be doing everything in their power to triangulate us."

Annika wrinkled her forehead. "How do they do that?"

"They lay out three listening devices along the edges of an area. The listening devices have a compass that points to the strongest signal on a given frequency. Then it's simple geometry. Inside, where the lines intersect, is where they'll look for the transmitting radio. The army does it regularly to identify where an enemy headquarters is located."

She watched him quietly as he prepared his code. Just as Rory put the headphones on she said, "If you're concerned, why not wait a day. You had a feeling about the road back to the canal. Maybe it's the same thing here again. We can stay an extra three or four days here if we have to."

Rory stood a moment considering her advice, then put the headset down. "I think you're right." He pushed the telegraph key pad away from him. "I really don't want to send the message tonight, and if it doesn't feel right tomorrow, we'll have to go somewhere else to send it." He packed up the set, and sitting back in the chair said, "I don't know about you, but I'm hungry. Is there anything to eat?"

Annika smiled. "There's a bit. After I got back here this morning, I couldn't sleep. I thought there might be a faint chance you'd come back, so I prepared myself to stay for a few days. I went out and bought some food. I'm not sure if it was guilt or hope that motivated me. I bought some cold cuts, bread, fruit, and wine. We can last a few days."

They lingered over their meal talking for what seemed like hours. Although there was an easy rhythm to the conversation, to Rory it seemed as if they talked of everything but the biggest problem looming in front of them: what to do in their immediate future. Eventually the conversation faltered and Annika became quiet. "What's bothering you?" Rory asked.

"I've been thinking. What happens if for some reason we can't get out on the Lysander? What if it doesn't arrive, or it can't land? How would we get out of here?"

Rory stared at the candle, impulsively watching the flame flicker and the wax melt, bead, and drip to the base of the candle holder. "I think we'll be okay. I've given it some thought too. If the Lysander can't make it on the night we plan for the pickup, we'll try to arrange another night. We discussed this briefly before, but if for some reason we lose communications, then we'll have to give up the idea of getting out by plane. In which case, we ditch the radio, make our way to France, and get ourselves out through Spain. We've got plenty of money and lots of time, so if we have to, somehow we'll get through the Belgian and French frontiers; and if necessary, we can walk across the Pyrenees into Spain.

"You're not serious."

"I am. It's our only alternative. Our first and biggest problem would be how to get out of Holland. We study a map and establish a route and a series of points where we should meet in case we become separated. Once we're out of Holland, travelling together shouldn't be too much of a problem. But I think we should work out a more detailed plan tomorrow, after we've had some sleep. We'll both be thinking more clearly then. Now isn't the best time to plan this. I think we're both tired. We shouldn't worry ourselves about problems down the line. Our first problem is getting ourselves to the landing strip. That's got to be our first priority."

"Martin." Annika laid her hand on top of his. "We may be tired but I'm not sleepy. Let's talk for a while yet."

Rory gave a distant smile. "What else is on your mind?"

"What happens in England? What will they do with me?"

"I think they'll treat you as a legitimate refugee. I'm certain of that. I'll tell everyone I meet what a heroic job you've done—and it'll all be true. But once you're there, you'll be able to do whatever you want." Rory whirled the contents of half a glass of wine. "You could become a concert musician again, teach." He looked up at her. "You should get on with your life again."

Annika looked back blankly. She didn't speak for a few seconds. "I've said it before, but I feel I have an obligation to come back here and keep up the work that you ... that you and I have started."

He continued to stare at the candle. "I was afraid you were going to say that. Annika, there are a lot of other things you could do that would further the war effort. You know you don't have to put yourself in danger again. You've already lost a lot, and you've already done more than your share. Besides, I don't want to lose you." He shifted his gaze to her. "There, I've said it."

Annika reached out again and put her hand on top of his. It was almost a friendly, sisterly gesture. "Martin, what can I say? I think I need time. This has all been so fast. Saul and I had some problems, not big ones, but I still loved him, and he didn't deserve what happened to him. Then you came along. I feel lucky. I feel guilty. I feel sad, terrified, exhilarated. Everything's been so intense, so unexpected and sudden. I'm not overwhelmed, but everything has been just rushing up at me."

"I know." He reached out and touched her cheek.

"Thanks, Martin. I just need time."

There was a silence between them and they both stared at the dying candle.

"I don't know what we should say now." Annika laughed sheepishly. She grabbed Rory's arm and leaned her head against it. "What a terrible mess this world is. Do you think it'll ever get better?"

"Yes. Yes I do. But now, we're at a low point."

"I'm glad you're an optimist. It's so depressing. I trust your judgment. I think I should go to bed now."

Annika stood up. She kissed Rory gently on the forehead and went into the bedroom and closed the door.

He rooted around and found the bedclothes that he had left folded in the corner two nights before. It seemed a lifetime ago.

As he lay on the floor trying to get comfortable, he listened to the sounds of the boat creaking and rocking gently in the canal. The rain had stopped and the light was beginning to show the faintest shades of grey. He knew he couldn't sleep. Somewhere off in the distance a bird began an insistent chirping. He closed his eyes and a short while later he heard the bedroom door open. Annika padded into the room. She had a light blanket wrapped around her. She knelt beside him and smiled, drawing him upward. "This is crazy, you being down there. Come with me. Maybe tomorrow when we send the message we might be captured. We may not have a lot of time left together."

* * *

THE ONLY ALCOHOLIC DRINKS Laurina had in her apartment were two large bottles of Grolsch beer and half a bottle of red wine. Tonight Neumann was disgruntled; he wanted something stronger, and that was unusual for him. He was barefoot, wearing his uniform trousers and a white sleeveless undershirt. He poured wine into a juice tumbler and walked over to the kitchen window. It looked out on a tired street in a seedy section of the city. Down below, he could see his driver and a guard smoking and chatting idly beside his car.

He rocked back on his heels and sniffed. Now that Laurina was in the secretarial pool she should be able to afford something better than this place.

He took a long sip of wine. He wasn't normally a heavy drinker, but in the last week or so he had found himself wanting a drink at the end of the day, just to loosen up. On days like this, he needed something to help him think straight. It was ridiculous. He knew it: drinking to think clearly—how stupid! But lately he'd been frustrated, and the occasional good stiff drink relaxed him and made it easier for him to focus.

He didn't like what was happening to him. He felt frustrated. It was as if he was no longer in control of things. For a while now he'd had troubling sleeping, and each day he was getting progressively more tired. At night, as he lay in bed, his mind raced. His thoughts just whirled around inside his head endlessly. He had no one he could share them with. He thought of Maida and the children. Despite her actions, he didn't like being cut off from his family—and he didn't have anyone else. He wasn't in contact with his parents or siblings either, and he had no friends. It was hard to admit to himself, but he worried that he had never been able to keep a friend longer than a year or two. There was no one in the Gestapo either. He thought about the fact that nobody he worked with liked him or trusted him. Now all he had was this foolish, unsatisfying relationship he had entangled himself in with Laurina.

No, that wasn't true. He had his career. That was one thing he was certain about. It had become the focal point of his life. He wanted to get out of Amsterdam and get onto Reinhard Heydrich's staff in Berlin. Things would certainly be better as he went higher in the system.

In a few months, if he made no major mistakes, he should be in Berlin. In his heart he knew that getting out of Amsterdam had to be his next step. More than anything now, he wanted to be posted into a senior position in Department E of the Fourth Service of the Reich Main Security Office. It was the one he had his heart set on. Department E of the Fourth Service was the directorate that handled counter-espionage. That was one of the areas where the future lay for an ambitious and rising Gestapo officer. It didn't really matter which enemies you hunted: Communists, reactionaries, Jews, liberals, British, Americans, resistance leaders. There would be sufficient enemies of the Third Reich for as long as he lived.

Proving that you were efficient at eliminating undesirables and rooting out threats to the state was always going to be a vital prerequisite to getting ahead. It was the most important internal function in maintaining the health of a fascist state. He reasoned that for an officer who had unequivocally demonstrated his abilities in the field in wartime, the next step was to run a section in one of the key directorates. When the war was over, you wanted to be in a key spot in Berlin, because when the war ended, the game was going to change again and you didn't want to be stuck forever policing some European backwater. In Berlin, you could be noticed. People knew your name and your face. Amsterdam had been fine. It had served its purpose. He'd done well in Amsterdam, but if he stayed here, this Dutch town would quickly become his graveyard.

He sipped his wine and then, without thinking, finished it in a long gulp. Amsterdam was only a waypoint on his journey to the top. And the ticket to getting out of here, to proving that he was the man who should eventually lead counter-espionage, was catching the man who had shot Schmidt. The only snag in all this was that he needed to catch him soon. He wouldn't look so good if it took him several months to do it. He put the glass down and refilled it.

Laurina came in and rubbed his back. She wore a skimpy night gown that didn't flatter her. Neumann didn't like that.

"You seem so tense tonight, Reinhold. What's the matter? Let me try again. Come back to bed. Let me take your mind off what's bothering you."

It was the wrong thing to say. He didn't want some overweight Dutch cow reminding him that he hadn't performed adequately tonight. There was a nasty edge to his voice. "No, I simply want to have a drink by myself and think things through. Is that too much to ask?"

Laurina pulled her hand back as if she had been stung by an insect.

Without speaking, she left the kitchen and went back to her bedroom and closed the door. Neumann thought it was a good thing she
hadn't slammed the door. If she started getting insolent, she might
really have cause to fear him.

He dipped his head and smirked. Laurina was walking on thin
ice. She didn't know it, but she had become one of the symbols of
his being stuck here in Amsterdam. The real irritant to him, however,
the focus of all his discontent, was this German-speaking spy. There
had to be a solution to the problem. It was out there somewhere; he
just had to find it. He reached for his wine glass.

The hasty checkpoints had certainly been the right way to go.
The checkpoint at the train station had flushed him out in the first
place. His description and reward notices were all over the city; and
they'd worked, to an extent. There had been several sightings of him.
The problem was they couldn't sift the real sightings from the dozens of cases of mistaken identity that had been reported.

He expected to hear something from the radio direction-finding
units shortly. He had the military reserves standing by. His spy was
going to make a broadcast soon, and when he did, if he talked for any
length of time, the army had assured him that they would be able to
pinpoint him to within a hundred square metres—three or four hundred square metres if he spoke in short bursts. At least that's what he
was promised. If they got a fix on him, then he would cheerfully tear a
few city blocks apart until they caught him. But short of dismantling
the city brick by brick, he couldn't think of much else he could do.
He had considered shooting hostages until someone finally turned
the spy in. The problem was, that tactic would only further alienate
the population. And this spy probably went to some pains to conceal
his identity from everyone in the Dutch population.

Neumann put the glass down for a second and scratched behind
his ear. That was him last night at the burglary. It had to be him. It
was his old apartment and he'd clearly gone back for something big
and bulky. Somehow they had missed him. He had either evaded
the cordon or the searchers had missed him. Perhaps he got past
the cordon before they even set it up. That was possible but unlikely.

Perhaps he was travelling in an automobile of some sort and was long gone before the troops and police arrived. They had assumed he was either on foot or on a bicycle, simply because he was travelling on a train when they first flushed him out; but maybe that theory was completely wrong.

He walked into the living room and picked up the phone. He looked at the handset and then at the closed bedroom door. He was the one who'd had this phone installed. He had given it as a gift to Laurina, but he used it to maintain contact with his staff when he was here. Before he met Laurina, she couldn't even afford a phone, and now she had been offended by him. The thought made him angry. He dialled Ackerman.

"Ackerman, start putting checkpoints up for cars and trucks at all in and out routes to downtown ... I know we are running out of police. That's fine, tell the army to put another battalion on standby to help man the checkpoints. Ask for troops from the artillery. They haven't been manning their guns for weeks. Call the divisional operations staff. They're the most cooperative. If you go through the military police, they'll just bog us down in bureaucracy. I know you can do it, Ackerman. I'll call back in an hour. Oh, and Ackerman, you're a smart man, you've been to good schools. Put your mind to work. Come up with some more bright ideas as to how we should catch this man. We have to catch our spy within the next seventy-two hours ... Why seventy-two hours? Because that's our goal, Ackerman. That's all for now. I'll talk to you in an hour."

Neumann picked up his wine glass and took another long drink. He felt better, having given somebody some kind of direction.

"Oh, come on, Laurina! Come out here! Don't pout on me. I have a lot on my mind these days. Come on. I'll take that back rub now."

* * *

IT WAS THE SOUND of a kettle whistling that woke Rory. The canal boat was rocking gently from the wake of a passing barge; the sun was well up over the city and he could hear Annika busy doing something with dishes in the galley. He smiled to himself. Was this what the womb felt like: happy, secure, muted sensations, and a perpetual swaying motion? He lay back and stared at the ceiling above him. It was hard to imagine how quickly his life was changing. Yesterday seemed like a blur. He had been incredibly lucky to escape from the German Army. Not only had he been snatched from certain capture, but his rescuer had promised to raise a resistance cell. He wondered if that was how most of the Dutch felt. He admired their bravery, though he conceded they might be forced to change their outlook as the occupation wore on.

Above all else, the thing that stood out from that most improbable of days was the change in his relationship with Annika. Going to bed with her had actually come as a surprise to him. They had both been acutely aware of the energy building between them, like a powerful electromagnetic field that you couldn't see or touch; but the physical and emotional hunger it created was entirely real. Their understanding was unspoken and mutual. Rory could not have been the first to act. At first, there was a frantic intensity to their lovemaking. There was neither reserve nor shyness, only an aggressive desire to satisfy and to please; they both understood that this might be their last night alive. When it was over, Annika whispered, "I have to move on," and then she wept silently for a moment. Rory merely squeezed her in acknowledgement. At dawn they awoke to the sounds of the first barges chugging past them. They made love a second time, both drifting back to sleep, pleased and content.

Rory got up and draped himself in a bath towel.

Annika called out, "Are you up? No, stay there. I'm bringing our breakfast in on a tray."

He went back to the bed and propped himself up with a pillow, waiting for her. He hadn't had a morning like this since before Ruth had fallen sick. It was nice. It felt as if he was living again. He was relaxed and refreshed and oblivious to the world outside of this room. This was life as it should be: invigorating, satisfying, full of promise.

Annika came in holding a tray piled with toast and jam and tea things. "I was hoping that you wouldn't wake up before I brought this in. Did you sleep well?"

"Better than I have in months and months. And how about you?"

Annika raised her eyebrows and laughed. "I don't know about you, but it wasn't the sleeping that was great about last night." She poured them both mugs of tea and they chatted about nothing in particular for a quarter of an hour, but then the conversation faltered and Annika became quiet and began to chew her lower lip.

"What's wrong?" Rory asked.

"Nothing. It's just me. It's not you. You're wonderful, but I started thinking about how things used to be. It's taking me a while to get used to things being different. This all seems so unreal, so strange." Annika turned her head away.

Rory pulled her closer. "I'm sure it is. What can I say?"

"Nothing." They lay together quietly and after a few minutes Annika said, "Wouldn't it be nice if we could be doing something normal today: working in the garden or going to work or fussing around the house?" She didn't say anything for a time and stared beyond her tea mug at the rumpled bedclothes.

Rory stroked his hand down her arm. "We'll make certain that we have days like that again. One way or another, we'll get out of here safely. We've been lucky up to now." He tapped the bulkhead. "And, touch wood our luck will hold; and if it doesn't, we'll make our own."

"I hope so. You've got more experience in this sort of thing than I do." She sipped at her tea and bounced closer to him so that her side and thigh was burrowed up against him. Her voice was serious. "How did you ever manage to get through the last war? I can only imagine, but I'd guess things were incredibly dangerous and you lived through some terrible times."

Rory took a sip of his tea and was about to speak when Annika added, "I don't want you to talk about it unless you're willing to. I don't want to intrude."

"No, it's fine. I was just thinking about how I should answer that. I was in the war doing different things over a period of time. It was dangerous one way or another for almost all of it. But I suppose it's like anything else: you try to focus on the things that were good, the things that kept you going. After the war, well, memory is a strange thing. Remembering misfortune can depress you or inspire you. I try to be inspired. It doesn't always work, but most of the time I keep putting one foot in front of the other."

"What did you do?"

"At the start, I was in the infantry, just a common foot soldier."

"What came after the start?"

Rory wasn't going to tell her about his secret service in Germany but something inside told him that Annika was trustworthy, and something deeper than that wanted to trust her. "I was wounded. I was sent back to recover, and during my recovery I was recruited for some other work. I was sent to Germany. I was a spy. This isn't the first time I've done something similar to this."

Annika looked out in the distance. "That explains some things. You mean you've voluntarily done this more than once?"

He nodded. "People often ask why those of us who've been there go back and do it again. It's not that we want to. It's more like you said before: we feel obliged."

"You had a choice?"

"Yes, just like you did."

She put her head against his shoulder. After a few moments she spoke. "Where do we go from here?"

He smiled. "Well, I hope that after last night you'll see me again and we can get to know one another better."

She poked him. "I was serious."

"So was I." He shifted his weight and sat higher. "Okay, I think we call London tonight. And with any luck, we go out to the landing strip a day or so later to be picked up. Then we fly to England and we pick up our lives from there."

"Martin, do you think your superiors will be a little suspicious of you when you come back with me?"

"I've thought about that too. Yes. I'm sure they will. I would be. It would be easier if you weren't a pretty woman, but I hope, once they understand how things worked out here, we'll be fine. It's not as if we've broken any laws. The other aspect of this is—what are they going to do? If someone is angry or upset, so what?" He paused. "There's one other thing just now that I'm worried about, and that's calling from here. If we call from here on the boat, we probably lose our safe house. We'll have to move or they'll catch us."

"You mentioned that before. I've watched you set that radio up a couple of times now, and I think I have an idea that can help you fix that problem."

* * *

By 6:55 A.M., Major Sachs had six sections of his radio direction-finding units in place. He looked at his watch and then down the street. Oberstleutnant Neumann had said he'd be here to go over things with him in five minutes. He wasn't looking forward to the meeting. From what he'd seen, Neumann was a first-class bastard: ruthless, bullying, and arrogant. Most of the Gestapo were like that, but Neumann was especially dangerous. He was bright and had a spiteful streak: the kind of man who in an instant would cheerfully ruin your career, or just as swiftly, have you hauled off to a work camp never to be heard from again. He'd already developed a reputation here in Holland. It was rumoured that he had privately received some kind of SS commendation for shooting the hostages. He was a man to be avoided if you could.

Sachs was worried because his headquarters had promised Neumann seven detachments and there was only manpower available for six. They were scrambling back at his unit to cobble together another detachment. The seventh, however, wouldn't arrive until at least ten this morning. Sachs was aware that if things didn't go flawlessly this morning his head was going to be the one to roll.

Major Sachs looked at his watch and began to pace. The sooner he got this little police inspection over with the better. At seven sharp, a black Opel staff car rounded the corner and stopped beside Major Sachs's camouflage-painted three-ton command post van. Dressed in a field-grey officer's uniform and knee-high parade boots, Reinhold Neumann got out of the Opel. He looked just as Sachs imagined he would: unforgiving and scowling. Sachs came to attention, forced a smile, and saluted. "Good morning, Herr Oberstleutnant. I have the detachments in place and I'd be happy to show you their layout if you would care to step into the back of the truck with me."

Neumann nodded his assent and looked about him disapprovingly. The street, he noted, was empty of civilians. At either end of the road, Sachs had positioned a motorcycle and sidecar team armed with a machine gun to discourage any curious Dutch from coming too close to the van. Their presence wasn't really necessary, though. It was more a theatrical gesture designed to show Neumann that he took his safety seriously. The street was empty.

Inside the planning van, Reinhold Neumann squinted in the dim light. Sachs pointed to a map of Amsterdam on the wall. "Sir, we are here. The target area we spoke of is circled in red. You will see that we have six radio direction-finding stations covering this area. They are indicated by the blue lightning bolt signs on the map. They provide very good coverage of your target area."

"I was told there would be seven. Where's the other one?"

"Ah yes, sir, you were told that we have seven." Sachs paused and licked his lips. He noticed that Neumann had cut himself shaving. He looked in a foul mood. "The seventh one, I have kept in reserve ..."

"I didn't tell you to hold any back."

"Right, sir, but I have kept one back to deploy once we've got a feel for how the coverage works in this built-up area. Built-up areas can be tricky for radio direction finding. All these buildings create echoes and might give us a false reading. We're doing measurements now, and the seventh detachment will be deployed shortly to cover the area with the weakest reading. It will increase your accuracy."

Neumann looked suspicious. He looked closely at the map. "You'll be able to catch him the moment he starts broadcasting?"

Sachs thought Neumann looked a little unsteady and wondered

if he was drunk or hung over. He weighed his words carefully. "If it's technically feasible to pick him up here, we'll get him."

"So there's a chance you might not?"

"I think we'll catch him. It depends on how long he broadcasts. The longer he broadcasts the more precise our reading will be."

Neumann nodded faintly. "Good. I want to go and see one of your detachments."

Sachs walked Reinhold Neumann around the corner to the nearest detachment. He pointed out the radio mast and the large directional antenna temporarily fastened to the roof of a house. He showed him the signals truck down in the street with the radios and monitors in the back, and explained to him the technical issues involved in getting a fix. He was surprised that Neumann was paying such close attention to every detail.

Neumann looked thoughtful. "So, you mean to tell me that your signallers might not be able to pick up our man if he broadcasts on a frequency close to a commercial radio station?"

"Yes sir, that's why we hope he broadcasts a good long message ..."

Neumann interrupted him. "That won't be a problem." He turned to his driver. "Get a message back to my headquarters now. Tell them to have every commercial radio station in the city stop broadcasting, permanently. They must all be off the air in one hour or the owners will be jailed. Tell Hauptmann Ackerman I'll explain later when I get back." Turning to Sachs, he smiled. "I think that solves that problem for you, Major."

Sachs smiled. "Yes, sir, it certainly helps."

"Very good, Major Sachs. I'm happy with what I've seen. I expect you to catch him if he broadcasts. You and I may be working closely together for some time. This probably won't be the last illegal radio transmission to come out of Amsterdam. But together we will catch them all. Very good." He turned to leave.

Major Sachs snapped to attention and forced a smile. "That would be excellent, Herr Oberstleutnant. I look forward to working with you, sir. I've heard only good things about you."

Reinhold Neumann smiled and walked back to his staff car. Halfway there, he stopped and turned around. "Oh, and Sachs, I want a report to my staff of any radio stations that are still broadcasting at..." He looked at his watch. "Eight-fifteen. Good day, Sachs."

27

THE DAY HAD BEEN almost oppressively hot, but now the sun's light was a warm gold and the shadows inside the boat grew longer. The air over the canal was cooler. A breeze fluttered the curtains in the portholes of the cabin. Rory and Annika had not ventured out since last night. Here it was safe. They drank cups of tea, made love, and had long intense conversations about their past, their families, their upbringing, and the things they liked and detested. They didn't talk of the future.

Just after they cleared the dinner dishes, Annika sank into one of the barrel chairs opposite Rory and said, "When you think about us, it almost seems like a bizarre kind of honeymoon, doesn't it? It's as if we have things backwards, I mean ..." She felt awkward and struggled for words in English.

"I know what you mean. Everything seems hurried, almost as if we're in a movie with the projector running twice its proper speed." He shifted his weight and leaned forward. "But at the same time, it's as if we're trying to make up for time we never had together, or might not have in the future."

Annika pushed her hair back off her neck, "That's exactly how I feel; but it's strange all the same. Do you think we're being foolish?" Then, as if she could no longer keep it in, the fear that had been nagging at her all day surfaced. "Martin, what do you think our chances are of getting out safely?"

"First of all, no, I don't think we're foolish. We've been pushed by events beyond our control and we're both reasonably sensible adults, so I don't think we've been foolish at all. If anything, I'd say we've both been lucky, in every way." Rory leaned back heavily in his chair. "As for our chances of getting out, I really don't know what they are. That's the truth. Nobody's ever done this sort of thing before. Who knows if the Germans will monitor our radio. Who knows if we haven't already been betrayed by a spy or a traitor back in Britain. I really have no idea what the odds are. But so far we've managed to keep alive."

"I suppose they've sent you over here the same way they give miners canaries to carry down coal mines. If we die, it wasn't a good place to be or we did something wrong."

Rory looked pensive. "Unfortunately, you're probably right. That's definitely part of it. But there's more than that to it. Someone has to set up the beginnings of a resistance network, and what we've been doing is more than just feeling our way forward waiting for the canary to die. We knew it was going to be risky. When you volunteered to work with me, you understood it would be a lot more dangerous than just striking off on your own to get out of the country. And even if I ignore everything else that's happened, I admire you for that. You could have put all your efforts into escaping, but you didn't." He reached over and took her hand. "We'd both be dead without each other."

"Maybe I'm just being frightened and selfish."

"No. Not at all. You're right. Fear is a normal part of thinking through a dangerous situation. So, yes, I think we're a bit like canaries in a mine. Someone has to figure out what works and what doesn't. You think it through as best you can and then you do it. It won't be just you and me who have to do this. It'll be the same in every occupied country. And when things go wrong, which they will, then people like you and me will die."

"That's what I'm afraid of."

"That's normal. But we've been lucky and we're doing everything we can to stay lucky. I think we'll make it." He stopped talking and looked directly at her. She was lost deep in thought, breathing almost imperceptibly. "You're probably thinking I'm not frightened by all of this."

"You don't seem to be."

He leaned towards her. "Sure I am. But the truth is—and I've never admitted it even to myself—until I met you I was prepared to die. I didn't want to die but I was prepared to. I didn't do this as a suicide mission, but I wasn't as alive then as I am now. My reasons for wanting to get back safely are a lot stronger now than they were before I came here and I didn't realize that."

Rory leaned back and took a deep breath. "If I really believed that this was a hopeless mission, I never would have come here. I could have convinced the people in London that there'd be other ways to accomplish what we've already done. But I think what we've done …" He paused for a moment and looked away. "Even given the loss of the hostages, it will have been worth it. It sounds cold-blooded of me to say it, but when we get back, we'll have a lot of information we can use to help others: how the Germans react; how they conduct searches; how the Gestapo use the local police and the army; hundreds of details. We should be thoroughly debriefed. There'll be other things we haven't even thought of. The risks will have been worth it if it eventually helps shorten the war."

He leaned over and lifted her gently up out of the chair to him. "But once we're back in England, the war's going to be my second priority. I hope to spend most of my time with you. I plan on getting there safely."

As the sun dropped from the sky, Annika walked alongside the canal to where she had secured the runabout. Lights were already burning in most of the canal boats and in the houses across the street. There was no traffic. She unshackled the runabout and motored back to Wiesja's. While she lashed the smaller boat to the stern of the canal boat, Rory lugged the suitcase out of the cabin and placed it in the bow under the tarpaulin. It was not yet completely dark, so the two of them went back into the cabin and waited.

They sat in an uncomfortable silence for several minutes, deep in their own thoughts. Rory was the first to break the stillness. "You know, this was a stroke of genius on your part, Annika."

"Not really. I just saw you uncoiling the antenna and it gave me an idea as to how we could send our message and not give up our hide-out until it was time to go."

"It was still brilliant. It's the difference between getting caught and going free." Rory looked at his watch. "London will be on the air in a few minutes, so by the time we get there we should be okay to transmit. Are you ready?" He spoke cheerfully and forced a smile.

Annika got up without speaking. He gave her a hug and she smiled thinly at him. "I'm still scared."

"I know. You'll be wonderful. You're a natural at this sort of thing."

She untied the smaller boat while Rory fired up the outboard. As they were preparing to push off, two large German trucks loaded with infantry roared past and stopped fifty metres up the street.

"Oh my God!" Annika whispered.

Rory stood up and watched the soldiers. They looked bored and not particularly interested in anything going on in the canal. He gave a cheery wave and one of the soldiers on the rear truck halfheartedly waved back.

"Let's go," he said, with a wide smile stuck on his face.

They motored off. Rory motioned Annika to sit beside him in the stern. "You steer. I'll sit beside you. I don't want to talk too loudly—our voices travel a long way over water at night. They're out looking for something. It's probably us. We have to assume it's us."

Annika squeezed his arm.

A moment later Rory said, "You've been magnificent. If we had broadcast from Wiesja's canal boat, they would have caught us in minutes. But you know, that's the second time they haven't paid any attention to people in the canal. Someone's going to think of it sooner or later."

Once more Annika steered them through the canals like she was manoeuvring about in her kitchen. Rory quickly lost his sense of direction. "You've an uncanny ability to navigate these canals. I can't even tell where north is down here."

"No, I don't know the canals. I know the streets beside them. I grew up in this city."

He gave an agreeable shrug but the sense of inadequacy from not having a mastery of all the skills he knew he needed for the operation left him feeling vulnerable. She pointed forward. "Just up ahead, around the next corner, is the Amstel River. We go along there until we reach our spot, the Blauwbrug Bridge. I think it will put us about two and a half kilometres, as the crow flies, from Wiesja's."

As the lights from the bridge appeared in front of them, she eased back even further off the throttle while Rory moved forward and took the antenna wire from the suitcase. She guided the runabout around the bend and forward alongside the approach to the bridge. The bridge was a majestic structure, made with three large but low spans of concrete and stone. It was topped by a rococo handrail and eight sets of ornate street lights. At the mouth of the bridge was what appeared to be a fence, made of heavy wooden rails, that when closed formed a gate to prevent boats from travelling up or down the canal system. Tonight the canal gate was open. With its jaws disengaged, it resembled a massive minnow trap designed to feed boats under the bridge.

Rory tied one end of the antenna to the uppermost wooden rail, and Annika eased the throttle. As the boat glided under the span, she had to duck her head. Once under the concrete, she put the engine in neutral and grabbed onto a rocky lip jutting out from the concrete. She skinned her fingers trying to stop the boat's forward motion. The blood that oozed from her scrape looked black in the mix of incandescent light and the reflection from the water. Rory pulled out a flashlight and crawled under the tarpaulin. He inched himself out a minute later.

"You'll have to turn the engine off. I can't hear the keys properly with the noise bouncing off the bridge."

To Annika it seemed as if he were under the tarpaulin for an eternity. Half a dozen cars passed over them and each time her heart felt like it stopped. What could he possibly be doing under there? She watched his feet shuffle as he tried to make himself comfortable.

At last he emerged and scrambled to the stern. He hauled the boat backward to the wooden barrier and untied the antenna. "Let's go."

She eased the throttle out gradually and the boat moved forward. She was about to turn them around to go back the way they came when Rory grabbed her by the arm. "No! Keep going forward." He gestured behind them. Several vehicles, including a heavy military lorry and a police car with a blue flashing light, were heading towards the bridge from the Waterlooplein area.

Annika opened the throttle and the boat surged forward.

* * *

SACHS AND NEUMANN got out of the staff car and faced westward, looking at the line of houses and shops. "Sachs, are you sure they're in this area?"

Sachs looked over at Oberstleutnant Neumann. He was doing his best to look confident. "Herr Oberstleutnant, that's where the signal came from. Three of my detachments tell me they had a positive reading and they all picked up a response on the same frequency. My best guess is that this is what you are looking for. Somewhere over here in the area of Rembrandtplein. I would guess he's in one of those large blocks of houses on the west side of the canal. Yes, I think you will have your man before daylight."

Reinhold Neumann grunted. Sachs didn't like his response; it was the same sound a bull made as it pawed the earth before charging.

As they walked along the bridge, Sachs's stomach felt hollow. There were buildings on both sides of the canal and he had advised Neumann to search in the Rembrandtplein Square side of the Amstel River. He looked back behind him. Given the distance and the accuracy of his detachments, it could just as easily have been a contact that came from the other side of the river.

Neumann saw the doubt in the signal officer's face. "What's the matter? I thought you said you were certain we've come to the right place?"

Sachs chose to brazen it out. After all, he had a fifty-fifty chance of being right. "No, I'm just double-checking for you. It's this side of the river." He tapped the folded map in his hand. "This side of the river is the Jewish quarter. Which side do you think your spy would choose to hide on, Herr Oberstleutnant?"

"I'll ask the questions, Major Sachs. You may be right."

A taxi drove up behind them and, seeing the assembly of police cars and military vehicles, stopped and waited patiently. The taxi was soon joined by a truck, and within a few minutes, there were small lines of vehicles in all four directions, all waiting uncomplainingly to get through the cluster of German trucks and infantry.

Neumann turned his back on the buildings and faced the canal. He was annoyed, and his mouth twisted in frustration. He waved his hand indicating the Jewish side of the Amstel River. "Search all these buildings. Anyone with something wrong with his eye, bring him down to police headquarters."

He looked out over the canal and uninterestedly watched the wash slapping at the canal banks. There was no movement on any of the boats tied along the banks. He didn't feel good about tonight. Perhaps they had created too large an area to triangulate the transmission. He looked at the buildings on the two sides of the bridge. He could have been on either bank and scurried off east or west, north or south, as soon as he finished transmitting. Maybe Sachs had overestimated his capabilities. As tight as he thought his plan was, he had a sinking feeling that his spy had escaped him again. He knew in his gut they weren't going to catch him here. There would be no triumphant achievement to report to his superiors tonight. "Sachs, if you catch anyone here, call me. I'll be at my office." He slammed the car door behind him.

Sachs cursed the Gestapo officer under his breath as Neumann pulled away. Neumann had ordered him to travel here in his car; and now Sachs's staff car was back at police headquarters.

* * *

A FEW HUNDRED METRES past the bridge Annika swung the boat hard left at the mouth of the much smaller Nieuwe Kaiser feeder canal. "I don't think anyone is following us."

"Neither do I, but we should keep going for a while. They may figure out that the transmission came from the river and start searching along the banks." They motored on in silence and Annika nestled close to Rory. He put his arm around her. After a minute, he spoke without emotion. "Tomorrow night, London's going to confirm what date the Lysander is ready. We have to go back on the air again tomorrow." His tone changed abruptly. "I hope they give us a different operator. The idiot at the other end was trying to get me to respond to a lot of foolish questions."

Annika could feel his anger but was more concerned about immediate problems. "Do you think we should go back to Wiesja's boat? We'll probably have to go all the way around to the harbour and back."

"No, not now. Is there somewhere we can pull up in the next six or seven hundred metres? That'll be far enough away to lie up. We'll go back tomorrow morning. We shouldn't be out on the canal after dark more than we have to."

"Okay. Up here a little bit, then we'll go left and stop at the landing." Annika steered them on for another three minutes, turning past the peaceful-looking eighteenth-century burghers' houses with lights twinkling through sheer curtains in the upstairs rooms. She brought the boat up to a space a hundred metres from the next public landing. "How's this?"

"I think it's as good as we're going to get. You did a terrific job tonight, Annika." He gave her a squeeze. "We made it this far. Now, we still have to figure out what we do tomorrow night."

28

THEY WERE FAR ENOUGH AWAY from the public landing to be beyond the pool of light from the lamp post. The street behind them was empty. Rory rolled up the antenna and then spread the tarp out, folding it such that they would have a cover over them and a layer under them so they would not be lying on the boat's damp floorboards. He looked at his watch. "It's not twelve yet. We've still got to spend six or seven hours here. I'm glad it's not cold."

They passed the night uncomfortably, lying beside each other in silence listening to the ropes creak and strain and the slapping and sloshing of water against the concrete walls of the canal's bank and the wooden hull of the runabout. Annika fell asleep shortly after two. Rory forced himself to stay awake, listening to Annika's soft breathing—and for the sound of anyone approaching them. Just before four, the temperature dropped a few degrees; shortly after a wind came up and a gentle rain started to fall. Annika woke with the pattering of raindrops on the heavy canvas. She rolled into Rory and giggled. "This would almost be fun if it wasn't so dangerous." They both smiled.

Just before six o'clock, they could hear the sound of boats moving off in the distance. Rory lifted the canvas and strained to hear them. The boats he heard in the distance were probably travelling along the Amstel River. There were no boats moving here on the feeder canal.

They left their place of concealment, started the motor, and headed back to Wiesja's. There was early morning commercial activity on Amsterdam's canals long before the city's streets came to life. Rory and Annika were not alone. As they chugged back under a grey sky and turned into the Amstel River they met a half-dozen boats like theirs, with sleepy people heading off to conduct deliveries at daybreak. At the Blauwbrug Bridge, there was no sign of the drama of the night before. The streets on both sides of the bridge looked menacingly normal and quiet. By 6:30 they were back at the houseboat.

Inside the safety of the houseboat's cabin, they fell eagerly into one another's arms. Even though it was probably illusory, the cabin walls provided a sense of refuge. Rory closed his eyes and his whole body relaxed. Annika clasped herself tightly to him and sheltered her head against his chest. They clung to each other without speaking, breathing deeply, luxuriating in the security and warmth of the contours of each other's body. In a moment the tension they had suppressed for so long ignited in a physical hunger. Rory kissed Annika and guided her into the boat's stateroom. They made love with the ferocity of new lovers, but there was an additional intensity to this morning's passion. It was sparked by an unexpressed craving to forget their past and ignore their future.

They slept until close to eleven and were awakened by the sound and rolling wash of a heavy tug motoring on its way to the city's harbour. Annika rose first, dressed, and walked to the market to buy food. When she returned, she found Rory sitting in one of the barrel chairs with a cup of tea in his hand.

She put her cloth shopping bag down in the chair opposite. "Things are grim. When I was in the market, I saw one of the morning newspapers. Wiesja's radio isn't broken. Yesterday, the Germans outlawed all Dutch radio stations. This morning, they've got sound cars announcing a permanent curfew during the hours of darkness."

Rory rubbed his unshaven chin. For a moment he didn't speak. "I heard the sound car about twenty minutes ago, but I didn't understand what it said. They're tightening the noose on us and everyone else they're trying to pick up."

"What do you want to do?"

"I think we have to move out of the city. Last night your idea was inspired, but we can't do another transmission here. They moved in on us so quickly this last time, we just can't risk going on the air like that again. The next broadcast they'll figure out that we're using the canals."

Annika folded her arms. "So, let's think this one through. We can't stay here and we have to make our way to the landing zone anyway. In either case, we can't have you lugging a suitcase around with the radio in it. You'll be spotted immediately. We have to be clever about this one, and we don't have much time."

* * *

"I DON'T THINK THERE WAS any question, Oberstleutnant. It was not a coincidence. Someone was broadcasting from that area last night. Five of my detachments picked up their signal." Major Sachs was being guarded in choosing his words; you could see it in his face. At the same time, he wasn't backing down, and Neumann liked that. The man was obviously not comfortable around Neumann, but he managed to balance fear and caution with doing his job. Neumann liked his tenacity; he could work with such an officer.

"Sir, even if we were out in our fix by a hundred percent, we still would have narrowed the broadcast down to an area two hundred and fifty metres on either side of the bridge." He paused and looked grave. "I still think he was broadcasting from within one of the buildings west of the bridge. That wasn't a guess. I rechecked all the angles, and if you excluded the most easterly indication, which was probably the poorest calibration, the other four detachments put him inside a fix between the bridge and two hundred metres inside the Jewish Quarter. There's no disputing that kind of geometric accuracy."

Neumann didn't speak. Even with the curfew in place now, he knew that they might not catch the spy if he ventured out. And there was no guarantee his spy would broadcast again tonight or even this week. He wanted to catch him before then. He cupped his chin with his hand and walked over to the map. He stood there rocking back on his heels for a minute. "You know, we tore those houses apart last night. There was no radio there. Now, it's just possible that he could have escaped carrying a heavy radio in the dark, with him knowing that we would be looking for a man with a strange eye, but I don't think so. This man is too smart for that."

"Sir," Sachs began to protest, "I am positive we had an accurate fix on that broadcast last night."

Neumann waved him down. "No, Major Sachs, I think you were right. I believe you. I've seen your maps and your diagrams. Everything tells me you were right. You did your job well. We went in with over a hundred men within two minutes of his final transmission and we still missed him. Do you know why?"

"Sir?"

"He was right under our feet. It wasn't your fault."

Sachs said nothing and did his best to look at Neumann as if he actually thought he made sense.

"We didn't find him because he was under the bridge and we were looking everywhere else but there. Our man was in a boat. That explains the wash I saw in the canal. I thought nothing of it at the time because we were fixated on the Jewish Quarter."

Sachs looked intense. "It's also possible, sir, that he had a vehicle. He finished his transmission and drove away to the west as soon as he was done."

"I've thought of that. Normally, I would think you were right. But I don't think he has a vehicle. It's possible, but I don't think so." Neumann was looking at the ceiling. "No, no, if he had a vehicle, he would not have taken the train when he travelled from Hauwoud to Amsterdam—it's such a short trip. Our spy has no choice. He has to get around by other means, and I think he is on one of the canals. That's why he disappeared from us despite such intensive searching, and that's why we didn't catch him last night, even when your instruments told us he was there. We were in the right location but looking in the wrong place. He was literally right under our noses."

"That makes sense, Herr Oberstleutnant." Sachs looked relieved. He took a quick glance at the door.

Neumann didn't notice the other man's body posture and drew a circle on the map with his finger. "I have a hunch, based on all the other evidence, that our spy is to be found somewhere on one of these canals." He turned away from the map. "Major Sachs, go call Hauptmann Ackerman in here. In the next two hours, we are going to conduct an immediate search of every boat along the canals in the city centre. I don't want to waste a minute."

Sachs left the room and Neumann turned to look out the window. As he did so, his shoulders slumped. His spy, whoever he was, probably didn't even suspect that the search for him had become a personal vendetta. He probably thought it was simply a fight between the Germans and the Allies. Maybe that was part of the problem. Maybe he had let this become too personal for him. He inhaled deeply and lifted his head, as if he had been inspired by some insight. Perhaps that was it. Maybe all this had become too personal.

But when he exhaled and turned away from the window, he let his shoulders droop again. For the first time, he seriously thought that maybe this faceless spy with a bad eye was going to defeat him. Perhaps he might just slip through his fingers. Maybe he was gone already. Reinhold Neumann didn't want that. He wanted to be promoted out of Amsterdam. He wanted to move up in the organization, to go to the next level, to go to some place where he could comfortably write policy and give directions to a subservient staff around a conference table. And although he hadn't admitted it until this morning, he wanted to go somewhere where he could be reunited with his wife and children. He didn't want to stay here in a sordid relationship with a frightened Dutch woman. He wanted to be given a chance to make a new life of it and start things afresh in a place where he would have opportunities open to him. But this obstinate spy! He smacked his fist into his open palm.

And then the thought occurred to him. He had been doing the right thing all along. He had wanted to capture a live spy. But doing the right thing in these circumstances was simply foolish. He would catch him one way or another. A dead spy would serve his purposes just as well.

* * *

ANNIKA RETURNED WITHIN THE HOUR. She had left to go searching for, as she said, "the nearest second-hand shop to get some things to make the radio look a little less obvious." When she came back, she was pedalling an elderly rusting bicycle with a large wire frame cage on the back. She had a huge grin on her face.

"Until I met you, I'd never stolen anything before. Now look, this is the third bicycle I've stolen in a week. And you know what's worse? I enjoy it! I saw this one with the basket and thought it's exactly what we need. So, now it's ours. When we get to England, I think I'll quit music!"

Inside the bicycle's wire cage was stuffed a dark blue second-hand coat, a flat cap, and a pair of scratched tortoiseshell glasses. Rory changed into the coat, which was a touch large. He put on the flat cap and tried on the glasses. With the glasses on, the world seemed painfully out of focus. He winced.

With her head cocked to one side, Annika looked him over appraisingly. "No, it works. It makes your face strained, and with the clothes and the unshaven face, now you look like a poor Dutch farmer, not the stylish gentleman in a suit and hat the day we took the train. As long as no one stops you and looks at your eye, you'll be fine."

"I hope they don't get too close," Rory muttered. "Anything beyond fifty or sixty feet is a blur."

He pushed the glasses up on his forehead and they consulted a map. They agreed on three rally points where they would meet should they become separated on their way to Hauwoud.

Annika started out first with the suitcase strapped beneath her wire cage. Rory loaded the food and blankets into his basket and set off after Annika. Hunched over the handlebars, wearing his coat and cap, with his unkempt beard and one trouser leg rolled up above the ankle, he looked years older than he was. He kept a blurry two hundred metres behind her. When Annika wanted to indicate she was about to make a turn, she scratched her head with her turning hand. Once she'd made the turn, she slowed down to give him time to follow her route. They looked like nothing more than two of Amsterdam's thousands of cyclists going about their business in the middle of the afternoon. In five minutes they were at the Jordaan Market.

Rory got off his bike and meandered slowly down the side of the street, pretending to look at the stalls, while Annika bought two live chickens and stuffed them clucking and fussing into her wicker cage. From where he stood, he wondered if people's curiosity would be drawn away from the suitcase or if they would be attracted to a pretty farm woman pedalling a bicycle with a ludicrous-looking cargo of chickens on the back. He frowned. An ideal criminal disguise should make someone disappear into their background, not stand out as something other than what they are. He had reservations. Certainly it was clever, though.

Out of the corner of his eye, he could see Annika making animated small talk with the chicken stall owner. She got on her bicycle and pretended to wobble slightly as she pedalled off in the middle of the market. Rory took his cue, and after stopping to peer at a tabletop of leeks and tomatoes, he swung back onto the narrow leather saddle and wove his way through the shoppers, hoping Annika wouldn't be so far ahead that he couldn't see her. A block away, he heard the two frightened chickens squawking and clucking before she came into view. When she came into focus, he saw her waiting patiently amidst a half-dozen other amused cyclists at the traffic lights.

As they left the downtown area, the swarms of cyclists steadily diminished in size until by the city's outskirts there were just the two of them pedalling away. The distance between them decreased as Annika led him out of the city and onto the side of the highway that led to Utrecht. She took the first turn onto the secondary road that led to Hauwoud, and after a kilometre, stopped to fix her chain beside a small poplar grove. Rory caught up with her and took off his glasses and rubbed his eye. He stretched his shoulders and turned around. Looking behind him, he said, "Don't look now, but there's a German army lorry headed this way."

Annika stood up quickly and looked from the approaching truck to Rory. "We'll be fine." Rory said quietly. "I'm your retarded older brother and we've just bought chickens at the market."

Annika stood tall and swallowed. She looked like a performer about to go on stage, willing herself to assume a difficult part. "Wish me luck."

The truck pulled up beside them and stopped. Rory was leaning forward over the handle bars. Under his coat, he could feel the sharp edges of the Webley biting into his back. His throat was dry. He put his head down and gawked vacantly at the radiator. He rocked himself ever so gently and waited several moments before looking up at the soldier in the passenger seat and then back down to the radiator. There was a man on a Prairie farm he had known years ago, a quiet and gentle soul who was easily frightened; right now he wanted to be that man.

"Why are you stopped out here?" the soldier snapped in German. Rory recognized the voice. It was the Gefreiter who had given him a lift. He slowly looked up vacantly and returned his gaze back down to the radiator.

"I speak German, a little German. Please speak slowly," Annika said in a slightly flustered voice.

"What are you doing out here?"

"My brother and I are going to our farm, back to our farm. We buy two new brood hens and my bicycle is ..." Annika pretended to struggle for words. She pointed to the dangling chain. "My bicycle, it is not so good." She shrugged and forced a smile.

"Does your brother speak German?"

"No, he speaks Dutch, but a few words only, though." Rory continued to rock himself and stare at the front of the truck.

One of the soldiers in the back of the truck shouted down to the Gefreiter. "We have a pair of pliers in the tool bag, Gefreiter. It'll only take a minute."

The Gefreiter pushed his helmet back off his forehead and made a face. He waved out the window and beckoned with one finger. "Hurry up."

One of the young soldiers at the back jumped over the tailgate brandishing a pair of pliers. He laughed and took the bicycle from Annika. He raised his eyebrows and looked into her eyes and then made a cheerful clucking noise at the chickens. The men in the back of the truck guffawed.

The Gefreiter shouted, "Hurry up, Pfeiffer."

Rory looked up as if in alarm and cried out. It was a muffled sound, the noise people make in bad dreams that they can't wake up from.

Annika grabbed his arm and spoke to him soothingly in rapid Dutch. Rory went back to his rocking and staring at the radiator.

"He is afraid with strangers."

The Gefreiter laughed and turned to the soldier. "Hurry up. We haven't got all day to spend with the village idiot."

Annika nodded coolly at the Gefreiter, and smiled at the young soldier as he stood up, wiping his hands on his trousers, the chain once again tight. He tipped his helmet to her as the Gefreiter smacked the side of the door.

"Come on, come on, Pfeiffer. This woman has no time for someone as ugly as you. Let's go."

The soldier clambered back on board. The truck lurched into gear and drove away with the summer's dust settling back onto the road behind it. Rory and Annika got on their bicycles and continued on their way.

When the truck was a kilometre away, the driver looked over at his section commander and said, "You know, Gefreiter, we've been patrolling out here for a long time now. I can't help but think that man back there, the simple-minded fellow, he looks familiar."

The Gefreiter smiled a thin smile. He looked in the side mirror.

The two cyclists were no longer visible. "Watch the road. We'd re-member her anyway if we'd seen her before. As for him, he probably reminds you of someone in your family." He laughed at his humour.

* * *

AS DUSK FELL THAT NIGHT, Rory and Annika sat in a small clus-ter of trees and shrubs with their backs against an old beech. They had been talking and laughing quietly for the last hour but gradually they grew quiet as they huddled together with one of Wiesja's blan-kets wrapped around them. The evening wasn't cold, but the blanket protected them from the clouds of mosquitoes rising from the water-filled ditch a few metres away.

The western sky was streaked with the last splinters of orange day-light. Rory shifted his weight and Annika moved closer to him. He enjoyed having Annika close like this. She was petite but sturdy, hot spirited, enthusiastic, and imaginative; but she was more than just sexy. Since meeting her, his energy and *joie de vivre* had resurfaced. Until recently, he hadn't even been aware those characteristics had diminished. Now it was clear he had only been going through the motions. It was as if he had been wearing sunglasses, and now they were off. It was the same world, but everything had a more vibrant and immediate appearance.

Even through all the magnificent years he'd shared with Ruth, he had never thought of himself as someone who needed somebody else to feel alive. That kind of need was a vulnerability, something that applied to other, less robust people, but not to him. He'd never doubted that he was anything but self-reliant. Now, with Annika, it was undeniable. His self-assurance and energy were stronger.

Off in the distance behind them they could hear an owl hooting. Despite the constant annoyance of the insects, both of them were cheerful. Out here, the possibilities of capture seemed remote. The exhilaration of their impending escape and the promise of a new life in England left them happy and optimistic.

Rory looked at his watch. "They should be on the air now." He got up and stretched his arms. "I wonder if our friends back in Amsterdam will be listening to us again tonight?"

Annika shrugged and tried to laugh. "We'll find out soon enough."

Earlier in the evening, Rory had found a small hollow in the ground and put the suitcase in it. While it was still light, he set up the radio telegraph handset and strung out the antenna. He ran the antenna wire up through the tree branches and then prepared his coded message. He opened the suitcase and took out the flashlight. He took the blanket from her shoulders.

"I'm afraid I'm going to need this for a bit."

She made a playful face. "I'll get eaten alive."

Rory got down on his knees and pulled the blanket over his head. "I'll be back shortly." The blanket stopped most of the light from escaping and Annika could hear the clacking sound of the keys as he tapped out his message. The clacking stopped and started again as he encoded and sent his response.

A few minutes later he emerged smiling. "They'll pick us up tomorrow night. The same field I landed in. We had a much better radio operator on the other end tonight—one who knows how to be brief. We'll be picked up between 12:35 and 12:40. Seems hard to believe, doesn't it? Almost like calling a taxi."

Annika was swatting at mosquitoes. "I'll be so glad to get away from here."

"So will I. We still have some tricky bits ahead of us, though." He folded up the blanket and handed it to her, and then swept leaves and twigs over the suitcase with the radio. He stood up and brushed himself off. "It's time for our next stop, but before that, I think we should set our chickens free. I don't want them hanging around our next hiding spot to give us away."

29

TONIGHT, THE FILE Reinhold Neumann tried to busy himself with wasn't holding his attention. It was little more than a series of poorly thought out summaries of crime statistics and security issues. For once, he wanted someone on his staff to at least think through a problem and give him some reasonable options. He closed the file and angrily threw it into the wooden out-basket on his desk. This kind of sloppy work was just another reason he had to get out of this place. The fools he had to work with still couldn't differentiate between routine crime and security. He wasn't interested in crime. The Dutch could handle that. He was only concerned with threats to the new order.

"Sir?" It was Ackerman standing at his door.

He grunted in response.

"Sir, Major Sachs phoned me. I've got him on line two."

Neumann grabbed the phone and wrenched the dial on the wooden switch box over to line two. "What have you got for me?"

"Good evening, Herr Oberstleutnant. I think we have him again. We just had a series of transmissions on the same frequency; and the stronger signal, the one coming from here in the Netherlands, had the same operating signature."

"Never mind operating signatures. Where is he? Have you dispatched the reserve?"

"Well, sir, that's the problem. The signal is not coming from anywhere in the city. He's moved. He's out in the country, somewhere to the south of us."

"What do you mean somewhere? What are you telling me, Sachs?"

Sachs took a deep breath. "I can dispatch the reserve companies if you want, sir, but our reading is only going to be accurate to within an area of five or six square kilometres. By the time they arrive, they probably won't find anyone in the dark anyway."

Neumann motioned with his free hand for Ackerman to come into the room. "Sachs, I'm looking at the map. Have the reserve dispatched now. Expand the area of your fix. He can't go too far from his transmission site. Have the reserve battalion seal off all the roads within a radius of twelve kilometres of the possible transmission site."

"Sir? I'm not sure ..."

"Sachs, don't waste my time. They have to move by road. All of the fields in that area are divided up by drainage canals and deep ditches. There are no dense forests or scrublands to hide in. Choke off all the roads leading into the target area and you seal them in. We will at least have him trapped in a known location. Then it's just a matter of time until we find him."

"Yes, sir."

"Call me back when you've done that." Neumann dropped the phone into its cradle and walked over to the map. "Ackerman, get each one of the roads in here patrolled by police cars, each with a German and a Dutch officer. I want this section of the map completely covered." He drew a large circle with his finger around Hauwoud. "I want it patrolled intensively. We're going to leave the cordon in place and search that area. We'll search and re-search every house and barn and under every haystack for as long as it takes to find him. He's there." Neumann took a deep breath and looked at the map with obvious satisfaction.

"Don't just stand there, Ackerman. Get moving. I want every car in the city out searching within the hour."

As Ackerman left the room, Neumann picked up the phone and dialled the duty centre. "Get me the army patrol reports for the rural

area twenty kilometres around Hauwoud for the last forty-eight
hours. Anything, anything at all that looked out of the ordinary or
unusual, I want to know of it."

He walked over and stared hard at the map for ten minutes. He was
eventually distracted by Ackerman, interrupting him by feigning a
cough. "What is it, Ackerman?"

"Sir, the army reports you wanted. I have verbal transcripts."

For a fraction of a second Neumann almost looked hurt. "Are the
clerks too frightened to give them directly to me? Go on, go on, never
mind. What do they say?"

"Nothing. There has been nothing unusual to report. The only
thing even remotely of interest to them was a pretty woman with her
retarded brother on bicycles on the road to Hauwoud today. They
claimed to live on a nearby farm, but nobody had heard of them in
the local village. Apparently she was quite good looking, and when
the patrol got into town, one of the soldiers was trying to get information to contact her." He raised the papers in mock frustration. "Stupid things that go into their reports. Other than that, they have seen
nothing whatsoever in the last two days."

"Wait!" said Neumann. "A pretty girl and a man stopped on the
road near Hauwoud today. We know our spy travelled with a pretty
girl before. Now, we have just heard for certain that he's in this area,
and then we get a report of a pretty girl with an unknown man claiming to be from the area, but nobody knew of them—there's something fishy there. We also know they are very resourceful at getting
themselves out of a tight spot. It could have been them, some kind of
a disguise. No, no, I think we're right."

"Sir, there are a lot of pretty girls in Holland. And maybe the pretty
girl didn't want to be pestered by some lonely German soldier and
she gave a false address. This sort of thing happens all the time."

"It's possible, Ackerman; but I don't believe in that kind of coincidence. We know he's out there and so is she. Aside from sending a

transmission, we have to ask ourselves—what are they doing? He's not a fool. He knows we are getting a fix on him. What are they doing out there, Ackerman?"

* * *

BY THE TIME THEY GOT to the landing field, it was dark and the sky had clouded over. By day, most of these fields and hedges looked the same. In the dark, the problem was worse. When Rory estimated he was close to the right area, he stopped and dismounted his bicycle, checking each gate. It wasn't until his third stop that he found the gate with the oversized brass screws fastened high up on the post. He turned to Annika. "How deep do you think the ditches are here?"

"Why do you want to know that?"

"Because we're at the right field and we have to hide the bicycles. We can hide ourselves, but the bicycles will be a dead giveaway. They're shiny and they'll draw attention, especially if they try to search for us from the air. The deeper the ditch the better."

"Most of the ditches are stagnant but I'd guess they're probably close to two metres deep in most places—but do you think they'll have an airplane searching for us tomorrow?"

"If I were them, I'd have one searching for us. I think they'll have an airplane and a lot more. They probably picked up our transmission and I'd guess that they'll be sending someone out to search the area right now. Our best hope is that they'll have to search a larger area, and that takes time."

Annika looked worried but she said nothing.

"I'm not trying to scare you. We still have a good chance of getting out; but even if we don't, I've got the Webley. We won't let them take us alive."

Annika looked startled but forced a laugh. "Oh, that's reassuring!"

"I know." He shook his head and looked away. "I'm just being realistic. I expect we'll get out. We've made it this far." He felt hollow, though, and wasn't nearly as optimistic as he hoped he sounded.

For the twentieth time, he did a quick summary in his head. They had pedalled as fast as they could for thirty minutes after making the broadcast. He estimated in that time they would have travelled at least seven or eight kilometres. He had to believe that any direction-finding station would have picked them up. What he didn't know was how accurate their equipment was, or how many troops the Germans had available to cordon the area. How big was the triangulated area made by their direction finders? And how big an area would the Germans cordon off around that triangulated area? He could only guess. Was the landing zone inside or outside a possible cordon? There was no way of knowing. There were too many unknowns. He had an uncomfortable feeling that whatever the distance was, they were close. They couldn't possibly get far enough away on their bicycles to be certain they were out of danger. Rory grimaced. If they succeeded in getting out, one of the lessons would be that pickup zones had to be a long distance from the broadcast site. That conclusion wasn't a lot of comfort now.

Rory broke the silence. "Our best bet is to dump the bicycles and hide until tomorrow night." He reached over and gave her hand a squeeze. "The odds are probably on our side but let's not put them too close to the gate."

"I agree," she said, pointing back along the road. "There's a patch of drainage ditch back there that looks pretty dark and deep."

They wheeled the bicycles back in silence and dropped them end to end into the black water. In the dark, it looked like the ditch had swallowed them. A film of tiny floating weeds drifted back to cover the disturbed surface. Rory hoped it would look as natural in daylight.

* * *

REINHOLD NEUMANN was preparing to leave the office. He gathered up papers to take with him. He'd need something to read to keep busy. Earlier in the day, he'd decided he wasn't going to stay in the city if his spy was trapped in the country. He had given orders that he was going to set up his temporary headquarters in the hotel at Hauwoud. If the action was all taking place somewhere else, he couldn't stand being here in Amsterdam at the end of a phone.

He stuffed some reports from his in-box into his leather satchel. As he did so, the thought crossed his mind that he never read anything that wasn't concerned with his work. These stupid papers and others just like them were the only things he'd ever read in the last ten years. It wasn't really a revelation. He'd had these moments before, but it struck him as odd that now, of all times, he should feel a cringe of inadequacy. For some reason, this simple act of gathering papers from his in-box made him aware that for years his entire belief system had been built on an incredibly narrow understanding of the world. He didn't know very much about history or literature or art or science. The only thing he really knew was police work, and most of that was in the simplified context of maintaining order within the Third Reich. Yet in all those years, he'd been absolutely convinced he understood things. He'd never really imagined himself as being on any other path than the one he was on. He sat back and tilted his head slightly to one side. Perhaps that wasn't true. But then what of it? He managed to get by all right. He continued to stuff briefing papers into his satchel and shrugged. What difference did it make? His outlook on the world was probably as good as anyone's.

The phone rang and interrupted his line of thought.

Neumann listened carefully and his face clouded. "What do you mean the army won't give us the complete reserve battalion? I requested that it be on standby a week ago."

The voice at the other end patiently told Neumann he could only have a reserve company. The rest of the battalion had been kept on a high level of alert for too long. The troops were exhausted from conducting endless checkpoints, roadblocks, and cordons. They were being pulled back to rest, clean up, and have a few hours off duty. If he wanted to protest the decision, he was free to speak directly to the officer commanding the Netherlands garrison.

He slammed the phone down. Assholes! They sat around doing

nothing most of the time, and when he needed them, they couldn't perform. No wonder Himmler was creating his own army in the SS.

He picked up the phone again. "Ackerman, we've just had our army cordon troops reduced. We now have only one company. Not to worry, though. I still want all roads in and out covered by road-blocks, and I want police patrols searching within the cordon as we planned. I'm going to Hauwoud now. Ensure that we have radio and telephone communications with the hotel." This time he put the phone down carefully. There was no point in losing his cool. He had the transmission area blocked off. No one could get out of there—and now he had all the time in the world. He would tear this part of Holland apart building by building until they got him. And if they didn't get him today, they would have more troops in twenty-four hours.

* * *

UNLIKE THE THIN SHRUBBERY that curled around the fence wires at the edges of the roads, this ragged hedgerow looked like it had origi-nally been planted to act as some kind of permanent divider between two fields. Over the years, a lone beech tree had grown from its cen-tre, and the hedgerow itself had been allowed to grow into a rambling but ineffective windbreak. Little more than a handful of scrub bushes and stunted Dutch juniper survived here. The hedgerow varied in width from two to six feet. As Rory wearily noted, it wasn't much, but it was the only natural cover in this stretch of bald pasture land. The hedgerow ran perpendicular to the gravel road and drainage ditch and continued past the two deserted outbuildings. It petered out near a rusted wire cattle fence four hundred metres from the gate. The hedgerow had the added advantage of being beside their land-ing field.

No one had thought of it back in England at the time, but as he was now beginning to appreciate, placing a landing zone in open country when one might have to hide there for a length of time was not a smart idea.

Rory and Annika settled into a spot in the middle of the hedgerow at what appeared to be its widest point. There, after they dropped the bicycles into the ditch, they had spent the last four hours of darkness lying together, wrapped in one of Wiesja's brown blankets. Now the edges of the horizon in the east began to turn grey, and behind them, from somewhere up near the old beech tree, a pair of robins began their excitable morning chorus. Rory struggled to his feet. The morning dampness left his legs stiff, and his back ached. He looked around them. In the growing light, it was obvious the hedgerow didn't provide much concealment. "If we expect to stay here all day without anyone seeing us, we'd better sort out some sort of camouflage."

They walked two hundred metres from their lie-up, broke several small branches from the shrubs, and then built a small fifteen-inch-high frame over the blanket. They covered the frame with grass and leaves. When they finished, Rory stood back critically appraising it. "We'll have to get under this before it's too light. No one is likely to see anything unless they come right up on top of us, or a wind comes up and blows all the grass away—or, they look for us with dogs. Other than that, we should be fine," he said with a grin.

Inside their tiny makeshift wigwam of grass and leaves, it was hot and sticky. Rory and Annika passed the morning without speaking much. It was surprising how much noise there was in an open country field. Birds and insects kept up a near constant chatter in the rising summer heat, and occasionally they could hear the drowsy lowing of cattle. Twice they heard the sound of what must have been a military motorcycle roaring down the gravel road, but it didn't stop or slow down. By noon, they thought they could distinguish between the sounds of individual cows and calves a few fields away. As the day wore on, they whispered in low tones and talked about dozens of subjects. Rory would periodically raise a finger and they would strain to hear whatever it was he thought sounded out of place.

It was around two in the afternoon that Annika raised the subject they had been avoiding for days. "I keep thinking about the hostages the Nazis shot. I know we couldn't have known, but I feel guilty. They died because of what we did."

"You're right. Innocent people died because I killed an unsuspecting German policeman in uniform in wartime."

"I'm not blaming you for it."

"I know. But I also know it's something that bothers you. That's fine, but this is how I view it. I killed an armed man in uniform because he was a mortal threat to us and there was no other way out of the situation. Before I came here, I thought through the morality of that kind of situation. I simply acted on what I believed was the right thing to do."

Rory stopped and looked up at the sky through the patchwork of the frame's grass. "The hostages were shot because I killed him; but I wasn't responsible for their deaths. I didn't know there would be reprisals. It's the most vicious sort of blackmail there is. There's a practical side to this too. We can't work it out right now. Sometimes it takes years. When we get to England and we're safe, I'll start thinking about it again and try to make some sense of it; but I can't let guilt cloud my judgment now. That will be fatal for us. For now, we've got to just put it out of our minds. It was a horrible tragedy that someone else was responsible for. You have to believe that." He turned and looked at her. "Unfortunately, I've been through something a lot like this before."

They lapsed into silence, but just as Annika was about to reply a motorcycle engine roared towards them on the road and then stopped abruptly outside their gate.

* * *

THE SMALL HOTEL in Hauwoud that Neumann had requisitioned made a perfect temporary headquarters. The food was good. The hotel was clean. It had a telephone, the reception for the police radios was excellent, and it was close enough to the cordon that he could have his police and military commanders report to him personally as they finished searching their areas. Even better, Hauwoud was near the centre of the cordon. He had the perimeter blocked off, he had patrols searching within the cordon, and they all reported in to him at the centre. That was good. Even though they hadn't discovered the spy yet, the sense of control these arrangements provided was encouraging.

The young Hauptmann commanding the infantry company was in the hotel's drawing room standing in front of a large map. He was in the process of describing how his attached motorcycle reconnaissance teams had been patrolling all the country roads since before sunrise. Reinhold Neumann juggled a cup of coffee and a pastry and then waved his hand.

"Fine. Keep patrolling the roads just as you are doing. The very fact that you are moving along the roads means they can't risk travelling. Wherever they are, they're bottled in. It's only a matter of time before we catch them. Tonight, we should be reinforced by another company of infantry, and then we can intensify searches within the cordon. I would guess we'll have our spy in our hands in the next forty-eight hours." He rocked back on his heels and wiped his mouth with the back of his hand. Turning to his police liaison officer, he said, "Now I want to go and witness how you search the next farmhouse. Get your things."

When Neumann's car pulled up on the gravel road, there was already a motorcycle and a police car waiting half a kilometre down the road from the farm they had selected to search. Neumann got out and walked to the policeman and the motorcycle team. "So, the farmhouse is just the other side of this scrub line, is it?"

"Yes, sir. Nobody has left the house, at least they haven't used this road in the last twelve hours. We have a roadblock in place five kilometres that way." He pointed with his gloved hand. "And of course you came through the roadblock six kilometres behind us."

"Good, let's get on with it." Neumann slapped his thigh for emphasis.

The two soldiers from the motorcycle team were out first and ran to the front door. The three policemen scrambled after them with their weapons drawn. From outside his car, Neumann watched the scene unfold: the shouting of orders, the frightened household pushed out onto the porch, the crash of things being overturned, the tears, small children clutching at their parents' legs, weapons brandished in faces, shots from inside as the searchers fired into places they could not or would not delve into.

The whole process began to repeat itself in the barns and outbuildings. Neumann leaned back on his staff car and folded his arms, enjoying the sunshine on his face. It was really a lovely day. He would rather have been somewhere else, though not because he felt badly about this kind of thing. He relaxed and kicked at the pebbles on the driveway. He looked across the fields. This afternoon, he felt strangely composed and philosophical. What he was watching was more violent and intimidating than most other types of behaviour, but he sincerely believed it wasn't much different. Everyone tried to exert some kind of power over everyone else. The cycle of dominance and submission was a completely natural thing. It was in man's character. The application of authority and power was as basic to humans as eating or sleeping. The rich dominated the poor. The strong ruled the weak. The intelligent controlled the stupid. It had been that way since the time men lived in caves. What society had ever seriously believed in compassion? Progress always came through conquest. Every time someone on this earth met someone else, there was an implicit understanding of who held the power. When that understanding didn't exist, there was conflict. This process of conflict and exploitation was as natural as the turn of the seasons. Neumann walked over to the edge of the driveway and pulled out a long stem of grass and chewed on it.

They weren't going to find the spy in this farm. He didn't know how he knew, but he knew he wasn't here. He looked out over the fields. There was nowhere to hide out there. As far as the eye could see, there was only one scrubby stunted line of a hedgerow and you could see through that. There was no place to hide in this country.

Maybe in one of these farms there was a secret room. He scoffed at the idea. Nobody had thought of that yet. Nobody had needed a secret room.

He turned around and frowned. There were shots fired inside the barn and terrified cows were bellowing and streaming into the farm-yard. What were these idiots of his up to now? Ruthlessness was one thing, but he didn't want his police to look stupid. Fear had to have a purpose. He wanted a search done, not mindless vandalism. You could tell from the faces of this family that they weren't hiding his spy. Fear was just a tool you used to extract information, and you had to know how to use it. Once people were frightened, they normally couldn't control their other emotions. If you saw fear with a sense of evasiveness, it usually meant you had to dig deeper. Fear and bewilderment usually meant innocence. That's what was going on here. He would have these clowns search the disused outbuildings and then they would move on. There was no point in wasting time here.

30

AT DUSK, THE MOSQUITOES came out again. Beneath the camouflage frame, Rory lay on his back and watched them with irritated fascination as they bobbed and hovered just above his face. He wondered if mosquitoes could smell humans.

Annika lay beside him, absorbed in her own thoughts. She brushed an invisible bug from her face. The two of them said nothing. As each minute crept by, they were closer to rescue, but they refused to speak about it. Talking about the plane would only jinx them. Rory shifted his weight and turned onto his side. Annika smiled at him in the gloom and instinctively he smiled back. He was still worried about being caught. There had obviously been some kind of commotion at the farm next to them. Vehicles, shouting, and shots: some poor farm family being terrorized. But in a perverse way that was good news. It meant they had moved on to look elsewhere.

At ten, it was dark. They broke cover and stood up. The night was warm. Tattered clouds slithered across a crescent moon. By eleven, a wind had risen and the moon was barely visible behind a fast-moving stream of mist. Rory chewed his lower lip and Annika looked up at the sky. It was more than she could bear to avoid the subject any longer. "I think the plane will still come tonight, don't you?"

Rory stood behind her, put his arms around her, and gave her a squeeze. "If they don't come tonight, it'll be another night. But if for some reason it's not tonight, we'll have to be patient. We'll just hide here until we can go back and telegraph them for another pick-up. We might be a bit hungry. It won't be anything we can't live through." He said it with as much cheer as he could muster, but they both knew there were obvious holes in his optimism. How would they get back to the radio with the Germans covering every inch of the country-side? What would they eat and drink? The longer they stayed out here, the greater the risk of being caught. They both knew the Germans had boxed them in on this flat farmland. Tonight's flight was a one-shot chance.

At 12:20, Rory reached into his pockets and took out three matchbox-sized pieces of what looked like green plastic. "Here, take these." He handed Annika a book of matches and one of the pieces of plastic. "The green square is a highly flammable piece of...I don't know what's on the outside, some kind of combustible covering...but inside, it's mostly some sort of phosphorous compound. When you light it, after a second or two it burns with an incredible intensity for five minutes. Be careful when you light it—it can give you a nasty burn. When we hear the plane, I'll light two of them up by the road and you light yours by the bottom of the fence. You become the base of a T. The pilot will key in on your flare and land keeping himself in between the two flares that I light. When he touches down, run up along the left side of the field, keeping close to the hedge-row until you're even with the plane. I should be at the plane, but don't approach it until I wave you forward. If more than one person approaches without the pilot's okay, he has orders to shoot them and get the hell out. I'll wave you forward and help you in and then we're off. Don't run so fast that you trip in the dark. We only get one shot at this. Any questions?" He looked at her intensely.

"I think I can remember that. Should I practise?" Annika was smirking.

"I wasn't being condescending. I've seen smart men screw up simpler things under pressure."

"You probably haven't noticed. I'm not a smart man."

Rory didn't answer immediately. Instead, he reached out and gave her a hug. "I've noticed. One other thing: when you're at the centre of the field, the plane should come in right over top of you. I'll light my first cube when I hear his engine. We won't have much time."

Rory kissed her on the forehead. He held her for a few seconds, then said quietly, "Wish us good luck." She was the first to push away and walk to the fence line.

At his end of the field, Rory couldn't see Annika, which was a good sign. She was probably crouched down in the grass keeping a low profile. At 12:30, he could hear the drone of an aircraft. He looked at the faint luminous glow of his watch. It was earlier than he'd expected. He hesitated for a second, then dropped to one knee and struck a match. He held it against the small plastic square and jumped backwards as the square instantly burst into an intense blue flame. He ran over to the other side of the field. As he did so he could see Annika's flare blazing in the centre of the field. He lit his second flare and hurried over to the hedgerow. The engine noise was louder now, and he thought he could see the plane's silhouette approaching in the eastern sky.

Annika ran up to him. "He's taking longer than I thought he would to get here."

Rory nodded and swallowed. "I expected him to come straight in on the flares. Maybe he's double-checking his position." He felt a sickening feeling in his stomach. Off in the distance, above the sound of the plane, he thought he could hear the unmistakable sound of a motorcycle moving at speed on a gravel road.

* * *

THIS WAS GEMEINER KARL LOTTINGER'S first command. Just yesterday, he had been driving a motorcycle, and now he was sitting in the sidecar as the acting commander of his detachment. If he didn't screw it up, the Unterfeldwebel told him that he might even be promoted to Gefreiter in the next few days. They were short of good junior noncommissioned officers in the company; the Unterfeldwebel had told him that himself. Tonight he was a part of the advance guard from the new battalion that was taking up picket duties searching for some kind of spy out here in the countryside. The Unterfeldwebel had told him to go out and relieve the motorcycle team at the cross-roads just down from the old windmill on the gravel road.

That was fine. It all seemed so simple back when he had been briefed. But out here in the dark, he must have taken a wrong turn. He didn't remember seeing the track on the right, and then he kept going and turned right when he realized he'd gone too far. He'd been hoping to double back around behind the way he'd come, but the road didn't go where he thought it would; and then he took a couple of other turns, and now he didn't know where the hell they were. The Unterfeldwebel would be furious. He was late in relieving the outgoing motorcycle detachment. Instead of being promoted, he was going to be the laughing stock of the reconnaissance com-pany.

From the sidecar he motioned for the driver to pull over. He pulled out his map. He wasn't even certain which way north was now. The driver was no help. He just sat back and tugged at the chin strap of his helmet and grinned. He knew they were lost and the jeal-ous bastard was enjoying his discomfort.

Gemeiner Lottinger needed to take a compass bearing. He couldn't do it from the motorcycle: the sidecar's machine gun and the metal in the motorcycle threw off the magnetic needle in the com-pass. He jumped out and ran twenty feet down the road, struggling to get his compass out of his pocket. North was off to his right! How was that possible? Now he was more confused than ever. It was then that he saw the strange lights off in the distance in the field. What the hell could that be? Seconds later, he heard an airplane buzz-ing somewhere. God almighty, he had no idea what this meant. He should send a report on his radio, but he couldn't do that because he couldn't tell them where he was. He'd look like a fool. One thing was certain: if it was a spy, he wouldn't be setting off flares to let everyone know where he was. It had to be something to do with the search party. They would know about it anyway so there was no need to send a report.

As he climbed back into the sidecar, the radio crackled into life. The operator at the other end was asking him what was going on with all the lights to the east of them. And where was he? He should have been back twenty minutes ago.

Gemeiner Lottinger cleared his throat and looked around him as if some miraculous voice in the darkness could give him an answer to get out of this mess. "I am just north of the search party operations, with the lights in the field by the gravel road. I will be in your location in ten minutes." He put the radio handset down and turned to the driver, trying to sound as confident as possible. "Keep going. I think our sentry post is just up the road."

* * *

WHEN THE REPORT of the lights came in, Reinhold Neumann had just turned out the lights in his room and was on the verge of falling asleep. Now Ackerman was standing at his door jabbering away about the army using search lights and the Luftwaffe having an airplane in the area. Neumann leapt from his bed and threw on his dressing gown. He rubbed his eyes, and gave his head a shake. "Ackerman, what are you talking about, 'search party operations'? Is someone out there using flares to find the spy?"

"Sir, the report just came in that we have a search party on the ground and they have the field illuminated with flares. An airplane has circled the field. You never told me of any operations with the Luftwaffe scheduled for tonight."

Neumann stood still for a moment, then spoke slowly. "No, we have no aircraft in support today, and what's this about our people illuminating the field with flares? We have no one back inside the cordon until we resume search operations at first light. It's not us."

Neumann and Ackerman looked at one another and they both raised their eyebrows simultaneously. "They must have an extraction planned," Neumann said. "They're taking the spy out with some kind of airplane that can land in a field. Get on the radio. Tell them to shoot down the plane immediately!"

* * *

THE LYSANDER CAME IN low and fast from the west, flying directly over the three flares. Eric jerked himself around in the cockpit. Over his shoulder he could see some kind of vehicle with its running lights on. It was moving fast and heading away from the field towards Amsterdam. That seemed unusual. He would have thought anyone dropping off passengers would have departed the airfield location long before this. On the other hand, someone had certainly set the flares in the correct spot. He bit his lip as he banked the aircraft. Perhaps this was a trap.

As he rounded the loop, heading back to make his final approach, he gained altitude and noticed, off to the northeast, a line of vehicles with their running lights on. They were stopped, evenly spaced out and staggered on alternate sides of the road three or four kilometres away. That was certainly a strange coincidence for this time of night in a rural area. Farmers didn't do that; organized groups of soldiers did.

Eric instinctively rubbed his chin, a habit he'd developed as a small child whenever he was perplexed or worried. His fingers brushed against the microphone hooked into his leather flying helmet. There was no one he could radio to query about what was going on. He couldn't break radio silence, as a transmission coming from this location might compromise the agent on the ground as well as give away their modus operandi. But those vehicles waiting down the road certainly looked like a set-up; no one would blame him if he turned and headed back for England. In fact, heading back in doubtful situations was the suggested reaction in the squadron's standard operating procedures. In the likelihood of a compromised landing you abort the mission and reschedule.

It wasn't that easy in practice, though. The Canadian seemed like a decent enough sort and Eric didn't want to leave him hanging out for the Germans. But, if this was a compromised landing zone, they could always re-confirm the pickup by radio and come another time.

Eric curled his lip and flared his nostrils. His hands involuntarily squeezed the control wheel. "Fucking hell!" He didn't want to make the decision. A good man was waiting for him down there but he was surrounded by German soldiers. It was worse when you had to make a life or death choice about someone you could put a face to. Eric opened up the throttle and started to climb.

* * *

THE LYSANDER BANKED in a long lazy curve and flew back, reversing its original course and paralleling the field. Annika's hand went to her mouth. "What do you think he's doing?"

"I hope he's checking out the landing field, but he seemed to gain altitude pretty quickly as he passed." Rory felt stunned as it dawned on him that the Lysander might not be touching down. Suddenly he turned his head. "The motorcycle on the road, did you hear it? He stopped, then continued on. I don't understand that."

The sounds of the Lysander and the motorcycle receded in the distance, leaving the field illuminated by the harsh light of flaring and hissing phosphorous cubes. The two of them strained to hear the plane as it disappeared into the night, as if somehow by intense concentration they could will it to return.

"He's gone," Annika said, raising her head as if in acceptance of an unwelcome verdict. The two stared up in silence at the night sky, the exhilaration of the previous minutes draining from them as if some unseen hand dialled back their energy levels.

"I don't hear the plane, but we should wait here anyway. He might come back." Rory didn't believe what he was saying and knew his voice betrayed him. "The pilot must have seen the motorcycle. I'm sure he's seen other Germans nearby. He's probably decided it's too risky to land. Besides, there's nowhere to run now. But if we leave, and for some reason the plane comes back, we'll have missed our only opportunity. We'll give him a couple of minutes, at least until the flares go out."

Rory put his arm around Annika. They stood in silence. The flares began to sputter and the edges of the field receded into darkness. Rory thought it looked as if someone was dimming the lights on a stage at the end of a play.

Annika turned around and looked towards the farm buildings. She spoke softly. "There are lights shining a long way off over on the road. I think the Germans are coming."

Rory nodded. He was going to say something, but suddenly grabbed her arm instead. "Listen. Listen." Off in the distance was a faint but unmistakably growing sound of an aircraft engine. "He's coming back!" Rory stared into the dark eastern sky but Annika paid him no attention. She was transfixed by the steadily brightening lights on the gravel road.

Rory exhaled heavily, his excitement turning to disillusionment. He couldn't believe the sound. He was about to say it was probably a German plane when the Lysander flashed its lights once. He whooped with joy. "The Germans wouldn't flash at us. He's coming back!"

In seconds, the Lysander swooped past them, roaring down over the wire fence and bouncing heavily on the turf. The sound of its massive radial engine in the night was deafening. Rory was about to sprint out to the plane when Annika yanked him by the arm, pointing to the north. The lights were much closer now. Rory waved his arm excitedly. "Okay, wait here. I'll call you forward as soon as the pilot gives me the recognition signal." He dashed out, making the V for victory sign with both hands. A shadowy pilot gave him a thumbs up and he waved Annika forward.

Annika scrambled across the field. In seconds Rory was boosting her up the fixed ladder and clambering after her. He had only one leg inside the cockpit when the pilot pushed the throttle forward, pivoting the Lysander in the soft dirt. The aircraft lurched forward, the engine revved, and Rory pitched backward like a rodeo rider, hanging on with all his strength to stop himself from plunging to the ground. Straining muscles in his back and chest, he pulled himself inside. The Lysander bounced repeatedly and then lifted into the air, making an ear-splitting but reassuring roar as cool air blasted against him.

Rory straightened himself out, and as he pulled the cockpit cover closed, he looked through the heavy glass canopy into the blackness. His mouth went dry as several red streaks flashed past. Someone was firing machine guns at them. It was odd, for there was no accompanying noise. Though it was hard to tell in the dark, the tracer looked uncomfortably close.

31

"I COULD HEAR THEM going over last night. It woke me just after eleven. I was drifting off to sleep and I sat up in bed thinking to myself, 'I hope our bombers give the bastards in Berlin the same they gave us two nights ago,' and here it is." Harold Thornton smiled as he tossed a copy of the morning's *Daily Mirror* onto Ewen Crossley's desk. Two-inch headlines screamed, BERLIN HIT, 2ND RAID!

Crossley sat back and sipped at a steaming mug of tea. "I suppose it was inevitable. In a fight to the finish, we'll eventually end up destroying one another's cities. Better theirs than ours, I suppose. But I wouldn't get too excited about this. This is just the beginning." He looked sceptical.

Thornton sat himself heavily in the wooden chair in front of Crossley's desk. "Oh, I know that, but as you said yourself, we should have crushed the buggers ten years ago."

Crossley smiled as Thornton took off his glasses and began to rub them vigorously on his shirt. "That's a rough paraphrasing, Harold, but you've got the gist of it correct. What's on your mind?"

Thornton sat forward and smiled too. "Ah, you public school boys. You know you shouldn't be upset when grammar school boys call a spade a spade. We both know the Nazis are dirty buggers. Why not say it?" He shifted his weight. "Anyway, I've come to talk to you about our agent from Holland."

"Rory Ferrall? What seems to be the problem?"

"No, no. No problem, as such. I was just wondering what we have in mind for him." Thornton licked his lips and looked sideways. Crossley traced a finger across the scar on his cheek; it came to rest sceptically on his lips.

"Ewen, I know he's an old friend of yours, but some of the new staff are making jokes. They seem to think that, uh ..." Thornton wanted Crossley to interrupt him but knew his silence meant he was being left to skewer himself with his own words.

"What I meant was, some of the new people have some serious concerns about the man's reliability. He goes off on a short mission to Holland and comes back with a pretty girlfriend, and he's giving us some weak-kneed story that the Netherlands isn't a good place to develop a resistance. Not exactly Winston's idea of roaring defiance now, is it? And the girlfriend, well, no one's said it yet, but I think people see it as being, well, self-serving. I hear they're a couple and ..."

Crossley frowned and picked up his mug of tea. "Harold, I'll say this once. Thank you for raising the subject, as I expect you to be completely candid with me, so don't interpret this as a reprimand." He sat forward. "Against our better judgment, we sent an easily recognizable man into an occupied country where he doesn't speak the language. As we requested, he made contacts and then set up the beginnings of a resistance cell, and he did this after he had been identified by the enemy. I should also tell you that we've had Dutch expatriates who have independently verified the reprisals and the shooting that led to his identification. And what's more, he's a man with a proven track record who has brought a valuable contact with him. She has, by the way, volunteered to go back into Holland and he has volunteered for further service abroad. Nothing too self-serving about that. Lastly, they return with bullet holes in their aircraft and you tell me that some of the new staff find it amus-

ing or are scandalized that they just happen to be a couple. Is that
the problem?"

"Well, I didn't know about the bullet holes in the plane or the
verification of the reprisals," Harold admitted. "What do you have
planned for him?"

"The first thing I want is for you to put an end to any rumours
about him, and her. He's a valuable resource and we're going to use
them both again, as they've both volunteered. It's in the interest of
this organization that people have confidence in them. Does the fact
that they are a couple pose you any kind of a security risk?"

"Well, no. No, not at all."

"Good. So Harold, get out amongst our new hires and quash
any rumours and sniggering. There's a war on and we have serious
work to do." Crossley sat back and pushed one of his massive hands
through his curly grey hair. He didn't look happy. "We'll keep them
here for a while yet and then they'll both likely go back into occupied
Europe. He won't be going back to Holland." Crossley looked at his
watch. "I've got to give the new director a briefing on the new concept of operations in ten minutes and I need time to review my notes."
He forced a smile and raised his bushy eyebrows cheerfully. "Harold,
anything else I can do for you?"

* * *

"THERE IS NO EVIDENCE of a spy ring working any longer in Amsterdam, gentlemen. There is no evidence of any resistance in Amsterdam. The city is as safe and tranquil as any city in Europe, and it is
now becoming a productive and important part of the Reich. We
can safely say that Oberstleutnant Neumann has provided us an
excellent example of how a major city can and should be run in the
Reich's occupied territories." Oberst Schröder was smiling and the
candlelight reflected off his reading glasses. He stood at the restaurant table holding a glass of champagne in a toast with the other eight
men seated with him. Reinhold Neumann looked up at the Netherlands Gestapo chief.

Neumann was doing his best to look suitably modest, but at the same time he wanted to look flushed with pride at the praise of his superior.

"I am sad to say," Schröder continued, "we will shortly be losing Oberstleutnant Neumann. He is leaving us for better things. In a few weeks, he will be taking up a new post in Berlin, where he can be reunited with his lovely wife and family, and provide us all further service in a challenging new job in planning the growth of all SS police services."

There was a small, polite round of applause, and Neumann was asked to say a few words. He shook his head and smiled as if to say, "Oh, what was all this fuss for?" He stood up and looked about him, smiling happily at his fellow senior Gestapo officers. The trick was to make yourself believe your own disinformation. He beamed and bowed his head in gratitude to all around him. Yes, there was no resistance network for now in Amsterdam. True, his spy had escaped, but shortly afterward, he'd had a Socialist Jew who lived beside the Waterlooplein near the Blauwbrug Bridge arrested. Under interrogation, the man had admitted to being the leader of the spy ring and implicated all his ring's members. Arrests had been made, reports had been filed, and although he hadn't been promoted, he now had the posting that would secure his next step up the ladder.

Neumann bowed his head again and smiled broadly at his fellow policemen's appreciation. It was a good thing they were fulsome in their praise for him. Some day soon they would be working for him. He pulled a card with his notes from his pocket. He was confidant in what he was about to say; his speech had been well planned.

* * *

THEY WERE SITTING TOGETHER at a corner table in the Red Lion pub in the village of Wendover. They were lucky to get a place to eat and much luckier to get a room. The pub was noisy, smoky, and filled with blue uniforms, most of them young men from the nearby

RAF station. Annika had her arm resting on the table with her hand on Rory's in a reassuring gesture.

"Everything's fine. I'm going to be sent to do my training at Ramsford House, and someone told me that apparently I'll have the room next to the one you had."

Rory had a distant look in his eye.

"You shouldn't worry, I'll be fine."

"There's nothing I can do to make you change your mind?"

"Rory, it's not because of you I'm going. I don't know why, but I feel I have to go. The Nazis have done so much: they murdered Saul, bombed Rotterdam, the occupation. I just can't sit back and watch others fight for my country." She paused and whispered, "Don't forget, you're going back over there some time too. I've thought about that a lot."

"It's going to be very dangerous for you, you know that."

Annika laughed and squeezed his hand. "You're the last one to lecture people about taking risks; and anyway, I'll come back. We'll be together again." She took a sip from her beer and, doing her best to sound cheerful, changed the subject. "You know the worst thing that's happened to me since I came here? One of the green grocers in our village reported me to the police as a possible German spy."

They both laughed. Rory put his hand on Annika's. "So what's the immediate future hold for you now?"

"I'll continue my training for a while yet. I'm not permitted to tell anyone outside my case officer what I'm doing or when I'm going back, but we should manage to be together for a couple of days next month. Some time after that I'll be gone. Don't look so glum. I intend to come back, you know. We'll be together then."

Rory looked defeated. He gave a tired smile. "Of course you will. I'm just being selfish. Let's just enjoy the time we have left together. Shall we order?"

Postscript

The incidents in this novel have been drawn from real events that happened to Special Operations Executive agents in Europe during the Second World War.

Given the nature of clandestine operations, Allied unpreparedness for the war was arguably much more extensive in its intelligence services than it was in the woefully ill-prepared armed services. As a result, the early days of covert warfare were uniformly marked by a series of calamities.

With the Venlo Affair, the British lost all their intelligence assets in the Netherlands before the outbreak of war. In several countries, agents were inserted who did not have a solid grasp of the local language or were otherwise conspicuous in their appearance. Operations in Holland went from bad to worse when the German army captured an agent and forced him to send messages back to Britain. A careless radio operator in London ignored the absence of a key code word signifying that the agent had been captured and was broadcasting under duress. As a result, the ensuing German counter-intelligence operation, the "Englandspiel," captured all fifty-four agents who were subsequently inserted into the country. All of these heroic men and women were either murdered outright or, after torture, sent to concentration camps. Only three survived the war.

MICHAEL GOODSPEED has had careers in business and in the army as an infantry officer. He has lived and worked across the Americas, Europe, the Middle East, and Africa. He has degrees in English literature, business administration, and strategic studies.

The author of numerous articles and newspaper columns, Goodspeed wrote a major 2002 non-fiction book, *When Reason Fails: Portraits of Armies at War*. His first work of fiction, *Three to a Loaf: A Novel of the Great War*, also featured *Our Only Shield* protagonist Rory Ferrall, on a dangerous mission inside Germany.

Michael and his wife, Shannon, have three grown children and live in an old farmhouse in the Eastern Ontario countryside. His hobbies include reading, music, fitness, writing, travel, and skiing.

Interview with the Author

You began your writing with works of non-fiction, including such important books as When Reason Fails: Portraits of Armies at War. *Why did you decide to switch to fiction?*

MICHAEL GOODSPEED: I suppose it's because humans have a tendency to study life through stories. As children we love them, and as adults we carry that over into news, novels, movies, and TV shows. We try to make sense of our problems through stories. We crave someone else's context; and fiction readily provides not only context, but also an alternate perspective and someone else's personal understanding of a situation.

Do you see similarities between these different styles of writing?

GOODSPEED: In both types of literature, fiction and non-fiction, you examine issues and present a case. Non-fiction serves primarily to inform, while fiction serves not only to inform, but also to entertain and make a statement about your subject. So in this sense, I think that writing fiction and non-fiction are probably two sides of the same coin. Besides, I'm certifiably human and a sucker for a good story.

Your character Rory Ferrall is back now for a second tour of duty, having learned skills in military espionage in your Great War novel Three to a Loaf. *Did you as an author find he'd developed new qualities or attributes in your mind, or is he essentially the same character?*

GOODSPEED: For me, in writing a novel, the characters become real people. I suppose it's a kind of self-imposed delusion. When I work out the plot and imagine the characters and how they develop in the circumstances they find themselves in, I end up with a well-defined image of who these people are and how life has sculpted them.

In Rory Ferrall's case, he's an interesting guy, someone who has lived intensely, personally experienced some of the most catastrophic and formative events of the twentieth century, and of course he's been influenced by them.

So a character grows and changes?

GOODSPEED: I see a person's life as being similar to a body of water. If it flows and doesn't stagnate, it changes shape, it takes new directions; and over time its character changes, sometimes subtly, sometimes wildly.

In this book Rory is twenty-two years older. He's been a Mountie in the North, he's lost his wife, changed careers, and now he's thrown into another set of challenging circumstances. He's the same person, but the world has made some changes in him. He's been wounded and hurt in his life; he's had some quiet triumphs and grown stronger in some ways, more vulnerable in others. He's learned a lot, he's savvier and less naïve; but there's still a core sense of decency and diffident stoicism about him.

Readers of Three to a Loaf *will note you've shifted voice here, to a third-person narrator. Why?*

GOODSPEED: I wanted to explore in detail two other main characters, and to do that I wanted to view them in situations Rory couldn't have witnessed. So, the point of view changed.

Many readers say that once they start your novel, it is very hard to put down, which is a compliment you must find gratifying as a writer. Yet you consider your works more than just page-turning thrillers, isn't that so?

GOODSPEED: Thanks for the compliment. I certainly hope people enjoy my books.

I've always thought that the best stories should leave the reader or the audience thinking and mulling over the underlying issues after they're finished. And to do this, you can't propagandize your themes. You absolutely have to respect your reader's intelligence. Themes have to be balanced and fairly presented.

The reader has to believe that your settings, plot, and characters are credible; and then the themes you weave in through the characters' conflicts and their moral quandaries should relate somehow to your readers' lives and their world. In this way, good novels should be more than just entertainment.

A lot of the best themes are timeless and endlessly multi-dimensional: love, loyalty, fear, integrity, courage, ambition, how to respond to evil. I believe that if a story is going to connect, its themes should say something about the world we live in; and the themes that you develop have to surface naturally in the characters, the setting, and the plot. That's what I aim for; but it's up to the reader to tell me if I hit the mark.

In your first Rory Ferrall novel and now in this one, he is en-gaged in high-stakes intelligence operations behind enemy lines. While that is a constant, the Great War and the Second World War themselves are very different conflicts. What to you is the essential difference?

GOODSPEED: We should never have fought the First World War. It was a colossal miscalculation on everybody's part. Nobody envis-aged the scale or the duration of the destruction, and the issues we were fighting over could and should have been resolved by other means. The Second World War was very different. Nazism had to be thoroughly extinguished, and that could only be done by force of arms. People like Winston Churchill understood that fact as soon as Hitler came to power. But it was almost too late when we finally went to war, and by then everyone went into that conflict with their eyes wide open.

How does that difference impact on Ferrall?

GOODSPEED: I think it had a huge impact on Rory Ferrall, as it did on the rest of the world. Those generations had suffered enor-mously; they sincerely wanted to believe that war was completely ineffective, that the threat to them wasn't really an existential one, that somehow things would all work out for the best. Rory Farrell has seen the true face of the Third Reich, and despite everything he's been through, he knows we absolutely have to win this conflict. At the same time, he's also unhappy about having to fight a second time. On a private level, his own world has just been shattered; and on top of this, in the early days of the war, he's not at all certain that we're going to win.

Readers might be interested that between writing these two novels, you served for a year in Kosovo. What was that experience like?

GOODSPEED: It was a fascinating time. A lot was going on. It was highly rewarding, with a very intense work schedule. I was on the Military Civil Advisory Team and I was privileged in my own small way in helping to build Europe's newest country and help patch up a troubled part of the world. It was a people-watcher's paradise. I got to meet scores of interesting individuals, not only from Kosovo, but from almost every nation in Europe. It was a tremendous experience; the only down side to it was that it was a long year away from home.

 Did you find any time for writing?

GOODSPEED: I did, usually very late at night.

 Can we expect to see another return of Rory Ferrall?

GOODSPEED: I certainly hope so. The man led a remarkable life.

More great reading from Blue Butterfly Books

If you enjoyed *Our Only Shield*, you might also like the following Blue Butterfly titles. Your local bookseller can order any of them for you if they are not in stock, or you can order direct by going to the Blue Butterfly Books website:

www.bluebutterflybooks.ca

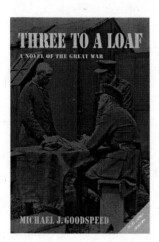

THREE TO A LOAF *is the page-turning drama of Rory Ferrall, a young Anglo-German Canadian smuggled into Germany during the First World War to discover the Imperial General Staff's top-secret plan to break the deadlock on the Western Front.*

Three to a Loaf: A Novel of the Great War
by Michael J. Goodspeed
Soft cover / 6 × 9 in. / 374 pages
ISBN 978-0-9781600-6-7 / $24.95 U.S./Cdn.
Features: author interview

Francis Pegahmagabow was a remarkable Canadian aboriginal leader. He served his nation in time of war and his people in time of peace—fighting all the way. In wartime he volunteered to be a warrior; in peacetime he had no option. His story needed to be told.

Pegahmagabow: Life-long Warrior
by Adrian Hayes
Foreword by Hon. James Bartleman
Soft cover / 6 × 9 in. / 165 pages
ISBN 978-0-9784982-9-0 / $19.95 U.S./Cdn.
Features: photographs, maps

When *impoverished, disheartened, poorly educated, but well-armed aboriginal young people
find a modern revolutionary leader in the tra-
dition of 1880s rebellion leader Louis Riel, they
rally with the battle cry "Take Back the Land!"
Co-ordinated attacks on Canada's strategic but
vulnerable energy supply facilities soon have
the armed forces scrambling and the country's
leaders reeling.*

Uprising: A Novel, by Douglas L. Bland
Hard cover / 6 × 9 in. / 507 pages
ISBN 978-1-926577-00-5 / $39.95 U.S./Cdn.
Features: author interview, maps

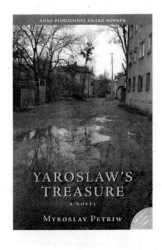

*When Yaroslaw leaves his Canadian home to
spend a short holiday in Ukraine searching
for family heirlooms buried by his grandpar-
ents during the Second World War, he has no
inkling his explorations will draw him into a
dangerous quest for Europe's greatest treasure,
or that he will be caught up in the swirling in-
trigues of Ukraine's "Orange Revolution."*

Yaroslaw's Treasure: A Novel
by Myroslav Petriw
Soft cover / 6 × 9 in. / 293 pages
ISBN 978-0-9784982-7-6 / $24.95 U.S./Cdn.
Features: author interview, maps

About this book

SET IN THE DESPERATE DAYS at the outset of the Second World War, *Our Only Shield* brings back Rory Ferrall, the resourceful Canadian spy from Michael J. Goodspeed's debut novel, *Three to a Loaf*.

Hastily recalled from a successful career in the Royal Canadian Mounted Police, Rory arrives in Britain only to find a war that is being prosecuted with political indecision and wishful thinking. The skills he displayed as a spy in the Great War are once again sorely needed by a small group of far-sighted but frustrated military planners.

Our Only Shield is a fascinating journey that takes us from an early wartime Britain still reeling from a string of catastrophic defeats into the once-peaceful Netherlands.

In 1940, Holland was a prosperous country where an industrious and innocent population simply yearned for peace and the chance to lead tranquil lives. Believing they could escape the havoc and violence of a world gone berserk, they awoke to find themselves governed by a new, terrifyingly brutal regime. Inserted into this shocked and traumatized community, Rory Ferrall soon finds himself caught up with two unforgettable characters: Annika Hammerstein, a gifted musician who refuses to watch passively as atrocities are inflicted on her family and her country, and Reinhold Neumann, a dangerously anxious but clever and ambitious Nazi policeman whose aspirations are unrestrained by conscience.

Our Only Shield is a meticulously researched story of how ordinary people marshal their talents to fight against ruthlessly efficient evil. Rich in historical detail, peopled with enduring characters, this powerful narrative gains steadily in momentum and tension and moves to a gripping conclusion. It's an enthralling and satisfying story as well as a meditation on the timeless nature of organized violence.